A New ROSE Novel
by **Laura Parker**

Author of the bestselling
Rose of the Mists and
A Rose in Splendor

In an unconquered
and he would teach her
sweet surrender...

THE
SECRET
ROSE

WARNER BOOKS $3.95 U.S.A. 32639-9 ($4.95 CAN. 32640-2)

ISBN 0-446-32639-9

>>$3.95

"About us, lass. We're man and wife. 'Tis time we acted the like."

Aisleen's fists clenched in her lap. "We are sharing our first real conversation. I thought we were proceeding quite nicely."

"Then ye'd best be thinking again," he muttered. "I'm a man wed and that gives me certain rights."

"Which you agreed not to lay claim to."

"Never I did!" he answered hotly.

Aisleen closed her eyes. So there it was, plainly said. She could no longer evade the moment. "I would rather you leave me in peace," she said low. "Yet I have sworn before God to submit to you." She swallowed with difficulty before adding, "I beg you, do not use me as you would your whores!"

The pleading statement should have touched him differently, Thomas suspected, as laughter struggled in his chest for release. His whores! Did she believe him to have been the ram in the paddock before they wed? Poor, wee thing. "I will be gentle," he said.

☆　☆　☆　☆　☆

THE WONDERFUL PLEASURES OF THE ROSE NOVELS...

Also by Laura Parker

ROSE OF THE MISTS
A ROSE IN SPLENDOR

Published by
WARNER BOOKS

THE SECRET ROSE

Laura Parker

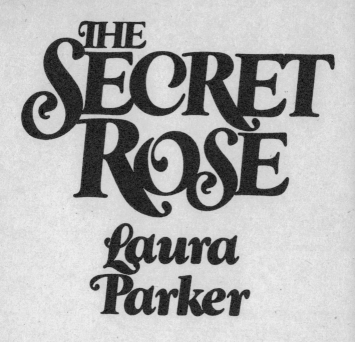

WARNER BOOKS

A Warner Communications Company

WARNER BOOKS EDITION

Copyright © 1987 by Laura Castoro

Cover illustration by Bob McGinnis

Warner Books, Inc.
666 Fifth Avenue
New York, N.Y. 10103

W A Warner Communications Company

Printed in the United States of America

First Printing: May, 1987

10 9 8 7 6 5 4 3 2 1

This book is dedicated with love to my mother.

ACKNOWLEDGMENT

The saying goes that reading about a place is the next best thing to being there. With the help of friends, I was able to "visit" Australia. Thanks to Laurie Smart, a delightful Australian native living in the U.S., who lent me books and shared her perception of her country with me. A very special "I couldn't have done it without you!" salute to Pat Bradford, an American living in Melbourne, who provided me with wonderfully informative letters, maps, and books that made all the difference. Thanks to Joe Strickland, who cared enough about the project to find an Australian link for me. Thanks, mates!

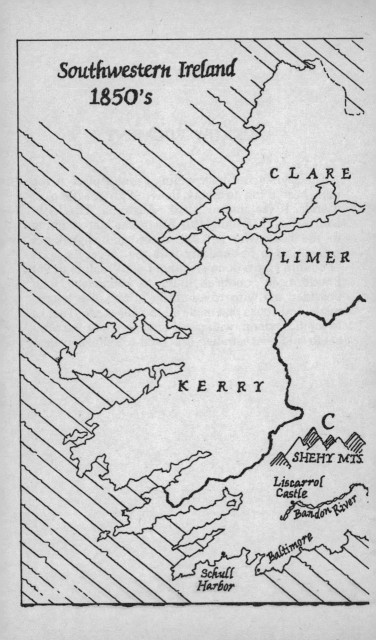

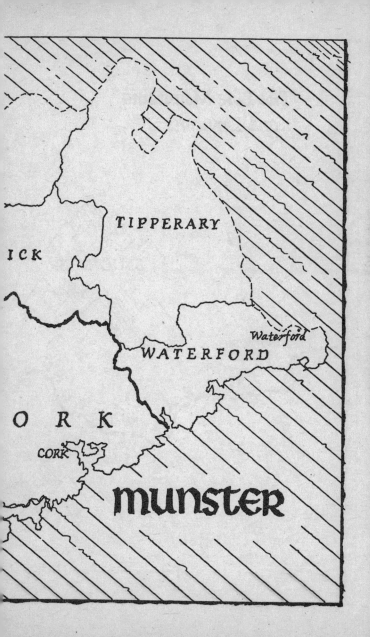

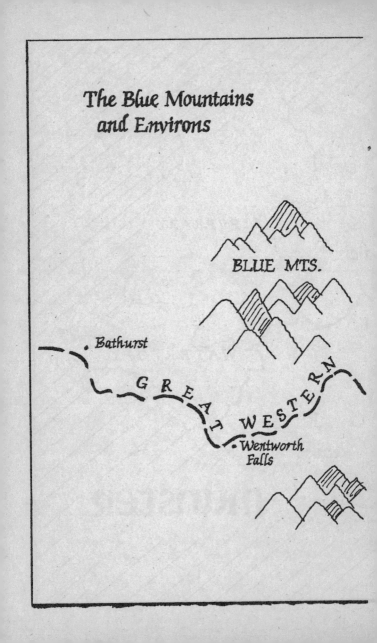

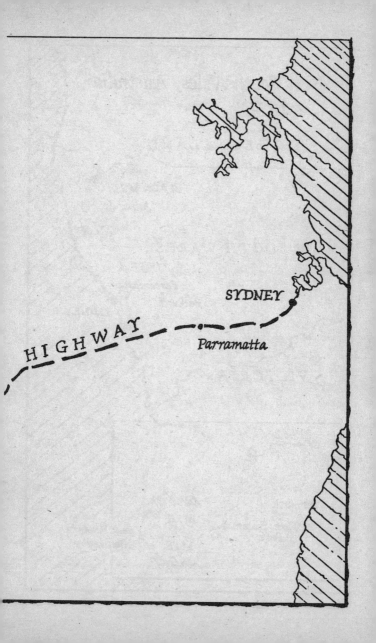

New South Wales, Australia
1850's

QUEENSLAND

BLACK MTS.
Armidale
Gara R.

NEW SOUTH WALES

• Hill End
Parramatta
Bathurst
SYDNEY

VICTORIA

Hill End
Turon R.
Bathurst
Three Sisters
Peak
BLUE
MTS.
Great Western
Highway

Sing of old Eire and the ancient ways:
Red Rose, proud Rose, sad Rose of all my days.

—To the Rose upon the Rood of Time
W. B. Yeats

Chapter One

Liscarrol Castle, Western Cork: 1844

A silver sickle of moon rocked itself to sleep on the slumped shoulders of Nowen Hill in the west. To the east the golden-veiled sun rose beyond the hills, shining down upon the blue-white mists undulating through the valley. Through the incandescent light of early morning came the clear piping of an unseen blackbird, stirring other less eager creatures to their awakening.

There was one who did not need the call to another day. Deep in the heart of the valley, not far from the lichen-scarred granite walls of the somber ruin known as Liscarrol Castle at the edge of the river Bandon, a girl squatted in the tall grass and waited until the cow herder had passed beyond the bridge.

"I can so, if I wish it!" she whispered and stood up.

Ye cannae, ye foolish lass, came the reply in a boy's rude country accents.

Twelve-year-old Aisleen Meghan Deirdre Fitzgerald jutted out her chin and balanced a fist on each narrow hip. "I can, and I will!"

Quick and agile as the mountain hare she startled from its hiding in the dew-cooled grass, Aisleen raced up the short embankment of the river. She wore no shoes, and her gown was too small and worn to offer much protection against the chill kiss of the mist. Yet she did not heed the damp nor the cold as she ran toward the distant slope of the hill beyond the river. Gorse bushes, their tough branches sprouted with golden buds, tugged at her sodden skirts. Rocks lying half-hidden in the boggy ground bruised her feet.

She did not think of these things. She had made a bet that she could climb Slieve Host, the hill that had gained its name more than a century earlier when a priest had hidden there and had whispered Mass on the isolated slope of this western Cork hillside. Without pausing to catch her breath she hurried on, allowing nothing to induce her to pause before she had accomplished the task.

Not until she reached the very top did she stop. "I've done it! Did I not say I would?" she cried in breathless joy. "I've conquered the mountain!"

Aye, ye did, lass, came the answer as clearly as the blackbird's song.

Aisleen turned her face to the east and breathed deeply. There was so much to see and smell and feel. The spring morning . . . the odor of fresh drying grass . . . the rippling movement of the breeze . . . the startling warmth of the sun . . . the deep, cool shadows slinking down toward the valley to disappear until dusk brought them creeping back. Below, in the valley, sunlight turned the surface of the Bandon into a thousand dark-gold mirrors. Above her head the air and clouds streamed in an endless fascinating flow.

This day is like no other, Aisleen thought. *It is special, just as I am special.*

In her life each day was different, unconnected to past or present, holding only a brimming magic of its own. The grass was greener, the stones sharper and grayer, the morning air sweeter and clearer than ever before. And if she missed it, the day would be gone, gone forever. That was why she could not sleep. Why could no one else see things as she did?

Would ye be forgetting me, then?

Aisleen smiled. "No, *bouchal,* I would not forget you. You are my very best friend."

Small praise that is, came the retort. *Best friend, only friend. Could it be that ye're feeling a wee bit sad, then, colleen?*

Aisleen shook her head. No, she must not be sad. How could she be sad on the best morning that ever was? There was in the air an excitement, a tremulous anticipation of momentous proportions. Something very important was about to happen; she could feel it tingling just under her skin.

That was why she had called on *bouchal* to share the anticipation with her. He was the best friend one could have, and nothing and no one could keep them apart, not even her father.

Aisleen frowned as she thought of her father. He would not allow her to play with the children of the cottagers. He said the Fitzgeralds were too good to mix with commoners, but she suspected that he forbade her to have friends as a punishment. From a very early age she had known that her father disliked her and that she could do nothing to please him. But he could not stop her from seeing *bouchal,* who had been a part of her life for as long as she could remember. No one else knew of or saw or heard him. That was because he was not real.

"Race you to the altar stone!" she cried suddenly and,

muddy heels flying, ran up over the shoulder of the hill to the place where a wide, flat-topped boulder lay on its side.

"I won! I won!" she crowed, jumping up and down until she was tired.

Ye've a sad lack of sportsmanship, bouchal taunted. *But then, 'tis to be expected, ye being but a poor wee bit of a lass.*

"I'm not a poor wee lass! I'm the last of a proud and ancient line. Me ancestors were kings!" Aisleen replied.

So ye've said. And so much the worse ye are for that, came his sour retort.

"Go away!" she snapped and turned her back on the place where she imagined he stood.

And leave a deeshy lass the likes of ye muttering to herself?

Aisleen swirled about. She could see him clearly in her mind's eye: his patched knee britches and knotted rope belt, his long legs and arms streaked with grass stains and mud, and his thatch of black hair half-hidden beneath his wool cap. He was older and a head taller than she was—at least he would be if he were real—with a ready grin and clever hands that fashioned for her toys from twigs and bracelets from wild flowers.

She had named him *bouchal,* the Gaelic word for "boy." He was always full of adventures and escapades. One of the things she liked best about him was that he never seemed sad, or lonely, or afraid. They did not talk about her da nor her ma. In fact, many times her parents seemed far less real than *bouchal* as she lived and played in a world all her own.

She turned and climbed up on the altar stone and flung herself back until she lay flat gazing up at the sky.

"Today I will be Queen of Beltane. Make a crown of May Day flowers for me, *bouchal!*" Even as she said it, she closed her eyes to wait.

Insects hummed in the grass beneath her, too faint to be

heard until every other sound was hushed. With each breath and heartbeat the sounds quickened until she was no longer attached to the earth but floated softly, lazily above her own flesh.

She became a cloud... shining as sunlight... rippling with the breeze... smooth as the amber river... rich with fragrances of earth and grasses... within the moment of the morning... pierced with the aching, sweet sadness on the cusps of the fading moon.

Ye've mud on yer face. The jeer struck the moment as clean and deadly a blow as a sword's edge.

Aisleen sat up, a frown riding her brow as she scrubbed at the dried spot on her cheek. "You're a beast! All men are beasts!"

A beast am I, and me thinking that ye cared for me!

Laughter trembled about her: goading, taunting boyish laughter. She looked about for something to throw at her imaginary jester, but when she looked down the impulse was forgotten. Laced about her wrist was a delicate bracelet of fairy foxglove. She did not remember picking them nor fashioning them into a rope. A special day, indeed.

Well, will ye nae say thank ye?

Aisleen touched one of the deep pink flowers. "I wish you were real!" she said suddenly.

He was silent for a moment, the air vibrating about her as shimmers of his ethereal presence. *But I am real,* he answered at last. *As real as ye want.*

Aisleen bit her lip. No, she would not think about what she wanted. In moments of solitude like this she could pretend that she had all she needed. "You're real to me, *bouchal,* as real as can be."

She reached into the pocket of the apron she wore. "I brought buttered bread. Come and share with me." Soon the milking of the cows would be finished, and the cow herder would be leading his cattle back to the fields, and she would be expected in the kitchen for her porridge. She made a face. "I hate porridge!"

So do I!

"One day we will be grown and rich and we shall have cream and strawberries, and oatcakes and rhubarb and ginger jam—"

And ham.

"And ham, every morning for breakfast."

And cocoa.

"And cocoa," Aisleen amended. One day she would have everything she wanted.

Nuala Murray, the cook at Liscarrol Castle, clucked her tongue when she saw the muddy, grass-stained young lady of the house. "*Wirra!* Would ye be looking at the sight ye are!"

Then she glanced up at the girl's face, and her jaw went slack. Dirty she was, and mud-stained, but nothing could dim the brilliance of Aisleen's smile or her red hair. Backlit by the sunlight streaming in the doorway, it shone like polished copper.

Nuala still believed in the old ways, and one look at the Fitzgeralds' daughter was enough to reaffirm her belief that the lass was blessed by the fairy host. Everyone knew that bright red hair was a gift of favor from the *Daoine sidhe.* "Why, lass, ye'll be looking as if ye've swallowed a spoonful of sunshine!"

Aisleen giggled, for she felt as if it were true. "I've been to the very top of Slieve Host."

"I would nae be telling that tale abroad," Nuala answered in a lowered voice. "There's those about who would nae care to hear it."

Aisleen glanced back through the doorway to the castle which was her home. "He's back, then?"

"Aye, and Himself madder than a gelded bull by the sound of it." Nuala shook her head as she described the mood of the master of Liscarrol. She cocked an arched brow at her daughter, Alvy, who was helping out with the morning baking. Alvy was simple and not very clean, but she had a comely figure. "Some people would do well to make themselves disappear altogether."

At the sound of her mother's disapproving tone, Alvy looked up, well aware of what she hinted at. "He's asked for her!" she said, and jerked her head at Aisleen. "Said she was to come right in to him."

Nuala snorted her disgust and then wiped her hands on the apron. "Well, that's it, then. Come along, lass. Ye've a bit of tidying up to do before yer da sees ye."

Aisleen felt a funny plummeting within. Her da was home. He had been gone longer than usual, nearly two months this time. Was his imminent return the event that had set her blood rushing and her skin tingling before dawn? "Do ye think he'll be happier now, what with his trip behind him?"

"God knows I wish Himself struck blind with rejoicing, but the devil if I know what's happened to him. He's rushing about giving us all every great rock of English, 'til our ears are ringing with the sound of that devilish tongue."

"English is a very fine tongue for an educated person to speak," Aisleen answered in Gaelic, the language she spoke when her father was not about. "But I do prefer our own."

"Aye, and ye should, being a true daughter of the sod," Nuala replied as she began vigorously scrubbing the girl's face with a damp cloth. "What's to become of us when the place is gone, that's what I'll be asking? There now. Where's yer ribbon, lass? *Och,* don't I know! The *coolyeens* are dancing fair to a jig about yer head, and never a fire was ever so bright a red. *Ochone!* In ye go, and God bless!''

Aisleen stood rigidly before her father's hide-bound chair in the Great Hall of Liscarrol Castle. Once it had been a fine room. Now it was moldy and nearly bare. Not even the peat fire glowing in the great hearth could alleviate the chill. Her father looked different from the way he had last she saw him, more tired and agitated. His black hair was more thickly streaked with white, and his usual ruddy complexion was strangely pale. He was not a heartening sight.

''Well, daughter,'' Quenton Fitzgerald began, ''have ye nothing to say for yerself?''

''No, sir,'' she answered softly, her gaze warily upon his face.

Her reply, given stiff-lipped and self-possessed, did nothing to improve Quenton's ill temper. The mere sight of his daughter was often enough to provoke his anger, and never more so than in recent months. She was a reminder that nothing had gone right since the day he had inherited through marriage the Fitzgeralds' ancestral home. Why, he had even changed his name to Fitzgerald so that his heirs would be Fitzgeralds, whose ancient bloodline reached back to Gaelic kings. He wanted sons, but what did he have to show for fifteen years of marriage? A single, useless lass.

The midwife had proclaimed Aisleen's birth a portent of good luck. Then his wife told him of the legend that lay behind the rose-shaped birthmark on his newborn daughter's tiny hip. When such a mark was borne by a member of her family, it was said the possessor had the power of creating miracles.

On that day he thought he had bested those who murmured behind his back that he was not good enough to be a

Fitzgerald. Had he not produced from his loins the bearer of the Fitzgerald mark? It was to have been the beginning of a new age of prosperity for himself and his family. Yet Aisleen had done nothing to fulfill her promise. Her birth had marked the beginning of his ruin.

With active dislike filtered through the haze of the generous portion of poteen he had consumed, Quenton eyed the cause of his unhappiness. Tall for her twelve years, with coltish legs and arms, Aisleen had none of the diminutive softness of the lady who was her mother, nor was she likely to achieve real beauty, he surmised. Her nose was short and turned up at the end, and her chin was too stubborn. She had missed her mother's subtle coloring of gold and cream. Hair, eyebrows, lashes, and freckles: Aisleen's coloring was the most striking shade of copper red. She had not even had the luck to inherit his own brilliant blue eyes. They, too, were an odd shade of golden brown shot with green. Nature had burdened him with a daughter as brilliantly hued as an exotic parrot, and as useless.

A frown puckered Quenton's forehead as he recalled that from the cradle she had not liked him, had cried when he held her and later balked at sitting on his knee. Perhaps even then she had sensed his aversion to her. She was more Fitzgerald than he, and the people of the countryside never allowed him to forget it, which was why he kept her hidden away. His jealousy was never long suppressed, and it grew with every day. If only he had a son, she would be left with nothing.

"There's no need to recount the matters between us," he mused aloud. "I've given voice often enough to my opinion of ye."

Aisleen lifted her chin at her father's tone. She hated these interviews. Nothing she ever said or did pleased him. He despised her. Why did he not simply leave her alone? The thoughts became words and escaped before she could prevent it. "Nothing I have ever done pleases you. Why should today be any different?"

"Bald arrogance!" her father cried. "*Musha!* I hate ingratitude more than stubbornness!"

Anger mottled her father's face as he lurched unsteadily to his feet. Aisleen trembled as she spied the silver flask on the table by his chair. He had been drinking again. Had she suspected that, she would have bitten her tongue before speaking. "I beg your pardon," she said, the words sounding stiff and clumsy in her ears.

"Aye, that ye'll be doing before I've finished with ye," he answered.

Anxiety pricked her as he reached to unbuckle his thick leather belt. She clenched her fists. She was not afraid of him. No one lived long under Quenton Fitzgerald's domination without suffering his temper in one form or another. He often threatened, but he had never used his belt. She could stand the slap or two he usually doled out.

It was her mother who concerned her. Timid, frail of health, and heavy with her third child in five years, Kathleen Fitzgerald spent most of her time in bed in the hopes that she would not lose or give birth to yet another stillborn son. If she heard them arguing, she would try to intervene; and when Quenton had drink in him, there was no guessing what he would do.

Quenton took a deep, calming breath. A beating was not what he had in mind when he sent for Aisleen. The idea had come to him as he rode home from Dublin. Over the years he had seen the sudden wariness in her eyes when he came upon his daughter in solitude. He did not know why it had not occurred to him before. She withheld some secret from him. If there was the slightest chance Aisleen possessed the Fitzgerald "gift," then he must not allow anger to prevent him from benefiting from it.

He brought all the force of his gaze to bear on her even as

he lowered his voice to its most charming and persuasive best. "These last three hundred years and more, we Irish have flourished despite the English. We've dodged their laws when we could, defied them when possible. Ye know the reason why the Fitzgeralds survived with more than most. Ye've heard the stories.

"Yer family triumphed over their enemies because they had the blood of the *Daoine sidhe* in their veins. Meghan was the first to bear the mark of the rose. Then there was Deirdre, yer ancestor who fought to bring Liscarrol back to the Fitzgeralds. She, too, had the mark.

"Now there's ye. The proof is there on yer hip, lass, the mark that proclaims ye to be the guardian of the 'gift'."

He leaned in close to her, excitement animating his expression. "The English devils are hard upon us. They've squeezed 'til there's nothing left. The taxes come due next month, and they'll be taking Liscarrol if there's nae money to give them. Ye must help us, daughter. Ye must use yer power, the power of the *Sidhe*, to save yer da from debtors' prison and Liscarrol from the English!"

As he gazed at her expectantly, Aisleen began to quake. From the moment she was old enough to understand, she had known the legend behind the rose-shaped birthmark on her right hip. The legend had been treated lightly by her mother, the birthmark seen as a good-luck charm rather than as an omen of absolute belief in ancient ways. Oh, she had pretended with *bouchal* that she was someone special, but there was never any proof.

Tears of helplessness filled her eyes as her father stood before her, watching and waiting. She had no magic at her disposal. Would he believe her? "I've no magic power, Da. I cannot help you."

"Cannot or will not?" Quenton countered. He struck the chairback with his fist, and the blow made Aisleen recoil a step. "Aye, so ye fear something, do ye?"

He withdrew a sheaf of papers from his pocket. "The days of Fitzgerald ownership of Liscarrol will come to an end when I've affixed me name to these. The damned English demand taxes only a leprechaun's pot o' gold could pay! But then, ye'd nae be knowing of such things, would ye?"

He tossed the papers on the carpet. "If ye will nae willingly help me, then I must make another use of ye. Aye, and with the Gilliams' help."

"Ye hate the Gilliams!" Aisleen answered, forgetting the danger in which she stood.

"Aye, they're English landlords and Protestant into the bargain, but they've one thing I've a fondness for, and that's gold, lass." He nodded. "Aye, they're willing to pay well for Liscarrol."

"You'd not sell our heritage to the English for a few coins?" Aisleen asked in disbelief. Liscarrol had been a Fitzgerald stronghold since the days of the Normans. The loss of it was unthinkable.

Quenton saw the horror in her face, and his resolve momentarily weakened. "Ye'll nae blame me for what's to come! The mark and the burden of the rose is on ye! It came down from yer mother's ancestors to protect Liscarrol, but, for hatred of yer own father, ye'll nae use it! If Liscarrol is lost to the Fitzgeralds, forever after the blame will be yers!"

Aisleen opened her mouth to protest, but her father's hand slashed the air only inches from her face, and the violent gesture silenced her. "Nor will ye sit and gloat while yer da is driven from his rightful inheritance. The Gilliams have a daughter they've a mind to send to England for schooling. She'll be needing a maid and companion. Yer mother's put a bit o' reading and writing into ye, so the Gilliams are willing to take ye."

"No!" Aisleen whispered in horror. "Ye . . . ye cannae mean to send me away."

"I can and will," Quenton replied. "Ye're to be packed and ready in a week's time, I say!"

"Pl-please..." Aisleen swallowed and nearly choked on her anxiety. "Please, I'll do anything, only do not send me away."

Quenton's eyes glowed strangely. "Then work yer magic, lass! Save Liscarrol!"

"But I cannot..." Aisleen's voice trailed off into nothingness as rage distorted her father's face.

"What of the fairy I've heard ye speaking to when ye thought no one knew? Ah!" he cried as her face paled. "Why would ye not be asking the fairies for aid?"

"Th-there's no fairy," Aisleen answered, so frightened she shuddered. "You will nae allow me to play with the village children, so I sometimes pretend to—to have a friend. 'Tis not ma-magic!"

"Useless bitch!" he roared, frustration and disappointment merging. "No man has ever had so stubborn and useless a daughter! Ye do it to spite me! Ye're like all the others who think yer ma did wrong to marry the likes of Quenton McCarthy. Ye think I'm nae good enough to be the owner of Fitzgerald land. Well, if I cannae have it, neither will ye!"

Only just in time did Aisleen raise her arms to shield her head as he freed his belt with a *snap*. She told herself that she must not cry out, but as he brought the thick leather belt down across her arms and back again and again, she buried her face tightly in the crook of one arm to muffle her cries of pain.

Quenton had not set out to beat his daughter, but she had provoked him beyond all reason. Life had cheated him of every pleasure. He had deliberately set out to marry into Irish nobility in hopes of becoming a gentleman of leisure. Instead he was the impoverished recipient of a castle ruin and a wife who repeatedly lost his sons but had given birth to this strange daughter whose only purpose in life seemed to be to defy him. He must have his revenge, and he would.

Reason slowly reasserted itself, scoring through the whiskey fumes of his mind. If he injured or crippled her, he would lose the opportunity for revenge against her. The Gilliams expected a quiet, modest lass as their daughter's companion. What they would get was Aisleen. It was a fitting curse on them. They would come to rue the day Aisleen Fitzgerald came into their lives as much as he did the day she was born to him.

His arm fell heavily to his side, and the belt slipped from his grip. "Get out! Get out of me sight, lass, before I kill ye!"

Aisleen rose from her knees, onto which the blows had forced her, and brought her hands tightly over her mouth. For a long moment a rage to match her father's pumped blood heatedly through her abused body. Something seemed to catch fire within her soul, to burn and blacken and shrivel as she fought against the consuming pain of his hatred. He hated her and she . . . she hated him.

The thought so frightened Aisleen that she turned and ran out of the room.

When she was gone Quenton Fitzgerald sank heavily back into his chair and reached again for the silver flask. Seeing his daughter's fearful, tear-blurred face had not given him the satisfaction he thought it should have. There had been something else in her expression, and it had quite astonished him. In the golden brown depths of her eyes he had seen strength and courage, a determination more powerful than his own. He had not bested her; he had only made her hate him.

A shadow passed before the sun, casting the Great Hall in shadow, and Quenton shuddered. Someone had stepped on his grave.

Quickly he tipped the silver flask to his lips and drained it.

"If the twelve Apostles in heaven came down asking me to say a single kindly word about Himself, I could nae give them satisfaction!" Nuala muttered as she bathed the long red welts on Aisleen's exposed back. "The devil knows what's to become of us! Skelping bairns with a great ugly belt 'til they bleed! May the devil choke him!"

Aisleen lowered her head onto her crossed arms on the table, tears running down her face. Her arms and back stung horribly, but she did not whimper as Nuala applied a cool lard and laurel-leaf poultice to her skin. The effects of the beating would heal, she told herself. Yet the wounds caused by her father's words gaped wider with every heartbeat. If Liscarrol was lost, forever and ever future generations of Fitzgeralds would remember the name of Aisleen Fitzgerald with a mutter and a curse.

She squeezed her eyes shut to prevent more tears. Was there nothing she could do to change that? She was not the son her father desired. She was not the obedient daughter he demanded. Worst of all, she was not the magical creature he needed. Because of her lack was she doomed to dishonor and shame? "Do you believe in magic, Nuala?"

Nuala's brow rose halfway up her forehead. "Now why would ye be asking such a question?"

"Da believes," she said very softly. .

Nuala exchanged enlightened glances with Alvy. "Poteen's addled him, that's what!" she said. "Ye're to keep shy of yer da these next days. Alvy and me will be making a place for ye at our cottage. Aye, that'll serve."

Aisleen lifted her head. "I cannot. I'm going away."

"Of course ye are," Nuala agreed, "and never soon

enough, I'm thinking. Meanwhile I'll be having a word with yer ma about ye stopping with us." She winked. "On account of ye come down with the ague and her so great with child."

Aisleen shook her head. "Da's sending me away. To England."

Nuala's hearth-reddened complexion blanched. "Away? To great bloody England? The man's that mad!"

Aisleen's dark-honey eyes shone with tears, but her voice was calm. "You're not to tell Ma. He might hurt her if she pleaded for me."

Nuala balked. "I'd like to see Himself raise a hand to the lady of the house!" Instantly she realized what she was saying, and her eyes slipped from Aisleen's. "Oh, the Lord save us!"

"Can I go now?" Aisleen asked as she pulled up the shoulders of her gown.

"And where would ye be going?" Nuala asked suspiciously.

"Down to the river," Aisleen answered. "I like dangling my feet in the coolness."

"Stay away from the castle!" Nuala called as the girl slipped out the door. " 'Tis a queer business, that," she said to Alvy. "And Himself as drunk as any lord before the sun's good and proper in the sky. Magic, is it, he's thinking about? Himself should steer clear of the doings of the *Sidhe*. If 'tis true and the lass is one of their own, they won't take kindly to the morning's business. Mark me words, Alvy, dark times ahead! And nae just the bairn will suffer!"

A week later Aisleen lay in the tall grasses which shielded her from view and chewed a spearmint leaf she had plucked from the herb garden by the kitchen door. The sharp tang of it tickled her tongue as she lazily dragged her toes in the bracing water. She did not think about the fact that she was crushing the new velvet gown her father had bought especially for her journey to the Gilliams. She did not think about the grass stains that were seeping into the white silk stockings she had cast aside. Nor did she care that her new dress shoes, black and hard as iron pots, were soaking up the damp. She thought only of the moment, with no past and no future, only the deep resonant hum of insects and the incessant bickering of birds.

Colleen? The question was tentative, as if the poser doubted her reply.

Aisleen closed her eyes. "Go away! I did not call ye!"

Aye! Ye did, and ye know it.

Aisleen rolled over onto her stomach. It was true. Without realizing it she had allowed herself to drift into thoughts of *bouchal* for the first time in a week.

Colleen?

"Aye," she answered reluctantly.

There was a moment's pause. *'Tis been so great a time since ye called me I thought ye was terrible sick or hurt. But then I always feel that, ye know?*

Aisleen did know. He knew things about her not another living soul knew. That was why she had deliberately closed him off. If he knew what had happened, that Liscarrol had been lost forever and that it was her fault, then he might curse her name, and she could not bear that.

His voice was strangely hesitant as he said, *There's something I've been wanting to tell ye.*

Aisleen sat up. "What is it?"

I'm going away.

The words came matter-of-factly from him, yet Aisleen shivered as though the sun had suddenly slipped behind the shoulder of a rain cloud. "Going away? Why?"

Come with me.

She felt his presence surrounding her, as warm and

enveloping as a summer breeze. He smelled of sweet grass, sea air, and—Aisleen wrinkled her nose—fish.

Ye hate it here. Ye're paining and 'tis yer da's fault. Do nae lie. I know he beats ye. Ye've called out to me though ye did nae know it. I could nae take the pain away, but now I can free ye. Come away! We'll have grand adventures, ye and me. Say ye'll come!

Aisleen sat perfectly still. It had never before occurred to her that she could escape her father's plans for her by running away. Da was sending her away, but that was different from running away. Besides, there was her mother. Her father might not ever want to see her again, but her mother would write to her, perhaps be allowed to come and see her. If she ran away . . .

Come along! he pleaded with a hint of impatience. *Are ye afraid, then?*

Was she? For years she and *bouchal* had plotted and planned and dreamed of the things they might do if only they could. But it was only make-believe. It was not real. It was impossible. "You're not real!"

She had not meant to say that, had not even meant to think it, but it was out. "No! I did not mean it!"

It was too late. She felt *bouchal* withdrawing from her. "Don't you see, there's no magic. It was me who made you and . . . and—"

And if you don't believe, then I don't exist, he finished in a sad, weak voice that trailed back toward her like a distant echo.

"Go then!" she cried in frustration. "See if I care!"

Appalled, she clamped both hands over her mouth. He was gone. Would he ever speak to her again? The fear that he might not overrode the suspense of what lay ahead of her. Would it not be better to run away, even with a phantom friend, than to be carted off to a strange place to live among strange people?

"Wait! *Bouchal?* I've changed my mind! Take me with you!"

For a long moment there was silence.

Before she could cry out to him a second time, the reeds parted and Alvy appeared. "Ye best be coming quick! Himself is calling for ye." She looked at Aisleen's rumpled gown and muddied stockings and water-logged shoes and shook her head, glad that the master was not waiting for her.

Aisleen gathered her stockings and shoes with a heavy heart. The moment was gone, gone forever, and with it *bouchal*.

"I did not mean it!" she whispered fervently as she cast a last look at the place where *bouchal* had been beside her. "Even if ye never answer me, I did not mean it when I said that you're not real. I believe you're real! Please take me with you! Please!"

Only the breeze sighed in answer, and she knew in that moment that she had lost everything: her home, her family, and *bouchal*.

The sad, the lonely, the insatiable,
To these Old Night shall all her mystery tell...

—The Rose of Battle
W. B. Yeats

Chapter Two

Somerset, England: 1844

Miss Emilia Burke regarded her two new pupils with dispassionate interest. Ella Gilliam, the elder of the girls, was plump, with a weak but pleasant face that bespoke the personality of a spaniel, eager to please and simply directed. Miss Burke always summed her girls up by attributing to them the character of an animal. It made it much easier to remember how to deal with each. The pugnacious bulldog must be dealt with differently from the stubborn mule or the skittish colt.

She reached out and rubbed one of the girl's golden curls between her fingers. The hair was of good quality, the cheeks rosy, the mouth small and pink. "Show your teeth, miss," she directed and nodded in satisfaction to see a full set on display.

As she walked slowly around the girl who stood ramrod

straight in the middle of the office, Miss Burke took note of each and every detail of her clothing, frowning when she detected the frayed edge of her collar. Really, it was too much to expect her to perform miracles on an Irish-reared English lady. She smiled a tight self-satisfied smile. That was why the Gilliams had paid handsomely for the girl's entrance. They hoped for a miracle that only she could work.

At fourteen, Ella Gilliam was late in coming under her tutelage. Every effort must be made to further her quickly, for the parents expected much more of Miss Burke's Academy for Young Ladies than simple schooling in deportment, art, and music. Girls who finished her course were meant to set a standard, to become a divining rod between what was acceptable in polite society and what was not.

Miss Burke nodded finally. "You will do very well if you study hard and work hard and pay the strictest attention to the other ladies who have had the great good fortune to be under my care a number of years. Your posture needs improvement. Your speech is lacking in the vowels and your hands, well, the less said the better. Miss Crockett is quite brilliant with cremes and softening agents. We shall see, yes, Miss Gilliam, I believe we shall see rapid improvement."

Less interestedly, she turned to the second girl. There was little to be seen beneath the brim of her bonnet: a round chin, short nose liberally sprinkled with freckles, downcast eyes. "State your name, child."

"Aisleen Meghan Deirdre Fitzgerald's me name," Aisleen answered proudly as she lifted her eyes from the carpet.

"Gracious!" Miss Burke exclaimed at the young girl's thick accent. "What sort of heathen gibberish does the child speak?"

" 'Tis English, I'm thinking," Aisleen answered, not realizing that she had been spoken of, not to.

Miss Burke's usually serene features puckered, betraying the age lines about her mouth and eyes. "Do not speak until spoken to!"

"But you *did* speak to me," Aisleen replied, puzzlement clouding her eyes.

"Impertinent chit!" Miss Burke said, mentally attaching the designation "sly fox" to the girl's character. "Remove your bonnet."

Aisleen reached up to do just that, her eyes curiously on the tall woman in black who stood staring down her long nose at her. When she slipped her bonnet off she saw the woman's mouth form a perfect "O" of surprise and her brows—"Why, miss, you've been drawing brows on your forehead with a pencil!"

Miss Burke's mouth snapped shut and then opened on a torrent of words. "Lower your eyes at once, my girl! At once."

Aisleen did as she was directed, smothering her curiosity behind lowered lids.

Miss Burke regarded the bent head in wonder. Was there ever another with hair so bright? The tresses positively glowed, even in the gloom of the study. Like a magnet her hair drew every beam of light and wound it into a fiery halo. Was it possible that it was natural? And the girl's eyes—there was clear reasoning in those golden depths. Intelligence and self-possession in a servant child, a companion to one of her paying pupils? It would never do.

"I see that the Irish have sent us a most difficult task," she began with a pointed look at one of her assistant teachers who stood near the doorway. "Only the sternest measures will do for her. 'Tis plain enough that a blind man might see it."

She grabbed a handful of Aisleen's hair, making her yelp in pain. "Miss Gregory, you must see to it that the false vanity of our sly fox is scrubbed out and the method of the coloring discovered. This is a respectable establishment. We will not tolerate Covent Garden tricks here.''

Ella Gilliam spoke up, her blue eyes as wide as plates. "Aisleen's hair is real, Miss Burke. I've seen her wash it myself. 'Tis good and truly red.''

Miss Burke turned an appraising gaze on the elder girl. So that was the way of it. The spaniel was fond of the fox, was she? That would never do. One fox among the flock, an Irish fox at that, and discipline would be destroyed.

"Miss Gregory, take this Aisl— No, no. Even the name is heathen.'' She caught Aisleen by the chin, her nails digging painfully into the girl's cheeks. "You shall answer to the name Alice from this moment, though I must allow that even that is too fancy a name for one of your station. Miss Gregory, into the washroom with her, and let us pray that a scrubbing does the trick.''

Aisleen met the woman's pale stare with dry-mouthed fear. "You'll nae hurt me?''

"I will do what is necessary to remove the taint of Ireland from you, child, whatever methods are demanded. Take the pair of them out, Miss Gregory.''

When the door had closed, leaving her alone, Miss Burke took two turns about her office before she came to a stop. Ella Gilliam would fit in quite well. As for the Irish papist who had been dropped into her midst, well, only time would tell if the girl could be maintained beneath this roof without the sacrifice of discipline.

"Red hair!'' she exclaimed in wonder of it. "Horrid! Indecent!'' And quite wantonly beautiful.

Aisleen lifted another bowl of peeled potatoes onto the table beside Mrs. Greesham and then mopped her damp brow with the back of a hand.

"Feeling poorly, are ye?" the plump woman questioned.

Aisleen shook her head. In the six months since her arrival at Miss Burke's Academy, she had learned not to complain to anyone about anything. Kitchen duty was much preferable to scrubbing cisterns or hauling water from the well. Punishments varied according to the transgressions, and at least the kitchen was warm.

The bell over the door jumped agitatedly.

"That'll be for ye," Mrs. Greesham said. "Run along. Ye can finish them taters after yer lessons."

Aisleen untied her apron and carefully folded it twice before laying it aside. When she had wiped her hands and patted her face dry, she left the kitchen by way of the servants' stairs.

"A shame what they set that girl to do," Mrs. Greesham grumbled when Aisleen was gone. Miss Burke did not like the child and that being so, her life was less enviable than that of many of the domestics who served the academy.

On the stairs, Aisleen paused to catch her breath. Every indrawn breath made her throat ache. Every step made her feel light-headed. Yet she dared not complain.

She loosened the strings of the bonnet she was made to wear from the moment she rose until she retired at night and pulled it off. Her hair clung in damp curls to her brow. *Hurry up,* she told herself, but she did not move. Instead she pressed her cheek to the cool stone of the stairwell and closed her eyes. She did not know why the tears began. She had not shed them in the six months since she waved good-by to her mother in Dublin. Six long, lonely months that seemed like six years. And not a word from home. Had her mother begun to believe her father, that she was the reason for their troubles and that she was wicked and accursed?

She had tried, truly tried to be good, to make Miss Burke like her, and the other girls as well. But none of them did.

She did not dress right, or speak right, or even think right. Every word out of her mouth brought new instances of misconduct. If she did not hurry, she would be late, and tardiness was a great sin in Miss Burke's book.

But her feet would not move, and the effort only made the tears flow faster. She was so tired, so very, very tired. If only she could lie down a moment on the cool stone steps and rest.

"You found her where?"

"In the servants' stairwell, Miss Burke, unconscious. She's feverish. I fear she's seriously ill."

Miss Burke looked down on the pale girl with two bright spots of fever burning on her cheeks. Each rapid breath filled the small room with its rasping sound. Doctors were expensive, and the Gilliams had not given specific directions about their willingness to pay for extras regarding Alice Fitzgerald. "I will send word to Dublin about the girl's condition. The Gilliams will make the decision about what's to be done."

Miss Gregory looked at her employer across the width of the sick girl's narrow bed. "If it's contagious or if the child should die before word can be returned . . ."

She let the sentence hang, but Miss Burke did not need it finished. "Very well, send for the doctor. But I warn you, if she's brought pestilence into my school I shall have her removed immediately!"

Aisleen nearly gave up the effort to breathe, but suffocating was worse. Once she had nearly drowned in the Bandon, and this was very much like it. Her lungs seemed filled with water, leaving no room for air.

"Mama?"

A cool hand found its way between hers, and she gripped it tight. "Mama?"

"No, darling. It's Miss Gregory," a soothing voice said close to her ear. "You must sleep, and you will feel better in the morning."

Aisleen gripped the hand tighter. "I want...to go...home. Please. Please!"

The room dimmed, leaving her in a nether world of painful breathing and racking chills. Why did her mother not come for her? Why did no one come to take her home?

Is that ye, colleen?

Trembling, Aisleen whispered, *"Bouchal?"*

Aye, came the reply that was no more than the whisper of the wind.

Her eyes opened wide. "You came back!"

"Who, dear? Who came back?" Miss Gregory questioned.

Never gone, lass, and didn't ye know it!

Aisleen's lids dropped over her feverish eyes as a smile curved her mouth. "Stay with me."

I cannae, the voice murmured in regret. *I must go. But ye must live, colleen. There're things ye've yet to do. Ye bear the mark of great promise. Never forget me!*

"No," Aisleen murmured. She was not alone after all. She had her memories.

"She's fallen asleep," Miss Gregory reported as Miss Burke entered the sickroom. "I think she's breathing easier."

"Ella's fallen ill. That makes seven," Miss Burke said. "I've learned that the outbreak of scarlet fever is worse in London. Amy Lester is believed to have brought the disease back from her holiday.'' She nodded at Aisleen. "I do not wish to see any of God's creatures suffer, but I believe the doctor's remedy was a blessing in disguise.''

Miss Gregory glanced at Aisleen's scarf-wrapped head and wondered again at her employer's enmity for the child.

Aisleen lay back against her pillow in something akin to wonder. Her tiny room, once the sleeping quarters of four girls, was completely her own. The aching throat and itching had subsided a few days earlier, but she had not been allowed to set even a toe out of bed.

Impatient with waiting for her breakfast tray, Aisleen threw back the covers. No one was here to tell her that she could not get dressed; therefore it must be permissible.

On rubbery legs she crossed the floor to her cupboard and pulled out her black wool gown. She pulled her nightgown over her head and replaced it with a clean shift and drawers. When she had completed those tasks, she was suddenly bereft of strength, and her legs began to tremble. She caught herself by grabbing the cupboard door, and it swung wider under the pressure of her weight, revealing the mirror that hung inside.

For an instant Aisleen stood staring in mute disbelief at her reflection, and then she was tumbling, tumbling, falling into a deep abyss.

When her rap on the door was not answered, Mrs. Greesham pushed the door open with her elbow and backed in, carrying Aisleen's tray. The sight that greeted her when she turned around made her drop her tray with a cry.

Aisleen lay sprawled on the floor in a shift. All the girl's lovely red hair had been shaved off, and her fragile skull was as smooth and pink as a newborn babe's.

*   *   *

Aisleen shifted uncomfortably from foot to foot. Three months had passed since her illness, but she was still very shy before others. Surreptitiously she touched the short curl that had escaped from beneath her cap. She had a head of ringlets now, as bright and curly as before. The fact annoyed Miss Burke, but the woman had not mentioned it except to remind Aisleen to keep her head covered.

"Very good, Jane. You may step down. Next!" Miss Burke called crisply.

Aisleen stepped forward to stand before the class, her chin lifted in defiance of the fear she felt at being singled out before the other girls.

Miss Burke looked up in surprise. "Alice Fitzgerald! I did not expect you to stand forth for the year-end examination. Your illness required you to lose many hours of class work."

Aisleen took a deep breath. "I have studied for it, ma'am."

"Have you, indeed? We shall see. Let us begin."

Half an hour later Miss Burke looked up from her tally of Aisleen's answers, and a begrudging respect lit her eyes. "You have qualified to advance to next year's class, Alice. I am quite amazed."

Aisleen smiled shyly, not certain that any reply was required.

Mis Burke turned to the class of girls. "It is my hope that you will report this girl's proficiency to your parents as an example of the remarkable work that may take place under my tutelage. Alice came to us a veritable heathen with a detestable brogue. And while we have not yet broken the back of that deplorable habit, we at Burke Academy have been able to instill a modicum of other skills in language, mathematics, and the graces in her. It is my hope that further studies shall advance her to the degree that any of her acquaintances will not blush to be seen in her company.''

With this dubious compliment ringing in her ears, Aisleen descended to her seat. She had learned something valuable in the last minutes. The way to win Miss Burke's approval was to excel in her studies. If she worked very hard at her lessons, perhaps there would be fewer potatoes that needed peeling in future.

Spring 1847

"As you have heard, your father is dead these past two weeks,'' Miss Burke continued in an even tone. "The Gilliams were unable to reach us in time for you to be sent home for the funeral, and it is my belief that it is just as well. Your studies would have been interrupted, and you would not have been present to pass your term exams. Do you have any questions?''

Aisleen held the scrawled note from her mother so tightly that it was crimped. "How did he die?''

"Run down by a dray cart in Dublin,'' Miss Burke answered, her tone implying what she thought of so ignoble a death. "It is believed that he died instantly. Tragic, of course, but preferable to a lingering death.''

Aisleen nodded slowly. Preferable. He was drunk. She did not need anyone to tell her that. The Gilliams had been quite frank in their letters to their daughter, and through Ella she knew that her father had moved to Dublin as soon as Liscarrol had been sold to the Gilliams. Her mother had lost yet another child and been sent to recuperate with relatives in Waterford.

"May I be excused, ma'am?''

Miss Burke nodded. "You may have the rest of the day to

yourself. But no dawdling come the morrow. The Gilliams have indicated to me that they are well enough pleased with your progress to continue to sponsor you for another term. They feel it is their Christian duty, particularly since your mother is in poor health, to provide for you until you are of an age to earn your own keep. Count yourself lucky, Alice. You might be alone in this world.''

Aisleen stared out of the window of her room. It was past the dinner hour, and she did not doubt that the girls had eaten without her. She did not care.

After three years of waiting and praying and despairing, her mother had written at last, to say that her father was dead.

Dead. Done to death under the wheels of a Dublin dray horse.

Aisleen bit her lip. Why now, after three years of silence, had her mother written to her? Where were all the answers to the dozens of letters she had written over the years?

She opened her hand and allowed the letter to fall to the floor. She had read it over and over until every word of it was imprinted in her brain, and yet it explained very little.

Me dear, darling daughter,

I write ye not for the first time, but I fear that these may be the first words ye've received.

'Tis sad I am to say this letter brings terrible news. Yer da, God bless him, is dead. Run over on a Dublin street, he was. The constable says he was killed instantly, the iron shoes of the horses being the murderous things they are.

'Tis me hope that ye'll be forgiving him his hard

heart these last years. And that ye'll be comin' home where ye belong.

Yer loving mother

"No," Aisleen whispered defiantly. She would not go home. Home? She had no home. Her father had sold Liscarrol out from under her in the same stroke with which he had exiled her. She was an orphan in fact now, but in her own mind she had become one three long years ago when her father had betrayed all her hopes for happiness, permanence, and security. Even her mother was a stranger. The letter had not said so, but it must be true that her father had blocked the letters her mother had written. Another betrayal, another instance of his hatred of her.

"I am alone, no more or less than I have ever been," she murmured resolutely to the night. For three years she had managed alone, and survived. Only in being strong, in relying on herself alone, had she existed. Nothing had changed with the news she'd been given. If the letter had never reached her, she would not have cared. It brought no sadness or gladness. She felt nothing on learning of her father's death.

So why did her heart hurt? Whence came this aching rift that threatened her world? She did not want this pain, this sorrow for what might have been if only she were loved. It hurt too much to care, to care when her caring was not returned. She felt torn by tongs, buffeted by desires that could not be met, starved for that which could never be hers.

She bent and picked up the letter and carried it to her chiffonier, where she placed it in a drawer. In the morning, when she had recovered, she would write to her mother, the stranger who had borne her, and be the dutiful daughter. Perhaps, in time, they would become friendly once more.

But she would not seek her mother's love. That way led to pain, this shattering, splintering ache that made her catch her breath sharply.

No! She felt nothing. Nothing!

She tasted blood and realized that she had bitten through her inner lip. The metallic taste of blood was quickly joined by the saltiness of tears as they streamed down her cheeks and into her mouth.

"Da! Da! Why could you not love me?"

September 1850

"A post?" Aisleen repeated. "Here at your school, Miss Burke?"

Miss Burke nodded. "I know that it comes as a shock to you, Miss Fitzgerald, but shocks are not always unpleasant events. You have shown yourself over these last six years to be of sound, if forward, temperament and a reliable, if somewhat passionate, nature. Were you to return to Ireland, I daresay you would find yourself educated quite beyond those of your past acquaintance. You would not find a post worthy of you. As for marriage, well, you must know how little hope there is of obtaining a suitable match, things being what they are. In short, you have few alternatives. Ireland is prostrate from the effects of famine and mismanagement."

"You refer to the years of starvation that England saw fit not to prevent?" Aisleen questioned.

"That kind of talk will land you in the gutter," Miss Burke rapped out. "Ungrateful chit! Always were, always will be!"

Aisleen could scarcely contain her smile. She had never sought Miss Burke's favor, only her respect. Now she did not need Miss Burke's approval any longer. "For the past two years I have worked as a teacher without benefit of salary or title. In that time I have not asked for nor received from you in the form of benefit a single sum. You will understand that I could not well refuse your dubious charity until now.''

"Until now? Why now?" Miss Burke asked.

"Because, Miss Burke, I have obtained a post." Aisleen withdrew a paper from her apron pocket. "It's a post as a governess for the Beetons of Salisbury. I have agreed to their terms and will leave on the morning coach at the end of the week.''

"Ungrateful chit!" Miss Burke repeated hoarsely. "After all I've done for you! You'll regret leaving here. You're not fit for the world beyond these doors. You'll regret it!''

"Perhaps," Aisleen agreed. "But I feel that it is my right to test myself against the world's measure."

"There's a man in this," Miss Burke said suddenly. "You believe you shall catch yourself a husband, that's it!''

Aisleen shook her head firmly. "One thing I would not wish for myself is matrimony. Nothing I have ever heard or seen of it persuades me to believe that marriage is a fit institution for a woman of good morals and sound mind. You yourself have never married, and yet you prosper. So shall I.''

Miss Burke regarded the young woman before her in mingled pride and rage. "I have made you! You must never forget that. I turned you from a Gaelic heathen into a well-bred young lady. If you ever forget yourself, you are lost. As for marriage, it's a trap for fools and dullards, and you're neither, my girl, and do not forget it!''

Aisleen smiled. "I do not intend to, Miss Burke."

* * *

Beeton Cottage, Somerset: 1851

"Such a serious creature, Giles," Mrs. Beeton said as she buttered another slice of breakfast toast. "I do wonder that the children are not thoroughly frightened of her."

Mr. Beeton peered over the edge of his newspaper. "Of whom do you speak, dear?"

"Of Miss Fitzgerald, of course. She's quite the most daunting nanny any child ever had. I find myself correcting my own posture when she's about." Mrs. Beeton smiled coquettishly. "She's positively a replica of Miss Burke!"

" 'Tis why you hired her," her husband answered reasonably. "I've not seen much of the young woman these past months, but I defer to your tastes in such matters."

Far from mollified by his answer, she said, "I had hoped that a young woman of whom Miss Burke approved would prove beneficial to the girls, but I had forgotten quite how miserable I was my first year at Burke's Academy."

Mr. Beeton lowered his paper a fraction more. "Are the girls unhappy with Miss Fitzgerald?"

"Oh, no. I would not tolerate a single day of their misery, as well you know. All the same, I wish you would speak to her, Giles. She appears to be quite bereft of the finer feelings of nurturing that one would expect in a young lady. Why, I wonder if that explains why she has not wed. She's passably pleasant to look at. One does wonder, Giles, why she has not formed an attachment."

Giving up, Giles folded the paper. "I suppose her lack of suitors would have something to do with the lack of opportunity, my dear. A young woman closeted behind the doors of Burke's Academy for six years would have little opportunity to meet gentlemen. As for the future, you must remember that she's Irish and, well, there will be few of her kind who are her equal.''

"That's true,'' Mrs. Beeton mused. ''Educated above her class and Catholic into the bargain. I suppose we performed an act of charity by taking her on.''

"I suppose,'' her husband murmured, regarding his poached egg with distaste. ''I do abhor poached eggs!''

"All the same, you will speak to her?'' Mrs. Beeton urged.

Mr. Beeton looked up. ''If you wish it, dear. A letter arrived for her in the morning post. I shall take it to her the moment breakfast is done. You will, of course, tell me what to say to her?''

"Of course,'' his wife agreed in a pleasant voice. ''Servants of her caliber are difficult to obtain. They must be handled carefully.''

At exactly half past ten o'clock, Mr. Beeton found himself crossing the topiary garden at the rear of his home in search of his governess and two daughters. The sound of laughter drew him to the wall that separated the gardens from the orchards.

"Up you go, Miss Hillary. Now hold on. I won't allow you to fall. Pick the shiniest, reddest one! Pull hard. That's my girl!''

Mr. Beeton entered the orchard just as his younger child was being swung high in the arms of the governess. Startled to find his stern governess caught in a moment of play, he paused in the shadows to watch.

"What a clever, clever girl you are!'' Aisleen cried in approval when she had set Hillary on the ground. She bent forward to observe the treasure in the girl's small hands.

"Why, I do believe that this must be the biggest, juiciest apple in all the county."

"Mine's bigger!" Mary called down from the branch onto which she had climbed. "See? Mine is the biggest apple of all."

"Miss Mary, you come down from there this instant," Aisleen said firmly.

Mary tossed her apple onto the ground and began to shinny backward until her sash caught on a limb. "Nanny! Oh, nanny, I'm stuck!"

"Serves you right for being a very naughty girl," Aisleen replied, but she quickly added, "Don't cry, dear. I'll climb up and get you."

To Mr. Beeton's surprise, his very proper governess reached down and pulled the hem of her gown up between her legs and tucked it into her waistband. Then, using the stone bench at the base of the apple tree, she reached up and pulled herself into the lower branch of the tree.

His lips twitched as he spied a slim ankle encased in a black stocking. Was this the young lady his wife thought of as a termagant? She seemed more like one of the children than the severe lady his wife's words had painted in his mind's eye.

Aisleen grabbed Mary about the waist and handily returned to the ground with her charge in tow. "Now then, Miss Mary, what have you learned from today's adventure?"

Mary looked down at her torn sash, and then a pair of dimples appeared. "That the biggest and best apples in all the world are at the top of the tree!"

Aisleen tried to keep a straight face, but it was impossible and she laughed. "You should be scolded. Your mother would be horrified to learn that her daughter climbs trees."

"Then you must not tell her," Mary said precociously.

Aisleen's copper brows lifted. "If I do that, then you must do something for me in return."

"What?" Mary asked suspiciously.

"You must promise never to climb a tree again."

"I think that a jolly good pledge!"

Aisleen swung about at the sound of a man's voice and saw Mr. Beeton striding toward them. Blushing furiously, she shook out her skirts and then folded her arms primly. "Mr. Beeton. Curtsy to your father, Mary. Hillary."

The clipped toned surprised Mr. Beeton, for it was quite different from the voice she had used with the girls before he appeared. "I trust you are adjusting well to your new life here," he said kindly.

"It is sufficient to my needs," Aisleen answered softly, embarrassment making her feel awkward. She was so seldom in the company of men that she did not know how to behave.

Mr. Beeton stared at the brim of her bonnet because she had lowered her head before his gaze. Where was the young woman who had moments ago climbed a tree with abandon and laughed freely? His wife believed her to be a tartar. In reality she appeared as tongue-tied and shy as any green girl. "Are there any changes that you would make?"

Aisleen shook her head, her eyes still downcast. "No. Thank you for inquiring, but I am quite content."

At a loss, Mr. Beeton remembered the letter he carried and offered it. "This came for you in the morning post." When Aisleen lifted her head he smiled encouragingly. "It's from Ireland—a relative perhaps? I hope it's good news."

To his amazement she turned white as her gaze fell on the postmark. "Thank—thank you," she said unsteadily and clutched the letter in her fist. "If I may be excused . . ." Without waiting for his permission, she turned and walked rapidly out of the garden.

"Was it sad news, Papa?" Hillary asked.

"I don't know, child," Mr. Beeton replied. "Perhaps it's delight that overcame Miss Fitzgerald." But he doubted it. What a strange young woman she was. Perhaps his wife was right, that she bore watching.

Aisleen impatiently tore open the letter. It was from her mother. As she frantically scanned the lines, her heart slowed. There was no crisis, no emergency. It was nothing more than a friendly note.

Aisleen cast it angrily away, annoyed with herself for reacting so foolishly. Her mother was well, not ill or starving. And yet she felt responsible for her, as if her father had been correct when he said that the burden of her family had been placed at birth on her shoulders.

"I've never had a say in family matters. I have no family!" Aisleen murmured as she paced her small room. Yet this feeling of dreaded anticipation came over her more and more frequently in recent weeks. At every turn Miss Burke's final words echoed in her mind: "If you ever forget yourself, you are lost!"

Why did she so often feel on the verge of forgetting herself? The impetuousness of climbing an apple tree was forgetting herself. Laughing and running and glorying in the beauty of the day were threats to her peace of mind. Why should that be so?

She had found a safe haven, and if she were smart she would settle in gratefully and never hope for and think of the possibility of anything else. After all, what else could there be?

Love.

Aisleen spun about. "Who said that?" she demanded angrily of the room. The chirping of the canary in the wicker cage in one corner of the nursery was the only reply.

"Foolish whims!" she murmured in an imitation of Miss Burke's acerbic voice. "Foolish whims, Miss Fitzgerald, and well you know it!"

She wanted nothing more than to make a success of her post. That, and nothing more.

But the young queen would not listen;
She rose in her pale night-gown;
She drew in the heavy casement
And pushed the latches down.

—The Cap and Bells
W. B. Yeats

Chapter Three

Yorkshire, England: 1856

Aisleen slammed the door to her attic room and twisted the key in the lock an instant before a fist hammered upon it.

"Open up, Miss Alice! You know you want our company!" The latch was tried, and then the sound of masculine laughter exploded in the narrow hallway beyond.

Aisleen pressed her weight against the door, silent but for the pounding of her heart. She had made a grave error in visiting the kitchen after dark, but she had thought the house empty except for the Maclean servants. That was her mistake. Nicholas Maclean, the elder son, who was home from Oxford on holiday, had returned unexpectedly and with him was a male companion.

"Alice! Pretty Alice," Nicholas called in singsong fashion.

Drunk, Aisleen thought as her lips tightened in disapproval. It seemed it was a detestable habit that many men shared in common with her father.

"Go away!" she whispered in an angry hiss.

"Ah! She abides therein!" the second man voiced in amusement. "Shall we serenade her?"

"Nay, she's not the sort of lass a man woos with songs, are you, Miss Alice?" she heard Nicholas ask just before the latch was tried again.

After checking the key to make certain it had made a complete turn, she stepped back and folded her arms across her bosom, only to notice her left sleeve gaped away at the shoulder, where an aggressive hand had torn it.

Righteous indignation fired her resolve. She had waited and prayed for this post for more than six months after the Beetons had been forced to let her go in the wake of a reversal in their finances. She was not about to lose it because of a drunk young lordling. "Step away from that door, Mr. Maclean," she said in a stern voice, "or I shall be forced to call for aid."

"She sounds serious," the companion cautioned. "There'll be Roberts to deal with if he hears us."

"Roberts is a servant and knows his place," Nicholas answered, but whether it was real doubt or merely the slurring effects of too much whiskey, Aisleen thought she heard hesitation in his voice.

"Good night, Mr. Maclean!" she said in a tone that brooked no defiance.

"Silly old bitch!" she heard him grumble under his breath before retreating footsteps sounded on the narrow stairwell.

A sudden blast of winter wind rattled the shutters and despite her outward calm, Aisleen jumped and turned to-

ward them. All at once her shoulders drooped, and she
brushed from her face a strand of hair.

"Fools!" she muttered and crossed the room and picked
up the poker to stir new flames from the dying fire. She
would not be able to sleep now. The unsettling effects of
having been attacked must have curdled the warm milk she
had consumed, for she felt decidedly queasy.

When the flames had licked into the new scoop of coals
she placed in the fireplace, she turned away and began to
undress. She pulled the bodice from her shoulders and
paused to inspect the tear. Luckily the threads had given
way at the seam, and the damage could be easily repaired.

When the young gentlemen had first entered the kitchen
she had seen their disappointed expressions. No doubt they
had hoped to corner younger, prettier game. After all, she
was not a silly young scullery maid of eighteen but a
twenty-five-year-old spinster who had been the Maclean
governess for well over a year. She had not truly believed
that they would touch her. But then Nicholas had winked at
her and offered her brandy while his companion reached out
to stroke her sleeve as if she were some—some strumpet!

"Really, it is too much that a woman is not safe beneath
the roof of the house she serves!" she muttered, so furious
her hands shook. She stepped quickly out of the dress and
hung it up on a peg, adding her petticoats and corset to hang
from the others. Frigid drafts swept over her as she hurriedly slipped her nightgown over her head.

The Maclean estate was situated on the cold, barren flats
of northern Yorkshire. Outside her window the storm of the
previous day had passed, and the velvet-black night was
lightened by an iridescent white blanket of snow. Drifts
pillowed the house and changed the familiar landscape into
an eerie, white-duned scene. The weather was the reason
none of the Macleans had been expected to return this night.
Roberts, the butler, had informed the staff at supper that the

Macleans would extend their Boxing Day visit with the Ventnors until the treacherous weather abated.

After tying a rough wool shawl over her nightgown, Aisleen pulled off her white cap, plucked out the combs that held her hair in a tight bun, and reached for her brush.

In the dimly lit room the firelight struck bright red sparks from the billowing cloud of red-gold hair she brushed out. One and all, people were struck by the color. When she first came to work here, the younger of her charges, three-year-old Michael Maclean, had dared to touch a curl, expecting it to be warm like a candle's flame, he had explained. She had noted in displeasure the gleam of interest in Nicholas Maclean's eyes, but he had left almost immediately for college and she had not seen him for months, until this night.

Aisleen set her brush aside to massage her brow. For five years she had been her own mistress, and never in that time had she been assaulted.

She shook her head. She had taken this post out of desperation. Though the Beetons had been generous in their recommendation of her, she had been turned down repeatedly, often without explanation. Gradually, after countless interviews, she began to understand why. Being Irish and Catholic were handicaps, but her youth and striking appearance were greater impeachments to cautious wives. The Yorkshire Macleans had offered her employment at a time when she faced starvation. They were country-bred gentry with little respect for her excellent education beyond the status it gave them in the community. Yet until tonight, she had never been afraid to live on these desolate moors.

Even so, she wondered how she would tolerate another year in the north, where in winter nature succumbed to the colors of death: black, brown, and white. Winters in Ireland were cold but not bleak. She had never ached with chilblains until she came to Yorkshire. Now her fingers were blue and swollen, and she tried to warm them by working

them in the folds of her shawl. When she had saved enough
money, perhaps in a year, she might be able to afford the
luxury of seeking other employment. The old restlessness
was never far away. .

She had not heard footsteps, but all at once there was a
jiggling of her key in the lock. Even as she rose to her feet
the key fell to the floor on her side with a distinct *clink*.
Moving toward the door with a look of disbelief, she heard
the scrape of another key and realized too late that someone
was unlocking her door from the outside. She turned and
ran toward the mantel to pick up the poker as the door
swung open.

"There she is!" Nicholas cried triumphantly as he reeled
across the threshold.

Ordinarily she would have credited Nicholas Maclean
with more than an average measure of handsomeness, with
his fair hair and tall, slender form, but his unwelcome
presence made him repugnant to her. She addressed him as
though speaking to a boy of six. "Your cravat is askew, sir,
and your collar is unbuttoned."

He smiled crookedly, putting a finger to his lips as he
came forward into the room. "Sh, mustn't wake Roberts,
Miss Alice. Yo-you're— My God!"

She lifted her weapon, unaware as she did so that she was
backlit by the fire, which threw into silhouette her figure
beneath her nightgown.

Nicholas's smile deepened into a leer as he took in the fiery
halo of hair and enticing outline of her body. "Bloody hell!
You ain't as plain as you seem! You've a right fine figure!"

She was prepared for his lunge but did not strike him a
hard blow. After all, he was the son of her employer. The
blow caught him on the tender flesh where the shoulder and
neck meet. He went down hard on one knee with an "Oof"
of pain, and she backed away. "Go away, Mr. Nicholas, or I
shall strike you again! I swear it!"

He looked up, the firelight reflected in his hungry gaze. "Stewart?" He glanced back over his shoulder to the doorway. "Stewart!" he called more impatiently. A flushed young man appeared in the doorway, and Aisleen recognized him as the one who had torn her sleeve. Lifting her poker again, she faced him as he came in.

It was a mistake. Nicholas grabbed her ankles and with a jerk pulled her feet out from under her. Aisleen screamed as she fell, and then her head struck the corner of the hearth, stunning her.

"Got her!" she heard Nicholas cry triumphantly as he dragged her across the floor toward him.

"Not on the floor, old boy," Stewart said disapprovingly. "'Tis devilishly cold for such sport. On the bed. There's time enough for the amenities."

Caught between shock and pain, Aisleen could not protest as she was lifted from the floor.

"A bit old for virgin flesh," Stewart suggested skeptically, "but I'll do the honors if you're certain she's game."

Nicholas's laugh came out as a snort through his nose. "Look at her! With hair that flaming color she's as hungry for a man as any strumpet! You can go first, but hurry!"

The lifting of her nightgown brought Aisleen back to reality, and she reached up with screams of rage, scratching and clawing at the men who held her.

"What is this!"

Miraculously Aisleen heard Roberts's gruff voice from the doorway.

"Please! Please help me!" she cried, scrambling away from the hands that suddenly freed her.

Nicholas turned toward the doorway, piqued that his game had been spoiled. "What the devil brings you here, Roberts? You've no business in the governess's room."

Clutching her shawl to her, Aisleen turned pleading eyes on the butler. The slight, balding man refused to meet her gaze as he said in quiet dignity, "Neither, Mr. Nicholas, do you."

Nicholas shrugged and rose from the bed. He glanced back over his shoulder at Aisleen. "Do invite me again, Miss Alice," he said with a sneer. "Come on, Stewart. Events have come to a sad end when a man cannot find a friendly bed beneath his own roof."

Aisleen did not move until both young gentlemen had withdrawn, and then she rose from the bed. "You are a witness, Roberts," she said forcefully. "You saw what happened. I am innocent!"

"What I saw will not make much difference to the outcome." Roberts's neutral expression did not alter, but she thought she saw sorrow in his eyes before he turned away.

As he started to close the door he paused to add, "I'd lock the door if I—"

She saw that he was staring at the key inserted in the outside lock. He took and pocketed it. When he looked up at her again his expression had softened. "You'll not be troubled again this night, Miss Alice. I'll see to it myself."

When he was gone, Aisleen poured water into her basin, stripped off her gown, and began to wash herself. Water ran in chilling rivulets over her thighs and arms, but she did not care that she shivered so hard that her teeth chattered. Any sensation was preferable to the shrinking revulsion of moments earlier. They had dared to touch her, the pair of them, had put their hands on her legs and waist and thighs. If Roberts had not appeared when he did . . .

"Oh, God!" she moaned. Dropping the cloth, she sank to her knees, her body trembling in the aftermath of the assault.

The tears did not last long, and soon she retrieved a handkerchief from her belongings and mopped her face.

Long ago she had accepted the fact that one's life was seldom ordered to one's desires. To be powerful, one must first be born a man, like her now-dead father or Nicholas Maclean. Yet physical assault was new to her. Never before had she felt so vulnerable, so helpless, so utterly useless in the face of a threat.

"Well, it's done," she murmured, but as she climbed into her bed she knew it was not. Only minutes earlier she had considered seeking a new post. That was not the same as being discharged for misconduct and without references. She was a spinster without recourse and without support. Her situation was not unlike the plot of some tawdry melodrama. If it were not so pathetically real, she would scoff at her circumstance.

With a sinking feeling, she realized that she was once more at the mercy of forces beyond her control. The Macleans were likely to believe Roberts, but they might also, like most people conscious of their position in society, be quite willing to deprive her of employment in order to keep scandal from beneath their roof.

"Oh, Holy Mother, what shall I do?" She had not yet saved enough to live on while she sought a new post. If she were dismissed she would be destitute.

Waterford, Ireland: February 1857

Aisleen sat stiff-backed in her chair as her mother ladled a generous serving of Soup Meagre for the man who had asked for her hand in marriage.

"*Och,* won't that set a man up just fine," Patrick Kirwan declared in a hearty voice tainted, in Aisleen's mind, by an uneducated brogue.

Aisleen stared down at her own soup plate, where bits of

cabbage, parsnips, onion, and sorrel swam in a creamy purée. Fresh vegetables were difficult to obtain. Only the wealthy could afford to pay for their importation from England. She had already appraised Mr. Kirwan's well-appointed dining room, noting that it was larger than the combined tiny rooms she shared with her mother. Mr. Kirwan was a man of parts. What was his interest in her impoverished mother?

She had been horrified when she arrived in Waterford three weeks earlier and found her mother talking excitedly about the man. Their marriage was all but accomplished, and she had not even been informed.

"Will ye not say grace for us, Aisleen?" Kathleen Fitzgerald asked when she had served them all.

After a quick, reassuring smile at her mother, Aisleen recited grace, noting from under lowered lids that Mr. Kirwan made the sign of the cross with the easy grace of a man accustomed to the gesture. So he was Catholic. That was small comfort. What was his interest in her mother?

"Well now, isn't it as fine a supper as ever any man had set before him?" Patrick Kirwan praised as he reached for his spoon. "Gracious company and gracious surroundings; a man could think himself apace with kings."

Aisleen looked across at her mother and, to her consternation, found her blushing. Kathleen Fitzgerald looked radiant and very pretty with her rich golden hair caught back from her face in a black hair net. Her gown of green-and-black check accentuated her slender waist and full bosom. Except for the fine lines about her mouth and eyes, she might have been a young girl with her first beau.

Aisleen glanced again at Mr. Kirwan and saw that he was smiling boldly at her mother. He was big, broad-shouldered, and deep-chested and had a quick, engaging smile. She understood her mother's interest in a man who wore a splendid frock coat when much of Ireland remained ill fed and nearly naked from the lingering effects of the famine years. But what were his reasons for pursuing her mother? When he suddenly looked across at her, Aisleen looked away.

It was the flash of good humor in his gray eyes that she suspected most. Nicholas Maclean had had charm, and yet he had cost her her job without regret. Never would she forget his smirking salute as Roberts handed her up into the carriage that took her away. He had smiled as though they had shared some great lark that was at an end. Her own father had been charming to a fault, until he began to drink. Charm was suspect.

To keep her thoughts at bay, Aisleen lifted a spoonful of soup to her mouth. "Why, Mother, this is delicious."

"Thank ye, dear, but part of the praise should go to Mr. Kirwan. He's responsible for the fresh vegetables as well as the slice of veal and oysters from which I've made our supper pie."

Mr. Kirwan smiled. "Were little enough, yer mother refusing the salary I offered her."

"What salary?" Aisleen questioned sharply.

"Didn't she tell ye?" Patrick Kirwan asked. "Kathy, darling, ye promised ye'd talk it over with the lass. And being the right sensible lass I see her to be, she'll agree with me."

Kathleen Fitzgerald pinkened a second time. "I wanted to wait until the two of ye had met." She looked beseechingly at her daughter. "Aisleen, ye'll remember that I wrote ye about the gowns I copied for Mrs. Gorham from the London fashion plates she showed me. I sketched them myself and even made a few small changes in the designs before I cut the patterns. Mrs. Gorham was so pleased with the results that she gave me permission to shop for her and charge her personal accounts."

"That is how we met," Patrick Kirwan said with a wink at Kathleen. "She's as meek as a mouse and as clever as a cat, yer ma, but she's nae head for business. I told her that the first day.''

Ignoring the comment, Aisleen waited patiently for her mother to continue.

"Mr. Kirwan owns a fabric shop as well as Kirwan Mills,'' Kathleen continued after a moment's hesitation. "We met when I was in his shop to select a bolt of cloth.''

"A fateful day that was,'' he added. "One look at yer ma's sketches told me she's as clever as she is pretty.'' He smiled at Kathleen. "She gives them away, did ye know? Nae, ye couldn't be knowing or ye'd have said the same as I. She should make her customers pay for the sketches. Sold three of them in me store, but she won't take the money.''

Aisleen turned to her mother in amazement. "I knew your sketches were splendid, Mother, but why did you not tell me that people were willing to pay you for them?''

Kathleen smiled. "They are willing to pay Mr. Kirwan for what hangs in his shop.''

" 'Tis the same thing,'' Patrick maintained. "Five shillings each, and she could make more if she heeded me advice.''

Aisleen saw the intent expression on his face, and all at once she understood his interest. It was so simple she nearly smiled. Mr. Patrick Kirwan wanted control of her mother's talent, and marriage was the quickest and easiest way of ensuring that he would always have it.

"I agree that your advice is sound, Mr. Kirwan,'' she said with a direct look at him. "I shall begin at once to encourage Mother to set up a business of her own.''

"That's the ticket,'' he answered with a smile she did not expect. "Did nae I tell ye she'd see my way in it, Kathy?''

Kathleen shook her head with a small smile. "Perhaps Aisleen should consider setting herself up in business. As for myself, I am quite content.''

For the first time, Patrick Kirwan regarded Aisleen with a

deep, penetrating gaze. "Are ye not satisfied with yer post in Yorkshire?"

Aisleen felt her cheeks warming with embarrassment, but she held his gaze. "I am no longer employed there. I am seeking a new post." She glanced at her mother. "Perhaps in London."

"London? Ye cannot be thinking of returning all the way to England, not when I've not seen ye these last twelve years," Kathleen protested. "Can ye not seek a situation closer by?"

Aisleen flashed her mother a look of annoyance. She did not want to discuss her private life before a stranger. She had seen the look of surprise Mr. Kirwan quickly masked when they were introduced. She was nothing like her mother. That look had discomforted her. She did not want his approval, but neither did she want his pity. "I am ever resourceful, Mother, never fear."

"Well, I will," Kathleen answered in motherly concern. "Until ye're settled I cannae think of anything else."

"She's well spoken," Patrick Kirwan said. "One would think her English born and bred by the sound of her."

Aisleen did not look up, uncertain whether he considered that a compliment or not.

"The very thing!" he continued, as if struck by inspiration. "I could use a lass of learning in me shop."

Kathleen looked at him with gratitude. "Ye have such a place open in yer business?"

"*Musha,* I did not say that. But I'll be making a place, if that's what Miss Aisleen should want," he suggested with a broad smile.

Made. The thought hung in Aisleen's mind. A position could be made for her—not filled or earned by her, but made. She would be an afterthought in his business, like an extra flounce cut from a piece of leftover cloth meant to be swept up with the rest of the scraps. Was she always to be unnecessary to the world in which she lived: an extra piece, an afterthought, a redundant woman? Aisleen shivered.

" 'Tis a wonderful suggestion," Kathleen answered in delight. "It means ye could remain here, with us."

"Aye, we'd be a family," Patrick Kirwan added. "That is, if yer mother will have me."

Aisleen rose to her feet. "I—I don't feel well. It must be something I ate earlier. Do go on without me. I'll walk home—it's not far."

She saw the look of hurt crowd out the joy in her mother's eyes, but she could not remain. She had to remove herself from them before she began to vent her anger and frustration and hurt.

Fifteen minutes later, when the door to the rooms she shared with her mother had closed behind her, Aisleen rested her head against it. She did not cry. She had not cried since the night Nicholas Maclean attacked her and was determined never to do so again. What she needed was a plan to set herself and her mother free from the tyranny of their womanhood.

Nevertheless she could not keep back the ungrateful, small knot of hurt she felt at the thought of Mr. Kirwan's courtship of her mother. There had never been a suitor in her life, and it seemed there never would be.

"Wouldn't have him in any case," she said aloud and straightened up. She did not need or want any man's approval. She must convince her mother to think likewise.

Yet later, in bed, she wondered what it would be like to have a man look at her as Patrick Kirwan had looked at her mother. He had seemed besotted, as though he could not drink in enough of her beauty. Was that love or merely the lust that had gleamed in animal brightness in Nicholas Maclean's eyes?

Aisleen sighed in resignation. She was destined never to know. What she did know was that men could not be trusted.

*   *   *

"Whatever would I do with me patterns if Patrick did not sell them?" Kathleen asked the next morning as she and Aisleen shared a pot of tea in their parlor.

"You could sell them yourself," Aisleen answered, helping herself to a slice of soda bread.

"Sometimes ye have the strangest notions, lass," her mother answered with a gentle shake of her head.

"In England many women have their own businesses," Aisleen maintained. "Seamstresses who design gowns for the wealthy call themselves modistes, and they do very well for themselves. They drive elegant carriages and command their own servants."

"*Musha,* what would I be doing with servants?" Her mother chuckled. "As for a carriage, I cannae drive one."

"You would not need to," Aisleen replied patiently. "You would hire a driver, and a footman, and as many seamstresses as you like. You would sketch the designs, have tea with your customers, and leave the drudgery to others."

"Ye flatter me, Aisleen. Even if all ye say were true, it would nae be me wish to embark on so strenuous a venture at me age."

"You are but forty-two, Mother, and in better health than you've ever been," Aisleen countered.

Kathleen smiled as she regarded her daughter. "What'll ye be thinking of Mr. Kirwan?"

Aisleen smiled. "I can say without equivocation that he is not worthy of your consideration."

Kathleen's eyes filled with reproach, but she said quietly, "How can ye be so very certain of the man when ye've only just met?"

"One does not need a second whiff to know when a fish

is spoiled," Aisleen answered. She saw the hurt in her mother's eyes deepen, but she felt she must speak the truth. "He sees in your talent a means to increase his wealth, Mother. He did not even bother to hide his interest. Did he not claim that you could live well from the sums you might earn? What else could make him offer for you?"

"What else, indeed?" Kathleen answered softly.

Aisleen blushed. "You know that I think you are wonderful and clever and still quite beautiful."

"For a woman of my years," Kathleen suggested wryly.

Aisleen's cheeks reddened further. "You could have a life better than that you now live without giving up your freedom to a man who would use you and ultimately do you injury. If you do not heed me you will end up a prisoner of marriage once again."

"Where can ye have heard such nonsense?" Kathleen questioned in mystification. "Marriage is the natural course for a woman, unless the Church calls her."

"Was your life with Da happy? What did he offer you besides poverty, misery, and humiliation?"

"Ye have been listening to the English suffragettes!" her mother said suddenly. "They are unnatural women with unnatural goals. When ye find a man whose manner suits ye, ye'll understand 'tis nonsense, this talk of liberation."

"There'll never be a 'when' for me, Mother," Aisleen said abruptly.

Reproach filled Kathleen's eyes. "I know that the first years of yer life were hard ones, what with an ailing mother and a—a very troubled father."

Aisleen stiffened. "You may speak plainly, Mother. Da was a man who loved drink more than his own kin."

"Aisleen! Ye'll nae refer to yer father's weakness in that tone. He was a man of spirit and ambition whom the world did not see fit to endow with its riches."

"He was a despot and a drunkard who fell to his death

beneath the hooves of a Dublin dray horse because he was too sodden with drink to rise!''

"Aisleen!" Kathleen whispered in a shocked voice. She reached for one of her daughter's hands and held it tightly, saying quietly, "I blame meself for yer anger. I should have been better able to plead for ye when yer father sent ye away."

"Da would not have listened. He nearly killed you in his desire to sire a son," Aisleen returned calmly. "No, do not look away, Mother. He never cared for me, not from the first day of my life to the last day of his. I was not the son he desired, and for that we were both made to suffer."

Kathleen stared at her daughter. "Ye were hurt more deeply than I knew. I should have expected it. We're mother and daughter, yet we're more nearly strangers than any two people meeting on the street. But ye're home at last and we've many years to make up. So don't scold me for hoping that ye'll not wed too soon."

Aisleen blinked. "I have not mentioned marriage."

Kathleen nodded. "Ye've the heart of a Fitzgerald in ye. No man ye claim will ever be able to resist ye."

Aisleen stared at her mother. "Look at me, Mother, and see me as I am, a spinster lady with nothing to offer. I may be a Fitzgerald, but I will undoubtedly be the last of our line."

Kathleen was silent for a moment. It pained her that her daughter and only child had grown into womanhood without a proper appreciation for her unique beauty and spirit. She had known from the beginning that Quenton resented his daughter's strength and passion. At the time she had been too weak to stand between them. When Aisleen was sent away she hoped and prayed that it was the answer to keep her from being destroyed. But the young woman who sat before her now was different from the passionate, life-loving child who had gone away. This lady kept her inner feelings hidden, perhaps even from herself. Was it anger or fear that had her locked inside herself? Kathleen shook her head slightly. So many years separated them. Perhaps she would never know.

"Oh, Aisleen!" Kathleen exclaimed, rising to embrace her daughter. "Ye're young yet and the world is before ye. Many a lass has thought herself passed by just before her beau appeared."

She brushed an errant curl back from Aisleen's face, pretending not to see her daughter's stubborn expression. "Ye've a world of love and good sense to bring a man. Someday a man will see this and value ye for it."

"I do not wish to be valued as one values a rare jewel or a fine horse," Aisleen replied stiffly. "Mother, with me to manage your business we would soon be able to afford a small cottage of our very own. What more could a man offer either of us?"

"Companionship," Kathleen answered, her expression softening.

"Am I not as good company as your Mr. Kirwan?" Aisleen asked in a wounded tone.

Kathleen smiled knowingly. "Ye're so learned in so many matters that I sometimes forget how very innocent ye are, lass. I love ye as none other in all me life. But a woman needs another kind of loving, a love which only a man can answer."

Aisleen backed out of her mother's embrace. "You mean to marry Mr. Kirwan?"

Kathleen shook her head. "Ye're me daughter, and I will do nothing of which ye strongly disapprove. But ye're wrong if ye believe that Patrick wants only me cleverness with gowns. He could purchase that with wages. And well he knows it, though he pretends I'll not accept them. He's a widower and as tired as I of keeping company with a stool by the fire each night. If in exchange for his name I can offer him me talent, then I'll be thanking God for it. Me only regret is that I did nae recognize me gift in time to save yer da.''

Aisleen could find nothing with which to answer that. "If you are fixed on marriage, then I suppose it's useless for me to protest further."

Kathleen's expression brightened. "Ye're quite vexed that yer mother has desires that run contrary to yer own. I do not claim to be clever or wise, Aisleen, but I have a woman's feelings, and they are fixed on Patrick. Do not be so very angry with me. We shall make a neat little family. Patrick's home is quite large enough for three."

Aisleen shook her head. "I intend to seek a new situation immediately. You must not allow Mr. Kirwan to believe that I shall become a burden to him."

"He has offered ye a position," Kathleen reminded her.

"It is too late," Aisleen replied. "I am ready to answer an advertisement and hope for a quick reply."

"Is it a teaching post?" Kathleen asked hopefully.

"Yes," Aisleen answered shortly, wanting only to be left alone. "It pays quite well."

"Well then, isn't that wonderful?" Kathleen clapped her hands. "Things will come right for all of us, just ye wait."

After breakfast Aisleen went to her room and locked the door behind her. When she had set pen and parchment on the small table before her, she reached into her purse and withdrew a small ad clipped from the *London Times*. It had been pressed into her hand by Roberts as she climbed aboard the coach that took her from Yorkshire. At the time she had thought it an insult. Now it was to be her salvation. She could not destroy her mother's happiness by refusing to accept the marriage she so clearly wanted. But neither would she remain and watch the disillusionment that was certain to follow.

Aisleen spread the paper open and reread the blurred print.

SCHOLASTIC—A lady, long established in the
Colony, wishes to meet with an English Protestant
lady, either single or a widow without family, to
join her in the management of her establishment;
to a lady fully qualified to finish young ladies in a
sound English education: the Harp, Piano,
Drawing, Italian, French, and German. Very
advantageous terms will be offered. Emigration funds
available through Caroline Britten Colonization
Loan Society. Address post paid to Mrs. Britten's
Stationer.

Sydney, New South Wales, December 12

Aisleen's lips thinned. She was fully qualified by all the
standards of the terms—except for her nationality and faith.
She had never deliberately lied in her life. She would not lie
about the first but, she decided in a spurt of anger at the
world's unfairness, she would omit reference to her religious affiliation.

Without pausing to consider the enormity of what she was
doing, Aisleen picked up her pen and began to write.

When she was finished, she stared for a long time at the
address: Sydney, New South Wales.

The words evoked a shiver of anticipation she had not felt
in many years. Once, long ago, she had dared to dream of
adventure, of faraway places, of excitement and glory. Once
she believed it was possible to climb the highest mountain,
to be as grand and proud as her ancient ancestors. Loneliness
had been the only fear in the dreams she had dreamed.

Aisleen closed her eyes. It was so difficult to remember
herself as a wild-haired lass with dirty feet and the belief
that all things were possible. In her loneliness and isolation
she had made a bright world out of thin air. Could she do so
again?

The answer came not as words, yet the image was clear. The shape of a valley came to mind, a place she had never before seen, a deep green valley silver-laden with mist. At its heart a river raced, the clear surface betraying green-gold depths. Pungent and sweet fragrances of grass and spring flowers vied with the exotic aromas of spice and sea.

Come with me.

For an instant the old plea whispered wantonly in her ear. Once she had turned away from the dare that had come as a boyish taunt. She touched the browned edge of the crisping newspaper. It was as fragile as a wish, the words it contained as compelling as an ancient incantation.

Aisleen shook her head and withdrew her hand. She was too old for fairy tales and daydreaming. What she planned was daring enough for the bravest of souls, but her goals were eminently practical ones. England was overcrowded with women like her. Ireland could not support her. Her mother did not need her. She was alone; her future was her own to decide. If it must be, then she would make a new beginning a world away.

Yet when she had affixed a stamp to the letter she sat staring at the address as excitement trembled through her. *I have not forgotten, bouchal,* she thought with a smile. *I am seeking my adventure at last.*

Ah, Exiles wandering over lands and seas,
And planning, plotting always that some morrow
May set a stone upon ancestral Sorrow!

—Dedication...
W. B. Yeats

Chapter Four

Sydney, Australia: September 1857

Aisleen stood at the rail on the crowded deck of the sailing ship *Black Opal*, her silk parasol the only relief from the wilting heat of the Australian day. Overhead the sun shone with an intensity that made the air vibrate. The scene before her eyes danced in wavy lines as the fishy odors of Jackson Bay and the sharp tang of baked earth made her vividly aware that she was at last going ashore.

Perspiration trickled down her spine and between her breasts, dampening her corset. The petticoats she wore weighed her down more than usual. Beneath her silk bonnet her scalp itched with the heat. She hoped that her face did not reflect the discomfort she felt, for she expected to be met at the dock by her new employer.

For twelve weeks she had lived in the belly of this ship.

During the first miserable days, prostrating seasickness had confined her to the damp quarters she shared with a dozen young girls of the servant class. There she had spent hour after hour recalling her mother's arguments against the journey and her own cavalier replies that she was equal to the task. How puny those assurances had seemed then.

She had reached an uneasy truce with her stomach when the cold, austere face of the North Atlantic had given way to the balmy weather of the equatorial regions. If it had not been for the harrowing passage around the Cape she might have forgotten her fear of sailing. Now all that was behind her. Before her stretched out her goal: the colony of New South Wales.

"Have you seen them, then, Miss Fitzgerald?"

Aisleen turned to the bewhiskered middle-aged man who wore the red military uniform of a British officer. "Good day, Major Scott. To whom do you refer?"

"Why the aborigines, of course!" he boomed. "Dock's usually crawling with them." He moved forward against the rail, surveying the deck with a practiced squint, and then shook his head. "Nary a one. Must have scared them away, knowing you had arrived to teach them the curtsy and waltz," he finished with a chuckle.

Aisleen smiled slightly at the joke, which had grown very stale. At the beginning of the voyage the major had misunderstood when she had informed him that she sailed to Sydney to teach English manners to the native Australians. He had taken the statement to mean the aborigines. Since then, whenever they met he had never failed to mention the joke.

From the first she had summed him up as a self-important but harmless man. If not for the fact that she had been one of the first to recover from the seasickness, while the major's wife had scarcely left her cabin during the journey, they would never have struck up an acquaintance. "How is Mrs. Scott this morning?"

Major Scott pursed his lips, which made his mustache bristle. "Right enough to prepare herself for the occasion of disembarking. She's no sailor, I give you that."

"One must make allowances for her," Aisleen answered.

"Right!" he replied. "Still, will never understand why the missus chose to begin an addition to the detail before we reached our destination. Never leave a woman to plan a campaign, I say."

Aisleen ignored the comment. Gentlemen did not speak of pregnancy with unmarried ladies. It was indelicate at best, bordering on the objectionable. "Will we be allowed to leave the ship soon?"

"Certainly. But I'd watch my step if I were you, Miss Fitzgerald. 'Tis the shearing season. The city will be full of jackeroos and drovers, as well as the usual riffraff."

Aisleen looked toward the teeming dock, where drays stacked with fine, smooth, honey-colored lumber jostled carts loaded with grain sacks and barrels. Her gaze moved to the steady stream of ox-drawn wagons piled a story high with sorted and baled wool. Like a huge canvas-backed snake, the line of wagons wound a sinuous path along the dock front to the ships waiting to carry the wool back over the thousands of miles of ocean she had just traveled to the northern industrialized milling centers of England's Midlands.

She gave a fleeting thought to her mother and her new stepfather. They would soon be selling cloth made from the merino wool laded here in Sydney. The thought vanished as her attention was caught by another sight on the waterfront.

Dressed in gray canvas jackets and checked trousers, with caps partially covering their shaved heads, a group of men walked in clumsy unison. As the path cleared before them she saw sunlight glinting on metal links and collars and realized with a shock that these men were prisoners.

"A rare sight, that." Major Scott frowned as the men were herded up the gangplank of a nearby ship. "Must be bound for the salt mines, the poor beggars."

"What are they?" Aisleen asked, unable to turn her gaze from the sight of the miserable men.

"It's where the law sends the hard cases."

A whip cracked, slicing through the sounds of the quay, and Major Scott felt the young woman beside him flinch. "It's a shame, I agree. 'Twas hoped when the government of New South Wales put an end to transportation that we'd see no more convicts. Here's me advice to you. Give those men less thought than you would a stray dog, Miss Fitzgerald."

"Less—?" Aisleen caught herself and forced her gaze away. It was none of her business. She had chosen to come to New South Wales knowing full well that it had once been a penal colony. The major was right. She would have to become accustomed to strange sights and give them no thought. But she could not still the indignant feeling that had risen within her. Surely there were better ways of dealing with such men.

"Your bags have been lowered into the dinghy, Miss Fitzgerald." The steward doffed his hat as Aisleen turned to him. "If you're ready to disembark, I'm to show you the way."

"That won't be necessary," Major Scott cut in and offered Aisleen his arm.

The offer surprised Aisleen. She had not thought him the gallant sort. Yet, in her dealings with men, she had found they needed little or no encouragement to preen. Doubt dimmed her countenance. "Will you not need to see to your wife, Major?"

"When the rush for the quay has ebbed I'll collect her," he answered, still holding out his crooked elbow.

Aisleen looked down at the bobbing boat into which she was expected to climb and decided that perhaps she might benefit from a stout arm to help her on shore. "Thank you, Major," she said, accepting his arm.

"You've every reason to be cautious." The major took up his thought once they were safely ensconced in the boat that carried them the short distance to the quay. "Don't accept the first proposal that comes your way, that's my advice to you. Look the lot over before choosing a husband."

Aisleen stiffened as she sat by his side. "I have not come to Sydney to wed; I've come to teach."

Giving her a skeptical look, he said, "See that lot yonder?" He nodded toward the group of men standing to one side of the pier at dockside. "Bushmen mostly. Whenever they're in town they meet the incoming ships in hopes of finding themselves a bride. You'll be lucky to get past them without receiving at least one marriage proposal."

Aisleen stared at the throng of bushy-bearded men in floppy-brimmed hats as the boat docked at the pier, and her gaze was greeted by a cheer that made her blush even as she looked away. "Preposterous!" she murmured.

"I see a prime 'un! Get the clergyman!" one of the group called out, and his cry was answered by more raucous male laughter as Aisleen was handed up onto the wharf by two seamen. A moment later the major appeared by her side, and she did not hesitate to take the arm he extended.

"Bring her on, Major!" another jeered. "She deserves better than an old sod the likes of ye!"

"Do not quail before them, Miss Fitzgerald," Major Scott said under his breath. "They'll not lay a hand on you. Just talk, that's all they know."

Aisleen looked down her nose at the crowd of scruffy men as they started toward the dock. "Is that the fisheries of Port Jackson I smell, Major, or is it the population?"

The men accepted the comment with good-natured hoots of laughter.

"That's the spirit, lass!" a drayman called fom his perch. "Dinna let them jackeroos scare ye!"

She ignored the other sallies coming her way, glad that she had the major as her escort. To her surprise, once they reached dockside the boisterousness subsided. Several of the men who had teased her snatched their hats from their heads as she passed, their grins less leering and their gazes almost shy. Even so, she pretended not to notice, lifting her chin to stare over their heads.

Once on the dock she quickly became aware of other things, like the costermongers holding up food and liquid libation as their cries of "Two a ha'penny!" and "Shilling a toss!" split the air.

The major led the way through the lines of traffic until he found a patch of shade under the overhang of a warehouse. "Here we are, Miss Fitzgerald. A bit of respite from the heat."

Aisleen touched a gloved hand to her forehead beneath her corded bonnet, where a fine beading of moisture had formed. "I trust I shall learn to deal with the clime after a few days. The summer's heat certainly lingers in this latitude."

Major Scott looked at her with amusement. "September is the beginning of spring by Australian reckoning."

"Oh, that's right!" Aisleen sighed inwardly. How, she wondered with misgiving as she lowered her umbrella, was she to survive the climate if the springs were warmer than summers in Ireland?

"You'll get the right of it," the major assured her. "If you are not being met, please permit me to..." His voice trailed away as he spied his wife on the deck of the *Black Opal*. "Sarah! Sarah Scott! Pardon me a moment, Miss Fitzgerald," he called over his shoulder as he started toward the pier.

It happened so quickly Aisleen could not prevent herself from falling to her knees when she was shoved roughly in the back. The next instant her purse was snatched from her wrist.

"My purse!" she cried indignantly as she scrambled to her feet. "That boy—oh! There he goes! Stop him! Stop him!" Without waiting for aid she started after the thief. All her money and the address of her employer were in that purse. If she lost it, she would be destitute and helpless.

"Let me pass!" she cried to those who crowded the quay. To her dismay the thief's path was opening up before him as if by magic while the seamen in her way did not move aside but stood grinning at her. They were deliberately allowing the boy to escape!

"Out of my way!" she ordered again and tried to elbow her way through the wall of sailors. When they did not comply, without hesitation she stamped the pointed heel of her leather boot hard on the instep of the man nearest her. The burly man reeled away with a yelp of pain, and she dove through the opening he left.

Her height served her well, for it allowed her to keep sight of the boy. But, hampered by the weight of her many petticoats and the rubbery-kneed feeling left from having been a long time at sea, she could not keep up with him, and he quickly outdistanced her.

"Oh, no!" she whispered in dismay when he rounded the corner of a warehouse. Gasping for breath, she reached the corner only to find that he had disappeared. It was gone, all of it: her money, her instructions, and the crystal brooch her mother had given her. Anger swept her as she turned away from the empty alley. "Damn! Damn! Damn!"

"Do you hear that, laddie? The lass must be a fearsome dragon, for all she looks a lady."

Aisleen looked up at the sound of the amused masculine voice with the caressing lilt of an Irish brogue. The next instant her gaze locked with the vivid blue of a stranger's and she felt her world compress to the limits of those incredibly bright eyes.

A wild tangle of black beard hid half his face, and a hat with turned-down brim cast a shadow low on his brow. She could smell the unpleasant musky odor of dirt and sweat and sheep emanating from his worn and stained clothes. Yet, for a moment, something as familiar and comforting as a childhood memory rose to mind.

A scent like heather borne on a breeze from the Irish Sea suddenly enveloped her with poignant sweetness, faint at first and then nearly overwhelming in its pungency. The shadows of home reached out to her . . .

The sensation vanished more quickly than her senses could record it, and an instant later Aisleen realized that the bushman held her thief firmly by the hair. "You caught him!"

"That I did," the stranger replied, easily avoiding the kicks and blows the boys aimed at him. "What will ye have me do with him, then?"

She frowned at the boy. He was not as large as she had thought. He was nothing more than a filthy assortment of rags and angular bones topped by a thatch of sun-bleached hair.

"Don't hurt him," she cautioned when the boy finally landed a blow high on his captor's thigh and the man retaliated by smacking the flat of his hand against the side of the boy's head.

The stranger gave her a hard glance. "Hadn't ye better make up yer mind?" He jerked a cry of pain from the boy in an effort to restrain him. "Ye were giving fair chase after the lad. Was it to thank him for relieving ye of this?"

Aisleen looked at the purse he held out. "Thank you," she said with heartfelt relief. Careful not to touch the stranger's hand, she took it. When he smiled at her she knew he understood her reluctance to touch him and was amused by the fact. That annoyed her, and she turned quickly to the boy, her expression severe.

"Aren't you ashamed of yourself? What would your parents think were they to learn of your thievery? Do you realize what sort of impression your conduct makes on new arrivals?"

Before she could guess his intent, the boy kicked her in the shin. With a sharp cry of pain she stepped back.

A rude guffaw exploded from the black tangle of the man's beard. "Ye're wasting yer breath, m'um." He shook the boy roughly until Aisleen's teeth hurt in sympathy for the child, and then he gave the boy a box on the ear before releasing him. "Off with ye!"

The boy's feet had scarceless touched the ground before he swung back on Aisleen with a hiss of fury. "Ye bloody pommie slut!"

This time Aisleen was prepared, and her eyes narrowed in challenge as she hoisted her parasol. "Touch me again and I'll thrash you myself," she said in a tone she would never have used with a well-behaved child.

The boy hesitated, his widened eyes darting to the bearded man and then back to the lady. He was not accustomed to ladies who gave chase. Most often they could be counted on to scream and faint when he robbed them.

"Bleedin' pommie sow!" he called over his shoulder as he turned and ran.

"Keep away from the wharf or I'll have you arrested!" Aisleen called back.

"Good on ye!" the bearded man voiced in approval. "Threats are all he understands. As for his parents, wouldn't doubt their acquaintance was above an evening's."

Aisleen blushed at the crude remark. Because he had saved her purse, that did not mean that the bushman had the right to be familiar. "I thank you for your timely intervention," she replied in the same superior tone she had used with the major. "This should answer for your trouble." She opened her purse and offered him a coin.

She saw a flash of anger in his eyes as his gaze moved from the coin in her gloved palm to her face. Then his gaze moved down over the voluminous skirts of her navy blue traveling dress. A slow smile formed in his nest of beard as his gaze wandered back to her face. The smile widened in response to some huge joke that he did not share with her. To her astonishment, he reached out and pulled one of her curls which had come loose in the chase. "Can ye do no better, lass?"

Aisleen stepped back and self-consciously put a hand to her bonnet, only to realize that it had slipped from her head during the chase and now dangled by its ribbons down her back. Her hair, which had been carefully coiled into buns on either side of her head, had slid free of its pins and cascaded over her shoulders. Hastily she retrieved her bonnet and set it on her head.

"Do nae hide yer glory, lass," he said softly. " 'Tis bonny fine hair ye have. 'Tis the color of a sunset in the back of beyond."

She ignored the dubious assessment of her charms and turned away. Relief swept through her as she spied the figure of Major Scott bearing down on them.

"Good heavens, Miss Fitzgerald! You shouldn't have chased that larrikin!" He sounded winded as he reached her side. "A lady, alone in an alley—you cannot possibly imagine what might happen."

The major's scolding only added fuel to Aisleen's embarrassment. "Nonsense, Major! I am quite accustomed to dealing with children. Besides, I was hardly alone. I have Mr.—" Aisleen fell silent as she turned and found the bearded stranger had disappeared. "Why, that's odd. Where did he go?"

"The bushman, do you mean?" the major asked. "I

saw him. No doubt he thought better of braving an English officer. Did he make overtures to you, Miss Fitzgerald?''

"Overtures?'' Aisleen repeated in mystification. "I should think not! He caught my thief.'' She held up her purse as proof.

The major was not impressed. "Miss Fitzgerald, if you are to get on in the colony you must remain on your guard. That man might have been the thief's accomplice. They may have plotted together to snatch your purse to lure you away from the dock. Good God!'' he cried, forgetting that he was in the presence of a lady. "You might have been stolen out from under my very nose.''

"Stolen for what purpose?'' Aisleen asked skeptically as she readjusted her bonnet.

Major Scott's startled gaze rested on her a moment. Could she really not guess the reason? Her appearance was that of a pleasant but plain spinster lady, yet surely some man had once pursued her? And now, with her bonnet askew, her cheeks flushed, and the most remarkable red curls tumbling from beneath her bonnet, she was quite a fetching picture. All the more reason, perhaps, that he should admonish her.

"Miss Fitzgerald, I must be frank. Do not assume that life in New South Wales will be a pastoral idyll. There is civility among the city population but, unfortunately, you've already witnessed the other sort.''

Aisleen heard the censure of her behavior with faint irritation. "I suppose you refer to the man who saved my purse when no one else would.''

The major's cheeks reddened. "Perhaps, Miss Fitzgerald, I am less than fair in his case. But I warn you, do not be deceived by the rogues of Sydney. Men like those who greet the arriving ships and this bushman who saved your purse are not bound by the rules of decent society. They consider any female without male protection fair game.'' He did not see the gathering storm in Aisleen's expression or he would not have continued. "In any case, you would not wish to consort with convicts."

This declaration silenced Aisleen's intended remark about her lack of interest in a husband. "Surely you do not refer to the man who saved my property?"

"I do, Miss Fitzgerald," he continued. "Many a bushman and jackeroo is the descendant of convicts. He may be an ex-convict himself."

Aisleen glanced back at the deserted alley. The man was an Irishman. Had he once been a rebel transported for crimes against the English Crown? The thought both appalled her and piqued her curiosity, but it was not the major's business what she thought.

"Well, Major, I can say I've survived my first adventure in the colony," she declared with a sense of humor the major had not suspected.

"Indeed you have, miss," he answered with an arched brow. He had misjudged her in more matters than one, it seemed. "We should return to the quay. I must collect my wife, and you have your bags to look to."

As they retraced their steps Aisleen could not forget that pair of mocking eyes of brilliant blue. Was it admiration that shone in the bushman's gaze? Was it because she had given chase to the thief or merely because she, a lady, had spoken to him?

Aisleen smiled. The major's declarations about wife-hungry bushmen were beginning to influence her reasoning. The bushman had been amused by her disheveled appearance. And yet, she remembered with surprising pleasure, he had paid her a careless compliment about her hair; and she had been flattered. That in itself was remarkable enough to make him memorable.

The remembered scent of heather stirred briefly in her

mind. "Is there a flower garden nearby, Major?" she asked absently.

Major Scott burst into laughter. "How could one tell when the air reeks of the docks?"

Aisleen did not answer. She was mistaken, of course. It was the Irishman's brogue that had brought back memories of rolling green hills spiked with fragrant wild flowers. She was homesick and more than a little unsettled by the events of the last minutes. The reminder of home had been welcome. As for the bushman himself, he was no doubt the rogue Major Scott pegged him as. Only a fool or a pitiable spinster would allow herself to dwell on the hollow flirtations of a stranger.

When Major Scott had led her to her baggage Aisleen realized that she did not even know which step to take next. She knew nothing about the people for whom she had come eleven thousand miles to work. She had only a name and an address, thanks to the bushman's quick action. "I have an address here," she said crisply as she pulled the letter from her purse. "If you will find a hansom cab for me—oh, dear, there is such a thing, isn't there?"

"Indeed there is, Miss Fitzgerald," the major assured her.

"Miss Fitzgerald?" repeated a middle-aged woman who stood nearby. She turned to Aisleen. "Are you Miss Alice Fitzgerald of Dublin?"

"I am," Aisleen answered.

The woman extended a gloved hand. "My name is Mrs. Freeman. I am from Hyde Park Barracks. Welcome to Sydney."

Aisleen shook the woman's hand. "Thank you. Did Mrs. Britten send you?"

The woman nodded. "You are to come with me until arrangements can be made for you."

Before Aisleen could question her further, Mrs. Freeman

signaled a young boy to begin loading Aisleen's baggage onto a cart. "Come along now, we've kept the others waiting."

Aisleen looked up at the wagon onto which her bags were being piled and recognized one of her cabin mates from the ship. The girl smiled and offered her hand, but the major suddenly grasped Aisleen about the waist and lifted her up.

Aisleen looked back at the major with a slight frown. "I was quite capable, but I thank you, Major Scott, for everything. Give my farewells to your lady wife."

"Righto!" Major Scott answered with a wave. As the wagon rolled away he brought his hands together as he had around Aisleen's waist and grinned at the narrowness of the span. Nineteen inches and not a fraction more, with hair the color of flame; surely he had misjudged the young woman.

Sally Wilks smiled warmly at the man who entered the Cross and Crown, one of Sydney's more notorious drinking establishments. Amid the cluster of sailors and dock workers who filled the tavern, the man in moleskin britches and broad-brimmed hat struck a definite contrast. Anyone watching would have known instantly that he was in from the bush. But for her the sight had a special significance. After two years' absence, Tom Gibson was back in town.

At a little above average height, he was not the biggest man in the room, and he suffered from time to time with a gimpy leg; but he was as tough as any of them. She had known him to drink a roomful of seamen under the table and still complete a twelve-hour shift on the shearing floor of Parramatta, fifteen miles away, the next day.

Sally's gaze traveled over the solid muscles clearly outlined beneath his soft gray trousers. A clean plaid shirt clothed the upper portion of his work-toughened body. As he lifted his broad-brimmed hat, revealing a head of thick glossy black hair, her stomach jumped nervously. He had not changed. He was handsomer than ever.

She waited for him every shearing season, wondering if he had married or died during the intervening year. When he had not returned last spring, she had canvassed the few drovers and swagmen who came to the Cross and Crown for news of him. From them she had learned that he now owned a station in the north near Armidale. Some said he would soon be as wealthy as any man in the colony. Most important of all, he had not yet wed.

Anticipation tingled through Sally. She did not care. She would marry him be he swagman, sundowner, or shearer. She had been a child when they met, and because of him she had never given herself to any of the men who frequented the public house. From the first her heart had been fixed on Tom. This year she meant to have him.

" 'Ere! Sally! There's a swab dyin' o' thirst!'' shouted one of the sailors at a nearby table.

"Shove off!'' Sally called back, but she moved to draw the man a fresh pint. " 'E's a two-pot screamer, that one,'' she muttered. Couldn't hold his liquor worth tuppence, but he was a steady customer.

When she had delivered the order, she saw that Tom had propped his feet on the table. His chin had dropped forward against his chest, and she knew he had fallen asleep.

A few moments later, she was beside him with a tumbler of ale and a plate of stew. "Long season, luv?'' she questioned softly and gently shook his shoulder.

At the unexpected touch Thomas reached automatically for the pistol he kept tucked in his waistband. An instant later, he eased back in his chair. "Hullo, Sally! Didn't see ye when I came in. Thought ye'd deserted me for another man.''

"Evenin's young,'' she answered in the thick Cockney

accent which betrayed her origins. "A girl must earn 'er keep." She leaned forward to set the stew before him and then curved her hand against his cheek to stroke his beard. "Ouch! Ye're as prickly as a porcupine, ye are. 'Twould give a girl a rash."

As she bent forward to place his meal before him, her full-swelling breasts snagged Thomas's attention. Her skin was as white as goose down, and the edge of one ruby crest peeked over the edge of her low-cut bodice. She had been a scrawny child when they met, and he continued to think of her as a mere lass. As she straightened, his gaze moved first to her narrow waist, then her gently flaring hips. That was no longer true. A sudden stirring in his loins reminded him of how long he had been without a woman.

A secret smile softened the corners of his mouth. He had nearly forgotten the grazier's wife up on the Lachkan River. They had had a single night; but she had been as lonely as he, and the sleepless night had seen him well-satisfied... until now.

His gaze met Sally's and he saw that she was aware of the drift of his thoughts and, more, was not averse to them. Reaching up to scratch his jaw, he drawled, "Could be I'm willing to shave this off—for a proper reason."

Desire surged through Sally, tingling in her breasts and loins. Long ago her mum had told her that the Black Irish—with their black hair and blue eyes—were the best company a woman could want. She meant to find out for herself. "For tuppence, I'll rid ye of the itch."

"Certain ye know how to treat a man?" he asked doubtfully.

"I know a trick or two," Sally replied, but she did not meet his eyes. If he laughed at her blatant invitation she was certain she would die.

"Surprise me," Thomas answered and reached for his fork.

Sally's gaze lit upon his hands, the palms horn-hard with

calluses, and a jab of jealousy dug at her. The men of the Outback were notoriously high-spirited, playing fast and loose with the women of the settlements and then disappearing into the bush. She would have to find a way to keep Tom from going walkabout. That was why she had saved herself. Once he knew for certain that she was a good girl, he would have to do right by her.

Thomas looked up, surprised to find her still gazing intently at him. "Can't a man finish his meal first?"

Sally flushed a deep shade of pink that made her pretty face even more attractive. "I wasn't waitin' on account o' that." She glanced back toward the noisy room before whispering, "There was a bloke name of O'Leary in 'ere asking questions a couple of months back. Looked every bit a bushranger, let me tell ye! 'E was seeking an ex-convict by the name of Gibson from County Cork."

"Gibson's a common enough name," Thomas murmured.

The mild reply did not surprise Sally. Tom was not the sort of man who showed his feelings. "Just thought ye should know," she mumbled and turned away.

Thomas watched appreciatively as she moved away, but she was immediately forgotten when he glanced back down at his plate. For a man who made his living among sheep, beef stew was a far more tempting item than even ripe and eager barmaids. Potatoes and carrots were even rarer delights, and he cleaned his plate.

Afterward he contented himself with a slow but steady succession of tankards of ale. Only then did he ponder Sally's news. Strange, he had not thought of Sean O'Leary and the others in years. For thirteen years Australia had been his home. Thirteen years was a long time. During that time he had changed more than his convict status. He had become first a shearer and now a squatter with vast holdings. There was nothing to be gained by dredging up the past. He would not seek out the man. He wanted only to forget the past.

He had come to Sydney against his better judgment, yet he could not stay away. So here he would remain until he found the source of the whim that had impelled him to come to the port city. He had lived by his hunches too long to deny them now. He closed his eyes and leaned back in his chair. When the moment came, he would know the reason why he was here. If it was that he must face part of his past, then so be it. He would not shy from it, but he would not seek it out.

More than an hour later Thomas opened his eyes to find Sally standing over him, her apron tucked under her arm.

"Ye were sleepin'," she said unnecessarily.

"Resting up for me shave," he shot back with a grin. Then his face sobered. "What're ye charging, Sally? A man must be certain he can afford his pleasure."

Sally caught her nether lip between her teeth as her face flooded with color. "I'd never charge ye, Tom," she whispered, her eyes averted from his face.

The bashful whisper surprised Thomas. After all, she must have been with many men. "Come, lass, ye'll never earn enough to keep ye in silks and tucker if ye give so generously of yer favors."

Sally pinkened to the tips of her ears, but she was afraid to contradict him. If he guessed her secret too soon he might change his mind. "Whatever ye say, then, Tom."

Thomas turned away from Sally and sat up on the narrow cot to pull on his trousers. After a moment Sally's soft weeping made him turn back, acutely aware of his part in her distress. "There, there, lass," he said gently, awkwardly patting her trembling shoulder.

Sally lifted her tear-smeared face from the bed. "Why, Thomas? I—I don't . . . Am I not pleasin' to ye?"

The sheet shifted as Sally twisted toward him, revealing her breasts with the crimson nipples which he had held between his lips moments earlier.

"Cover yerself!" he ordered and stood up. He moved to the window and braced himself with an arm above the casement.

Almost at once he was sorry that he had been sharp with her. It wasn't her fault he was frustrated. Dear Lord! She had eagerly offered him the ultimate prize of her woman-hood. The realization that a barmaid was a virgin had startled him; and then cold, hard reason had had a chance to make him think of what he was about to do.

"'Tis sorry I am, lass. But it's better so." They were friends. He couldn't simply bed her, then forget her, and that is exactly what he would do. He had come to Sydney to set in motion events he did not fully understand. When they were over he would leave. "'Tis better so," he repeated. His voice carried slowly and with tender pity across the short expanse. "Ye want to marry, ye've told me so before. 'Tis yer husband who should have the gift ye offer me."

Sally sat up, looking more childlike as the tumble of honey-blond hair framed her naked shoulders. "Don't ye see, Tom? 'Tis ye I want."

Thomas shook his head firmly, his gaze focused on the field of ships' masts visible above the rooftops of the shops across the way. "I'm nae the one for ye, Sally, lass."

"A body should know when a man's the one for 'er." Sally slipped off the edge of the bed, dragging the coarse linen sheet with her. "Look at me, Tom. Ye wanted me, I could feel it. Ye were grand and hard against me belly. I felt ye with me own hand. Ye *did* want me!"

When she came up behind him and leaned her naked breasts against Thomas's bare back, his body's momentary reluctance vanished, and once more he could feel himself filling with urgent desire.

"Ye're a wee bold thing, Sally," he said breathlessly. "Were I to accept the soft cradle of yer thighs for a night, when the morning came I'd be just another satisfied man. And ye, Sally, ye'd be just another whore."

He heard her gasp as she pulled back from him. For a long moment there was only his own harsh breathing as he held himself firm against turning to her and committing the very act he tried to talk her out of.

"It—it don't matter what they call me in the morning, Tom," she said, wrapping her arms about his waist and hugging his back once more. "If marriage ain't in ye, I won't ask it. But I want ye to show me the woman in me. I want it to be ye."

Thomas groaned. Why hadn't be bought the favors of a practiced harlot and left the seducing of Sally to another man? Marriage was on her mind, while marriage was the last thing . . .

The breeze rose suddenly, the window curtains dancing in its wake. The scent of the sea surrounded him, and with it the poignant memory of a red-haired lass with solemn golden eyes flickered in his mind's eye.

"I'm getting married, Sally. That's what come over me!" The outrageous words left him in one long breath.

Sally was as astonished as he. She yanked her arms away. "Ye're what? I don't believe ye!"

Thomas turned slowly, his mind fastening with absolute conviction on a truth he had not recognized until this moment. "I've come to Sydney to marry." In the dim moonlight he saw skepticism lift Sally's brows. "I've picked her out this morning, sort of."

"Ye're a lyin' bastard, Tom Gibson!" she spat.

"Nae," he countered softly and smiled. He had come to

Sydney to find a bride. That was the urge that had sent him
to the docks to watch the arriving ships.

"Her name's Fitzgerald." His smile deepened as he
recalled the name by which the redcoat had addressed her.
"She came on the *Black Opal* from Cork. Eyes like gold
dust from a miner's purse, she has, and hair as red as a
cypress forest ablaze."

Sally's mouth fell open at this unexpected eloquence.
There really must be such a woman, she thought, as painful
reality swept through her. "Ye're lyin'!" There was a
dangerous wobble in her voice that threatened new tears.

"Nae, lass. She's a bit fine for the likes of me, but I'll do
her proud. A lady deserves that."

At the word *lady,* Sally's humbling self-pity shriveled
under a flare of rage. "A lady, is it? And what o' me? Am I
an unskilled tart that ye may spurn?"

Screaming invectives, she flailed him with fists and feet
until Thomas lifted her off the floor and dumped her on the
bed. "Mind yer tongue, lass. Ye've the mouth of a gutter
wench when it suits ye."

Sally fell back against the bed, her rage broken, and cried
the broken sobs of a child.

"Ah, Sally." Thomas's sigh held a world of regret as he
reached for his shirt. He was doing the right thing, even if
he hurt her now.

The image of the red-haired young woman flickered again
in his mind's eye. His bride. She was not a great beauty, but
there was a fine brave spirit in her. She had not backed
down from the larrikin who had snatched her purse. That
was the kind of wife he needed, one who looked every inch
a lady and yet had the spirit to stand up to the brood of
hoodlums he would no doubt sire on her.

A new thought struck him, and his features hardened
momentarily. He hoped she was not related to the redcoat
who had come to her aid. He could not see an English

soldier without the old hatred simmering within him. That was the reason he had turned into a nearby doorway when the major appeared. Yet he had been fascinated enough by her to remain close until they left the alley. If only he knew where to find her.

She had come in on the *Black Opal* from Cork. There must be some swab on the waterfront who would remember her, this Fitzgerald from County Cork. The irony of it was not lost on him.

Thomas's laughter startled Sally, but she was too numb with misery and the collapse of her own thwarted passion to question its cause. When the door shut quietly behind him, she turned her face to the wall and sobbed herself to sleep.

Come near, come near, come near—Ah, leave me
    still
A little space for the rose-breath to fill!

                        —To the Rose upon the Rood of Time
                        W. B. Yeats

Chapter Five

Aisleen opened her eyes to the night. She had heard
laughter, masculine laughter, and then the closing of a door.
She sat up in bed, staring at the door at the end of the
barracks room where she had been assigned a bed for the
night. She saw nothing. It was too dark. Straining her ears,
she finally heard voices, both feminine. They came from the
bed across the aisle. From where had the man's laughter
come? Were some of her roommates entertaining a man in
their quarters?

The Hyde Park Barracks consisted of twelve government-
run dormitories for young women immigrants who had not
yet found work and shelter. From what she had observed in
a single day, most of these young women were from the
lower classes come to serve as servants, cooks, and laundresses
in the better homes of the colony. Much to her consternation
and disapproval, many of them had spent the entire evening
meal talking about men and marriage, winking and nudging

one another when the conversation turned bawdy. The matron had quite rightly put an end to it.

Footsteps sounded on the walkway outside the window that flanked her bed, a light tread but nothing secret in it. Did those footsteps belong to the man whose laughter she had heard? Indignation overcame modesty, and Aisleen drew back her sheet and slipped from her bed to the door without reaching for a wrapper. If there were a Peeping Tom about, she did not care if he viewed her nightgown or glimpsed a bare ankle if it meant he was apprehended. The door opened with a loud *crack* that halted the night walker.

"Are you all right, then, miss?"

A young woman stood on the flagstones outside, a candle in hand. Aisleen recognized her as one of the matron's assistants who had shared her table at dinner. "Yes, I'm fine, Miss—?"

"Warren, Ophelia Warren."

"Good evening, Miss Warren," Aisleen said politely. "I thought I heard . . . well, I would have sworn I heard voices just now, and laughter."

"That may be, miss. Some of the girls are regular owls, up until all hours. Matron does her best to keep them quiet, but they do not always listen."

Aisleen shook her head slightly. "I do not refer to women. I heard masculine laughter."

"A man?" Ophelia voiced in surprise. "That couldn't be, miss. We do not allow gentlemen callers after dark. There's a guard and the gates are locked. Perhaps you were dreaming."

"Perhaps," Aisleen conceded. "I do not sleep well in strange places."

"You'll come round quickly, miss. All our girls do. Good night, then."

As Aisleen retraced her steps past the rows of beds, she wondered at herself. She was not given to fanciful thoughts.

As a rule she never dreamed. Yet, as she slipped back beneath her sheet, she was shaken by the realization that she had been dreaming just before she heard the laughter, and the dream had been quite shocking.

She dreamed of a man. She could not see his face; neither could she describe him in detail. It was dark and he had been standing with his back to her.

Aisleen closed her eyes and pulled the sheet up higher. No, she had not "seen" him; she had felt him like warmth radiated in the image of a man. Her impressions of him and of the night had been sensed as subtle pressures and eddies of breath and breeze upon her skin. The man himself had been so close her nostrils had quivered in response to his odor.

Aisleen began to tingle in a manner quite unique in her experience. The tingling deepened with every remembered image of the masculine shadow which strode the edge of her consciousness. He had been naked, though the darkness hid his exact form. She had had the tantalizing urge to touch his warm, flushed skin and . . .

She sat up with a gasp as blood rushed warmly into her cheeks. What she remembered, what she thought of as a dream, was sinful. No wonder she had dreamed the laughter. It was a fitting end to so wicked a reverie.

"A nightmare," she whispered to herself and lay back. Not since childhood had she had so vivid a dream.

Bouchal. Once he had seemed more real than anything else in her life. She still thought of him occasionally and marveled at the power of a child's imagination. Now, of course, she realized how the family legend of magical ancestors had led a very lonely and unhappy young girl to half-believe that she had willed into being a companion for her very own. But that's all it was, imagining.

In years since, whenever she was tempted to yearn for something beyond her reach, she called to mind her father's whiskey-sodden ravings about magic as an antidote against the longings of her own heart. There was no magic, only the realities of life. Those who believed in anything more were doomed to disappointment and despair.

Aisleen turned onto her side, smoothing the wrinkles from the bottom sheet as a matter of habit. A long day in a strange place. No wonder she had allowed nonsense to capture her for a moment. Now that she knew its cause, she certainly would not allow it to happen again. She closed her eyes, determined to sleep.

"I do not understand," Aisleen began in annoyance as she produced the letter from her purse. "I have in my possession a reply from Mrs. Sarah Britten herself accepting me as a teacher in her school. Here it is."

Mrs. Freeman nodded her head, not taking the proffered letter. "I do not doubt it, Miss Fitzgerald. After all, you are here, aren't you? But you must hear reason in the matter. The post has been filled."

"How is that possible?"

Mrs. Freeman pursed her lips as she regarded the young woman who sat across from her. She, too, was vexed with Mrs. Britten's sudden change of plans, but it would not help matters to indulge this young woman's indignation. "There is very limited colonial demand for ladies of refinement. As a rule we discourage the immigration of ladies such as you unless they are moneyed or have friends in the colony to support them."

"I do not see what your colonial difficulties have to do with me," Aisleen answered more sharply than she meant to. She had had a miserable night. She had slept fitfully after the shameful dream and had awakened with a dull pounding at her temples. "I did not come as an immigrant but to fill a position for which I have been hired. Where may I find Mrs. Britten? I shall apply to her in person."

A pleasant woman by nature, Mrs. Freeman found herself growing quite annoyed. "It won't do you a bit of good. Mrs. Britten has hired a local lady of a prominent Sydney family."

"I have a contract," Aisleen insisted.

"Might as well be a lamb's tail for all the good it'll do you!" Mrs. Freeman answered roundly, her plump cheeks trembling. For nearly four years she had assisted young women immigrants. Most of those who came through Hyde Park Barracks were farm girls culled from the rural areas of Britain and Ireland—clean, respectable girls accustomed to the hard labor required in a frontier outpost. Often they worked only a short time before succumbing to marriage with some sheep herder or shopkeeper. For that reason there was always a need for female labor.

Only once before had she had to deal with a lady, and it had ended badly. Impoverished gentlewomen were, as a rule, both haughty and disobliging, expecting to be housed separately from the domestic servant girls who lived in the barracks. To her credit, Miss Fitzgerald had not yet mentioned her quarters. "My advice to you is to return whence you came. There's little Sydney has to offer you."

"Return? To Ireland?" The enormity of the suggestion stunned Aisleen. "Surely there are other schools, other cities in Australia which might find my services useful."

"There's Melbourne and Brisbane," Mrs. Freeman conceded.

"Either of those would do nicely," Aisleen answered. "How do I make arrangments to go there?"

Mrs. Freeman's irritation came to the fore. "Melbourne is more than four hundred miles south. As for Brisbane, it lies more than six hundred miles to the north. I would not advise the trains, for they require frequent changes and the schedules are most irregular. As for a coach, without a male companion you will find yourself confronted with the worst caliber of ruffians and rogues. Then there is the fare to consider, which is considerable."

Aisleen felt her purposefulness deflate. "I do not possess the money for travel of that distance at present," she said slowly, hoping that her words did not sound like a plea for funds. "Therefore I must remain in Sydney and look for employment."

Mrs. Freeman nodded, warming to the young woman. Nothing pleased her more than a girl who was not afraid of work. "We've jobs aplenty, but I warn you they are not the sort to which you're accustomed." Then, because she was not at heart a cold woman, she added, "My dear Miss Fitzgerald, if you would remain in the colony might I suggest that you look for a patroness who will introduce you into society? Marriage is preferable to drudgery."

Marriage. Why did that word keep cropping up when one mentioned life in Australia? Aisleen wondered in annoyance. "I have no wish for nor need of a husband," she answered curtly. "I came to find employment. I am a teacher."

"We've jobs available for laundresses, cooks, domestics, and seamstresses," Mrs. Freeman said promptly, her concern evaporated by the young woman's rebuff. "At which would you care to try your hand?"

"None," Aisleen answered truthfully, and saw the older woman's brows lift. "It's not that I'm afraid of hard work, Mrs. Freeman. I am not. My last employment was as a governess in Yorkshire, and I assure you that I cooked for my charges, carried firewood, and washed nappies, as well as saw to their educational requirements. But, as you have said, I am better suited to more cerebral pursuits." She glanced about the small office. "Perhaps I could assist you.

I write a legible hand, am familiar with both numbers and the management of children.''

Mrs. Freeman's expression was a study in frozen politeness as she said, ''Those of us who volunteer our services at the Immigrant's Home do so as an act of charity for those unfortunate souls who arrive on our shores without adequate means.''

Aisleen blushed. She had insulted the woman. ''Forgive my ignorance. As a lady who has found it necessary to earn her way in the world, I thought only of seeking a position of respectability.''

The older woman's face softened slightly. ''Very well, Miss Fitzgerald, but I must repeat that your skills are not those sought in the ordinary course. It is to be regretted that you do not have relations or acquaintances among the local population. Of course, you shall remain here with food and lodging taken care of until you find a situation.''

Aisleen rose. ''Thank you. I assure you that I have not come all this way to become a ward of the state. I fully intend to live a useful life in the colony.''

When she was gone, Mrs. Freeman sat a moment behind her desk, a thoughtful expression on her face. The young lady had looked so stricken when told that her post was lost to another, as if it were her last hope. Miss Fitzgerald was a puzzle: well-educated, remarkably so for an Irish woman. What on earth could have brought her halfway around the world without a friend or relative on whom to rely?

Mrs. Freeman frowned. She had cautioned Sarah Britten against sending all the way to Ireland for a teacher when one might possibly be found here. And so one had, but not before the *Black Opal* set sail with Miss Fitzgerald aboard.

''What could Sarah have been thinking of to give the post to someone else?'' Mrs. Freeman murmured to herself, and then a smile rounded her features. Her husband always gave sound advice. She would ask him for guidance in the matter of what was to be done about Miss Fitzgerald.

Aisleen patted the perspiration from her brow with a handkerchief as she paused in composing a letter. Sighing, she adjusted the portable wooden desk that rested heavily on her knees. Twice she had had to blot a drop of perspiration from her correspondence. Her supply of paper was small, and she could not afford to waste a single sheet.

Mrs. Freeman's warning aside, she knew she must make an effort to find employment. She was thousands of miles from home with five pounds between her and destitution. Five pounds would not buy a return ticket to Dublin.

There were other needs as well. Two days in Sydney had convinced her that the woolen gowns that served her in Yorkshire would not do here. Once she found a post, her first purchase would be calico cloth to make summer gowns.

Aisleen glanced up as a jewel-bright fly darted past, its rapid wingbeat humming in the still, oppressive air as it soared out of the open window of the barracks.

For a long moment she stared out at the stark brilliance of the day. From beyond the faded pink brick walls that surrounded the barracks came the sounds of the city. The voices were English. The rumbling of wooden carriage wheels and clip-clopping of hooves were familiar city sounds. Yet the vague, confused sense of utter abandonment settled over her.

What on earth was she doing here? What had she thought to accomplish by the impulsive act of immigration? *Independence:* how hollow the word seemed now. Pride had brought her to this place. Determined not to be a burden to her mother, she had chosen to strike out on her own. Did she have the courage to see the course through now that her plans were in ruin? She did not need much to make her comfortable, but surely she deserved more than this.

"Ye've a guest, Miss Fitzgerald."

Aisleen turned her head to find one of the barracks girls standing in the doorway. "Are you certain?"

"Mrs. Freeman said to say 'e asked most particular for ye." The girl eyed Aisleen curiously. "I seen 'im. A right toff, 'e is. Took 'im for a pommie, the likes of ye."

Aisleen did not pretend to follow the girl's speech. "Who is this gentleman who has asked for me?"

"Didn't give 'is name. Ye'll find 'im waitin' in Mrs. Freeman's office."

"I see. Thank you."

Aisleen gently patted her brows and cheeks dry, feeling better with each moment. Major Scott must have come to visit her.

"Does the gentleman wear a—?" she began, but the girl had disappeared. Oh, well, what did it matter? She was not alone, after all. She had a friend in the major. She had thought of appealing to him for help before. It would be bad manners to impose on so slight a friendship. Yet if he should inquire about her situation, that would change things. Perhaps he would offer to assist her in finding employment when she learned what had happened.

After carefully smoothing her center part with both hands, she drew on a pair of white lace gloves and then adjusted the matching lace collar at her throat.

She entered the matron's office with a complaisant smile on her lips. "You sent for me, Mrs. Freeman?" she asked politely, but her gaze had already strayed to the man standing at the open window. He stood in the sun's full glare, which overshadowed his features, yet she realized with disappointment that he did not wear a uniform, nor was his figure that of Major Scott. He was taller and slimmer, and he wore a tweed suit.

"Come in, Miss Fitzgerald," Mrs. Freeman said warmly. "Mr. Gibson tells me that you are just the person he has been looking for."

"Indeed?" Aisleen answered, turning toward the man with a neutral expression.

As he crossed the room toward her, Aisleen noticed that he favored one leg, and she wondered fleetingly if it were a momentary discomfort or a continuing malady. Belatedly she lifted her gaze to find that he smiled at her.

He was clean-shaven, his skin satiny smooth as only a man's could be after the application of a razor. From the ridges of his cheeks upward his skin was sun-darkened. Below, his cheeks and chin were pale. She surmised that he had worn a beard until recently. His eyes were beautifully ringed with sooty lashes that matched the jutting brows and shock of shiny black hair he had only partially succeeded in taming. His nose was boldly shaped, a trifle wide but well formed, the perfect balance for a firm mouth and strong chin.

She had always admired in others the beauty which she felt she lacked. Looking at this gentleman was like gazing at a glorious sunset, or the dappled brilliance of a trout as it slipped through the green-brown depths of a stream. As he neared she offered her hand, and until his hand closed over hers, conveying through his warm, rough flesh the reality of the man, she did not give a thought to how her gawking must seem to him. Suddenly he was human, not an objet d'art, and her pleasure vanished.

"Sir," she said stiffly, looking away even as his smile widened, "I am certain we have not met before."

"Miss Fitzgerald, that honored I am to make yer acquaintance," she heard him say with a lilting Irish accent that brought her gaze quickly back to his face. The eyes . . . too blue and too bold—

"I do know you!" she said in vexed surprise.

"Is there a problem?" Mrs. Freeman questioned. From the moment the man arrived she had been fascinated by his connection with Miss Fitzgerald, for the young lady had been quite insistent that she knew no one in the colony. The tale he had told her left her more curious than ever.

Thomas turned to the matron. "The very morning of Miss Fitzgerald's arrival in Sydney a larrikin stole her purse. A lucky thing it was I was there to retrieve it." He smiled encouragingly at Aisleen. "Isn't that so, lass?"

"Yes," Aisleen answered woodenly. She had been pleased at the time, but that did not explain why he was here. Had he changed his mind about her offer of a reward?

"I know what ye're thinking," Thomas continued when he saw the frozen look on Aisleen's face had not thawed. "Ye're wondering why a stranger has come calling when ye did not give him yer direction."

Aisleen merely nodded, aware that Mrs. Freeman watched her.

"Well, I'll be frank for I've little time for niceties. Me name's Thomas Gibson and I'm seldom to be found drinking tea or strolling the streets of Sydney. I've a station to see to most of the year. When I see something that attracts me eye, I stake me rights or let it pass. Do ye follow me?"

"I think not," Aisleen answered honestly. "Would you care to sit, Mr. Gibson?"

"No, but seat yerself, lass, if ye've a need for it," he replied with a fine disregard for the imformality of his speech. "What I've come to say is that I've a need for a lady of yer refinement on me station."

"You have come to offer me a post at your . . ." Aisleen turned to Mrs. Freeman. "Forgive my ignorance, but what is a station?"

"Mr. Gibson is a sheep grazier," the woman answered.

"Two thousand, one hundred and forty-three acres, five thousand sheep, and two hundred cattle," Thomas added proudly. "That makes me a man of consequence, does it not, Mrs. Freeman?"

"Indeed it does," the lady answered enthusiastically, seeing a solution to the problem of Miss Fitzgerald. "Mr. Gibson, if you are seeking a young lady of education and refinement to—"

"To look after me station," Thomas cut in hastily. His gaze flickered measuringly over Aisleen. He had gone over the matter in his mind a dozen times until he was certain of what he would say to her. But now, looking at the prim young woman perched on the edge of a chair, he wondered if he had been wrong about her. Nothing was left of the sense of rightness which had accompanied their first meeting. Seeing her glorious bright hair severely scraped back into an ugly knot made him frown in annoyance. From the high, tight neckline of her gown to the pristine white-gloved hands folded in her lap, she looked as pious and unreachable as any of the wooden statues of martyred saints that stood inside the doors of Saint Mary's Cathedral. Yet the feeling that she was meant to be his wife had been too strong for him simply to walk away now. He would see it through.

"I'm founding a dynasty," he said, testing the sound of that and finding it to his liking. "Aye, that's it. I need a lady of quality to see to the running of me house and rearing of me children. Do you like children, miss?"

"I do," Aisleen answered evenly. At last she began to understand why he had come. He sought a governess. A man with thousands of acres could well afford one. "Do you have many children, Mr. Gibson?"

"Not yet, but I will. Six or seven, maybe. What would ye think of that?"

"I'm certain I think nothing at all of the matter," Aisleen replied primly, flustered by the impertinent question. Once more she was at a loss. If he did not yet have children, what interest could he have in her? *Don't be a fool,* she chided herself. She would accept whatever post he offered. "If you wish to be assured that I can properly care for as many as seven children, Mr. Gibson, the answer is yes."

The answer made Thomas smile. She liked children. While she was slim, she did not look sickly. Bearing children would round her out a bit, and he liked a rounded woman. "Do ye sing, Miss Fitzgerald?"

"Tolerably well," she answered.

"Irish songs, Miss Fitzgerald? I've a grand passion for the music of me homeland."

"I know a few and will learn others, if it pleases you."

"Would ye be knowing yer way around a piano?"

"I play and give instruction as well," Aisleen replied. Really, the man was quite impossible, questioning her education as though his had been one of the best when clearly he was little more than illiterate.

"Do ye dance, Miss Fitzgerald?"

"A little," she answered cautiously and added truthfully, "but I would not consider myself a dancing mistress."

"Perhaps a test of yer skill is in order."

Aisleen looked at him in puzzlement when he did not elaborate. "Do you mean here and now?"

"Would ye oblige?" he asked with a smile startling in its intensity.

"Well, I don't—" Aisleen bit off the thought. In confusion, she sought Mrs. Freeman's advice, but Thomas spoke up. "'Twas only me teasing ye, lass. There'll be time enough for dancing when there are fiddlers and a harp and the pipes to play the measure. Will ye promise me a dance when the time comes?"

The man had come to offer her a post of some sort. It was an opportunity Mrs. Freeman had warned her she might never be given while she remained in Sydney. Was she to quibble over a night of dancing? "I'd be delighted to, Mr. Gibson, if you are certain that it will not be out of place."

Thomas nodded in approval. She was so proper, nothing at all like the winded and flushed young woman who had first attracted his eye, but she was exactly what he had waited for: a lady. "Ye are that different, Miss Fitzgerald, and everyone will comment on it, but we'll give it a go for 'tis the way I mean to go on."

Aisleen was astonished when he reached for her hand and bent over it as though he might kiss it. He did not. He had nearly forgotten, she supposed, that she was to be his employee. But when he raised up she saw amusement in his expression.

"I'm not a man of pretty phrases and fawning manners," he said forthrightly. "But then, ye're not the sort to need them, I'm thinking."

Aisleen gave him a polite smile. "Indeed, you are simple and direct, which I prefer, Mr. Gibson."

Thomas smiled. Looking at her closely, he saw again the fine gold-flecked eyes that were direct, inquisitive, and very alive in her serious and quiet face. When she blushed, the pinkening of her cheeks added youth to her face. "How old are ye, lass?"

"Five and twenty, sir," Aisleen replied. It was his right as her prospective employer to ask questions, however unusual this interview. "I'm of sound health and hardy disposition, too."

"Glad to hear it," Thomas answered. "After all, a man would ask as much of a horse he's buying, now wouldn't he?"

Aisleen stared at him in silence.

"Ah, well now, I can see that I've insulted ye, and I did not mean such. I'm a plain man, ye can tell that for yerself, but I admire quality in others, that I do. And ye've spirit. The way ye gave chase to that larrikin when ye might have come to harm, I liked that in ye."

"Spirit had naught to do with it," Aisleen informed him

ruefully. "All that I possessed in the world was in that purse. Had I lost it I would have been destitute."

The answer pleased him. "Then ye're not displeased that I've come for ye?"

Aisleen supposed that this frankness was one of the things she must become accustomed to if she was to be in his employ. "I am quite indebted to you for your interest in me and hope that I may serve you in the manner which you require."

"A pretty speech," Thomas said with a hint of laughter. "Me bairns will speak as ye do, without the damning brogue of their sire."

"My parents were Irish born and bred," Aisleen answered. It was a thing she seldom mentioned, but, contrarily, she wanted him to know that she was not the English lady he thought her to be. "I was the recipient of an English education, else there'd be no difference in our speech or manner."

"Ye are Catholic?" Thomas prompted.

"I am," she answered forthrightly. If this was to damn her in his eyes, then so be it. To her continued amazement he laughed.

"Ye're not as pretty as some perhaps," Thomas voiced, thinking of Sally, "but looks have never mattered to me."

"I see," Aisleen said in a tight voice because his pause seemed to beg an answer of her.

"No, ye do not." Thomas squared his shoulders. This was the moment. "What I'm saying to ye is I'm a man who knows it's time he wed and who knows what he wants in a wife. That'd be a lady of refinement and good breeding who can turn me station house into a home and educate me children as is fitting for a man of property and wealth. The minute I laid me eyes on ye I knew ye were the one."

"What one?" Aisleen asked in confusion.

"The one I mean to marry."

"Marry?" she repeated stupidly.

"Aye, proposing is what I'm doing, Miss Fitzgerald. Is this not the way these things are done?"

"I'm sure I wouldn't know," Aisleen said stiffly and rose to her feet. All at once, she understood. This was a joke! But who could have put him up to it? Who knew that they had met? Major Scott! He had a deplorable sense of humor, but she had not thought him capable of ridicule. Yet had he not advised her not to accept the first marriage proposal that came her way, after slyly insinuating that one would? It was more than cruel, it was a humiliation not to be endured. Without a word she turned to leave.

Thomas called after her, "Does this mean ye'll nae consider me?"

Aisleen turned on him, indignation flaring in her gold-bright eyes. Poor she might be, and a spinster with no hope of marriage, but she had her pride. "I do not understand why you wish to torment me. I am a spinster, that is true, but that fact does not make me a fool, Mr. Gibson. I find your jest more than vile. It's beastly and undeserved!"

As she pivoted away his laughter trailed after her, lifting the hairs on her neck. How despicable he was, to find her misery amusing. She took no more than three steps when blazing anger made her spin about a second time. "Sir, you are contemptible! Were I a man and carried a pistol, I would shoot you!"

She could not believe that she had spoken so outrageously, but his hand moved to his waistband and opened his coat to reveal the pistol stuck in his belt. Fear splashed through her, drenching her in a sea of alarm. From afar she heard Mrs. Freeman's cry of fright and her own indrawn breath as he removed the pistol and strolled toward her. She backed away until the barrier of the closed door halted her flight.

"Ye've a bold spirit, Miss Fitzgerald, and I've already said I like ye for it. Here, then, take yer revenge."

Before she could prevent it, he took her right hand in his and slapped the butt of the gun against her palm. "If ye think me a liar and cheat, that I do not mean to marry ye, then pull the trigger."

Aisleen stared at him, her mind too muddled to make coherent thought. She held the gun gingerly, as if it might recoil on her and bite. And well it might, for she had never touched one before.

"Well, then?" Thomas encouraged. "Either ye're believing me to be the lowest of rascals or ye know I've made ye an honest proposal. Which is it?"

The ludicrous situation both frightened and exhilarated her. She brought a hand to her lips and discovered that they were trembling. But it was not in fear. She was near laughter. At any second she felt it would burst out in loud, ringing peals. The realization appalled her. She detested dramatics, particularly her own, but the man before her had driven her so far from self-possession that she no longer trusted herself.

"Since I'm not lying on the carpet bleeding, I take that to mean ye believe me," Thomas said quietly. He gently pried her fingers from the butt of his pistol and casually thrust the barrel back under the loop of his belt.

"Well now, that's better. I can see I've surprised ye, Miss Fitzgerald, and I know a lass will have her way in such matters. So here it is, then. Ye've until Saturday three weeks hence to turn the matter over in yer mind. Then I will come for yer answer."

He turned to the matron as Aisleen slipped sideways away from him. "G'day, Mrs. Freeman. G'day, Miss Fitzgerald, until the end of the month." As the two women remained silent and motionless he walked out, closing the door behind him.

"Well!" Aisleen turned an incredulous look on Mrs. Freeman.

"Dear me, dear me!" Mrs. Freeman sank heavily back

into her chair and reached for a paper with which to fan herself. "I've never seen the like. Pistols and proposals. What will James say?"

Aisleen bit her lip. She was not altogether convinced that the man was serious. "I do suppose I should be grateful that he came here and spoke in your presence rather than accosting me on the street," she mused aloud. "I was warned about the eccentricities of bushmen, but I must say I did not take the warning seriously, until now."

"The man must be mad!" Mrs. Freeman answered. "It's the sun that turns their minds. Scraping and lurking about in the bush, no one to talk with for weeks on end, it's enough to turn the hardiest stock."

"Oh." Aisleen resisted the urge to glance out the window, where she knew she could have seen him crossing the promenade. She had stared quite enough for one day. She only hoped he had not misunderstood her glance. She had been in awe of the perfection of nature's craft, nothing more. The man himself, she well knew, could be the soul of Satan come to life. "He proposed!" she murmured in stunned amazement.

"So he did, Miss Fitzgerald," Mrs. Freeman replied and broke into a chuckle which made Aisleen wonder what the woman thought of her to have aroused such passion in a stranger.

"Well, it is finished. He will not come again," Aisleen said firmly.

Mrs. Freeman did not respond, for she was not at all certain what the squatter named Gibson would do next. Perhaps the third Saturday of the month would bring the answer.

He bore her away in his arms,
The handsomest young man there...

—The Host of the Air
W. B. Yeats

Chapter Six

"This passes all belief!" Aisleen said in bewilderment as
she sat on the side of her bed with her arms folded tightly
across her bosom. The light of dawn lay in a long, faintly-
veined stream across her pillow. In its flood motes as bright
as tinsel drifted lazily. All about her the inhabitants of the
barracks lay supine, cherishing their final minutes of sleep.

But not I! Aisleen thought angrily. She had awakened in a
cold sweat with the suffocating thickness of smoke clogging
her nose and mouth. At least, she thought she had smelled
smoke. Yet all about her was bathed in utter peace. The
freshness of the morning air mocked her burning throat and
stinging nose. There was no fire. It was only another dream.

During the past three weeks scarcely a night had passed
without her sleep being interrupted by some discontent. A
few nights earlier she had been dragged to consciousness by
an excruciating pain in her left calf. The agony had passed
almost immediately, but for the rest of the day she had

limped about, forced to explain the inexplicable malady as a muscle spasm.

I am not a child, Aisleen chided herself, only to wince in pain as she swallowed. If she had drunk scalding tea her throat could not hurt more. She was well past the age for hysterics. The sheer fabric of nightmares should not bind her in fear. Yet their disturbing aftermath lingered in physical expression: first the pain in her leg and now the parched aching of her throat.

"Nerves, that is all it is," she whispered huskily to herself. She had every right to be anxious. Another day was beginning, and she was no nearer a solution to her problem than the day she arrived.

She had answered every likely advertisement in the *Sydney Morning Herald,* including those for a lady's hairdresser, seamstress, and clerk. This last was addressed to men, but it offered the highest wages and she was qualified for it. Not one of her inquiries had elicited so much as a note in response. Yet a majority of the other women residents in the barracks had found employment, while new ones arrived daily.

The morning bell broke the stillness. Aisleen clenched her teeth as it jangled her spine. Immediately the girl in the bed next to hers groaned in protest. Cots creaked as other sleepers rolled and stretched to awaken.

Aisleen turned and gazed steadily out of the window to hide the distraction she knew was expressed in every line of her face. She was the source of much gossip and speculation among the other women. It had begun with the arrival of that impertinent Mr. Gibson. Within half an hour of his visit, everyone in the barracks had heard of his audacious marriage proposal. It had made her a celebrity of sorts among them, a fact she found quite distressing.

"Wretched man!" she muttered and again swallowed painfully. At least that matter had resolved itself. No further word had been heard from him, and she was now convinced that he would not return as he had promised to do. After all, the actions of a man so obviously disturbed were not to be trusted.

"Breakfast, Miss Fitzgerald," one of her roommates called as she passed Aisleen's bed.

Aisleen nodded, not turning from the window. Only when the final footsteps had faded away did she turn from the window. The emotional whirlwind had died, but its ravishment left her feeling drained. The thought of porridge made her stomach contract. That aside, she doubted she could swallow a single spoonful. Smoke or dream, her throat was raw.

A quiver began at one corner of her mouth. She had never before been the victim of a nervous complaint. Hysteria was not unusual in women in her rank and circumstance, she knew, but she thought of herself as having far too practical a nature ever to succumb to the weakness.

So, being practical, she went to the foot of her bed and extracted from her trunk the medical volume which she had carried since the day she began supervising children. She turned unerringly to the section entitled "Nervous Complaints" and ran a finger down the paragraphs until she came to the one marked "Fits." The term "Apoplexy" did not apply to her symptoms but, with a small gasp, she read the following under "Hysterics":

> The patient may suffer warning symptoms: headache, weak pulse, and often believe himself the victim of all manner of maladies, suffering false symptoms of disease. These are apt to follow great depression of the spirit and shedding of tears.

She closed the volume with a snap and replaced it.

"Enough of that, my girl!" she said decisively. She simply did not have time to languish about in a state of hysterics. If her throat was sore, she must be sickening. The best remedy for that was rest.

Lying down on her cot, she fell instantly into a deep, troubled sleep.

Thomas flopped belly first on the hard-baked red earth, gulping air into his starved lungs. He had groped his way blindly through the inferno, some instinct for survival driving him to this place from which fresh air was being bled by the flames. Smoke hung heavy in the air. He heard nothing but the omnivorous roar of the nearby blaze. Bush fires were unusual along the Hawksbury River in the spring months but no less dangerous. When they occurred, every able-bodied man for miles around came to the aid of those who stood in the path of the blaze.

For three days he had worked without pause, and then it happened. In a single blast the fire had leaped the fire line where he had been digging a trench, hemming him and the men who worked beside him between twin walls of flame. It was one of the peculiar dangers of fire in the colony. The volatile oils of the eucalyptus trees often exploded, sending balls of flame shooting across the sky like earth-born comets to light new fires in bush hundreds of feet away.

He coughed repeatedly, dislodging a shower of soot and ash from his hair. The action rubbed his shirt against his shoulders and red, raw pain radiated across them. He was burned and singed in a dozen places. His lungs felt scrubbed out by steel wool, and his eyes ran continuously in their effort to flush the detritus; but he knew he should not remain in what, for the moment, seemed a safe place. The fire lines had lost their definition when the new blazes sprang up. At any moment he might feel the lick of flame once more.

Curling his hands against the red earth, he pushed himself

up into a half-sitting position, only to groan as his left calf
muscles contracted in protest. Reaching back, he began to
massage it gently with the knuckles of his blistered, broken-
skinned hand. The weak limb did not always cripple him,
but a week earlier he had wrenched it while stacking
supplies. He hoisted himself up, using his good leg, but he
could not gain his feet. His left leg trembled under his
weight and threatened collapse if he put his full weight on
it. Swearing under his breath, he balanced on one foot and
looked around. It was daybreak. Moments before the explosion, the eastern horizon had been showing pure pastels in
counterpoint to the livid red-orange flames reflected in half
the sky. He had to move, even if it meant hopping about like
a kangaroo.

"Tom! Tom, you bastard! Answer me, you bloody get!"

Thomas grinned as the profanity reached him over the
roar of the conflagration. He should have known Jack Egan
would find him. "Jack!"

A short distance away a man appeared out of the swirling
smoke, a gigantic figure against the gray-white haze. Thomas
tried to hail him, but a racking cough unbalanced him and
he tumbled to his knees.

Without a word the man ran forward and lifted Thomas
and carried him, childlike, in giant strides across the flame-
scarred ground.

"Thanks," Thomas croaked.

"Keep yer bleedin' trap shut!" came the gruff reply
above his head.

"The other lads?" Thomas rasped.

"Safe enough. Only one damned fool doubled back on
the fire."

Despite the caustic words, Thomas closed his eyes and
concentrated on his breathing. That was what a mate was
for: companionship and dependability.

Suddenly they broke through the pall of sickly sweet

rosin and dry cinders, and a cheer went up from the men camped in the clearing beyond. Thomas grinned. A man needed his mates, he did that.

Jack dumped him none too gently on the ground beside a dray wheel, but his huge face, blackened by dirt and smoke, was etched with concern as he bent over Thomas.

He shoved a tin cup he'd taken from another man at Thomas. "Drink."

Thomas did as he was told, only to gasp and choke as the raw whiskey fanned new flames from his burning throat.

Jack hunkered down and grabbed Thomas's chin, turning his face this way and that. Then he reached for Thomas's hands, examining them. Finally he grabbed the cuff of Thomas's left pants leg and shinnied it up to the ankle. With surprising gentleness he felt along the calf, testing the bulk of muscle and then delving into the unnatural hollow of the scar tissue.

Thomas sucked in a quick breath as Jack began massaging the crippled muscles, but he said nothing as the man worked out the knotted flesh.

After a moment Jack pulled down the pants leg and rose to his feet. "What bride'll want a man who's shod of his hair and hide?"

Afraid that it had been singed off, Thomas grabbed his hair with both hands and then touched his brows. They remained.

"Flaming fool!" Jack spat and abruptly walked away.

Thomas gazed after the man a long time. He had known Jack for nearly five years, yet the man remained as strange and unpredictable as the bush fire they had fought for the past week. There was a violent intensity in his pale eyes that kept most people at bay. Jack was not a good man or an easy man, but he was reliable.

Thomas drained the whiskey in his cup. Jack did not approve of much, and he disliked women most of all. Well, with or without his mate's approval, he was going back to Sydney at the end of the week and wed Miss Fitzgerald. She was what he needed to fill his loneliness. It was quite simple once he thought about it. He had always wanted a family, and for that he needed a wife.

He had seen the priest, and the banns had been read each Sunday of these past three weeks. Miss Fitzgerald would be angry, he suspected, when she learned what he had done without her consent. But then, he did not expect anything else. That was one of the reasons he had not remained in Sydney to court her. Five minutes in her company had convinced him that his presence would only antagonize her. He had taken her measure, knew what he wanted, and taken steps to ensure that he would get it. If not for the fire, he would have returned to marry her a week earlier.

He raised a hand to suck his bleeding knuckles. At first he did not credit it, the splatter of wetness upon his face. Then he heard the gentle rumble of distant thunder followed by a round of hoarse cheers from the weary men about him. A second later heavy, cold rain splashed down, raising feathers of red dust from the ground. The break they had prayed for was at last upon them. Rain would do what they could not—smother the flames.

Thomas closed his eyes, allowing the whiskey to pull him down into the deep sleep of exhaustion.

October 1857

The days moved much too quickly in New South Wales, Aisleen thought as she tied the strings of her seventh starched petticoat about her waist. Underneath them she could already feel the chafing itch of her horsehair crinoline. Twice she had paused in dressing to apply talc to her shoulders, arms, and bosom. The heat had drawn more moisture to the surface of her skin, and the headache that had threatened all morning had blossomed into pain.

Major Scott's invitation to tea could not have come at a better time. His note said that he would introduce her to the families of his fellow officers. She cast a doubtful glance at her gown. It was lighter in weight than any of the others she owned, but she was not certain she should wear it.

The gown was lavender taffeta, the bodice made of white lace with a sash of deep pink. It was a present from her mother, a wild extravagance sewn in secret. She had been embarrassed by the gown and suspicious that the expensive material was a gift from Kirwan Mills. Weeks of fruitless effort had worn down her reluctance to solicit Major Scott's aid in her search for employment. Even with the support of the Immigrant Fund, she was nearly penniless. But what would the major think if she came dressed in silk and lace? It was a fashionable gown—everyone would recognize it as such—and far too nice for a maiden lady who was without a post or independent means.

Regretfully she decided against the gown and reached for her serviceable green wool gown with the black velvet banding on skirt and sleeves. When she had affixed the last button she looked at herself in the mirror. What she saw did not please her. Her cheeks were flushed and shiny, and her hair had lifted from her brow to form a foam of coppery curls above her forehead. With a murmur of annoyance she turned and searched through her trunk until she found a small white lace collar. Beside it lay the rock-crystal brooch her mother had given her.

She picked up the stone framed in lacy filigree, pleased by the facets of rainbow light it drew to its center. Reds and greens, blues and golds, they danced before her bemused gaze. It was as if the stone held within its depths a tiny treasure in topazes, rubies, and sapphires. Once it had been

a minor gem in the collection of ancient Gaelic jewels that
had adorned the hilt of the treasured O'Neill skean. One by
one they had been sold or bartered for the sake of Liscarrol
until only this inconsequential stone was left. Now it was all
that there was of the Fitzgerald legacy.

A sharp pain jabbed her temples, and Aisleen dropped the
stone back into her belongings and covered it. When she
had pinned her collar in place she smoothed her hair and put
on her bonnet. She tied the ribbons and looked at herself
once more. The deep black brim of her bonnet seemed to
enfold her like the ominous wings of some bird of prey. Her
head felt woolly, dull, and achy.

" 'E's here, miss!" a young girl called from the barracks
door. " 'E's come in a carriage!"

Aisleen started at the sudden voice but bit off the rebuke
that came to her lips. It was not the girl's fault her head
ached. "Thank you. I'll be along in a moment," she
answered and heard the tremble in her voice. Major Scott
was her last hope. If he could not help her, what would she
do next? Where would she go? Where could she turn?

It came from nowhere, a sudden careless breeze upon her
cheek, a sweet morning breath of anticipation that was at
odds with her own mood. She glanced about sharply. From
where had the sensation come?

"Are ye all right, miss?" the girl asked.

"Yes," Aisleen answered quickly. "Yes, of course." She
picked up her purse and black lace shawl. "Is there something wrong?" she asked when she noticed that the girl was
staring at her.

The girl blushed. "It ain't mine to say, miss, only I'd
wear a gown fit to turn the head of a Sydney lad were one to
come calling on me."

"I have not been invited to turn the heads of the Sydney
lads, as you put it. Quite the contrary." Aisleen turned

quickly away before the girl could see her angry blush. Turn heads, indeed!

When she reached the doorway she was startled to find the walkway beyond filled with barracks girls. Elbows dug into sides and giggles suddenly erupted behind feminine hands when they noticed her. They parted immediately but stood lining either side as if she were a parade about to pass by.

Annoyed at being once again a source of diversion for them, Aisleen ignored them as she stepped onto the path. No doubt they had been drawn by the sight of a red-coated officer. At least Major Scott had been spared this vulgar display of curiosity by waiting outside the gates.

"Good luck, miss," one of the girls said shyly when Aisleen passed her.

"Aye, have a go at 'im, that's what I say!" called another as girlish laughter rippled on the afternoon air.

"Good luck! Good luck!" came a chorus of cries.

Aisleen walked on, growing more and more annoyed with their good wishes. One would have thought this a momentous occasion. How easily excited these girls were.

Beyond the gates Thomas impatiently paced Queen's Square before Hyde Park Barracks, working out the stiffness in his leg. As he waited he repeatedly dug a finger between his starched collar and his neck. The stiff linen had rubbed a welt on his skin, and his cravat threatened to strangle him.

"Bloody hell!" He seldom put himself to this torture, but he was certain that Miss Fitzgerald would not approve if he arrived in his moleskin breeches and shirt sleeves.

When he had completed another turn about the square he cast a look at the barracks gates. "Where is she?" he murmured. He had nearly stopped on the way to fortify himself with a tankard or two at the Crown and Cross until he remembered Sally. The night before she had thrown a tankard at his head when he entered.

He brushed an arm across his brow, leaving beads of sweat on his broadcloth coat sleeve. He was not an indecisive man. Yet here he was pacing and sweating like some green lad, wondering if he were about to make a fool of himself. He was satisfied with Miss Fitzgerald, but what if she refused him? After all, he was a colonial squatter without manners or refinement. Ladies, he had been told, regarded some things above money. If she refused him what would he do?

"Mr. Gibson!" a feminine voice declared with distinct displeasure.

Thomas turned sharply on his heel, so lost in his thoughts he had not heard her approach. He took her in in a single glance. Buttoned up to her chin in vile green wool and a black bonnet more fitted for a wake than courtship, she looked twenty years his senior and about as approachable as a wart hog. It was what he expected: she had come but she was not pleased. "Miss Fitzgerald? 'Tis glad I am that ye agreed to see me."

"See you? I agreed to no such thing!" Aisleen answered stiffly. His appearance at the barracks was the embodiment of her worst fears. She glanced right and then left, but, mercifully, Major Scott was nowhere in sight.

She turned her haughtiest look on the object of her displeasure. "What do you mean by tarrying before the barracks? If you wish to speak with me then I suggest you approach the matron, but I warn you I do not intend to speak to some . . . some swagman who waylays respectable ladies on the street!"

Thomas grinnned as her petticoats rustled in response to her agitation. She had enough starch in them for two ladies. "That being so, why did ye come in answer to me summons?"

A niggling suspicion burrowed its way quickly through

Aisleen's simmering thoughts. The wide-eyed stare of the girl who had summoned her . . . the troop of girls on the path . . . their boisterous good wishes. She turned sharply to discover several suspicious shadows lurking just inside the gates. The girls had known who waited for her, yet none of them had warned her.

Regaining her composure, she turned back to him. "Perhaps I am in error, Mr. Gibson. I expected someone else, you see, and when the girl told me that a gentleman had arrived for me, naturally I assumed . . ."

"Ye expected another gentleman?" Thomas questioned. "What gentleman?"

Aisleen squared her shoulders. "I do not see where that should concern you."

"Then ye've a thing or two to learn about me, Miss Fitzgerald, for anyone who has to do with me intended, particularly when he wears trousers, is me business."

"Really! This is too much!" She glanced up the street in hopes of spying a red uniform coming their way. "I am waiting for someone else."

Thomas nodded his head and hung a hand over the edge of the carriage door. "I'm nae always a patient man, but I will wait until ye've said yer regrets."

Aisleen stared at him as if he had suddenly grown a second head. Of course he had not. In fact, the one he had was quite as attractive as she first remembered it. Far from mollifying her, the fact fed her annoyance. He knew he was a handsome devil. In her experience men thought themselves handsome when even a hog would show to favor against them. Charm and regular features could not tempt her to be civil to him. "Mr. Gibson, if you do not remove yourself from my presence immediately, I will call for assistance!"

"Ye're angry because I did not return sooner," Thomas mused aloud. "As a man who hates to wait himself, I can understand yer peevishness. But I'm here now, and here I will remain until we've tied the knot proper. Is that to yer liking?''

"Mr. Gibson," she began in a withering tone, "you are laboring under a misapprehension. Through a method of reasoning I find quite incomprehensible and irrelevant, you have decided to court me and believe that I have given you the leave to do so."

"Ye've a grand way with words, Miss Fitzgerald, which I do admire," Thomas said pleasantly.

His smile was the most charming Aisleen had ever witnessed, and it made her furious. "Sir, I did not, do not, and never intend to be courted by you. Do you understand?"

"Me name's Thomas," he answered with irritating good humor. "There's no need to simper and humble yerself to make me like ye better. I like ye well enough to post the banns these last weeks at Saint Mary's."

"You—? Oh, my!" She spun away from him, as if once he were out of her sight he would cease to exist, and walked briskly toward the gates. When Major Scott came, he would announce himself.

"What am I to tell the priest?"

Aisleen disliked herself for slowing her step, but she could not resist questioning his statement. "What priest?"

"Father Jacob, of course," came the reply from behind her. "He's to marry us, ye see, come Monday."

Aisleen turned back slowly, her thoughts as intense as the sunlight slanted down on her. People were listening, the barracks girls and the coachman. Anything she said would be fodder for gossip for weeks to come. "This has gone quite far enough. You cannot expect me to believe that you've duped a priest into taking part in this—this destestable jest!"

Thomas swung the carriage door open. "Come and ask him for yerself."

"I'm not mad enough to go anywhere with you!" Aisleen raised a gloved hand and pressed it tightly to her forehead. Her head throbbed to near bursting; perspiration dribbled down her temples and snaked down her neck into her high, tight collar. All the while he stood before her grinning like a boy who had won a prize. It was unseemly, it was vile, it was . . .

Thomas realized just in time that she had begun to sway. He reached her quickly and caught her by the elbow. "Steady, Miss Fitzgerald," he said bracingly. "The midday sun is hard on those not accustomed to it."

"Of course," Aisleen whispered, closing her eyes against the giddy rush threatening her.

"Perhaps ye'd like to sit a moment?" he encouraged, drawing her toward the carriage. "That's it, lass. We'll be finding a shady spot to have a dish of tea."

Aisleen heard in his voice a comfortable, vaguely familiar anchor for her dazed senses. Tea, yes, tea sounded delightful. But should she go? There was someone else who had offered her tea. "I must be sensible," she said to no one in particular as he handed her up into the carriage.

"Aye, ye'd be that, sensible," Thomas said. "Windmill and Fort streets!" he called to the driver and then climbed in beside her and shut the door.

To Aisleen's amazement he sat down beside her on the narrow seat rather than on the opposite bench. She twitched her skirts aside to make more room for him, but she could not keep her elbow from brushing his. The casual contact startled her, but he did not seem to notice.

Closing her eyes, she leaned back against the seat and willed her heart to slow. Heatstroke, that was what she suffered. In a moment, she told herself, her heart would find its regular rhythm and her head would clear and then she would demand that he return her to the barracks. But not just yet. The infernal heat of New South Wales combined with her own agitation was making her heart palpitate and her head feel as though it were caught in an ever-tightening vise.

Thomas watched her intently, wondering what he should do. Had she been in the bush, he would have removed the ugly bonnet she wore and loosened her collar. Yet here on the streets of Sydney, he was not at all certain that she would understand. So, against his better judgment, he did nothing, simply watched the slowing rise and fall of her bosom as she drifted into slumber. After a moment he smiled and gathered her against his shoulder.

When the carriage rocked to a halt, Aisleen opened her eyes, not quite certain where she was or how long she had been there.

"Ye dozed," Thomas said in answer to her puzzled expression.

She became aware of several things at once. She was slouched down in the carriage seat, her head resting scandalously upon a strange man's shoulder, and his arm supported her. She bolted upright on the seat, conscious that he smiled at her in that vile, charming manner he had. "Where are we?" she demanded tartly.

"Lord Nelson's," Thomas answered. "Never been inside meself, but there's certain to be a place to order tea."

Aisleen doubted the propriety of the venture, even more so when he had handed her down into the street. "Why, this is a hotel!"

"So it is," Thomas agreed. "A fine one, too. Tea, Miss Fitzgerald?" He offered her an arm which she reluctantly took.

Once inside, she permitted herself to be mollified by the decorous surroundings. The foyer of the small building was neatly appointed; the tavern room into which her host steered her was neat and quiet and occupied by several other couples. It was all quite proper and quite harmless.

"Tea," Thomas ordered when they had seated themselves in a corner. "Seen much of Sydney, have ye?" he questioned politely when the order was taken.

"No, I have not," Aisleen answered faintly, for he had turned toward her and his proximity made her feel more flushed than the heat. She reached for her fan and flicked it open, plying it between the scant space that separated them.

"Aye, well, then, we'll have to give ye a look round before we leave."

"Before we leave?" Aisleen pinned him with a cold look. "I have no intention of leaving Sydney."

Thomas gazed at her flushed face, wondering how to talk her out of that ugly bonnet. "Ye've no liking for the country, then?"

"Quite the contrary." Aisleen answered too quickly and felt her cheeks burn as he lifted a single black brow. "I came to New South Wales for the express purpose of employment. I am a teacher, sir. It is what I do, the thing at which I excel."

"Are ye now?" Thomas answered and fell silent as the waitress approached. He was not adept at small talk. When cups were set before them and the tea poured, he lapsed into an uncomfortable silence.

Several minutes passed, but Aisleen did not touch her cup. Finally the suspense became too much. "What exactly, Mr. Gibson, do you want from me?"

"Why, to make ye me bride, Miss Fitzgerald."

Aisleen gave her head a slight shake. "You must understand that I find your singular interest in me quite unreasonable."

"How's that?"

"I am scarcely the sort of woman to be pursued. I am not the marrying type, Mr. Gibson. I am a spinster who has had to make her way in the world as best she can. Never once have I entertained the hope of marriage. When you came to the barracks on the first occasion, I assumed that you sought a teacher or governess for your children."

"I offered ye better than that."

"Mr. Gibson, I am not at all convinced that marriage to you or any man is preferable to an offer of regular employment."

Thomas regarded her in silence. When he spoke there was no smile on his face. "Ye refuse me proposal of marriage, yet ye would have considered an offer of employment from me? Do I have the right of it, Miss Fitzgerald?"

At her nod, his mouth softened. "Well then, here's me new offer to ye. I'm weary of living me life alone. I want a family to come home to, a house that's felt a woman's touch, and meals to share with someone other than sheep and jackeroos. I want music and laughter and gentleness. In return I'm offering ye protection, a good home, more than enough to see to yer needs, and me name."

"That is a proposal of marriage," Aisleen maintained.

"I had nae finished," Thomas replied. "I see that ye've need of proof of me intentions. I will pay ye a salary. Ten pounds a month for keeping me home and hearth. Will that be sounding fair to ye?"

"Well, I—"

"There'll be bonuses for attending shivoos and weddings and such. And a hundred pounds sterling at the birth of each of me children."

"You're mad!" Aisleen whispered low. "Quite and thoroughly mad!"

"Mad, am I, when ye said yerself ye'd work for me?"

"Employment is not the same thing as being a paid wife," Aisleen replied. "Why it's nothing short of—of whoring." The last was scarcely audible.

"I'd not pay a whore so much," Thomas answered calmly. "As to that, ye may name yer price."

Aisleen stood up. "I've never been so insulted in my life!"

"Insult!" Thomas roared, irritated out of his good humor as he came to his feet. "Insulted? Because I've asked ye to marry me and have me children? If that's an insult to a lady like yerself, 'tis no wonder ye're not wed!"

The ringing words brought every face in the tavern swiveling toward them. Aisleen sank into her chair, too ashamed of her own lack of control to reprimand her companion. Likewise Thomas sat, but after a wink at their audience.

When she thought she could control her voice, Aisleen raised her eyes to Thomas. "It's not marriage you offer me but a position as a wife for hire."

"I thought that's what ye wanted," Thomas answered. "I'd wed ye and no difference to be made; but ye would regard it as a business proposition, and I respect that."

"I—I—" Aisleen sighed. What *did* she want? Was she really ready to scrub floors or be a barmaid in a pub before considering marriage? "If I were in your employ I would be free to leave my post at any time. Marriage is different."

"Would ye prefer a trial period? We could say we were wed with none but ourselves to know. If ye did nae like it, ye'd be free to leave at any time."

"And you'd be free to desert me!" Aisleen answered bitterly, remembering her father and his whoring days before his death. "I'll not be your whore."

"Then you'll be me bride," Thomas answered simply.

"We would be married in a church?" she asked faintly, scarcely believing that she was beginning to consider his proposal.

"Aye," Thomas said, holding back on his inclination to smile.

Aisleen looked at him, at his too-blue eyes and remarkably handsome face. Was it possible that she could wed such a man? Was it not insanity even to consider it? She looked away. She disliked and distrusted the motives of all men. Why should Thomas Gibson be any different?

Say yes!

Aisleen glanced over her shoulder. "Who said that?"

"Said what?"

Aisleen shook her head. She had heard the Gaelic words distinctly, yet no one was there. "Nothing." She wet her lips and looked down at her hands clasped tightly in her lap. "I will wed you, Mr. Gibson, on the condition that you treat me as an employee—with respect and a regular salary."

It was a mad scheme but one that would pay her passage back to Ireland within a few months. "Ten pounds is a generous sum for a governess, but as this is an unusual arrangement, I accept it. Ten pounds to be paid into my hands at the beginning of each month."

She looked up into his face to be struck again by his pleasantness and took a deep breath, feeling as though she were stepping off a high cliff. "In return, I will keep your home, act as your wife. However, I will not accept brutality at your hands nor suffer shame. If you subject me to either, I shall feel myself free to dissolve the bond between us." She paused. "Do we understand one another?"

"Oh, aye, Miss Fitzgerald. That we do."

The hour of thy great wind of love and hate.

—The Secret Rose
W. B. Yeats

Chapter Seven

Aisleen slipped the final button of her lace-bodiced gown into place. Her fingers unconsciously tightened at her throat as she gazed at her reflection. She was as pale as the white lace she wore, her nostrils pinched and her mouth drawn. Her eyes, always clear and serious, were on this morning dull and puffy from lack of sleep. Only her bright red hair tumbled colorfully about her shoulders in riotous waves.

"Altogether I look like a banshee braving the light of day," she murmured. She could not imagine a picture that was less bridelike. She felt no elation, no eagerness. How could she? She was about to marry a man about whom she knew nothing.

She picked up the rock-crystal brooch. The large stone sliced rainbow flakes from the morning light and shattered them upon the floor and wall. She ran a finger lightly over the gold filigree and wondered how her father had allowed it to pass unnoticed and unpawned. But, of course, it was not a diamond and was not of much value. She supposed that she should be grateful that there was anything left of the once proud Fitzgeralds. Everything else gone: the land, Liscarrol, even the belief that they would withstand and endure. Even her name was about to change, and she would be a Fitzgerald no more.

With infinite sadness, Aisleen reached up to pin the brooch at her throat, wondering what she should tell her mother about her marriage. Should she tell her the truth? While she had not changed her low opinion of marriage, she was capable of viewing wedlock as a reasonable alternative to starvation. It was a marriage of practicality, mutual need, a transaction in which both parties gained. Mr. Gibson would have his lady wife, and she would have the management of her own household.

No doubt her mother and Mr. Kirwan would choose to believe that she had fallen under the romantic spell of some colonial rogue when, in reality, she cared nothing for the man she was to wed. No, she would not mention her marriage to her mother.

Aisleen ignored the guilty flush that climbed her cheeks. Not even marriage would hold her if she chose to forsake her vows.

The idea had come to her in the middle of the night as she lay waiting for dawn. It should be a simple matter to gain command of Mr. Gibson. After all, he was a simple fellow. No man of sound reasoning would have offered his name to a stranger. While she would have preferred to wed a man whose vigor had been tempered by the years, his youth might well be an advantage. Immediately after the ceremony she would take him in hand just as she would any new nursery charge placed in her care and begin molding him into a gentleman. She would rid him of that embarrassing brogue, pare the rough edges off his manners, and teach him how to treat a lady. In time, and if she were half as clever as she should be, she would domesticate Mr. Gibson. If that proved impossible, she would gather her monthly salary and leave him without regret or misgiving. After all, theirs was a contract, and contracts could be broken.

"You will bend to the rules of society, but then, Miss Aisleen Fitzgerald, you shall bend those rules to your own purposes!" she whispered to the gaunt-faced reflection in her mirror.

"Are you ready—? Why, Miss Fitzgerald!" Though Mrs. Freeman had known the young lady a month, she scarcely recognized her in the gown of lace and lavender silk. The flattering cut revealed the youthful figure she kept hidden. Absent, too, was the shrouding bonnet or frilled house cap she usually wore. The blazing head of hair revealed was quite the most lovely shade Mrs. Freeman had ever seen. She wondered if Mr. Gibson were aware of his bride's crowning glory and doubted it. What a nice surprise he had in store.

The matron nodded in approval. "You're the very picture of a bride! How fortuitous that you had such a gown in your possession."

"Thank you," Aisleen answered, embarrassed and not quite certain of what to answer. "My mother forced the frivolity upon me." When Mrs. Freeman's smile dimmed she knew she had said the wrong thing. Why could she not accept the compliment? Because she knew what Mrs. Freeman was thinking: that despite her claims to the contrary she had brought the gown like an item in a hope chest in the expectation of attracting a marriage proposal. If it had been five degrees cooler, she told herself, she would have resorted to the gray wool. She quite ignored the tiny voice inside her head which whispered, *Liar!*

"Mr. Gibson has sent a carriage for you," Mrs. Freeman said. "Are you packed and ready?"

"Yes, thank you. You may send the fellow for my baggage. I have only to put on my bonnet." Aisleen quickly gathered her fire-bright cloud of hair into a ball and pinned it into a knot.

Mrs. Freeman hesitated as Aisleen picked up the straw bonnet with matching pink and lavender ribbons. She looked down at the garment in her hand. Should she make the gesture? Of course she should. "Miss Fitzgerald, I have a gift for you." She held out a length of white lace. It was a wedding veil. "The girls of the barracks purchased it for you when they heard you did not have time to buy a proper trousseau."

Aisleen gazed blankly at the lace veiling. She had not made a single friend among the barracks girls, nor had she attempted to do so. "Why should they give me a present?"

Mrs. Freeman's lips thinned. "I wonder myself," she murmured and cast the veil upon the cot before folding her arms. Really, the young woman had a great deal to learn about graciousness. "We wish you well, Miss Fitzgerald," she said stiffly. "If at any time we of the Immigration Society may be of further aid to you, do feel free to contact us."

Aisleen blushed. She had offended the lady once more. "Thank you, Mrs. Freeman, and I ask that you thank the others for me. When I am done with it, I would like to return the veil to the barracks." She saw Mrs. Freeman stiffen further and hurriedly added, "That it may be used by other barracks brides."

Mrs. Freeman thawed slightly. "A generous gesture, Miss Fitzgerald, but the girls would be hurt if you did not keep it for your own daughter's wedding."

This time Aisleen held her tongue and merely nodded. There would be no point in saying that she doubted she would ever have a daughter. That was another of the matters she meant to take in hand.

She picked up the lace veil and carefully folded it. After a final glance in the mirror she turned to the matron, and suddenly she needed very badly someone's assurance. "Do you think I'll do, Mrs. Freeman?"

The feminine question, posed as any bride might, disarmed the older woman. Bridal nervousness would account for the young woman's pallor and skittishness.

"You look very fine, indeed, Miss Fitzgerald." She reached out and took Aisleen's hand in her own. "I know you've had a bad start in New South Wales, but you've shown yourself to be a most sensible young woman. Marriage is the best thing for you. You'll see. You must come and visit when next you're in Sydney and tell me how you've fared."

"I will," Aisleen answered and gave the woman's hand a quick squeeze. "And thank you."

"Now hurry along, dear; your groom awaits you."

The carriage ride to Saint Mary's was quickly accomplished. Aisleen alit reluctantly, wishing she had given in to her impulse to ask Mrs. Freeman to accompany her. There would be no friendly faces at the ceremony. Mr. Gibson had informed her that his friends lived too far away to ask to Sydney on short notice. She did not have any. In fact, she was not at all certain that Mr. Gibson himself was present as she entered through the vestibule.

She paused uncertainly, dazed by the sudden gloom after the glare of the Pacific sun. Gradually her vision adjusted. The chapel was cool and dark, with too few candles lit. The altar was bare, without flowers or witnesses. With a leap of relief she at last saw her groom, talking with the priest near the entrance to the sacristy.

Thomas forgot the dignity required within the holy walls when he spotted Aisleen. Laughing in relief, he started down the aisle toward her. With every step his grin widened. He had wondered when she would arrive, had been half-afraid that she would not. While it was considered bad luck to see one's bride the morning before the ceremony, he had nearly ridden in the carriage to pick her up. Yet she had come, dressed as he had never seen her.

She was gowned in a most becoming shade of lavender, with a tight lace bodice and pink sash that showed off to advantage a trim waist and, well, a remarkably healthy bosom.

His grin stretched even wider as new possibilities danced through his head. An arranged marriage did not have to be a sour one. "Miss Fitzgerald, so glad I am to see ye!"

For a nervous moment, Aisleen thought he would embrace her, but he did not. He merely took her hand in his and squeezed it with surprising energy.

"Good morning, Mr. Gibson," she replied, taking in a glance his dark blue broadcloth frock coat, starched cravat, and gray-and-navy plaid trousers. She suspected that he had visited a barber, for his unruly hair lay docilely about his head. He was handsome, she gave him that.

A seldom consulted, feminine part of her could not help but wish that Nicholas Maclean could know that the poor spinster governess he had sought to ravish was about to marry the most handsome man in New South Wales.

Aisleen squelched the thought. It was unworthy of her. Handsome or ugly, old or young, Mr. Gibson represented nothing more than security. To gain that, she would marry him were he cross-eyed and fifty. And better so, she told herself, but did not dwell too long on the boast.

"Shall we?" Thomas questioned with a nod toward the altar.

"Just so," she answered. The sooner the better, for she was beginning to entertain the oddest notions.

"No, wait!" With a quick tug at the ribbon tied under her chin, she loosened her bonnet and lifted it off and placed it in a pew. With a quick shake, she freed the veil from its folds and draped it over her head. "Now, sir, I am ready."

"...I, Thomas Finnian Butler Gibson, take ye, Aisleen, as my lawful wedded wife..."

Thomas Finnian Butler Gibson, Aisleen mused as she gazed at the gold band he held poised at the tip of the third finger of her left hand. She had not even known his full name until this instant.

"...From this day forward, for better or for worse, in sickness and in health, until death do us part..."

As the ring slid onto her finger she noted that it was a good fit.

"...I, Alice—Aisleen Meghan Deirdre Fitzgerald, take thee, Thomas, as my lawful wedded husband..."

Aisleen heard herself saying the words of the marriage vows in faint wonder. Was it real? Was it possible?

Aye, 'tis possible.

"Until—until..."

"Until death do us part," the priest prompted.

"Until death do us part," she repeated very softly as the fateful words tolled in her head.

As she knelt for the final blessing she ceased listening to the words of the ceremony. Something quite inexplicable was occurring. A warmth enveloped her. Unlike the heat of Sydney, it was a comforting warmth, a thrilling, buoying enfolding that wafted about her and bound her in a swaddling of contentment. And words: something or someone whispered to her, in a voice too subtle to be audible, a benediction on this meager ceremony.

She closed her eyes, aware that for the first time in nearly a month her head had ceased aching. She felt relief and comfort. Yes, she had done right to wed.

"...now pronounce you man and wife. You may kiss your bride, Thomas."

Thomas rose and turned to Aisleen, his face growing

concerned as he gazed down at her. On each cheek was the slick of a single tear's path. The sight was so unexpected that he acted without thinking. Gently clasping her by the shoulders, he bent and kissed each dewy track. "Fear nae ye," he whispered against her ear and for an instant pressed his cheek to hers.

Too stunned to react, Aisleen stood docilely beneath his touch. His hand moved to frame her cheeks. As he bent toward her, his eyes closed. For a fraction of a second she saw with wonder the thick black lashes lying snugly against his sunburnt cheeks. An instant later, she turned her head away, and the soft impression of his lips grazed her cheek. It was a light touch, a casual brushing that nonetheless made her draw a quick breath. And then it was over.

"Congratulations, Mr. Gibson, and my felicitations to your bride," Aisleen heard the priest say, and then she was being propelled down the aisle on the arm of her groom. From the corner of her eye she thought she saw a shadow move at the far end of a back pew, but then she was stepping into the bright, blinding light of the Australian morning.

"Do ye not care for the beef?" Thomas questioned solicitously when he realized that Aisleen had scarcely touched the wedding breakfast he had had prepared especially for them in a private dining room of the Palisades Hotel.

"I am not very hungry," Aisleen answered, aware now that he had cleaned his plate with astonishing speed while she had been lost in thought. "But do allow me to serve you."

She reached for the bowl of green beans and spooned a generous portion onto his plate. "Potatoes?" Deftly she scooped up several pieces swimming in buttery cream sauce.

"And now a nice piece of sirloin." She picked up the carving knife and fork and with expert ease cut two thin slices and transferred them to his plate, ladling oyster gravy over them. "It's a nice cut of beef, not too grainy or overdone, as the English are wont to do. But the fried veal patties are a cold meat dish; I've made it before. Quite likely the veal was a part of last night's dinner fare. I advise you not to pay more than five shillings for it."

Thomas smiled at her. "Ye'll make a grand wife, ye will, looking after yer husband so. I did not think to ask if ye cook, but glad I am to hear that ye do. Ye're a clever thing, Aisleen."

Aisleen nodded primly, uncomfortable with his use of her Christian name, but she did not correct him this time. After all, he had complimented her. But as she watched him spear a piece of potato with his knife and poke it into his mouth, she mentally added his table manners to the list of changes she must make in him.

"I will do my best to see that you are fairly treated by tradesmen and domestics," Aisleen began. "Further, I will keep an orderly account of all household expenses, which you may wish to peruse as regularly as you do your foreman's business books."

Thomas nodded and chewed, undecided if he should tell her that his foreman did not keep records and that he could not read them even if the man had. "I'll take yer word for the expenses. As for records, we'll see."

Aisleen picked up her fork but after a moment's thought laid it down again. "Forgive me, Mr. Gibson, but I really must know something of your immediate plans. In order that I may formulate my own, you understand."

Thomas swallowed. "Is that what's had a frown riding yer fine brow? Well, 'tis easy enough to answer. We'll be spending the night in Sydney. A little time to ourselves would not be amiss, I'm thinking," he added with a grin that made Aisleen blush.

"I see," she answered faintly. Her task of taming her new husband would begin sooner than she hoped. First of all, he must be made to understand that she was not immediately to become his brood mare.

"Do ye, lass? I wonder." Thomas reached across the table and placed his hand over hers. He felt her try to withdraw and curled his fingers over the back of her hand to hold it still. "Do nae be afraid of me, lass. I'm yer husband now."

"I find intimacies in public to be singularly distasteful," she answered in a breathless voice and was relieved that he released her. The warm, rough touch of his callused hand had not been unpleasant but somehow unnerving.

Thomas held her shy gaze. "There's none to see us. A man might be excused a small liberty or two, seeing as how 'tis his wedding day."

Aisleen looked away from his cocky smile. Those too-bright eyes spoke with an eloquence their owner lacked, and their meaning was clear. "We are not the ordinary sort of bride and groom," she said, carefully choosing her words. "We are little more than strangers, sir. I am unaccustomed to the company of gentlemen and find your attentions, however well meant, disconcerting."

"We'll soon be taking care of that," Thomas answered easily. "From this night forward, ye'll be having me in yer bed. 'Twill make the knowing of me that much quicker."

His answer brought her gaze flashing back toward his face. He could not be serious? Yet the answer was there in his confident male grin. Dismay quickened her heartbeat. She had no intention of sharing even a room with him, this night or any other. "I believe it will take time, nothing less than that, to change us from strangers to companions," she replied with more conviction. "I reiterate, we are little more than strangers. We did not wed because of personal suitability or sentiment.''

"Loving, do ye mean?" Thomas questioned in surprise. *"Wirra!* It never crossed me mind to think that a lady of yer refinement would consider love a proper reason for marrying. Love's easy enough to come by. I thought ye saw clear the reason I've not wed before now.''

"In truth, I do not," Aisleen answered cautiously.

Thomas shrugged. "I won't lie to ye. I've known me share of women— Aisleen, lass, do not be screwing up yer face the like. 'Tis a monstrous sight. As I was saying, I might have wed a dozen times, but I didn't, as none of the lasses had a pedigree to match yers.''

"Are we speaking of buying cattle again, Mr. Gibson?" Aisleen asked coolly.

Thomas did not misunderstand this reference to their second meeting. "Aye, and so many a more sound marriage would be made were the parties to bring the wariness of a buyer into the choice. A man would not buy a horse, nor a cow, nor a bullock, without first seeing the stock. I saw ye and knew ye to be to me liking. And ye did the same.''

But did I? Aisleen mused. She picked up her fork again, ploughing her creamed potatoes with the tines. She should have been better prepared for his pleasant but obstinate nature. She had seen it work to remarkable effect. She was wed to him with less than two days of acquaintance between them.

Thomas watched her smear her plate with what was, to his mind, quite nice tucker. The hand holding her fork was gloved, and he wondered how she managed to eat without getting gravy stains on the tips. His perusal moved from her hand to the attractive straw bonnet she wore. She had replaced her veil with the pretty thing in the carriage, but he had hoped she would remove it now that they were alone. Remembering his single glimpse on the dock of her incredibly bright red hair, he nearly suggested it. The tiny frown puckering her brow changed his mind.

It was his wedding day, a day that a man had every right to look upon with pride and anticipation. The worst was over, the vows said, and now he wanted to celebrate with the lady who had consented to be his bride. So why did she sit there staring down as though she were on her way to an execution?

He wanted to put her at ease, but he did not know what to say. Words were never easy for him, particularly when she knew so many more of them than he did. His inclination was to put his arm about her shoulders, but he was certain that she would shy away if he did. She had turned her mouth from his kiss after the ceremony, offering him the cool, damp velvet of her cheek instead. He could scarcely remember the feel of her skin, and it rankled.

Give it time, Thomas, lad. Give it time, he counseled himself.

Aisleen looked up suddenly. "Do you mean that?"

"Mean what?" Thomas questioned, surprised to find himself staring into a pair of poteen-colored eyes, as rich and warm an amber as any whiskey this side of Dublin.

"That we have time, that you will give me time to become accustomed to marriage?" Aisleen replied.

"Aye, we've a lifetime for that," Thomas agreed, but puzzlement resonated in his words. He did not remember speaking his thoughts aloud. He must be more anxious than he realized.

The desire for whiskey that he had been denying himself for two long days suddenly loomed as an overpowering need. He rose to his feet. "There's a matter or two of importance that I should have out of me way before nightfall. If ye will not think badly of me, I'll be leaving ye some short while to attend to it."

Aisleen rose instantly to her feet. "By all means, see to your business. I shall deal splendidly well alone."

Thomas removed his cravat and opened his collar, too caught up in his own desire to leave to hear the relief in her voice. "I may not be back before dark, but I have the landlord's word that ye'll receive anything ye may wish. We're staying the night and then it's for Parramatta tomorrow, where we'll meet me mate who's waiting to accompany us home."

He reached for his floppy-brimmed hat and then crossed the room and opened a door, motioning with his head. "The bedroom's in here. They brought our things up before we came up to eat."

Aisleen moved to the doorway, stepping carefully past him to keep her skirts from brushing his legs. The room beyond the door was small but neatly appointed with printed wallpaper, a chair, valet stand, and, dominating the small space, a narrow brass bed with a crocheted cover.

Blood stung her ears as her gaze slid from the bed to the baggage stacked in one corner. It did not seem possible that two human beings could share that tiny confine and long remain in ignorance of one another. How should she broach the subject?

When she turned back and saw that Thomas's complexion had turned strangely red beneath its heavy tan she knew she could not. "Very well, Mr. Gibson," she murmured.

"Thomas, Tom, or just plain Gibson, but ye've no need to call me Mister anything after the morning's work," Thomas answered shortly. He set his hat on his head at an angle that shaded his eyes from her view. "G'day, then, missus," he said and walked to the door.

"Good day to you, Mis—Thomas," she replied. She was not surprised that he turned to smile at her, but, to her astonishment, he winked at her!

"Well!" she let out in a great sigh when the door was closed behind him. That man had no manners at all.

Thomas was in fine high spirits as he ordered the third round for the company of the Wallaby Tavern. It was quite gratifying, he reflected through the haze of amply imbibed grog, to know that a man could walk into a tavern a stranger and within moments have the entire assembly drinking his good health. Marriage had made him a roomful of new mates.

The rousing chorus of "Carroty Kate" sung to the tinny accompaniment of an upright piano filled the air with boozy conviviality as man after man slung a fraternal arm about the shoulders of the man nearest him to form a circle about the player. Thomas's rough baritone underscored the Irish tenor of Michael O'Casey as they sang

> ". . . Her hair was the color of ginger,
> She could reckon you up on a slate.
> My colonial, she was a swinger,
> And they called her Carroty Kate!
>
> "She was very fond of riding,
> As you can plainly see.
> For one fine day she rode away,
> With a chap from the Native Bee!"

As the next verse began, Thomas fell back from the circle to reach for his cup, but froze as Jack Egan's mighty frame filled the doorway of the tavern. Jack did not cross toward the singers but walked over to a table in an empty corner and sat down.

"Will ye nae give us another chorus, Tom?" Michael O'Casey cried, clamping a hand on Thomas's shoulder.

"Nae. Ask Tim there, he's a fine voice," Thomas answered. "I've a mate just come in."

Thomas made his way smilingly among the revelers, who were two-thirds drunk on his coin. *Ah, well, that's as it should be,* he thought. When he reached Jack's table he asked preemptively, "Are ye mad? What are ye doing in Sydney?"

Jack had drawn his pipe from his pocket and continued to tap tobacco into it. Knowing that he would answer in his own time, Thomas sat down and folded his arms across his chest.

When the tobacco was to his liking, Jack pulled a straw from his pocket, stuck one end into a blazing lantern that hung nearby, and then lit his pipe with the smoldering end. "She'll be right plain looking, Tom," he said finally, releasing a puff of smoke.

In that simple sentence was the answer to his presence in Sydney. Jack had been at the wedding, a silent and unseen witness. "Perhaps, but did ye hear her, Jack? She's a lady, a thoroughgoing lady."

"Manners will nae keep a man warm at night," Jack said shortly. "But 'tis none of my affair."

Thomas's eyes narrowed at the curt dismissal of his bride. "I'm not asking ye to like it, Jack. I'm asking ye to give her a chance, that's all."

Jack exhaled a huge cloud of smoke. "Open up the station to her like, and what will ye get? Respectability, civilization, and the *law.*" His voice was low but edged with rage. "Next thing, she'll be building a bloody church and calling the drovers in for prayer!"

"She's going to the station with me," Thomas said flatly. "She's me wife, and ye'll give the respect she's due. By the by, it's not safe, ye being in town. Or have ye forgotten the wee matter of the Macquarie murder?"

Silence stretched between them as Jack continued to suck

on his pipe. After a moment he stood and started for the door.

"We'll be in Parramatta tomorrow night," Thomas called after the retreating man. "Ye'll be there to meet us?"

Jack did not slow his step or reply.

"Bloody hell!"

Aisleen retied the bow at the neck of her bed jacket for the twelfth time. "Oh, bosh!" she exclaimed as she peered into the mirror that hung above the wash basin in the bedroom. She jerked the ribbon free. It looked horrid. Everything she had was horrid. Why had she not thought of what it would mean to share close confines with a man?

"Because you did not expect that eventuality to occur," she murmured. Absently she began to massage the pain from her temples.

The headache that had retreated during the ceremony had returned not long after Thomas had departed. The ache had increased in intensity as she had spent the afternoon going over again and again in her mind what she would say regarding the double bed and the single bedroom when he returned.

At dusk, a knock had sent her nervously to the door, but it was only the landlord's wife with her evening meal. She wondered if her husband had been considerate enough to order it for her before he left or if the landlord had simply taken the initiative. She had not inquired. Instead she had asked for an extra pillow and blanket, saying that she was cold by nature.

She had waited until the meal was cold before eating a portion of it. At any moment she had expected a tread to pause at her door. Now it was fully night and he had not returned.

Her mou...   ...immed at the memory of the landlady's
words when she ... brought up the extra bedding. "Ducks,
ye'll not be ... needin' much cover after this, not with that
brawny man ye wed to keep ye warm."

This giddy anxiety was alien to her nature, yet she could
not still the wake of quivering that followed her thoughts.
She had chosen a practical answer to a very trying situation,
but that did not quell her nervousness. She had bargained
away her freedom for comfort and she did not yet know if it
would be worth the price.

She closed the bedroom door and sat down on the edge of
the bed, reviewing her strategy. She would feign sleep, if in
fact she was not truly asleep when Thomas returned. She
doubted he would awaken her. Perhaps he might not even
enter the room. She had left a pillow and blanket in a
conspicuous place in the outer room. He could scarcely
misunderstand her intent. In the morning they would discuss
future arrangements.

The noisy rattling of the parlor door latch made her jump.
Thomas had returned. With an agility and swiftness rarely
resorted to, she tiptoed to the lamp and blew it out. In
heart-stopping anxiety, she heard the door creak as she crept
back to the bed and slipped off her bed jacket. She raised
the sheet and slid under the bedding as she heard her name
called.

"Aisleen? Aisleen, me love," Thomas called as he stood
on the threshold gazing at the empty room. Squinting, he
looked about. She was not there. He stepped back, peering
down the hall at the other doors along the corridor. No, he
was not mistaken. This was where he had left his bride.

He entered, liquor singing in his blood. He felt absolutely
wonderful. Gone was the anxiety, the doubt, the gnawing
concern that Jack's appearance had planted squarely in the
midst of his joy. Aisleen: the name was Gaelic for "vision."

His Aisleen might not be a beauty, but then again he had not seen her properly yet to know.

Properly. He chuckled. Improperly would be more like it. He had waited nearly twelve hours to claim his bride, and though his thoughts were less coherent than they might be, one singled itself out. She would not be his until he had bedded her.

He shut the door behind him with exaggerated care. She must be in bed. How neglectful a bridegroom he was to keep her waiting. Poor lass, was she wondering if he would ever return?

He removed his hat and tossed it carelessly aside. "Aisleen, lass. I would not desert ye. Not ever," he called through the bedroom door. There was no answer.

"Poor wee lass, must be sleeping," he murmured as he struggled to remove his coat. One arm was caught. He gave a hard tug and heard the broadcloth tear as his arm came free. He did not care. He had no intention of ever wearing the fancy coat again.

"Boots," he whispered to himself, then put a finger to his lips to remind himself to be quiet. But the whiskey was humming louder, warming him and whispering to him of the delight that lay waiting for him beyond the door.

"Me wife," he murmured as he bent to pull the first boot from his foot. Aye, he liked the sound of that, a woman of his own, for himself alone. That was something he had never had. His first woman had been an aging whore who had taken pity on a rangy convict boy without a penny. Over the years he had known a number of women, but they had always been for sale to any man or belonged to another. Only Sally had offered herself to him alone.

Thomas sighed as his first boot came free, and he moved to the second. *Dear, sweet Sally,* he mused, remembering her soft, full breasts and the warm scent of her skin. She had been a virgin. He sat upright. So was Aisleen. What did he know of virgins?

"One woman's made the same as another," he said in answer to the whiskey murmurings. It would sort itself out.

When the second boot came free he walked to the bedroom door and turned the latch, only to remember the lantern. Padding on bare feet, he crossed the room and pinched the wick. From the corner of his eye, he spied bedding piled on a chair, but the darkness eclipsed it before he thought much of it. Immediately he retraced his steps and opened the bedroom door.

The cry of the hinges sounded in Aisleen's ears like the mighty blast of Gabriel's trumpet, but she remained perfectly still. When she heard nothing more, she opened an eye.

He stood in the doorway, his shirtfront luminously white in the gloom. Aisleen held her breath. How long did he intend to watch her sleep? Did he know that she faked sleep? Did he hope to catch her? The very idea made her angry. She was not a small child seeing to escape the eye of a governess. She was a grown woman. A married woman.

Go away! Go away! she thought anxiously.

"Aisleen, love?" she heard him call softly, and his words strummed the chords of tension within her.

When he moved inside, she lowered her lids, afraid that he would detect the gleam of an eyeball in the dark. Scarcely breathing, she heard him move toward the bed and then a rustling. What was he doing? Why did he not simply go away like any sensible person would?

The answer was suddenly clear as the bed creaked under his weight and a callused hand came to rest on her shoulder. He was not going to leave. He had come to sleep with her.

Aisleen's eyes flew open, all pretense abandoned. "What are you doing!"

"'Tis only me, Aisleen, lass," he answered softly, patting her shoulder. "'Tis only Tom, yer husband."

"I—I did not expect you," she answered, pulling the sheet up tightly under her chin.

"Did ye not? And me thinking ye could think of nothing else but me return." He reached up and touched the ruffle of the nightcap she wore. The lass had more covers for her head than any woman he had ever known. "Did ye miss me?"

His breath brushed her face and Aisleen's eyes narrowed. "You, sir, have been drinking whiskey."

"Aye, that I have," Thomas agreed pleasantly, "and never had a man a better reason than in the celebrating of his wedding day."

"I do not approve of drinking spirits," Aisleen maintained as his fingers worried the lace of her nightcap.

"Ah, well, that may be because ye've never drunk them yerself, lass. It would nae come amiss, a wee drop every now and then." He bent forward to get a better view of her. "Are ye happy, lass?"

"Happy?" Aisleen whispered faintly, keenly aware of the intimate pressure of his chest against her breasts as she lay under the covers.

"Aye." Thomas nodded. "I'm a happy man. I've everything I need. I would that ye were happy, but I hear in yer voice a sadness that I cannot understand." His fingers moved to the curve of her jaw. "I can make ye happy. I know a way to make ye smile."

One moment he was leaning over her, his boyish grin a pearly gleam in the darkness. The next Aisleen felt with stunning surprise the warm pressure of his lips against her own.

A shiver went through her, a sensation not entirely unpleasant but one that sent panic fleeing after it. She put up a hand to shove him away but encountered the hot flesh of his shoulder. Appalled, she jerked her hand away. He was naked!

Thomas reached out to catch her chin and bring her face to his. "Do nae be shy, lass," he murmured as he bent to her once more. " 'Tis yer lawful husband ye kiss."

"Please!" Aisleen muttered against his mouth, beginning to struggle. He was drunk. Too often she had witnessed her father in a drunken stupor, or worse, when the liquor had released the pent-up anger and violence in him. To the day she died she would remember his beating. Now her husband was drunk and bent on physical assault. She struck out wildly at him with her fists. This was not what she expected. It was so unfair, so unfair!

Thomas caught her hands and easily pinned them to the bed on either side of her head. "Easy, lass," he crooned, moving his kisses from her mouth to her ear. "Ye taste so sweet, never like the tart berry ye seem." He felt himself filling, tightening, rising. "I know how to give ye what ye need. I know."

"Get off me, you beast!" Aisleen cried. Frightened beyond care for propriety, she kicked at him as she thrashed about.

Thomas responded by holding her down with his weight. She was new to lovemaking. She would be shy and frightened, he reasoned, until he had proved to her that she would receive only pleasure from him. With deliberate slowness, he walked his lips back from her ear to the side of her mouth, tasting the freshness of her skin. She was a woman, a soft and warm woman who was his wife.

He released one hand, his own wandering down over the covers until he discovered the mounded fullness of a breast through the covers. "Don't fight me, lass. Let me make ye my wife."

"No! Please!" Aisleen begged, but her words were crushed in the embrace of his lips. His kiss was long and hard, not like the first. His lips parted on hers, forcing her mouth open, and then the incredible heat of his tongue slipped through to touch the tip of her own. She gasped, unable to believe that anyone would want to do something so, so intimate. The beating of her free hand on his back was useless. She did not want to touch him at all.

Finally the pressure of his kiss lightened, and with tormentingly slow movements he dragged his lips back and forth across hers. This time when she tried to turn away, he caught her nightcap in his free hand and with it a handful of hair. Exerting a slight but firm pressure against the hair at the sensitive juncture of her temple, he held her still. "Kiss me, Aisleen," he mouthed against her lips. "Kiss yer husband."

Aisleen caught her breath in a sob. She would not cry, would not allow him that victory. When at last his lips moved aside to climb the summit of her cheek, her breath was ragged. "Please. I beg you! Spare me," she whispered, afraid that a loud voice would anger him.

When he answered he did not sound angry, even to her fear-shocked senses. "Stop? How can I?" he questioned in good humor. "We've just begun. Just begun."

He found the top of the coverlet and pulled it from her hand, rising up long enough to strip it from between them. "That's better," he said softly as he settled down over her and reached for the long row of tiny buttons that closed her gown.

"Lass, ye do like buttons," he said reproachfully. Without a second thought he grabbed the collar and jerked, sending pearl buttons flying and rolling and skipping in all directions.

The casual violence frightened her and she went limp under the heavy, feverish weight of his body. She had not realized the extent of his strength or the casual ease with which he could use it. She shrank back into the bedding in a foolish attempt to keep his naked skin from contacting her own. But it did, everywhere. She felt the rough furring of his legs as he embraced her gown-clad limbs between his own. His chest, hard and satin smooth, crushed her.

None of her fears transmitted themselves to Thomas. He found the opening of her gown and with eager interest slipped his hand inside. She was so soft he could scarcely credit his first light touch of her, and he wondered fleetingly if ladies were indeed different from other women. His caressing hand grew bolder, heavier, until his fingers brushed the peak with its unbudded nipple. Her gasping response made him repeat the gesture, and this time the bud rose. Again and again he stroked the soft peak until a hard little bud stood at the apex.

The whiskey whispered urgently, urging him to hurry before he exploded. *Gently,* he cautioned himself, but his body was not listening. It was too late. She was too soft, too sweet, too much of what he had not dared to hope for. He had expected her to be as thorny as a rosebush. Instead, she was as soft as new-budded petals. His own flower, his secret rose.

With quick, near-violent movements that gave no thought to her needs or fears, he stripped the gown from her body. She was not unlike a young heifer brought to stud for the first time, he mused, as he savored his body's response to her seductive writhing.

He murmured broken whispers of assurance to her, not realizing when he traded English for the older Gaelic tongue of his ancestors. His hands swept over her roughly, quickly, wanting to touch every part of her but knowing that there was little time. Next time, he told himself, he would be better able to explore and pleasure her. But not now.

Aisleen cried out in fear as he plunged a knee between her own, separating them. Panic jackknifed her up in bed, but he was there, pushing her back against the bedding and mumbling endearments that had no effect on the terror churning her middle. His hand slid between her thighs and for a long, mortifying moment she prayed that she would die. But she did not.

Inexplicably his probing fingers brought her not death but a sinful pleasure that made her want to weep in shame. Appalled by her ignorance of her own body, she did not know why he should do this nor why it should feel pleasant despite her anger and embarrassment.

Thomas smiled as he reached in to stroke from her the moisture of desire. She was so hot there, so impossibly soft. His bride. His wife.

He plunged into her with an enthusiasm that made no provision for her virginity. He held her tight, not really hearing her cries nor feeling the pummeling of his head and shoulders by her fists. He was home, she was his.

Aisleen felt she would smother when he stopped her cries with his mouth. He plunged again and again into her abraded flesh. The unrelenting rhythm continued as he buried some hot, hard part of himself inside her. *I will die,* she thought. *He will kill me!*

Thomas arched himself higher and harder into her, aware only of the summing of tension swelling the flesh he buried deep within her. Never had it been like this. The sudden bursting of his seed from his body made him moan in pleasure and pain, the shooting forth a release and regret as he collapsed upon her.

"Macushla!" he whispered harshly into her ear. "Ye are now me own flesh and blood!"

All true love must die,
Alter at the best
Into some lesser thing.
Prove that I lie.

—Her Anxiety
W. B. Yeats

Chapter Eight

Aisleen awoke to the thin milkiness of first light, her arms and legs tangled with those of the man who had shared her bed and her body. The heavy blanket of his embrace kept out the chill of the dawn but, recalling the events of the night, she trembled. Her new husband had done more than destroy her innocence; he had destroyed her peace.

In her ignorance of his character she had not believed him capable of overriding her protestations and violating her modesty. To her shame she had learned the truth.

Her body ached in a dozen places, each a taunting reminder of the superiority of his strength. He had taken her with an utter disregard for her feelings, her embarrassment, or her virginity. And that had not been enough. Once his lust had spent itself, he had not been content with that victory. Later, in the black abyss of night, he had set about destroying her last shred of pride.

Silent tears broke through the golden thicket of her lashes and raced silently down her cheeks. He deserved nothing but contempt for his actions. If only that was all. It was not. To her everlasting shame, she had allowed him the second victory. No—God help her!—she had participated willingly in her own ruin! That was the worst humiliation.

Even in the light of day the damning images and sounds would not release her. Aisleen threw an arm across her eyes to blot out the memories but, unwillingly, she was pulled back into a remembrance of the night past . . .

A moan escaped her as he plunged his tongue again and again into her open, unresisting mouth. This was sweet torment, the lick and stroke of passion-fed kisses soothing away the last of her doubts.

She was on fire everywhere his lips touched . . . her lips . . . her shoulders . . . her breasts.

She whimpered as he caught the crest of a breast between his lips. This miraculous feeling, this dry suckling, fed not him but the liquid tension than ran in an ever-rushing surf from her breast to the secret sea tide rising in her lower belly.

"Aye, touch me there! 'Tis a fine feeling, yer hand on me, colleen dhas," she heard him encourage with the careless charm he wielded with such assuredness.

His hands were on her back, sliding down over her hips to lift her up against him. One hand moved even lower, over the curve of her buttocks, dipping into the narrow canyon below. Fingers spread, parting her legs, and then he was delving once more into her wet warmth. And she did not try to stop him. Did nothing. No, did more than nothing. She

*sighed in guilty pleasure and joy and desire, wanting . . .
wanting . . . wanting . . . more.*

*She stretched exploring fingers over the taut expanse of
his smooth chest, finding the wide, solid slopes of his
shoulders strangely comforting. The heavy corded muscles
of his arms no longer held her in check but trembled under
her caress as she did under his seeking fingers.*

*Every breath he drew came harshly by her ear, punctuat-
ing his thrusts that carried her a fraction higher off the
mattress. This rutting, this deep plunging of his body into
hers, carried less anguish and more pleasure than the first.
The near-violence of his rhythm chased her retreating senses.
No, no, she mustn't, she couldn't feel pleasure in this. And
yet she did: hot, searing, swelling, flooding pleasure that
flowed from her in breath-catching cries of mindless abandon.*

Aisleen sat up with a jerk, tumbling Thomas's body from
her own. He snored in the long, slow rhythm of deep sleep
and did not move. His long, naked limbs sprawled in
boneless contentment on the bed sheets were lightly furred
with black hair. Unerringly her gaze sought and held an
instant upon that part of him folded softly now in a nest of
black curls. For this she had lain beneath him panting like a
whore, begging his pleasuring.

Anger and shame pulsed hot and cold by turns through
her. She had been uncertain of the details of the act which
bound a man and wife together, but she had known that the
consummation of their vows would mean that she was
bound to the stranger beside her forever. Why, oh why had
she not thought of that before this minute!

She turned abruptly and rose from the bed, reaching for
her gown, which lay on the floor. As she lifted it by an arm
she spied the gaping rip from the neckline to hem, and she
dropped the obscene reminder of the night.

She shot an angry glance at her sleeping husband. *Drunkard! Defiler of women! Rutting boar!* The epithets came quickly to mind, but she held all of them at bay for, far beyond her desire to vent her rage on him, she feared his awakening. What would he say to her? Would he gloat over his victory of her body and her spirit?

"Of course he will," she muttered low. What man could resist? He had mastered her body, and she, fool that she was, had allowed him to betray her with her own emotions. Her stomach lurched. If a single night in his embrace was any measure, he would want her again . . . and again . . . and again . . . until he grew tired of her.

He had been drunk, as her father had been so often. Memories darted about in her head, memories of her mother's haggard face the morning after her father had returned from one of his journeys. Then she had been too young to suspect the cause of the teary eyes and sleepless puffiness. Now she knew too much. Her father had kept a mistress in Cork while bedding his wife in hopes of siring a son. He, too, had demanded and bullied his way when the drink was flowing freely through his veins. He, too, had been capable of violence. He, too, had possessed the charm of the Irish when it suited him. Horror hammered her chest. Had she married a man exactly like her father?

"No!" The agonized breath was torn from Aisleen. As she spun away from the bed her gaze fell upon the pistol butt lying half-hidden beneath a trouser leg. Once Thomas Gibson had placed that weapon in her hand and dared her to pull the trigger. She bent and picked it up. Then she could not entertain the idea. But now . . .

She turned back to the bed, her eyes once again on Thomas's naked body. His mouth was open, and the garbled sounds of an animal lowed forth. What more should she expect? He was an animal, a vicious, low brute who would use her again and again until she was haggard and broken.

What right had he to lie so peacefully when she would never again know complete tranquillity? She raised the pistol, using both hands to steady the steely weight.

He had demeaned her in a way that she never thought possible. He did not deserve to live. With her teeth braced against her lower lip, she pulled back the hammer.

Perspiration gathered in her brows and trailed down her temples as she sought the courage to pull the trigger. She took a step forward and then another, closing the distance and improving the odds that her shot would have fatal results.

As she took a third step a whisper came softly, unexpectedly upon the morning breeze. *Macushla!*

A knock on the bedroom door sent Aisleen spinning about, the pistol poised to confront the intruder.

"Breakfast!" she heard the landlord call cheerfully from the parlor. "It won't keep long," he added with a chuckle. "Be back later to collect the dishes."

When the parlor door closed, Aisleen swung back around. From the corner of her eye she spotted movement, and she glanced right to see herself, pistol in hand, framed in the gilt mirror which hung over the wash basin.

Without realizing it, she lowered the pistol to stare at the harridan in the reflection. A wild tangle of red hair framed a pallid face. Eyes swollen with tears and smudged by misery stared back at her. She looked quite and thoroughly mad.

Unwilling to believe that it was an accurate reflection, Aisleen glanced down at herself. She had not bared herself to the light of day since she could remember. At Miss Burke's Academy bathing had been accomplished in darkness or under the cover of a wrapper.

The color and shape of her own breasts were unfamiliar. She had not realized that they were quite so full, the nipples so pink. She looked at her stomach, still tender from her husband's unfamiliar weight, and then spied a thin, dull red streak on her inner thigh. Nearby she spotted the bluish coin of a bruise.

Aisleen began to tremble. Fear had made a beast of her: an unthinking, senseless, frightened creature, cowered and cornered and mad enough to consider murder as the only escape. But she was not a beast. Nor was she a coward. She was married, and nothing could change that. Yet she would not allow Thomas Gibson to bully her into submission. She would stand and fight . . . because she had nowhere else to go.

The pistol fell with a thud onto the floor. Numbness replaced the anger as she bent to pick up and then don her ruined gown. When she had gathered her nightcap and slippers she crept out of the room.

Thomas awakened to the rare sensation of complete contentment. His arms and legs were heavy with sleep, and he savored the moment by keeping his eyes closed. Dawn usually meant the beginning of another endless day of work. But this day was different; he sensed it even before memories came stealing over him.

He had been drinking with his mates. They had toasted his good health and wished him the best of luck in his new venture. That venture was . . . marriage.

Thomas's eyes flew open on a room bathed in full morning's light. Slowly memories of the night came back to him, and he folded his arms behind his head, grinning. His thorny, red-haired wife had been his. His mind was too hazy from the effects of whiskey to recall in detail what she had done and said, but the lush, lazy feeling in his body told him that he had been more than satisfied with her. The discontent that had driven him to marriage was gone. In its place was a satisfaction that defied explanation. No, that was not true. The explanation was named Mrs. Thomas Gibson.

Thomas sat up and stretched his arms wide, arching his back until every vertebra snapped into line. Where was his wife? He would have preferred her to be within arm's reach, for already he was filling with need of her. He looked about, frowning, until he remembered the parlor. She would be up and dressed, he guessed. After all, it was midmorning. In future he would ask her to remain by his side until he awakened. He wanted to see her face after a night of lovemaking. He could not remember much—only vague sighs and moans of pleasure that could as easily have been his own as hers.

Fleetingly he recalled her resistance. She had been a virgin; the small stain he spied on the sheet by his thigh confirmed that. Resistance was to be expected. But she had been sweet to kiss, even sweeter to embrace. Too bad she had not remained, for he longed badly to see in the light of day all that he had kissed and caressed in the dark of night.

He swung his legs over the side. Perhaps he could coax her back to bed. She should not be so shy now that she knew the way of it. He stood up, giving in to another self-satisfied smile as he saw his clothes strewn about. He had been so eager for her that he had dropped them where he stripped them off.

As he bent to pick up his shirt, he noticed his pistol lying nearby. He frowned when he saw that it was cocked. Usually he was a careful man. Either of them might have lost a toe had they stumbled over it in the dark.

As his hand closed over the butt, an odd sensation traveled lightning quick up his arm, making the hair on his nape rise. Instinct made his skin contract and his senses quicken in recognition of the emotion affecting him long before his mind sorted out the response.

Rage: pure, consuming hatred was the sensation tingling through his body. In an instant it vanished.

He shook his head. There was no reason for concern. Jack had, no doubt, left town. It was his imagination. He carefully lowered the hammer back into place and laid the pistol on the table.

After a moment's reflection, he retrieved his trousers and stepped into them with consideration for his bride. She was a lady, he reminded himself. But if the night before was any indication, he mused as he rubbed his bristling chin, she was fast becoming accustomed to him. Feeling quite pleased with himself, he strolled to the door. He would bring her back to bed. They could talk later.

Aisleen had only a moment to compose her features as the latch of the bedroom door lifted. When the door opened, she was sitting ramrod straight, her hands folded primly in her lap, her expression implacable.

"Good morning, Mr. Gibson," she declared before she even saw him clearly. She did not blink an eye at the sight of his naked chest, wrinkled trousers, and bare feet. In the intervening hour, she had regained self-control and made up her mind how to handle the situation. She would behave as though nothing had occurred. If not for the hard thumping of her heart against her whalebone corset, she would have believed that his appearance did not affect her at all.

Thomas moved across the threshold with a lopsided grin on his face. "G'day, lass."

"Come in and have a seat," she replied in a formal manner. "Your tea is most likely cold, but I had no way of knowing when you would awaken. If you would prefer, I shall go below for more."

"Won't hear of it," Thomas answered easily, but as his gaze moved quickly over her what he saw disappointed him. There was no smile of welcome on her face. Far from it. Her gaze was distant and her expression was as reserved as the tightly buttoned-up gown she wore. He thought he had taken care of that clamshell posture of hers forever. How did she manage to look as untouched as the day before?

Aisleen poured a cup of cold tea for him. "Sugar? Lemon?"

"Both," Thomas answered readily as he sat down across from her. "They're hard to come by in the bush."

"Is that so?" she murmured in a manner that did not beg a reply. "I suppose it is difficult to obtain many things in the wilds," she continued politely. "If you will provide me with a list I will provision you accordingly."

Thomas gulped half the cup of tea, wondering where his plan had gone astray. He had meant to sweep his bride up in a long and thorough kiss that left no doubt in her mind of what was going on in his. Then back to bed for an hour or so. Afterward he would fetch the wagon for their journey to Parramatta, where Jack waited for them.

He set his cup down in its saucer too hard, and tea splashed over the rim. "Sorry," he mumbled when he saw her flinch and then instantly wondered why he had apologized. If he had broken the cup he would have paid for it. "About last night," he began.

"Best forgotten and never mentioned," she interjected.

"Forgotten?" A grin blossomed in the nettle of his new beard. "Lass, I would nae forget it were I to live a hundred years more."

"I see," she answered in a reluctant voice. "Very well, we shall speak of it. Once. What do you say in your defense?"

Thomas stared at her as understanding dawned. She was angry; how could he have missed the signs? Sitting there with her arms folded before her bosom . . . her nice, soft, rounded bosom—He reined in his wandering mind. "I do not know what ye'll be expecting a man to say."

Aisleen raised her eyes until she stared over his head. "I don't suppose you will apologize. No court of law would demand it of you. After all, we are legally and morally wed, until death do us part."

Thomas winced as she pronounced the last words, and unaccountably the cocked pistol came to mind; but he rejected the half-formed thought. "I did no more than any man would on his wedding night."

"That is no recommendation to me." Aisleen raised a hand to forestall his speech. Why, oh why must they discuss it at all?

He sat up straight. "Now, lass, a husband is entitled to certain rights."

"I did not understand that to include violence." The quiver in her voice betrayed the strong emotions she held in check.

Thomas looked down into his cup of tepid tea. Violence? Had he done her injury? Surely not. He remembered her cries as moans of joy. He had been drunk and he knew it. Suspicion trickled in slowly. Perhaps he had been too enthusiastic. He looked up sheepishly. "Did I hurt ye, lass?"

Aisleen lifted her torn gown from her lap and waved it like a captured banner. "Do you not remember? But, of course, you were drunk. So I will tell you. You ripped the gown from my back and treated me as callously as a whore!"

"Did I now?" Thomas whispered, his manner subdued at last. Harsher memories warred with pleasure in his jumbled thoughts. Yes, now that he thought of it, she had resisted him, had struck him with her fists and hurled abuse at him. She had fought and he had bested her. Yet he had thought her pleasured by his mastery. He had heard her pleasure, felt her passion. Or had he?

"Was there no pleasure for ye in me loving?"

"Certainly not!" She tossed the gown aside and clasped her hands tightly together in her lap. "When I agreed to marry you, I hoped our arrangement would spare me the sort of degradation to which you have subjected me. I know men to be brutes. My own mother—"

Aisleen glanced up, horrified that she had mentioned her mother. Her chin trembled slightly as she said, "I had hoped that you were different."

Her golden eyes blazed as she stared at him. "But as I am wrong and the events of the night before make it impossible for us to change our arrangement, we must alter our contract since we cannot nullify it."

The torrent of words left Thomas staring at her with a furrowed brow. Doubtful of his own memory, he could say nothing in his own defense. "I meant no dishonor of ye, lass."

"No, of course not," she answered. "You did not consider my feelings at all. I propose a period of separation that will give each of us a chance to think through the matter."

This last gave Thomas something to say. "No, lass, I'll not leave Sydney without ye. I cannot say with any truth what I did or did not do. When a man's traded whiskey for blood in his veins, he's not always as gentle as he might be." His face was hard and set as he looked at her. "I'm that sorry I frightened and hurt ye, but ye're my wife and ye will come home with me."

Aisleen stared angrily at him. He had every right to insist that she accompany him, and no authority would take her side against him. Yet there was something else pushing her to agree, something she could not yet face.

"Because I have sworn before God and man to be a helpmate and companion to you, I will agree to this. But I will not submit myself to further abuse from you."

Thomas held her gaze for a long moment. Only the day before he had thought her eyes were the rich, warm color of whiskey. Now they were as dull as stone. There was something more, something he had not seen there even on the morning she had chased the beggar child who had stolen her purse. It banked her expression. She feared him.

"Aye, that will do for now," he said at last and rose from his chair.

The rapping of a fist on the door broke the tense moment as Thomas moved to open it. "Sally!" he declared in frank surprise.

"I must 'ave a word with ye, Tom," Sally said softly. Her gaze went unerringly to where Aisleen sat. "In private."

Aisleen stared at the pretty blond standing in the entrance, taking in at once her youth, low-cut gown, and most of all, her hostility. The conviction came swiftly and undoubted. This was her husband's mistress!

Jealousy overrode anger as she rose to her feet. The bald arrogance of the pair! "Come in, Miss—?"

"Sally," the girl offered, tucking her shawl more protectively about her as she edged inside the door. "G'day, ma'am. I come to speak to Tom."

"So I heard," Aisleen answered icily as her hard gaze moved to her husband.

"Sally, this is me bride, Miss—Mrs. Gibson. Sally's an old friend," Thomas offered as he closed the door.

"But not a forgotten one?" Aisleen suggested in knife-edged politeness. "Do come in and sit down, Sally."

"No, ma'am. Thank ye." Sally glanced repeatedly from Aisleen to Tom, unable to believe that he was wed to this poker-stiff woman in the frilled housecap.

"What did ye want, Sally, lass?" Thomas encouraged, aware of the instant enmity between the two women but at a loss to defuse it.

"I come to tell Tom that the bloke that was looking for 'im a while ago is back in town, on account 'e 'eard ye was to wed," Sally said, her gaze never moving from Aisleen. "Thought 'e'd best know."

Thomas nodded. "Thank ye, Sally, for coming with the news. Not to worry. We're leaving today. Will ye be readying yerself for that?" he added with a look at Aisleen.

Aisleen nodded stiffly.

Thomas smiled in relief. "Well then, I'll just be accompanying Sally below to the street." He reached with one hand for Sally's elbow as his other grasped the door latch and lifted it. "Come along, lass."

"G'by, ma'am." Sally gave Aisleen one last measuring look before succumbing to Thomas's tugs on her arm.

When they were gone, Aisleen sighed as if all the breath would come out of her, and her shoulders drooped in defeat. Had they stayed a moment longer she might have shamed herself with tears.

Thomas had brought his mistress into her presence almost on their wedding day, and yet he expected her to do his bidding as a dutiful wife. She should be shocked, and yet she was not. She was angry and hurt and disappointed.

Aisleen dropped inelegantly into her chair. The interview had not gone at all as she had hoped. She had been afraid of so much: that he would not listen to her, that he would not agree to her wishes, and most of all, that he would throw in her face her shameless and wanton behavior. He had not. When she hurled her accusations at him, he had looked, well, ashamed. Hope for a compromise had blossomed...until the knock on the door.

Aisleen shook her head. She had read too much into the moment. He was a man, after all, and fully capable of parading his mistress before her eyes. His tenderness had worked to his advantage, for she had agreed to go with him.

"Fool!" she whispered to herself. Miss Burke was right. If she forgot herself, hoped for too much, then she would be lost. She must not lower her guard because of a kind look. For, more than him, she feared herself.

After the first rage of the morning had worn off, she had begun to realize the real source of her distress. Her husband had acted as any man might. That had not frightened her nearly as much as the truth she had gained about herself in the darkest hours of the night. She had wanted his interest, his desire. She wanted to be desired.

As he had sat across from her she had been taken by the strangest urges. Her body had ached with unnamable sensations—guilty sweet pangs that made her want to run away.

"I am no better than a whore!" she murmured. Even now, made palsied by rage from the emotional backwash of her confrontation with his pretty little mistress, she felt the urge to run downstairs after them and shout that Thomas was her husband and that she had better keep away from him.

Was this the emotion of which her mother had hinted? Was this every man's hold on the woman who desired him?

"I . . . can't . . . desire . . . him," Aisleen ground out, pounding her fists slowly on the table top. As a child she had watched her father's interest in her mother turn to indifference. The last years of his life he had lived openly in Dublin with his whore while her mother lived in shame and poverty in the famine-ravaged countryside.

She would not allow that to happen to her. Her only protection against desire was anger. He must never be allowed to persuade her through false charm and calculated kindness to care for him. She was too ripe for it, too needy, too fragile to withstand the daily assault of his embrace. In one short night he had stripped from her the veneer of respectability that she had worked more than a dozen years to cultivate. Gone was her self-respect, her peace of mind, her protection against a harsh and unfeeling world.

Never again, Aisleen vowed to herself. Never again would she allow him to touch her, for in his caress lay a trap and her ultimate defeat. She would be no man's slave.

*   *   *

"That's the lot!" Thomas announced as he heaved the last bag into the back of the wagon.

Aisleen gazed with misgiving at the numerous sacks. The implication of so many provisions was not at all to her liking. "Is it necessary to carry so much with us? Surely we will return often to Sydney."

Thomas shaded his eyes with a hand as he looked up at Aisleen. "We'll not come to Sydney again for some time."

"Why not?" she murmured in dismay.

" 'Tis too far a journey to make more than once a year. My station's well over four hundred miles from here."

"Four . . . hundred . . ." Her throat closed over the statement. "Dear God!" she whispered.

Thomas watched her with sympathy. "Aye, 'tis a fair long way. But we'll accomplish it, right enough."

The thought of the journey did not daunt Aisleen as much as the realization that she would be so far away from Sydney. How odd, she reflected fleetingly, that this strange city in a strange land suddenly seemed a refuge compared with what lay before her. "I hadn't thought we'd be so far away," she said slowly. "I have left some of my belongings with the landlord pending my return."

Thomas did not miss the reference to "her" return and did not like the fact that she was thinking of leaving him even before they had set out. He would give her no ready excuse. "There's no room here. I'll be sending another to collect them," he answered evenly.

Aisleen stood a moment in indecision, debating whether or not simply to ask him to leave her behind, bags and all. She moistened her lips, but the words would not come.

"It could nae be that the lass who's sailed a world away to Sydney is afraid of a wee journey through the bush?" he asked.

She unconsciously squared her shoulders. "Of course not."

"Good!" he answered and withdrew a pouch from his shirt and tossed it to her. "Here's the first month's expense."

Aisleen caught the purse and heard the clink of coins. Her first month's wages. He would not allow her to back out gracefully. Well then, she would not back out in a cowardly fashion. "I'm ready," she said and bent to pick up her portmanteau, aware of his victorious smile.

"I'll be taking that," he said and reached for the bag. The weight of the case surprised him and he staggered in exaggeration. "*Musha!* What'd this be?"

"Books. I came to Sydney prepared to assume the post of a teacher. If one is to teach one must be properly equipped."

"I see," Thomas replied, but he did not. What he understood was that a few extra pounds of unnecessary weight was being added to his provisions. It did not matter now, but once they traded horses for bullocks and the flat bush turned into hills and rain-swollen streams of the north riverland every pound would add to the difficulty of their journey. Still he lashed it in with the rest and then wiped the sweat from his brow with his coat sleeve before offering his wife a hand. "We're ready, then, lass."

"I can manage on my own," she replied and turned away from the frown that contracted his brow. Catching her skirts together in one hand, she slipped one booted foot into a spoke of the wheel and grabbed the edge of the wagon seat with her free hand to hoist herself up.

Unoffended, Thomas watched patiently. As she bent forward to lever herself up, her skirts pulled taut, revealing the curves of her hips, and he was once again aware that his wife was younger and more vulnerable than she often appeared. He allowed her to struggle until her foot slipped. With a quick and handy grace he caught her with a hand under her buttocks.

In quick succession Aisleen registered the strength of his hand under her bottom, the firm wall of his chest buttressing her lower hips, and most discomforting of all, the narrow-bladed pressure of his nose in the small of her back. The unwilling memory of the feel of his hands upon her naked skin flashed through her mind.

Immediately she began to struggle, but her muscles were melted by mortification. With relief she heard him say, "Up ye go, lass," as he pushed her from behind.

Her cheeks flaming, Aisleen was thrust up into the wagon. When she regained her balance, she slid quickly to the far side of the seat. She had made a spectacle of herself on a public street.

Interest in the public vanished as Thomas hoisted himself up onto the seat beside her. She pulled her elbows in against her body and pressed her right hip hard against the seat ledge until it hurt, but she could not completely remove herself from his touch. As he reached for the reins, his arm brushed hers. When he turned to her, his face was so close that she drew in a quick breath.

"Are ye ready, then, wife?"

"Yes," she answered and lowered her gaze from those blue eyes, only to meet yet another uneasy sight. Beneath the white lace glove on her left hand was a gold band spanning the third finger. Because of momentary weakness of character, a selfish fear of poverty, she was now bound for eternity to this man whom she feared and distrusted.

Mrs. Thomas Finnian Butler Gibson.

Aisleen tucked her hand into the folds of her gown to hide the taunting golden reminder of her impetuousness. What had she done?

As he snapped the reins to start the horses, Thomas glanced at her from under the brim of his hat, squinting as he strained to read her expression. She sat so still and stiff, as if she were made of marble or as if she were still afraid of him.

The thought did not please him. The more he thought

about what he had done, coming in drunk to bed his bride, the more certain he was that his memory of her pleasure had been nothing more than the hazy recollection of his own passion. She was a lady. What did he know of ladies? Nothing. Perhaps she was right to accuse him of treating her as he would a whore, for they had been his tutors.

He shook his head. He wanted to talk with her; a dozen questions trembled on his tongue, but he dared not disturb her.

Ye shy from the truth, Thomas, he chided himself. He was now a little wary of her. It had never occurred to him that they would not suit. Of course, they were different, but he had thought that would not matter once they were married. Perhaps he had been too hasty. After all, he knew nearly nothing about her, nor she about him.

There were many things he had not yet told her. Most important of all, he had not told her that he was an ex-convict, an emancipist. What would she say if she knew? Would she twitch her skirts aside as the proper ladies of Van Diemen's Land had done years before when he passed them wearing the canvas jacket and trousers of a convict laborer? Would her delicate features contort with revulsion and loathing when she learned that her husband had once been a convict?

For four years he had endured the blank stares of the gentlewomen of Hobart Town, the indifference or pretense that he did not occupy the same lane as they. Sometimes the urge to do something outrageous had seized him. He had wanted to stop one of them, to thrust his face in hers and make her acknowledge his existence. He had imagined clasping the delicate body of one of them against his filthy uniform and grinding his lips against hers until she sighed in pleasure or fainted at the outrage.

It would not have mattered to him what the lady's reaction would have been, as long as she had admitted that he was a man and not a stray cur to be gingerly bypassed. Only the fear of the lash had kept him from acting on the anger writhing within him. To have touched a lady would have meant death.

Why did he brood over old hurts? He had gained his freedom and more. He was respected by the men with whom he dealt. His future was assured.

He was lucky. His grandma had predicted that he would be. Luck had been with him when his sentence had been shortened from seven to four years because he discovered a talent for shearing sheep. When he had turned his hand to gold-digging, hadn't he found a strike worth a squatter's station in trade? He hadn't been like many others, made mad by a strike. He had bought what the gold-struck squatter had abandoned and earned respectability. Now he had gained the hand of a lady as good as any who had passed him with a scented handkerchief pressed to her nose. He was not about to lose her.

Sally's warning had come at an inopportune time. After the discussion of the morning, he had nearly been persuaded to remain a few more days in Sydney, where Aisleen could come to know him gradually, in civilized surroundings rather than the unfamiliar wilds of bush. Then he might have been able to tell her things about himself, things that might have answered many questions for both of them. But he dared not remain, not with the news he carried.

He glanced at Aisleen once more, but this time her features were hidden by the brim of her bonnet. All prim and proper, she was proof that he was as good as any colonialist. Yet to keep her, he must find a way to make her happy. What could he do? Sooner or later he would tell her his history, but not until they were at ease with each other, if they were ever at ease with each other again.

Pity, an aching head,
Gnashing of teeth, despair;
And all because of some one
Perverse creature of chance...

—On Woman
W. B. Yeats

Chapter Nine

Afternoon became evening and then a short, brilliant dusk rapidly gave way to a blue-velvet night as they rode toward Parramatta.

In the beginning Thomas had been talkative, but Aisleen would not answer his ramblings about places she had never been nor wished to see. After they left Sydney and entered a strange forest of tall, high-limbed, pale-trunked trees that flanked the road, he had lapsed into a thoughtful silence for which she was grateful.

Less gratefully, she had sat mile after mile while they paused for neither comfort nor refreshment. From the dark wall of the surrounding forest came the strange cries of unseen birds, their exotic chatter the only conversation on the lonely trail.

She glanced at him, wondering why he did not share her desire to have a drink of water, to stretch cramped muscles, or even to answer the call of nature. Though they shared a wagon seat it was too dark to see anything more of him than the sharp silhouette of his features, the pale gleam of a single eye, and the relaxed sway of his body as he held the reins between his fingers.

She could not bring herself to speak to him. With hours of silence between them, to speak would seem to require a need of some magnitude. The need to relieve herself was much too personal and humbling an excuse. She would manage.

He suddenly sat forward on the bench, and she carefully let out the breath she had not realized she held. "We're here," he said in a cheery voice that gave no sign of the strain between them.

Then she saw them, too—lights on the road ahead.

A few minutes later he drew the wagon to a halt at the edge of a clearing under the starry night sky. The clearing was filled with dozens of glowing tents. Laughter rippled across the night, rising and falling in counterpoint to the steady hum of voices. The aromas of roasting mutton, burning wood, and tobacco smoke misted the night air. Aisleen's stomach murmured in expectation. All the same, a makeshift camp was not what she expected to find at the end of a weary day's journey. "Why are we stopping here?"

Thomas cocked a brow at her, annoyed that her first words were tinged with rebuke. "Where would ye be having us stop?"

"Sydney would have been my preference," she answered ungratefully because her back ached and her stomach churned with hunger and he had not given a moment's thought to her discomfort. "As I have not been consulted until now, I will merely suggest that we look for a sound roof under which to sleep."

"Aye, we'll have that." He pointed at a tent which stood a little apart from the others. "That'll be our resting place for the night. A bit grand, perhaps, for our needs, but after this we'll be doing without the trappings of civilization.''

Resentment whipcorded through Aisleen. He was being deliberately rude. ''You cannot mean to suggest that we shall be without even the shelter of a tent after this night?''

''*Musha*, I did not suggest it, I said it.'' He knotted the reins about the brake lever and climbed down from the wagon.

This time he did not offer her a hand in assistance, and so she gathered her skirts in one hand and negotiated the steep descent with as much dignity as she could.

Thomas watched her, ready to help if she needed it but too proud to face a second rebuff, for he was smarting from the punishment of her long silence. And though he might have guessed it would be so, her first words to him had been ones of discontent. He was tired and hungry. His head ached from the rare, lingering effects of rum, and his muscles were sore from the cramped quarters in which he had slept the night before. The narrow bunk at his station was even less suited for two. A bigger bed was one of the first things he would order when he returned home. Aye, a big brass bed with fancy trim and a genuine feather tick mattress.

The thought of bed lingered in his mind. Aisleen had shown him the fine edge of her anger that morning, but she could not have meant all the things she said. She was his wife. When she had had time to think things over she would welcome him back into her arms.

The distant bleating of sheep momentarily drew his attention. Some of them would be the new flock he had purchased to increase the stock on his station. He would have to speak with Jack about selling them, for his plans had changed. But first he must settle his wife.

''Come along, then, and meet the folk,'' he said encouragingly.

Following the gentle prod of his hand in the small of her back, Aisleen crossed the yard, acutely aware of the road dirt which streaked her dark skirts. "You might have warned me that I would be meeting your friends."

"Ye did nae ask," Thomas countered in an even tone. "Ye did nae say much at all this day."

She let the remark pass. He was right. She had deliberately kept silence as a punishment for his behavior. Now she realized that she had been much more miserable than he. He had had the knowledge of their destination to look forward to while she had sat fidgeting and stewing.

As they crossed the grassy ground a man with a large Adam's apple and two missing teeth stepped out of the tent they neared and paused long enough to cry, "G'evenin', Tom!" He pulled his forelock at Aisleen, then hurried his partner, a rail-thin woman in a blue print gingham gown, past them.

Thomas took Aisleen's elbow to steer her through the shantytown of tents. "Smile, Mrs. Gibson. They'll nae bite ye. They're all me friends."

Aisleen nodded politely at the blur of passing faces, conscious that she was quickly becoming the center of attention for the people who strolled among the tents. Most of the glances were friendly, some merely interested; all were curious. Children paused to stare openly at her. They were neatly dressed, but most were barefoot.

Casting a look about, she noted that most of the women wore the simple cotton gowns of servants and the lower classes. Likewise the men wore shirts open at the throat and cloth breeches. None of them wore a jacket and soft black tie of the kind Thomas wore. They were obviously herdsmen and laborers.

"There's Ian," Thomas announced. "Ian, man! Over here!"

The man called Ian came toward them with the listing gait

of a sailor. "I won the ringer's prize, Tom! Damn ye for not competing!"

"Against ye, Ian? A man'd be a fool to do so," Thomas answered with a chuckle and offered his hand, which the other man grasped so tightly he winced. "Mind the hand. I'll not come against ye, but even a squatter has a need for his shearing hand."

"Aye, I hear ye've no need of prize money these days. Jack's claiming half the sheep in New South Wales as yers. All the same, there're those who remember when ye took the grand prize and set the record which stood six seasons. They'd have the others believe ye're still the better man."

Thomas grinned. "*Musha,* I *am* the better man!"

"Is that a fact?" Ian's gaze ran warmly over Aisleen. "Then why are ye hiding the lass?"

Thomas turned her and urged her forward with a hand on her waist. "Lass, I'll have ye meet Ian Rafferty. Ian, Mrs. Gibson."

"Gibson, is it?" Ian turned a surprised stare on Thomas. "Never tell me ye've gotten yerself married, lad?"

At Thomas's nod, Ian returned his widened gaze to Aisleen. "There's little enough to be seen under that wake bonnet." He reached out and tipped the brim back from her face with a flick of his forefinger.

"That's better!" he continued over her gasp of indignation. "Tom, man! She'll be a handsome one, for all she's wearing a pinched expression. She'll do me the honor of a kiss, I'm thinking." He swept her up in an arm and crushed her to his chest.

Startled out of her self-possession, she cried, "How dare you! Put me down!"

Thomas intervened with a smile but a firm hand on Ian's arm that demanded her release. "Ian, man, ye've frightened me lady."

"Lady?" Ian repeated, squinting down into Aisleen's

flushed face. "Marrying *ye,* I'd have thought her a girl of some spirit."

Aisleen backed out of his embrace. "You are impertinent, sir, and quite disgustingly drunk!"

"I dearly hope so!" Ian answered fervently.

"And here I've not had so much as a thimbleful," Thomas said regretfully, smoothly steering Aisleen behind him and out of Ian's reach. "Will ye be pointing out the direction of the kegs, Ian?"

Ian frowned, trying to focus his rum-glazed eyes. "Ye've truly wed, Tom?"

Thomas nodded. "Aye, I have. Now if ye'll be forgiving us, me wife has not yet met the other folk. Can't have her sweating and stinking before she's made the acquaintance of the others, can we? Evenin', Ian."

"I seldom perspire," Aisleen said in a horrified voice as Thomas hurried her away. "And I never stink!"

"Of course ye don't," he agreed pleasantly, "but I say there's no harm in Ian thinking it's possible. He's harmless enough except when he's spied a woman he fancies. When he's the whiff of a lass in his nostrils, he's little put off by sweat or odor, come to that."

Aisleen did not know how to answer the indelicate statement and so concentrated on righting her bonnet as he led her between the next tents.

Thomas sniffed the air. "The smell of stew has me belly rumbling. Same with you, lass?"

"What I should like is—is . . ." Aisleen stammered to a stop.

"The privies are yonder," he offered with a knowing grin. "When ye're done ye'll be finding me with Ian." He nodded toward the group of men who had gathered by kegs of rum stacked nearby. "I've yet to pay me respects to the lads."

"You don't intend to drink whiskey?" Aisleen asked,

anxious not to face a drunken husband for a second time. But he only waved at her as he walked away, and she could do nothing but watch him with misgiving.

She turned toward the tents behind which he had said she would find the necessary facilities. As she rounded the corner the stench of feces and urine rose up to meet her, halting her in her tracks. Clamping a gloved hand over her nose and mouth, she peered into the darkness. Where was the outhouse? Without the light from the dozen campfires, she could see nothing. And then she realized that there was nothing to be seen. The "facilities" were nothing more than a gash in the ground.

Immediately her imagination conjured up vivid images of what the scene must be like in daylight, and she began backing away. No need was so pressing that she could not find a better place than this.

Weak with hunger and slightly nauseated from the swaying wagon, she hurried back toward the center of the encampment.

She did not notice the man's approach, but suddenly she was lifted from behind, spun about, and set down. Expecting to encounter Ian's rummy gaze, she looked up in annoyance. A broad canvas shirtfront was where she expected a face to be. Her gaze rose and rose until at last she stared up into the rough-featured face of a seven-and-a-half-foot Goliath whose bright red hair and beard blazed in the lantern light. With a deliberateness that bore no glimmer of respect, the man's gaze moved down over her and then came back to her face, at which he stared in insolent silence.

"I beg your pardon," she said in what she hoped was a daunting voice, "but certainly you have mistaken me for someone else. Kindly allow me to pass."

Instead, like Ian before him, the giant tipped her bonnet back fom her face as though he had every right to touch her familiarly. This time Aisleen held her temper, but her golden brown eyes reflected anger held in check. If this were an example of the frontier manners which her husband hoped that she would amend, it seemed that she had her work before her.

The man stared at her a moment longer, his craggy features as immutable as stone, and then turned without a word and walked away.

"Mercy!" she murmured. "Insufferable man!"

"Jack Egan? Nae, only a bit rough for most tastes."

Aisleen spun about to see that Thomas had come up behind her. "Do all your acquaintances paw the women to whom you introduce them?"

Thomas shrugged. "He's a man whose respect ye'll nae easily win."

"It's an acquaintance I've no desire to further." Aisleen spied the cup in his hand and guessed the contents. "You're drinking rum."

He glanced at his cup and then offered it. "Ye would nae care for a nip, now would ye?"

"Certainly not!"

"I thought as much," he replied in a regretful tone.

"Drunkenness is a sin," she said righteously.

"A sip never hurt any of God's creatures," he maintained. "Ye do nae drink, but I do, and that's the way of it."

"Does that mean that you will—?"

To her vexation, he turned away and headed after Jack Egan. Because she would not lower herself to shout after him, she was effectively silenced once more.

Two women passed her, smiling and nodding. She smoothed her face into an unreadable expression and nodded in turn, her smile a frozen monument to civility.

"Aisleen, aren't ye coming, lass!"

She turned her head to see Thomas waving at her from a distance.

"Newlyweds," she heard one woman say in a carrying voice.

"Aye, she's a lucky lass to be claiming Tom Gibson for a husband."

Aisleen cringed inside as she walked toward him. She knew what the women were thinking, that he must be anxious to get her away from the prying eyes of others, to be alone to kiss and cuddle and—oh, all those things that made her squirm inside just to think of them.

"What'd be the reason for yer frowning now?" he asked as she reached him.

She stopped short. Was she frowning? If she was, the reason for it was too personal to be dealt with comfortably, and so she said derisively, "It would seem that some women believe you're quite a catch."

Thomas's eyes crinkled at the corners as he reached for her hand and inclined his head to whisper in her ear, "And a fair number of lads are wishing they were in me place tonight."

Aisleen felt her face catch fire and tried to withdraw her hand, but he held it tight.

"Ah, well, I've done it again—insulted ye when I meant to please ye," he said mournfully. "Now why do ye think that's so, lass?"

"I would prefer that you address me as Mrs. Gibson when we are in public," she answered coolly.

"And what would ye be having me call ye when we're in private?"

Startled and embarrassed by his question, she did not know where to look and so chose a spot above his left shoulder. But his hand moved to her chin to bring her eyes back to his. "Tell me, *colleen*, what does a man say to a lady like yerself that'd put a smile on her pretty face?"

Aisleen stared up at him in mute surprise. He was the one with the handsome face. Absently she wondered what other women saw when they looked at him. Did they respond to his attractive exterior in the belief that it made him a kinder, bolder, more romantic male than the men in their lives?

"Aisleen, lass, we should be friends," he said huskily.

He was so close that she could see the lights from the campfires reflected in his eyes . . . and feel his warm, rum-laden breath—a sudden, sharp reminder of the night before.

She turned abruptly from him. "You smell of the brewery, Mr. Gibson. I hope that does not portend a repeat of last night's humiliation."

Thomas heard the demise of his hopes in her frigid voice. "I'm nae drunk, lass," he said as he reached for her arm, but she jerked free.

"No, you've only consumed enough rum to drown your memory," Aisleen retorted. "Well, I have not! I remember everything!" Including the fact that he had left with Sally and been absent more than an hour, she added in her thoughts.

"Everything?" he repeated softly, but she turned away, and he did not know whether or not she had heard him.

He watched her cross the clearing to their wagon, wondering when she would realize that there was nowhere else to go. She stood a while by the wagon, her head erect and her arms folded tightly across her bosom. *Let her stew, then*, he thought. He had tried his damnedest to please her.

The call of nature that had momentarily receded had become too much for Aisleen to bear. She could no longer wait. In desperation, she sought the concealment of the trees that edged the clearing.

He waited, watching the place where she had disappeared, but she did not return. Frowning, he started toward the wagon. *Damn!* She must have gone into the bush. Trust a city lass not to have more sense than to leap into danger.

Ferns and bushes snagged the hem of her gown, but Aisleen did not stop until she had waded into the densest portion of the underbrush, where the lights from the clearing did not penetrate. Close by she heard the lap and gurgle of flowing water. When she turned toward the sound she saw that the river was only a few feet away, its blue-black surface gleaming under the stars.

As she tried to maneuver her voluminous skirts into manageable handfuls she began to envy the colonial women who wore fewer petticoats and simpler clothing than she. At last she reached the waistband of her drawers and pulled the drawstring to release them. They dropped to her ankles, but she could not squat without bracing her feet wider apart than the garment would allow. With a sigh of exasperation, she stepped out of them and squatted down.

She saw the intruder too late. For an instant she thought the glow was the reflection of starlight on wet stones, but then it changed color, becoming the eerie green glow of predatory eyes only two feet from where she crouched.

Her muscles locked in spasms of fear. She had never seen a bear or a wolf or a lion; but this was a wild country, and surely the wild creatures who inhabited it must be very dangerous.

"Aisleen!"

She heard her name called in relief. "Thomas?"

"Aisleen!"

His cry accompanied the thrashing of the bush as he made his way toward her. The sudden noise startled the animal and it leaped forward, right at her.

With a scream of terror, Aisleen flung herself to one side. Arms caught in the fullness of her skirts, she fell forward onto the riverbank with a force that knocked the breath from her and slid, headfirst, into the river.

Thomas broke through the bush just as he heard a splash and, without seeing her, he knew what had happened. Shucking his coat, he paused long enough to pull off his boots before he flung himself into the inky water.

Immediately he came to the surface, effortlessly treading

water. To his dismay Aisleen was nowhere in sight. Where was she? Why had she not surfaced at least once? Frantically he craned his neck about, swearing at the cloaking darkness. With creeping dread he wondered if she had been caught in the strong currents that carried the Parramatta River for miles to Port Jackson.

Aisleen broke the water beside him, gasping and clutching the air blindly as she fought the weight of her soaked gown, which dragged her under again almost at once.

He reached for her as the water closed over her head and was enveloped in a morass of cold, wet wool and petticoats as he drew her close. The weight dragged them both under as she grabbed him about the neck.

Automatically, his hand went to the knife he carried, and he began hacking at her skirts. Little by little the sodden clothing slid past her hips, freeing them, and they surfaced.

Both gasping for breath, he caught her to him and struck out for the shore with his free arm. The current was swift, and her weight pulled at him until his shoulder muscles threatened to tear under the strain; but he did not pause to rest until they reached the bank and he had pulled her up with him.

Too winded to move farther, he turned her onto her stomach and patted her back as she choked and gasped, spewing water from nose and mouth.

Aisleen submitted helplessly to his pounding, caught between shame and relief as she struggled to regain her breath. After a moment she said, "Thank you."

"Aye, a thank-you's a proper thing to say to the man who's saved yer life," Thomas answered in amused relief as he turned her toward him and hugged her. "But what I'd like to know is why ye jumped in in the first place, being that ye cannae swim a lick."

"But I can," Aisleen answered. "The wind was knocked out of me before I fell in."

Thomas continued to hold her, his patting reduced to long, slow strokes from shoulder to waist that were meant to soothe. "Is that why ye screamed?"

"I screamed because there was a beast—oh!"

Aisleen tried to sit up, but Thomas held her down beside him on the grass. "What sort of beast?"

"I—I didn't see it clearly," she admitted. All the same, she darted glances left and right. "We should go back to the others, before it returns."

"For meself, I quite like where we are." His hand curled down tight in the hollow of her waist as he bent forward to lay his lips softly against hers.

At once several things came clearly to Aisleen's mind. She was alone with Thomas, her hips were pressed against the hard pressure of his loins, and she was very, very cold because her skirts had ridden scandalously high. Appalled, she reached down to lower them. Instead she found nothing but naked thigh. She jerked away from his kiss, and he loosened his grip to allow her to roll onto her back. "My skirts!"

"Cut them off ye," he advised pleasantly. "They were drowning us."

"Cut . . . them . . . off!" She tried to scramble away from him, but he threw a leg across her, pinning her.

"There they are!" a voice cried jubilantly.

Thomas and Aisleen looked up to find a lantern weaving its way toward them.

"We're about to have company, lass," Thomas grumbled.

"Oh, no!" Aisleen closed her eyes.

Aware that more practical measures were necessary to protect her modesty, Thomas raised up and pushed her under him to shield her nakedness with his trousered legs just as the lantern bearer and his companions reached them.

"Goodness gracious!" cried a female voice.

"Will you look at that!" declared a man.

"Tom! That you?" asked another.

Thomas looked up from where he lay and smiled. "G'evening."

After one clear look, one woman turned away, giggling as she fled back to the camp. The other stood her ground, a plucked chicken of a woman with stooped shoulders and defeated breasts. "We thought we heard cries for help." Her gaze narrowed on Aisleen's torn skirts. "I see now we misunderstood." She turned away, but only after a whispered aside to her husband. "Coupling in the bush like savages. The poor girl is to be pitied!"

"If it's not asking too much," Thomas prompted with a lifted brow at the men who stood mute but vigilant.

"Aye. Should be getting back," one of the men offered, but they all reluctantly withdrew their gaze from the tantalizing glimpse of Aisleen's naked hip visible beneath her husband's provocatively draped leg.

"Good night, Tom. Missus," a man offered and then snickered. The snickering was picked up by others as the men disappeared into the bush.

"What's he done with her skirts?" one of them questioned loudly.

"Damned if I know."

"Tom weren't a shearer for nothing!" said a third.

Hearty male laughter turned Aisleen's face scarlet. "I'm ruined!" she whispered furiously.

"Ruined?" Thomas questioned, as amused as his mates by the situation. " 'Tis not indecent for a man and wife to cuddle in private."

"What privacy!" Aisleen cried, losing her last shred of dignity. "I've lost my—my, and you've mutilated my gown!"

"*Och,* well, I was about to be asking that. Where's yer knickers, lass?"

Aisleen stared up at his face in the darkness. "Release me at once!"

Thomas did not move. She was very, very soft. His hand beneath her buttocks tightened its grasp. Her wet skin was dewy with moisture, but beneath the chilled flesh he could feel the hot warmth of muscles and blood. For all her propriety, she was a woman, his woman. He rolled farther onto her, pressing his roused loins against her bare thigh as he bent to kiss her a second time.

Aisleen stiffened at his kiss, refusing to part her lips to the persuasive stroke of his tongue. She felt the deepening possession of his caress with a fear very different from the fright that had been aroused in her by the predatory gleam in the dark. His touch was no random threat but one of which she knew the exact consequence. In another moment she would feel again the melting desire that she could not think of without shame. It was so pleasant, would be so easy to yield to the tantalizing promise of his kiss.

"Please," she begged against his mouth. He must not touch her, not when she was too vulnerable to resist.

Thomas did not answer. His hand moved from her buttock, curving up and forward over the top of her hip, chasing shivers across her belly as he paused to rub slow, deep circles into her flesh. "Ye feel so nice I cannae leave ye be," he murmured into her ear. "I am yer husband. Ye must let me—"

"Force me again?" she spat, fear beating so hard in her blood that her ears hummed.

Thomas froze. He could not see her face well, but her voice had been full of loathing. She was repulsed by his lovemaking, abhorred his touch. He moved, rolled off her, and came to his feet in one continuous movement.

"Where are you going?" she cried as he turned and started to walk away.

"Where a man's welcome!" he hurled back over his shoulder as the night closed in behind him.

She sat up, too shaken by the last seconds to think of

anything. Only when the sound of his path through the bush faded away did she rise and begin searching for her drawers. She found, instead, Thomas's jacket where he had left it lying before he dived in after her, and she picked it up.

Embarrassment warred with anxiousness as she stood irresolutely on the riverbank. She could not stay in the bush forever, and yet the thought of walking into the camp without decent covering kept her rooted to the spot. Even if she had had a gown to wear, how would she ever face them? They were Thomas's friends. They had seen her lying half-naked on the ground. They must think her a depraved woman, a brazen harlot, to couple in the bushes with a man, even if that man was her husband.

"Mercy!" she whispered, her face stinging with shame.

The rustling of a nearby bush made her spin about. Heart pounding, she stared into the darkness, but whatever had disturbed the underbrush was as invisible as the wind. Without quite reasoning it out she began backing away, and then she was running toward the clearing.

With heartfelt thanks she saw their wagon parked at the edge of the bush. More surprising, her bag had been handed down and stood by the wheel nearest her. Had Thomas done that? The gesture of consideration was not what she had expected. After all, he was very angry, had left her alone with only an angry word.

Cautiously she searched the area for him, but he was nowhere in sight. Satisfied, she wrapped his jacket about her hips and tied the arms about her waist to clothe herself. After another look, she darted out from behind the protection of a bush, grabbed her bag, and pulled it back into the underbrush.

With dismay she found that the bag contained her underclothes and nightgowns. "Drat!" she muttered. What was she to do? What else could she do?

She pulled out a nightgown and lay it across a nearby

bush. Eyes ranging back and forth between the bush and the camp, she quickly stripped off the bodice of what had once been a gown and then unlaced her corset. The night air was warm but she was damp where the clothing had held the moisture, and her teeth chattered as she hurriedly pulled the nightgown over her head.

"Are ye ready, then?"

She spun about to find Thomas walking toward her out of the densest part of the bush. She voiced indignantly, "Is there no end to your revolting habits?"

His eyes narrowed but he said pleasantly, "I was keeping watch for ye. Ye're not accustomed to the bush, and being the skittish creature ye are, I did not wish to fish ye from the water a second time."

Aisleen stared at him. She wanted to believe him, but she could not shake the lingering, shuddering memory of his hand on her skin. He had touched her, kissed her, made his lust known, and she could not forget it. "After what you have done the help of a stranger would be preferable."

"Aye, and that ye'd be having in abundance if I were not keeping watch," he replied less civilly. "Ye'd be getting more than ye'd be wanting now that ye've paraded yerself before the lads in yer nakedness."

The accusation stung. "That's unfair! You cut my skirts away."

"Aye, I did, and will do so again if ever ye burden yerself with so bloody many petticoats!"

"Don't swear at me!"

"Then don't act a bloody ass!" he roared.

Aisleen shrank away from his anger as he caught her by the arm just above the elbow. He bent and picked up his jacket. "Put this over yer gown. I'll be escorting ye back to camp." He thrust the jacket into her hands and picked up her bag. "Well?" he prompted when she did not move.

Aisleen wet her lips. "I—I cannot face them."

Thomas frowned, uncertain that he had heard her right, and then he understood. She was ashamed, good and truly ashamed of what the men and women of the camp thought of her. His hand gentled on her arm. "About what I said before, about the lads, I did nae mean it. They won't do or say anything to insult ye."

"How can you be certain?" she challenged.

He grinned. "There's not a man alive who's met Thomas Gibson and doesn't know that he'd be answering for touching anything that's mine."

The speech was not calculated to appease in its implication, but she was too exhausted to argue. Her shoulders drooped in defeat. "It's been a most vexing day."

Thomas took the jacket from her hands and placed it about her shoulders, pleased that she did not pull away from him when he let his arm drop to her waist. "Poor wee *colleen*, ye've had a fright."

She *had* had a fright. Under the guidance of his arm, she allowed him to guide her back to the clearing. She did not look up from the ground as they crossed to his tent. Neither did she comment on the sleeping arrangements when he stretched out beside her on the bedding that had been laid out. Yet she sighed in thanks when he covered her with one blanket and unfolded a second for himself.

Curling up in a tight ball against the chill from the drenching, she listened to the sound of his easy breathing until her own matched his and she slept.

"Tom?"

Thomas sat up beside his sleeping wife. "Jack?"

"Aye."

Thomas quickly and quietly slipped from the tent into the

darkness. Jack's huge silhouette was visible several yards away.

"Ye've had news," Thomas said when he reached the man.

"Aye."

"O'Leary?"

"Aye."

"Sodding bastard!" Thomas sucked in a quick breath. "O'Leary will have heard about me station, so we'll not go there. Couldn't sell the sheep. I'm thinking we'll lift the mob over the Blue Mountains. Fresh meat will bring a good price in the gold fields north of Bathurst. Once we're across, we'll give O'Leary the slip." His smile was a pearly shadow. "Folks are less curious about a man once he's out in the bush."

"Aye." The voice held a question in reserve.

"The lass goes with us," Thomas answered.

This time there was no reply.

When an immortal passion breathes in mortal clay;
Our hearts endure the scourge, the plaited thorns . . .

—The Travail of Passion
W. B. Yeats

Chapter Ten

Aisleen held on tightly and gritted her teeth as one wagon wheel slammed into a rut and bounced out of it again. The man beside her gave only a low chuckle and flicked the whip over the backs of the horses.

They had not exchanged a single word in more than five hours. The driver was the camp cook; but as she sat beside the withered old man with enlarged knuckles and a missing thumb, she doubted she would be able to stomach anything he touched. Cellophane-thin flakes of skin peeled from his nose, cheeks, and brow. Even worse, she was certain she had seen vermin crawling along his cheekline where his grizzled beard thinned. Shuddering, she drew her skirts in against her legs.

Overhead the midday sun blazed down, making her scalp itch beneath her straw bonnet. The gingham gown she wore was two sizes too big, but she was too grateful for the circulation of air that the roominess provided to complain about it or the fact that she had no crinoline to make the skirts stand out properly. Along with her petticoats, the crinoline was at the bottom of Parramatta River.

The gingham gown was a gift from one of the camp women. She had been too embarrassed to ask what explanation Thomas had given the people of the camp for the incident the night before, but she was grateful to put her wools aside.

The wagon shimmied over the summit of another rut and then dropped heavily into the backswell. She clung determinedly to the side of the wagon seat, refusing to utter a groan of protest. She had learned within the first hour that the cook would not respond to her pleas. In fact, she suspected that he drove over the ruts just to annoy her.

Nothing had gone right from the moment she was awakened by Thomas's rough shake of her shoulder. It was not yet dawn when she stumbled from the tent. Even so, she had missed breakfast because the cook was anxious not to be left behind by the drovers. So here she sat even hungrier and thirstier than she had been the day before.

At least, she surmised with more cheerfulness than she felt, she was in no hurry to relieve herself. Still, her stomach ached with hunger, and she decided to brave another attempt at conversation with the cook. "Will we be stopping soon?"

The cook turned a baleful stare on her and issued a short, enigmatic grunt.

She recoiled from the rude syllable, but he did not seem to notice as his indifferent gaze wandered back to the road.

Thoroughly disgusted, she raised a hand to shield her eyes as she searched for Thomas. He had been riding right in front of them a moment before. Now she saw the backs of the drovers weaving in and out of a roiling sea of hundreds of sheep whose pink skins shone like bald men's scalps under the white ruff of their newly sheared wool. All the drovers looked identical. Like the others, Thomas wore a canvas shirt and moleskin britches. His shiny black hair was hidden beneath his wide-brimmed hat. Only the huge expanse of Jack Egan's shoulders set him apart.

When the wagon suddenly lurched off the road and came to a halt under the doubtful shade of the trees, she turned a surprised face to the cook, but he set the brake and climbed down from his perch without signifying that she existed.

"Well!" she declared in annoyance. He was as rude as any man she had yet met.

Gathering her too-long skirts together, she stepped over the side of the wagon and climbed down. She was becoming accustomed to the maneuver, which was just as well, she decided.

"Missus!"

She turned toward the back of the wagon just in time to catch the heavy iron skillet which the cook heaved at her. For the first time animation showed in the man's face as the weight of the skillet forced her to lower it to the ground.

"Weak, ain't ye?" he jeered with a snicker.

Anger caught fire in Aisleen's face. "How dare you address me in that manner!"

He turned toward the dropped tailgate of the wagon and reached in and dragged out a large billy. Patting it, he said, "Water's in the barrel on the other side. Put on the cha." He grinned, showing gaps between every tooth in his mouth. "Unless ye'd rather do the slaughtering."

Aisleen let the skillet drop. "I don't intend to do either."

The man's weathered face stiffened. "Tom said ye would help with the cooking. Well, it's time."

"Thomas said—" Aisleen's mouth snapped shut. Her husband had volunteered her for a job without seeking her consent or determining if she were equal to the task. "There has been a misunderstanding. I will speak with my husband."

As she turned away he exploded in profanity that shocked her more than he knew. Determined not to show it, she turned back to him. "The filth spewing from you will not solve my problem nor cook your meal. Therefore I suggest that you begin without me."

"Bloody pommie!" she heard him hurl after her.

The blowing dust surprised her, for the ground was grassy for the most part; but the passage of hundreds of small hooves had stirred up the layer underneath, and she sneezed repeatedly as she walked toward the flock.

The sheep had poured forth in a widening circle from the narrow column that they had been forced to maintain by men and dogs. Now they spread across the grassy spaces between the tall trees which flanked the road. Feeling awkward as the sheep swirled in about her, she continued toward the drovers on horseback.

The barking dogs did not surprise her; they had been constant company the morning long as they helped the men keep the sheep moving smoothly. A long, low growl to her right did not unsettle her until she turned to face the gold-and-white dog a few feet away who had bared its teeth. Sheep, sensing danger, flowed away, leaving her and the dog inside an empty circle.

Misgiving flicked her spine as the dog lowered its head and flattened its ears back, but she was not afraid of animals. "Nice dog," she said quietly, and tentatively offered the back of her hand for its inspection.

The dog's snarling lunge for her hand came as a surprise, and she stumbled back with a cry of fright.

An instant later the report of a gun split the air, and with a yelp of pain the dog jerked and fell sideways, its legs jerking spasmodically.

"Oh, God!" She swung toward the source of the gunfire. A few yards away Thomas sat astride his horse, a smoking pistol in his hand. Immediately he thrust the weapon back into his belt and dismounted.

"What the bloody hell were ye doing?" he roared as he caught Aisleen roughly by the arms.

"You killed it!" she accused, unable to believe that she had been in real danger.

"Bloody right I did!"

Aisleen stared up into his anger-distorted face, at his eyes bulging white about the deep blue irises. Rage trembled through his hands into her arms where he mercilessly gripped her. She had never before seen a man so angry, and the fierceness of it made her feel watery with fear. "I don't understand," she whispered. "What did I do?"

Jack Egan, his long legs dwarfing the size of the horse, road in close to the pair. "No good for the sheep, spooking them that way. Won't be worth piss, they drop dead of fright."

"Then ye'd best be calming them," Thomas shot back. He looked about and saw that the other men had stopped to watch. "I'm paying ye wages for work!" he said roughly. "Get that carcass out of sight."

He turned Aisleen away from the dead dog, pulling her along after him with a bruising hand on her upper arm. Only when they had cleared the flock did he pause and turn to her. "Never do that again, ye hear me?"

Aisleen nodded, unable to steady her voice for a moment. He was so angry, angrier than he had any right to be. "Is—is that all?"

The red cloud of rage that had overcome Thomas receded slowly. When her face was clearly before him he saw that her golden freckles stood out vividly on her too-pale skin. "Frightened ye, did it?"

She steadied her gaze on his. "You did."

"Me?"

"You killed that poor dog," she said, shrugging free of

his touch. "You killed it for no reason. It did not touch me. It was only doing its job of protecting the flock. That was no reason to murder it. How could you?"

Irritation needled Thomas. "I was protecting ye, lass."

"I don't need that kind of protecting," she answered and turned to hurry back toward the wagon.

He watched her go in mingled annoyance and chagrin. It had never occurred to him that she would do something as foolish as wade into the middle of a mob. What had brought her out here? That thought sent him striding after her, but Jack came riding up to intercept him, leading his horse.

"Sam'll bury the dog," he said, and he tossed the reins to Thomas. His eyes flickered over the younger man before resting speculatively on his face. "Leg's paining ye," he announced in a flat voice before moving on.

With a curse, Thomas lifted himself into the saddle, ignoring the twinge in his left calf. Perhaps he had overreacted. He had more cause than most.

He looked again toward Aisleen; but she was nearly back to the wagon, and he had things to do before they settled down for the evening meal. "Bloody hell!" he muttered, turning his mount away.

As she walked rapidly back to the cook wagon, Aisleen tried to put out of her mind the image of the dead dog. Yet it would not vanish, nor would the niggling possibility that its death was her fault. Had she provoked it? She had not meant to. The dogs she had known through the years were docile creatures, wagging friendly tails to elicit a pat on the head. The dust had confused her or she never would have waded into the center of the flock.

"Finish herding sheep, have ye?" the cook asked as she approached, and she knew that he had witnessed at least a part of the incident.

She crossed her arms and gripped her elbows, her voice

defensive. "The dog attacked me. It might have caused me serious injury had my husband not shot it."

"A man makes his choices. He can kill the thing that causes the trouble or kill the trouble. Seems like Tom took the long way round to it."

"Hold yer tongue, ye bloody get!"

Aisleen looked back to find Jack's long silhouette between her and the sun. "Ye'll do, missus?" His tone belied interest in her welfare.

"Yes, thank you," she answered, gripping her arms more tightly as she sensed his disapproval. She saw his gaze shift back to the cook.

"Tom says ye're to show the missus the way of camp cooking."

"Ain't known ye to want a sheila along on a haul," the cook ventured with a grin.

Jack's voice was dry as dust. "Might improve the swill ye serve."

"Bleeding better hope I stay!" the cook roared. "A pommie in the cha is as good as a dag on a sheep's arse!"

Jack did not answer as he turned away.

"Well?" the cook barked at Aisleen. "What're ye waiting for, yer majesty? Tom said I was to teach ye to cook and, by God, ye'll learn or ye'll flaming answer to me!" He picked up the billy can he had set near the fire and swung it across the flame to begin heating. "Get the tea."

"Where is it?" Aisleen asked.

"In the flaming wagon!"

"If you do not cease that filthy language this minute, I shall report you to my husband," she answered.

The cook unbent from his crouched position and took a menacing step toward her. "Ye do that, missus, and I've remedies that'll see to it yer husband cannae plow yer field for some good long time!"

Aisleen did not understand the implications of the threat,

but she did understand that it was a threat. "I am prepared to be civil, if you will. Kindly tell me what I must do instead of cursing me for not doing it."

The cook snorted and spat to one side. "Where's that blee—blooming tea?"

"In the wagon, of course," Aisleen answered with a smile as she lifted her skirts and went to retrieve the item.

"Bloody pommie sow!" the cook muttered and returned to his fire.

Aisleen sat on the burned-out stump of a tree and surveyed the contents of her tin plate. Chunks of lamb swam in a greasy broth along with bits of undercooked dumpling and some leafy green vegetable of unidentifiable origin. She speared a bit of meat and gingerly bit into it, discovering that it was every bit as tough as it appeared. With a resigned sigh, she laid her fork back in her plate and looked up to gauge the reaction of the other diners.

A little distance away, the drovers had hunkered down around the cookfire, conversing in low monosyllables and forking food into their mouths at a speed that left no time to chew. Thomas was among them, his back half-turned to her as he balanced his arms on his knees and ate. He was silent, seemingly listening to his men, but she suspected that he was aware of her and that his avoidance of her was deliberate. Two days had passed since the shooting of the dog, yet he had scarcely acknowledged her existence.

Disappointed, she waved a hand over her plate to discourage the flies who held her meal in greater regard than she. He was still angry and that disturbed her. And there was the dog. What sort of man shot a dog for no reason? She could not reconcile the action with the man she knew.

Or thought I was beginning to know, she mused. There was no explanation for his rage.

From the corner of her eye she saw him rise to his feet, his meal finished. She rose, too, resolved to speak with him, but then he started across the yard.

He limped, his left leg thrown out stiffly each time. She had nearly forgotten about his limp. He had not favored the leg so strongly since the first day they met. She knew nothing about the cause of his affliction or the things that made it better or worse.

He turned toward her as if he had felt her stare, and their gazes locked across the distance. He was too far away for her to divine the expression in his dark blue eyes, yet she had the distinct impression that weariness was there, and something more. He made no gesture, nor spoke. Suddenly he swung away from her, grabbed his horse's reins, vaulted into the saddle, and rode off.

She was not offended by his rudeness. She guessed the cause. She had seen his weakness, and he was too proud to accept the sympathy that must have been in her eyes.

"Tucker's done!" the cook called to Aisleen as the other men rose, leaving their plates on the ground. She watched the men troop silently toward their mounts until the cook's voice reached her once more. "If'n ye've finished, yer highness!"

The men's heads swiveled toward her in unison, and she heard the mumbling of a comment too low to be understood and then galling masculine chuckles as they mounted up. Lips thinned in annoyance, she walked toward her tormentor.

When she reached the cook, she shoved her full plate at him and said, "It's a wonder men eat the swill you serve. I, for one, cannot countenance it."

The cook bared his ragged row of teeth as his face turned alarmingly red. "Swill, it is? Can ye do better?"

Aisleen lifted an eyebrow. "I doubt I could do worse."

"Then, ye flaming slut, ye're bloody well welcome to try!" He slammed down the plate she had given him and marched off, cursing roundly.

She watched him climb onto the wagon to grab his swag and then leap off. He glared at her, roaring, "Tell Tom I'll collect me wages next time through!" before he set off on foot down the road from which they had come.

"Shouldn't have done that."

Aisleen looked up in unease to find Jack towering over her. Like an apparition, he unaccountably appeared when least expected. Had Thomas set him to spy on her? "Should not have done what?" she asked defensively as she gazed the long way up into his craggy face.

"Sacked the cook." As before, he turned his back before she could reply.

She had not sacked the cook. He had quit. Jack must have heard the entire conversation, so why would he say that? Unless he, too, enjoyed her misery?

"I don't care," she murmured under her breath as she bent to pick up the tin plates. She had had enough of the cook's insults and bad company. Certainly she could manage a meal that would not turn stomachs that had gulped down his inedible offerings.

When she had rinsed the cups and plates and put them away, she stacked the supplies in the back of the wagon and closed the tailgate, feeling quite proud of herself. But as she climbed up onto the wagon seat she realized the first of the problems the cook's absence presented.

She gazed in misgiving at the traces wrapped around the brake lever. She knew nothing about handling a team, had never held reins in her hands before. Someone else would have to take the cook's place on the wagon seat.

But when she raised her eyes, she saw that the sheep had begun to move, urged on by the whistles and cries of the drovers. Within minutes, men and sheep had disappeared around a curve in the road, and she was left all alone in the midst of the clearing with only the hum of insects and strange bird calls for company. Thomas would quickly miss the wagon, she surmised, and sat back to await the chagrin and the profuse apologies she was certain he would offer her when he learned of the cook's rudeness.

After the first ten minutes, she began to lose patience. Sunlight slanted down harshly among the tall, pale trunks of the trees, and small flies gathered to sip greedily the perspiration the heat raised on her skin.

When a full hour had passed, impatience had turned to worry. More and more annoyed, she swatted at her face and neck continuously. Where was Thomas? Had Jack told him a lie that had made him too angry to return immediately for her?

She heard the pounding hooves of the horse a moment before she saw the rider on the track. She stood up in the wagon and waved her arms frantically, but it was unnecessary. The rider was heading straight for her. Recognition of Thomas made her stomach quiver with joy, her annoyance forgotten. But before she could greet him he reined in his horse and cried, "Where's the cook?"

"He left," she answered, a little disappointed that he had not asked first about her. In fact, the stern lines of his face were less than heartening.

"Left? Where's he gone?"

"I do not know, nor do I care," she replied.

Thomas stood in the stirrups and surveyed the area. "That won't help," she informed him crisply. "He left before you'd driven the flock out of sight. He quit."

"Quit?" Thomas barked. "Why?"

For the first time in their acquaintance, she found she could not answer him with the complete truth. Her lashes fluttered down upon her cheeks. "He—he, I don't know. Ask him yourself!"

Thomas swore under his breath and, pushing his hat down hard on his head, wheeled his horse about and galloped off.

Another long, tedious hour passed before she heard a horse coming back up the road. To her amazement, she saw that Thomas rode double—with the cook.

When they drew up even with the wagon, the cook slipped off and turned an indignant look on Thomas. "A man can take only so much!"

"Ye're paid to cook, that's a beginning and an end to it," Thomas answered impatiently, his eyes on the road before him. "See that ye remember that!" Without a word to his wife, he kicked his horse into a canter.

Aisleen watched him in disbelief. He had brought the rude and vulgar man back without demanding so much as an apology to her from him.

Without a word, the cook climbed up beside her, unhitched the traces, released the brake, and, with an obscene shout and a flick of the stock whip, started the wagon rolling along the road.

"Ye'll be knowing who to thank for the late tucker," the cook said as new grumbles rose among the men who lounged about the campfire waiting for their evening meal. "City ways, mates. That's the style this year."

Aisleen ignored the snigger that accompanied his words as she tried unsuccessfully to lift the billy from its tripod without spilling water into the fire. The hiss of steam betrayed her failure, and the cook's snigger turned into a blue streak of profanity that she could no longer block from her thoughts.

She turned to him and dropped the billy, sending scalding hot water in a flood toward his boots. "I quit!" she cried and stalked off.

"Can't quit!" he called after her. "He's yer boss more'n mine!"

Aisleen hunched her shoulders against the laughter that followed. The day's journey had taken its toll. The jarring and lurching of the wagon had left her with muscles that trembled with fatigue and a head that throbbed. The cook's return was humiliation enough. His taunts were beyond enduring. She could not understand why Thomas had brought him back. At the very least she deserved an explanation.

She found Thomas with the horses. He had stripped off his shirt, and his back gleamed palely in the amethyst twilight. As she neared she saw that he rubbed the sweat from his horse's flanks with a cloth. The muscles of his back rippled smoothly as he worked, but that was not what brought her to a stumbling halt. All at once, she knew that he was not alone.

Her skin began to tingle. The moon had risen. High overhead the boughs shifted in the breeze, scattering the moon's pearly effluence over the violet shadows of twilight.

She saw him, no more than an adumbration before the softer shadows of the night. The scent of roses came strongly from him, blotting out the stink of horse and sheep and sweat. He took a step toward her, a hand outstretched, and moonlight cascaded across his tattered sleeve.

It could not be!

Thomas heard a gasp and swirled about. When he saw Aisleen, he reached for his sweat-soaked shirt. "Ye should warn a man when ye're about," he said nervously as he put his arms in his shirt.

Aisleen gazed at him blankly. What had happened? Had her eyes played a trick on her?

"Did ye want something?"

Aisleen blinked. Yes, of course, she wanted something. "I came to talk with you," she said in a distracted tone. "About the cook."

Thomas nodded and returned to his work. "He's back. That's an end to it."

"Hardly," she said tartly, drawn from her momentary confusion by his unsatisfactory reply. "He's rude and vulgar."

He looked up sharply. "He's not laid a hand on ye?"

"That is the only thing he has not dared. His language is coarse enough to strain the patience of a saint. As for his manners, he has none. He orders me about as though I were a lackey. I will not endure his bullying a moment longer!"

Thomas shrugged. "Ye'll learn to pay him no mind."

"I will do no such thing!" Aisleen moved closer to him. "You must dismiss him."

Thomas shook his head. "That I will nae do."

"I am your wife. How can you permit his disrespect? He calls me a—" Her voice dropped to a whisper. "A slut!"

Thomas sighed. So that was the problem. "I will speak to him."

"I don't want him reprimanded. Dismiss him."

He turned to her, his head cocked to one side as he folded his arms across his chest. "Maybe," he agreed, "when we've made the journey west."

"West?" Aisleen frowned. "You said your station was north of Sydney."

"And so it is," he agreed. "We're nae going home just yet."

"Then where?"

"West across the Blue Mountains to Bathurst. I've agreed to lift this mob of sheep to slaughter."

"Why did you not tell me?"

He shrugged. "It did nae concern ye."

"Of course it concerns me," she answered. "I think I should have been consulted."

"And I'm thinking ye should be helping with the tucker," he replied. "When a man's hungry his temper's less than reliable."

"Does that mean you will do nothing?"

"Ye have a fine way about ye. Ye'll win him round to yer way of thinking."

"If you will do nothing, then I must demand to be taken back to Sydney. Immediately!"

"Ye're me wife and beside me is where ye belong."

The simple, implacable statement made Aisleen angry. "I will not work beside that man. One of us must leave."

"If I was to sack the cook, who would be taking his place?"

"I would," Aisleen answered quickly.

Thomas grinned. "Would ye, lass? Can ye make damper? Slaughter a lamb? Skin a haunch? Who'd carry the water barrels and cure the meat? Can ye start a fire in the rain or drive a team of horses? When we trade them for bullocks..." Words failed him at the thought of his lady wife fighting to control four tons of snorting, intractable oxen as they traversed the Blue Mountains.

Every word he said made Aisleen feel more foolish and useless, but she resented his easy victory over her objections. "You think very little of my abilities."

"I think enough of ye to not be wanting ye worn and wearied to death." His grin deepened. "Ye might learn a thing or two from the cook or not. As ye please. Once we're home, ye can keep me house, cook me meals, and raise me children."

A blush suffused Aisleen's face. Raise his children? Did he still harbor the belief that she would agree to have his children when she had spurned his touch? Yet as she stared at his handsome face she was aware of confusion and unease that made her stomach jump and tremble.

When she did not deny his words, relief suffused Thomas. He had been right to hope for a change in her attitude. Instinctively he reached out to touch her, but she wheeled away from him.

"Don't you dare!" she said sharply, too aware of the need he brought so easily to the surface to temper her response. He had spurned her pleas for help. She must not answer his callousness with weakness or he would use it against her. "I've endured enough this day!" She turned and stalked away.

"Damn!"

Thomas kicked the ground. He had been so close to gaining her confidence until he rushed the moment by attempting to touch her. She was as skittish as a brumbie. He needed patience. But he had no patience. He wanted his wife.

He rubbed his jaw where a new growth of whiskers bristled. Soon he would have a beard, and that reminded him of a more pressing problem.

They had made good progress the first days, despite the bruising path that had unsettled Aisleen and made him the victim of her wrath. The cook was an irascible old devil but a reliable hand with the tucker. If he was rude, that was small discomfort in return for three hot meals. Aisleen would learn to appreciate that better as the days wore on.

Still, it rankled to know that she still shied from his touch. He groaned. The night was before them. How would she behave when he crawled into the wagon beside her? If she cried out or fought him, they would both be humiliated.

Uncertainty churned his middle. All he could think of was her sweet mouth and the feel of contentment he had awakened to the morning after their wedding night. She had been his only for that one night. And that was not nearly enough.

He turned and began resaddling his horse. When it was done, he walked back to the cookfire to eat the meal the cook had hurriedly thrown together. When he was finished, he volunteered for the first watch with the sheep.

"Makes a man wonder," one of the remaining drovers

mused and nodded toward the wagon where Aisleen had bedded down alone for the night.

"Wonder all ye damned well please," another drover answered, "but keep yer bloody gaze off his wife or Tom will make ye bleeding sorry ye ever saw her."

Aisleen turned from her side onto her stomach in her sleep, her mind resisting the tug of the dream; but it caught and held, drawing her slowly down into it.

... The smell of the sea freshened the breeze that swept the still, dark bulk of the hill. The damp ground beneath her smothered the pounding of her heart but not her starved gasps for breath.

Something was out there in the dark, waiting and watching, stalking her.

She lowered her head, praying that the unknown pursuer would pass her by. She did not know its shape or source, but dread crept up the back of her neck as she lay prone among the gorse bushes of the Irish hillside.

Suddenly the night was alive with the sharp yapping of dogs.

She scrambled to her feet and began to run faster and faster over the boggy ground that sucked at her bare feet and threatened to trip her.

They came upon her swiftly, yaps changed to snarls as she spun about to face them. She saw it from the corner of her eye, the gold-and-white sheep dog, an instant before it lunged and sank its teeth into her leg ...

Aisleen awakened with a cry. The canvas cover brushed her face as she tried to rise from the shallow space of the wagonbed, and she cried out again, fighting the material that would not allow her to sit. Suddenly it was lifted, and the cool breath of the night reached her as the spangled sky appeared.

"Lass! What's wrong?"

Hands reached out for her, and she slid unhesitatingly from the wagon into Thomas's embrace.

"A horrible dream!" she whispered as his arms enclosed her. "The sheep dog! Terrible! Terrible!"

"It's dead," Thomas answered and cradled her against his chest. "I killed it, remember." He reached up to stroke her hair tenderly. "Hush, lass, hush. 'Twas a sad thing ye witnessed, and I'm sorry for it. But 'twas only a dream frightening ye now. 'Twas only a dream."

Aisleen clung to him. The images had been so real. "My leg!" she said suddenly. She reached down and touched her calf beneath the tangle of her petticoats, half-expecting to feel torn flesh, but it was whole. "I thought—the dream. It was like one so long ago. I was just a child, but I remember."

Thomas stiffened. "What did ye say?"

"I dreamed I had been savaged by a dog. I limped for days." The words sounded so silly a small self-conscious laugh escaped her. "You must think me a foolish woman."

"Nae, lass," he answered in an oddly strained voice. "I've no fondness for dogs meself. Kelpies are quiet as ye like most times, but I've seen a pack of them take a dingo apart. When I think what could have happened to ye!" His arms tightened convulsively about her.

Under the cover of the canvas she had shed her gown to sleep in her chemise. The heat of his chest seeped through the thin material onto her skin as she stood within his strong grip. The intimacy was not repugnant to her. The flesh-and-blood reality of him was a welcome protection against the phantoms of the night. Yet even as she registered her change of heart, he withdrew from her.

" 'Twill be daylight soon," he said absently as he reached for the canvas cover. "This day will be harder than the last."

Reluctantly Aisleen climbed into the wagon and lay back as he pulled the canvas tight over her head. In the darkness she felt unexpectedly bereft. She had hoped that he would pull her back into his arms for a moment, perhaps kiss her. How strange. They had hardly spoken the last few days. When they had, the exchanges had been marred by argument and violence. He had refused to take her side against the obnoxious cook and chided her attempts to defend herself. Yet one brief instant of tenderness had eradicated her anger, her embarrassment, and her feelings of misuse. In his arms she had felt healed and safe. And that was the most devastating revelation of all.

Gradually she realized that he had not crawled in to sleep beside her as she had feared—and hoped—that he would. That should have pleased her, she thought as she drifted back to sleep. It did not.

He made the world to be a grassy road
Before her wandering feet.

—The Rose of The World
W. B. Yeats

Chapter Eleven

The first hint of dawn tinted the sky as Thomas leaned against the wagon wheel drinking tea from a tin cup. The voices of the drovers carried across the cool morning air. If he did not want to eat the dust of his men, he would have to move quickly.

Yet he did not. He had been awake the entire night, nursing the pain in his left leg, a pain that would only grow worse with hours in the saddle. Most often he shrugged off the discomfort, had over the years learned to carry the affliction with a certain pride of will over flesh; but during the night old memories had gathered. They circled now, darkening the bright morning with a past buried but not forgotten.

So long, it had been so long since he had allowed himself to remember.

... He lay on his belly in a bog, his heart thundering in his ears. It was black as pitch on the western Cork hillside above Schull Harbor; but dogs had sharper sight than men, and the English had brought dogs with them. The howls echoed eerily in the stillness, growing nearer with each minute.

He turned his head to one side and lifted it cautiously but saw nothing and dropped flat again. Sean and Virgil had been with him until the last shots rang out, and then he had lost count of the number of lads running beside him.

A bark sounded clearly to his left. He considered gaining his feet and running once more, but fear stopped him. The night was unusually still. Wherever his companions were, they were lying low, as he was. While he was not afraid of a good fight, the thought of being torn apart by the jaws of a huge dog made his bowels churn, and he pressed his body deeper into the mud.

Still, he could not resist a smile of satisfaction that cracked the mud which he had applied to his face to lessen his chances of being spotted. He was only fifteen, several years younger than the other lads, yet he had been a part of the night's work. The blaze from the military munitions hut had lit the sky with an orange flare bright enough to rival a sunset. No doubt it had been seen as far away as Baltimore Harbor across the bay.

He was a fisherman by trade and patriot by conscience. He was not an ambusher or cold-blooded murderer. Blowing up the shot powder was merely a warning to the English that they were an unwelcome presence along the southwest shores of Cork.

His father, too, was a patriot, but he was tired of the struggle. And there was his grandma. She disapproved of his fervent desire to exact retribution by force. She said he was marked for greatness but that he must be patient. She was dear to him but she was old, and patience was the weapon of the aged. Audacity belonged to youth.

As the minutes passed, the barking ranged closer and then

away, as if the animals were confused by the direction their prey had taken. He hoped it was the odor of his clothes that confused them. He had rubbed them with fish oil.

They came upon him with unexpected swiftness. The baying hounds erupted from the top of the hill with a suddenness that made Thomas shudder.

He did not have time to think. He was up and running in an instant, scarcely aware that his companions were doing the same. The darkness and rocky outcroppings made caution impossible, and he tripped repeatedly; yet the terror of the snarls at his back kept him from slowing down.

And then he heard a cry from the man at his left and the growling of a dog. A second later he felt a sharp pain in his left calf as if a knife had been driven through it, and he was jerked off his feet. As he tumbled helplessly forward he felt his flesh separate from the bone as the dog's grip did not slacken.

"... has been found guilty of acts of insurrection. It is the sentence of this court that you be taken hence to the place whence you came, and be thence drawn on a hurdle to the place of execution, and be there hanged by the neck until you are dead."

Thomas felt nothing as the sentence was passed on him: not the outrage expressed by the gasps and cries of the audience in the gallery or the fear that caused Sean O'Leary, standing on his right, to erupt in prayer.

Hanged. He was to die. That could not be right. He and his friends had done nothing that deserved so final a solution. Death in battle seemed a glorious end. Dancing at the end of the hangman's knot was ... obscene.

He swallowed with difficulty. Feeling was coming back and with it a sickening nausea. Somewhere behind him his parents stood. He should offer them some solace, reassure them that he was man enough to face his death, but he could not move. The room tilted. A roaring like the sea sounded in his ears.

Seated on a pile of moldering hay, his arms and legs fettered to the wall behind him by heavy links of rusty iron, Thomas waited for dawn and the hangman. Dirt, the beginnings of a beard, and long, greasy ropes of hair nearly obscured his face. His clothes, such as they were, were in tatters, and through the rents his painfully thin body was exposed. When the door creaked open he raised his head reluctantly to find his father standing motionless in the entrance of the windowless cell.

"Thomas, lad," Thaddeus said hoarsely.

"Stay back!" He raised a hand to fend off his father, but his weakness and the weight of the chain dragged it back to the ground. "I've prison fever. Keep back, Da," he added softly.

Cursing roundly, Thaddeus knelt in the straw and drew his son roughly into his arms. "Damn ye, Tommy, I told ye ye were a fool to go with them. Sean and the rest, they knew what they were doing. But ye, ye great fool, how could ye know 'twould come to this?"

Thomas allowed his head to sink against his father's chest. The tight embrace hurt him, but the pain was better than all the gentle touches he had ever known. "They . . . they're going to hang me . . . in the morning," he said between dry sobs.

"Nae! They'll not be doing that now," Thaddeus answered. " 'Tis why I'm here, Tommy. I've come to set ye free."

Thomas heard his father's voice, but his words did not make sense. He had known since his morning in court a week earlier that he was to die, to hang by the neck until dead.

"Did ye not hear me, lad?" his father asked, shaking him slightly.

Thomas moaned low in pain as the blessed peace of oblivion loomed, but he struggled to keep conscious. "Free?" he murmured.

"Aye, lad, that's the very thing I'm telling ye. 'Tis come in handy, that money I've been saving to take yer ma and the lasses to America. A few coins in the right hands has done it, Tommy. Yer sentence has been commuted to seven years' transportation. Do ye hear me? Ye're to live!"

Thomas stirred in his father's embrace, lifting his head to meet his father's gaze. "We're saved, then, Sean and all the rest?"

Thaddeus drew in a deep breath. "Nae, lad. Only ye."

Thomas smiled. It quite surprised him that he could do it. "Then I'll be staying with the others. They'll be expecting me, ye see. I'm nae afraid any longer. I'll not let them down."

The stars had never seemed closer, Thomas thought as he stared through a porthole of the prison ship at the star-spangled effulgence of the Milky Way. After a moment he weakly turned his head away. The stars were close, but his family and homeland were far away.

He could not remember much of the past weeks, only the pain and fever and a dread of dying that had ebbed into weary resignation. He had been too weak to understand what was happening . . . until now.

He was aboard a prison ship bound for the Australian colony called Van Diemen's Land. He looked down at the fetters locked about his wrists and attached to the bulkhead behind him with a length of chain. Other shackles chained his feet to the opposite bulkhead. Fear coiled in his belly and sweat broke out on his brow. Grandma was wrong. Marked for greatness? He had been marked for servitude and perhaps death under the indifferent eye of a foreign sun . . .

Thomas awakened with a start, sweat pouring from every pore. His cup had fallen from his hand, and he sat in a puddle of tea. He scrambled to his feet just as Aisleen emerged from the back of the wagon.

Aisleen started at the sight of Thomas. She had thought to brace herself against the cook's ill temper. But seeing Thomas's haggard expression and the guarded look in his eyes, she realized how unprepared she was to face him. Self-consciously she began smoothing her skirts with a hand. She hoped that he would speak first, but he did not.

"I overslept," she said finally, with a sideways glance toward the place where the cook prepared breakfast.

She started past him, and Thomas nearly let her go. At the last second, as her skirts swished his legs, he reached out and captured her wrist. "Wait!" He licked his lips nervously. "I—I'm sorry about, well, me temper the other day. I should have explained to ye what we are about."

Aisleen shook her head, unable to meet his eyes. "I should have realized that it was none of my business. I am a wife, bound to obey."

"Did ye sleep well, after the trouble?" he questioned for want of conversation.

"I suppose it seems a pathetic excuse to you, but dreams can sometimes seem very real," she answered, remembering how shamefully she had clung to him and had wanted to go on clinging.

Thomas regarded her solemnly. "I believe in dreams." He released her wrist. "There's tea in the billy for ye. We've a long day ahead, and there'll be no more till supper."

Aisleen watched him stride toward his horse, her eyes narrowing on the leg he still favored. What was the cause? She heard him groan softly as he mounted and promised herself that she would inquire about the source of his discomfort. The worst thing that would happen was that he would be angered and rebuff her. If he did she would comfort herself with the knowledge that she had inquired about her husband's death as any wife would and that he should not find fault with her for that.

With a resigned sigh, she straightened her shoulders and prepared to face the cook. Learning to cook in the bush was just another challenge, she told herself, and before the journey was ended she would have the mastery of it.

Aisleen awoke for the second morning in a row with the woolly-headed feeling that came from interrupted sleep.

"Missus!"

Of course. Aisleen moaned in protest and pulled her blanket up to cover her head.

"Missus!"

There was no denying that strident tone. In another moment she expected to be caught by the ankles and pulled unceremoniously from the wagon. In reality the cook had not dared that, but although he had never laid a hand on her, Aisleen felt she had been roundly abused by him. There was no appealing to Thomas either. He had been strangely absent from camp ever since the first day, riding out before the others and returning after she had retired for the night.

She stripped the wool blanket from her body and immediately remembered why she had wrapped up in it. Chill morning air invaded her body's cocoon of heat, raising flocks of goosebumps as she slipped into her gown. After days of wear the gown was stained with food, and the underarms and neckline smelled sour. Aisleen wrinkled her nose in dislike as she struggled with the buttons. She needed a bath and her gown needed washing, but that was not to be accomplished in the company of men.

A few minutes later she slid from the wagon. She saw at once that the drovers had already eaten and that the cleaning up had been left for her, a drudgery the cook particularly enjoyed passing on to her.

She bent and picked up a plate crawling with insects and knocked it against the wagon to dislodge them. The odor of rancid meat invaded her nostrils, and she jerked her head back. Spoiled.

When she had washed and packed the wagon she realized that the cook was nowhere to be found. Too relieved to think much of it, she sat down to enjoy the only part of breakfast she could stomach, a cup of tea.

A moment later the cook turned the corner of the wagon, his face so bright a shade of red that it looked burnt.

Flushing a softer shade of pink, Aisleen rose to her feet. "I've finished the packing."

"Aye, ye do well to be afraid of me." He took a step toward her, but the toe of his boot caught on a stone and he tripped and nearly fell. Swearing freely, he righted himself and pointed an accusing finger in her direction. "Ye keep outta me business or ye'll be sorry ye crossed me. Do ye bloody hear me!"

He was drunk! She was certain even before she spotted the bottle in his hand. Now she had drunkenness to add to the daily trial of journeying with the cook. "If you do not hurry, the others will leave without us," she reminded him.

"Swive the others!" He wheeled away from her and

staggered to the campfire, where he kicked dirt in to smother the flame.

With a resigned sigh, Aisleen drained her cup and put it away. She would not turn to Thomas for help this time. How quickly she had forgotten that she had learned to take care of herself a long time ago. She would manage.

Absently she brushed a lock of hair from her brow. She had forgotten to put on her bonnet, but retrieving it meant unpacking the wagon, and the cook was striding unevenly toward her. The bonnet would have to wait until the next stop. As usual, sheep, men, and dogs had gone on ahead. They would be out of sight for most of the day's journey.

The undulating ridges of the Blue Mountains had been visible from the outskirts of Sydney but had disappeared as they neared them under the covering of tall rose-and-white-trunked eucalyptus trees. Now, as they cleared a rise between the trees, Aisleen saw the dramatic drop-off into the valley below and the mountain ranges beyond.

The grand heights of the mountains rose abruptly as ragged peaks. Unlike the rocky granite mountains of western Cork, here were sudden high plateaus jutting straight up from sheer embankments.

The cook roared epithets and sawed the traces to bring the wagon to a halt. The drumming of hoofbeats came as a relief to Aisleen, for once the cook secured the brake he reached for his whiskey. It took longer for the sound of an approaching rider to penetrate his hazy thoughts, but he quickly tucked the bottle out of sight as Thomas appeared on the road ahead.

An involuntary smile came to Aisleen's lips as she recognized him. He wore a clean blue shirt with sleeves rolled back to reveal tan forearms and opened at the throat on the smooth, sun-browned planes of his upper chest. Though she could not see his eyes because of the shadow cast by the wide brim of his hat, his mouth was widened in a grin that quickened her pulse.

"Thomas!" she cried, standing on the floorboard and waving her arm.

Thomas's grin deepened at this unexpected welcome from his bride. He had kept out of her sight for the last three days to give her a chance to forgive him for his anger and impatience—and because he hoped that she would miss him a little. And so, it seemed, she had.

"Mrs. Gibson!" he greeted with a lift of his hat as he halted on her side of the wagon. "Top of the day to ye!"

"And the rest to you, sir," she answered, acutely aware that her pleasure at seeing him must be plainly visible on her face. She reached up to catch back her wind-tossed hair.

Cook grunted next to her, but she did not glance down.

"Have ye had yer fill of wagons?" Thomas inquired.

"Oh, yes!" she replied quickly.

Thomas reached out a hand to her. "Then come for a gallop, Mrs. Gibson."

Aisleen hesitated. She had never been taught to ride. Cook mumbled again and the chance to escape him, even for a short while, was worth a small risk. "I know nothing of horses," she admitted as she reached for Thomas's hand.

"Then ye must learn, lass. No lass can rightly call herself a squatter's wife until she can ride."

He took her hand and urged his horse closer to the wagon. "Throw a leg over and slide on," he instructed.

"Astride?" she squeaked.

"Coward," he chided as he smiled amusedly at her.

Very uncertainly Aisleen raised her skirts but again hesitated. The horse's rump seemed a very unladylike width to span.

Impatient with her tentative maneuvers, Thomas pulled

sharply on her hand. "Toss a leg over, lass, and be damned to propriety."

She took a deep breath and did as he directed.

"There, ye've done it!" he congratulated as she slid neatly astride and flung her arms about him.

Aisleen squeezed her eyes shut and tightened her grip as the horse danced away from the wagon.

"Pull yer skirts up," Thomas ordered. "He's a bit shy of them."

But Aisleen did not wish to unlock the arms she had wound tightly about his middle. She pressed her perspiring forehead into the valley between his shoulder blades and whispered in a tiny voice, "I can't! Oh! Oh! I don't like this!"

Thomas chuckled. "Very well, I'll be doing the tucking this time, but if ye're to ride with me again, ye must learn to look to yer own."

He gathered up the skirts on first one side and then the other, tucking them back under the anchor of her knees. As he completed the task he decided that perhaps he had spoken too hastily. She had quite nice legs, and any excuse to touch them should not be cast aside.

As the horse walked forward a few steps, Aisleen drew deep breaths to steady her heartbeat. She had not known that she was afraid of riding until this very moment. "It's not so awful," she said, mostly to herself.

"It's the best way a man can travel!"

Without warning, he urged his horse forward with a kick. The horse balked, displeased with Aisleen's extra weight; but Thomas dug his heels in a second time, and the horse moved forward into a gallop that sent them racing down the lane.

Aisleen kneaded handfuls of Thomas's shirtfront, gasping for air as the speed snatched the breath from her. Her heart thundered in her ears to match the horse's hooves as she felt the brawny haunches stretch and bunch under her with the animal's pace. The wind dragged at her skirts, and the action of the horse made her chin collide repeatedly with Thomas's back until she turned her face to one side and pressed a cheek against him.

His skin was warm and damp with perspiration and surprisingly less offensive than her own malodor. The suspicion that he had recently bathed crossed her mind, and she envied him the luxury. Beneath her left palm his heart beat in regular, slow strokes very unlike her rapid pulse. He moved with the horse, his body tensing and untensing in a rhythm that matched the animal's stride, while she bounced about like a poorly tied sack of meal.

Thomas checked his mount suddenly, and the horse danced back on its hind legs, unaccustomed to its master's hard pace.

With a cry of fright, she tightened her hold.

" 'Tis a grand thing, yer embrace," Thomas said huskily, "but, lass, ye're choking the life's breath out of me." He wedged a hand under hers, which were clasped, viselike, about his middle, and pried them apart. "There's naught to fear. Look about."

Aisleen reluctantly opened her eyes, and then they widened and widened. Before her was a breathtaking view of the mountains. Lit by shimmering sunlight, the sandstone summits rose from the pale blue ether which hovered above the deeper cobalt blue of the valley.

"We've begun our crossing."

"But how?" Aisleen voiced in doubt.

"Looks a bit rough," Thomas agreed, "but there's been a road through those mountains for more than thirty years. Thirty men worked six months to carve out a twenty-foot-wide road through seventy miles of those cliffs and chasms. A fair day's work, that."

Aisleen stared at the expanse and shook her head in wonder. "How did they do it?"

"Like many that came before and after, they had no choice." His voice lowered and hardened. "They were guests of His Majesty the English King, in a manner of speaking."

"Convicts," Aisleen said softly, recalling Major Scott's suspicions about Thomas after they had met in the alley on the Sydney wharf. What would he think if she told him of the major's suspicions?

Thomas turned within her embrace, his blue eyes gleaming more brightly than usual. "And were ye nae warned by a mealymouth Sydney lady to keep shy of the lot of them and their offspring?"

"Actually, it was an English major," Aisleen replied and was dismayed to see his lids shutter down over his bright eyes.

Tension stiffened his body, suppressed anger making rigid the wall of muscle she embraced. "Ah, well, I've no liking for the English. And when one wears a bloody red coat, well . . ."

She knew she should not ask, but she could not contain her curiosity. "Why?"

Thomas half-turned in his saddle. "Are ye not Irish, lass? When was that nae enough reason for ye?"

Aisleen pinkened. "Once I was like you, afraid and perhaps harboring hatred for people whom I did not know. But I long ago traded away many childish fancies. The English are among us. We must live with that."

Thomas stared at her a moment longer. He had not listened to her reply but used it as an excuse to hold her attention a little longer. The wind had blown her hair free from its bun, and it trailed down her shoulders in a fiery tangle of sun-spun flame.

Had any other head ever been so bright? he wondered

absently. He reached out to capture in his work-toughened fingers a few strands that clung to her damp cheek. Years of shearing had placed hard calluses over the sensitive nerve endings of his fingertips, but he could feel the resilient strands. They shimmered against his fingertips, softer than the combings of a ewe's underbelly, as fine as a spider's web.

His expression warmed as he looked back up into her eyes. Framed in marigold lashes were flashes of gold in the dark honey of her eyes. His fingers moved gently to her cheek that was liberally sprinkled with golden freckles. The Australian sun had added to them. But the rosy tint outracing his fingertip as it moved up the summit of her cheek was of his making, and it stirred him.

Aisleen held still under his touch. With her hands pressed against his abdomen she detected the sudden intake of his breath as his fingers lingered on her face. She knew she crimsoned, but she could not turn away. The breathless sense of being completely alone crowded out the reality of the day, the air about them, everything but his touch and the wide expanse of Blue Mountain blue that was his eyes.

Wild, exhilarating emotion tugged at her. Restlessness that had lain dormant since the days she ran free and happy on Slieve Host heaved to the fore. She had come to New South Wales a bitter, mistrustful spinster in search of security and self-respect. Now she was the wife of a handsome Irishman with a quick smile, ready wit, and heart-melting charm. Was it possible to trust her good luck?

She trembled on the brink of new knowledge about herself, but she could not push past the cowardice and dissembling of her own conscience. If she forgot herself, she was lost. There was no magic. Oh, but if there were . . .

He broke the spell. "Aisleen, lass, we've a way to go. We'll talk again. Tonight."

She nodded once, afraid to ask him what the subject was to be. She was all too certain that she knew.

She hung on as tightly as before; but as they rode she kept her eyes open, and the enchantment of the day won her over. The road dropped steeply a mile farther on, and in the valley into which they rode she saw a telltale sign of humanity rising from the densely wooded gorge—a thin column of smoke that could only be a campfire.

As they neared, the track they rode merged with another, wider road and she was surprised by the traffic on the broader lane. Several bullock-drawn drays formed a column stretching back down the road. Ahead of them an elegant town carriage, complete with red-enameled rims and spokes, bounced lightly over the wicked ruts. As the carriage sped past she thought she heard the distinctive notes of feminine laughter.

"There'll be fancy doings in the town tonight," Thomas remarked casually. "A good thing I rode in ahead to claim a room."

Aisleen brightened. "Did you say a room?"

"Aye, at the hotel. I do nae want me wife sleeping in a miner's tent."

A hotel in the midst of the wilderness? Aisleen smiled. Tonight she would have her very own bed and a roof over her head. There would be good hot food and water for washing and bathing. Just the thought of soap and water made her skin itch.

To her disappointment, Thomas did not whip up his horse. He slowed it to fall in beside the first of the bullock drays they met at the merge and then struck up a conversation with the driver.

The huge-shouldered beasts were harnessed with wooden collars behind their wide, flat brace of horns. They plodded along in seeming disregard of their master, neither quickening nor slowing their pace though the driver roared invectives at them with regularity.

Aisleen gave the wild-bearded bullocker in the distinctive wide-brimmed hat of the colony a quick look and decided that the animals he drove with the crack of whips and vitriolic shouts and curses were probably more reliable company.

When Thomas finally tossed his hand in farewell and kicked his horse into a canter, she was grateful, for she had learned several things: the pace of bullock drays was tediously slow, the driver's speech was even more alarming than the cook's, and bullocks attracted more flies with their foul smell than horses.

A few minutes later they entered a denser part of the forest, where the sheer number of trees formed a partial shade that was lacking in the less-populated areas of the bush. Suddenly the forest cleared and the road widened into the main street of a small community that teemed with bullock drays, wagons, horsemen, and pedestrians.

Ringing the cleared square was a row of wooden buildings interspersed with daub-and-wattle huts with string-bark roofs. Above each building hung a sign, and she read with amazement "Tobacconist," "Hair Dresser," "Barber/ Surgeon," and several marked "Hotel."

Thomas halted before the two-story building whose sign read "Bullock Hotel." Reaching back, he caught Aisleen by the waist and said, "Slide ye down, lass."

Aisleen dismounted with surprising ease, and then he dismounted after her.

"So, we'll be making a horsewoman of ye yet," he said in approval of her flushed cheeks. "Come in, lass. I've a fine thirst, and ye look like a meal would nae come amiss."

As they entered two gentlemen in frock coats and top hats were deep in argument with the large, aproned man who stood behind the registry desk. Beside the gentlemen two women in enormous crinolines stood fanning themselves against the heat.

"I demand that you make arrangements!" the younger of the two gentlemen said, pounding his fist on the desktop. "We've come forty miles in a single day. The ladies are exhausted from the heat. We'll pay you double what the damned rooms are worth!"

The beefy-faced publican shook his head. "As I've said, gov'ner, there's no rooms to let. Give the last one to a man this morning. Ah, there's the very one."

"G'day, Jeb." Thomas walked up to the desk with a small nod for the two men already standing there and picked up the quill.

"A moment, sir," the young man said as Thomas began to make a mark, and Aisleen saw as he turned that he was quite attractive with his blond mustache and seemingly wealthy, for he wore a pearl stickpin in his cravat.

Thomas turned a pleasant expression to the man, who was taller but slimmer than he. "G'day to ye."

"Is it true that you have a room?" the young man demanded.

Thomas's eyes narrowed at the absence of friendliness in his voice. "Aye, I've a room."

The man smiled, but the expression was too stiff to be pleasant. "I have with me my wife and my in-laws. I'm in need of a room. You do understand, do you not?"

Thomas lifted his hat from his head as he turned to the ladies and nodded smilingly to each. "I can see ye've a fine wife there. So have I. Give yer g'days to the gentleman and his lady wife, Aisleen."

Aisleen caught back her wind-ruffled hair and smiled shyly, acutely embarrassed to have been singled out by her husband's ringing voice. "How do you do?" she said softly.

"A lady!" the older of the two well-dressed women voiced in amazement.

Aisleen did not need their shocked glances to tell her that she was filthy and disheveled, but they added to her discomfort.

"She's a bit road weary but, for all that, she's as pretty a sight as ever I hope to see," Thomas said proudly. "Now I'll be seeing to her proper care."

The younger man took out his wallet, extracted several bills, and waved them under Thomas's nose. "Very well. I've been in the damned colony long enough to understand what is required. Here's five pounds for your trouble. With it I'm certain you will be able to find suitable accommodations elsewhere."

Thomas stared at him without a single glance at the bribe.

The blond man looked disconcerted. "We were told that this is the best hotel for miles about."

"I would nae be at all surprised that ye'll learn that they did nae lie to ye about that fact," Thomas returned smoothly.

The convoluted sentence took the man a moment to untangle and when he had, Thomas had already gained possession of the room key.

"Now wait a moment!" he cried, anger crimsoning his fair skin. "What will it cost me to buy you out? Whatever it is, I'll pay it! And the devil take you damned Irish!"

Aisleen saw Thomas's hand move toward his waistband, and even though she could not quite believe that he intended to pull his pistol, she rushed over and grabbed his wrist in both hands. "Tom, I'm very tired. Can't we go now?"

He angled his head toward her, his eyes strangely dark. "Tom? Please," she begged softly but squeezed his wrist as tightly as she could.

"Aye, aye," Thomas repeated slowly. "We'll be going up now." His arm relaxed back to his side, but Aisleen did not loosen her grip. She tugged on his arm to pull him toward the stairs, giving the two women a brief smile.

Thomas followed her without resistance, but the look in

his eyes made the younger gentleman back away as he passed.

"Ruffian!" the older of the two women called after them. "A lady like her wed to him. You can be certain there's a story of heartbreak for some poor mother in that!"

Aisleen did not care what was said about her, but when she reached the hallway on the second floor, she turned to Thomas and said angrily, "That was uncalled for!"

"I agree entirely," he answered with his usual charming lilt. "The things decent folk must deal with in the bush!"

"You are laughing at me!" she replied, caught between relief and irritation that his anger had passed so quickly.

"Aye, well, better a chuckle than I put a bullet through that English's black heart."

The hair lifted on Aisleen's neck. How casually he spoke of violence. "I do not agree with your decision. I think we should have offered the ladies our room."

The familiar cock of his head told her that her words surprised him. "Now why should ye be wanting to give up the bed yer poor body's yearning for?"

"Because those ladies appear to be, well, less suited to sleeping in tents and wagons than I."

Thomas's lids fluttered down. "If ye believe that they're better than us because they wear a finer cut of cloth, then ye've a thing or two to learn about life in the bush. They'd have taken yer room and told ye that ye did not deserve it, all in the same breath. Ye heard him call me a damned Irishman, and to me face he said it! I'd as soon lay me fist along the side of his head as spit on him!"

Aisleen blushed because he had made his voice deliberately loud and carrying. Defeated, she turned toward the hallway. "Which room is ours?"

Thomas came up beside her, wedging them in the narrow hall. He put a finger under her chin to lift her face to his. "Ye're as good as any of them, better to me mind. Ye'd have given up the room out of the goodness of yer heart when they clearly did not deserve yer consideration. Ye're a grand lass, and I'm a man with a bad temper and an empty stomach. Will ye be forgiving me?''

Aisleen stared up at him because there was nowhere else to look in that moment. It was a pretty speech calculated to gain favor with her, but she could find no fault in the contrivance. He had taken her side, something she could not remember anyone ever doing before in all her life. It was so small a thing, so very simple a pleasure, but it brought tears treacherously close to the surface.

She knew that he would kiss her, and she did not even try to escape. The gentle brush of his lips on hers was more disturbing than she could have imagined. When he moved away and his face came back into focus she remembered his promise that they would discuss the matter between them.

Shaking, she turned away. This was something to guard against, she told herself. She was beginning to like him.

I knew that I had seen, had seen at last
That girl my unremembering nights hold fast
Or else my dreams that fly
If I should rub an eye . . .

> —The Double Vision of Michael Robartes
> W. B. Yeats

Chapter Twelve

Aisleen sat by the window as she pulled a comb through her freshly washed hair. The pure blue of the mountains had intensified as the sun set until, with darkness, it faded into indigo. And with the change her mood had altered, gradually becoming as dark as night.

Gregarious voices, sudden starts of laughter, and the thread of a tune squeezed out of a concertina drifted in from the tavern next door. The bullock drivers had arrived an hour earlier. Thomas was below with them and his drovers, whom she had seen ride in at dusk. His laughter rang out clear and strong above the others, a sound she had heard often this night.

He struck up acquaintances easily, she mused. Why could she not be like him, more at ease with the world and herself? Most often she gave the matter no thought, but tonight, listening to Thomas's laughter magnified her feelings of isolation. She envied those who made him laugh and those who laughed with him.

She would have liked to have gone below, to sit quietly in a corner and listen to his conversation, but she did not have the courage. He found joy in the simplest things, like a ride on horseback. He had made a difficult day easy for her just by entering it. Would he remain nearby this time? Did she want him to?

She set the comb aside and leaned forward to cup her chin in her hands, braced by her elbows on the window-sill. The solitude of the night settled about her like the cool mountain breezes. In all her life she had made no lasting friendships. She was close to no one, had never been more important than necessary to the people in her life.

As a child, whenever loneliness had threatened to over-whelm her, she had escaped in dreams. Now she had a husband and a new life. It was just short of miraculous, and yet she was lonelier than ever before.

She shut her eyes tightly, quite unaware of what she was doing until it was done. *Oh, bouchal, you were right. Adventures are better if they are shared!*

The admission shocked her, and her eyes flew wide. What had she done? Addressing an imaginary playmate of child-hood fancy was preposterous. Was she so frightened of the future that a return to childhood was preferable? Whence had come this melancholy yearning?

Thomas came through the door at that moment, a strange look on his face.

Aisleen rose quickly to her feet, embarrassed to have been found sitting by the window like a neglected waif.

"Will ye nae come below?" he questioned. "There's a lass I want ye to meet."

"A lass?" Aisleen questioned, the image of Sally the barmaid flashing to mind. "What lass?"

A quick grin lifted his features. "Why, the sweet *colleen* who whispers to me in me sad moments. Did I nae tell ye?

I'm in league with the wee folk of the old sod.'' The jest did not elicit the smile he hoped for.

Aisleen's expression stiffened. If there was some woman whispering in his ear, no doubt she was all too human. Perhaps she had shared his company in the tavern. The reason for his laughter took on new, intolerable possibilities. While she sat near weeping for want of his smile he had—had— Humiliation stung her eyes. ''If you must cavort with women, please refrain from doing so in my presence!''

Thomas cocked his head to one side as he surveyed her. Her hair hung free, ringlets climbing her brow and shoulders as it dried. But the lass of the afternoon with rosy-hued cheeks damp with perspiration and dusted with Australian gold was once more hidden behind a reproachful gaze. Why was the elusive woman who lay behind those wary eyes so seldom set free?

''Where's the life in ye, lass?'' he questioned in irritation as she continued to regard him with misgiving. ''So prim and proper ye are, like all the breath and blood's been sucked out of ye. Were ye never a free-running creature, skipping through the bog, dirtying yer face and careless of yer dress because the heart in ye was a beating up so high and hard that ye feared nothing but that the day would end too soon?''

The barb hit too close and Aisleen turned to the window, afraid that he would see her anguish because she was just pondering that very question. Yet her voice betrayed her as she said, ''Yes, once I was very like the picture you paint with words.''

''What happened?'' he asked quietly.

Aisleen shrugged. ''I grew up, as we all must, learned to live as I must.''

He remained serious as he said, ''Ye must take joy in the living. There's no life, no real living, where there's no joy.''

"Is that how you see me, a joyless creature?" she asked a little desperately.

Thomas shifted uncomfortably from one foot to the other. "Maybe ye're just afraid."

"Afraid of what?"

"That's what I ask meself."

"Perhaps your life has been easier than mine," she suggested defensively. "Perhaps you've never been really alone or frightened, never wondered how you would live another minute if you had to endure—"

"If ye had to endure what, lass?" he encouraged softly.

Aisleen shook her head. It hurt too much to remember, even now—perhaps especially now because she felt so fragile. Like a spun-glass ornament, she feared that any sudden shock, a rough touch, and she would splinter into a thousand bright shards.

"Who hurt ye, Aisleen?"

She did not answer; she could not.

Thomas wet his lips. He did not know what to say to her in the serious moments between them. Laughter was easier, but she needed to be drawn out of herself or they would never settle into marriage.

"I believe that ye must have been a wondrous child," he said softly. "Any son of Ireland would be proud to say ye sprung from his loins."

The statement struck Aisleen's ears with stinging irony. "You are wrong," she whispered bitterly. "The man who sired me cursed me from my first breath to his last."

Thomas frowned. "Cursed ye, a bairn as bright and pretty as I'd swear ye were? Why should he be doing that?"

She flinched at the blunt question. Why had she spoken? Why had she not kept the pain buried? "I was not the son he desired nor the dutiful daughter he demanded."

"So, ye were always a contrary thing. I see how a man might grow wearisome of yer tongue were he nae convinced that there was more in ye than prudish airs and great parcels of words."

Aisleen turned to him, stunned. She had been too unwary, too unprepared for the possibility that he would turn her most painful admission into a jest.

Thomas's eyes narrowed at the sight of sick humiliation on her face. "Did ye never forgive him?"

She blinked at him in confusion. "Forgive him?"

"Aye."

She shook her head. "It was not his lack but mine that ruined him."

"How is that possible, with ye a wee bairn and him a grown man?"

Aisleen looked away. She had never told anyone about her feelings for her father. How could she share them with a near stranger? "My father was a dreamer," she said slowly. "He had grand plans for his life, and when they did not come true he could not accept it."

"That's a failing that may be laid at many a man's door," he answered evenly. "I have cursed me lot a time or two and then lived to know the folly of the oath."

"I saw none of his pain and much of his anger," she answered. "We grew poorer every year while my father spent what little there was for bottles of poteen. Things worsened, and he drank even more until even whiskey was not enough; and he turned to madness and magic."

"What magic?"

Aisleen shook her head. She had not meant to say that. "He was a drunkard who began to believe in the whiskey dreams at the bottom of the bottle."

"And ye, lass, what did ye believe in?"

She was silent for a long time before she said, "I have learned to rely only on myself. There is nothing more."

She was half-turned from him, her hands clasped tightly across her middle as if to press out a sudden spasm. In reality she had told him little, but he was not lacking in imagination. The thought of what a lonely child must have endured at the hands of a drunken father made him wince.

Anger pumped suddenly through his veins. He did not know her father, but he would swear to Saint Peter himself that she was guiltless of whatever sin her father had made her feel in his dislike of her.

"My grandma, a grand old lady if there ever was, had a saying for every occasion. I'm reminded of one that goes 'A good man is not without fault and there're two faults in every man.' Yer da drank a bit overmuch and he was a dreamer. For all that, he gave ye life, and at this moment I cannae think too badly of him because of that."

Aisleen looked up, seeking desperately to read his expression. There was no humor there, no half-hidden edge of a smile. Even so, she did not trust the feeling blossoming inside her. For the second time this day he had taken her side. He had complimented her without pity, yet his words left her trembling. Tears tangled in her lashes, distorting her view of him. How pathetic her defenses were against this man. One more word from him, one more kindness, and the years of work to build an impenetrable fortress about the crystalline shell of her heart would collapse at her feet.

Aware of the danger of the moment, if not the reasons for it, Thomas cast about for a safe topic. When his wandering gaze spied the copper tub in a corner of the room, he seized on it gratefully. "Ye've bathed. Now it's me turn."

Aisleen's eyes widened, and then she looked away as he went to pull the tub into the center of the floor. Without waiting for a dismissal, she headed for the door.

"Where're ye going?" he questioned when he noticed.

"Below, to the parlor," she answered and reached for the latch.

"In yer night clothes? I'd like to see that!"

Aisleen halted. She had forgotten that she was dressed for bed.

"*Och,* the water's still warm," he murmured in approval as he put a hand in it. "Won't be needing more."

She turned to suggest that fresh water be brought in any case, but the sight of him stopped her.

He had already pulled his shirt from his britches and unbuttoned it. As she watched, first one bronzed shoulder and then the other appeared as he peeled the shirt back and slipped his arms free. Mesmerized, she saw him reach for his belt buckle. "Stop!" she cried suddenly. "Stop that this minute!"

Thomas looked up in bafflement. "What have I done?"

"You know," she said accusingly. "You know very well it's what you were *about* to do!"

"Bathe?" he asked innocently.

"You were about to—to bare yourself!"

Thomas tried to sober his expression. "The water's cooling. If ye are afraid of offending me modesty then there's nae need. I'll trust ye to be turning yer back, for I cannae wash meself in me britches." Grinning, he loosened his buckle and began unbuttoning his fly.

Aisleen turned away from him and again set her hand on the latch, but it was an empty gesture. She would not leave the room in her bed clothes, and they both knew it. *Very well,* she told herself, struggling for composure. She would remain and keep her dignity.

When she faced about she kept her eyes from straying to where he stood, but from the fringe of her vision she saw the pile of his dirty clothes and mud-caked boots and the governess in her took over. Head erect and spine straight, she crossed over and scooped up the offending items and carried them to the pile of her own gown and boots which lay by the door.

"Why'd ye do that?" he questioned, water splashing as he stepped into the tub.

"These things need washing. The hotel has a laundress who promised to have them ready by morning."

"Ye'll not be giving her me boots!"

"Why not?" She stood them beside the garments. "They need the mud scraped from them, and a shine would not do them any harm."

"They'll nae leave the room and that's an end!"

She swung about at his stubborn tone. "Oh, my!" She had only a swift glimpse, but it was enough to send her rotating back to the door. He stood bare, hairy legs and all, in the basin. And curls—who'd have thought to find curls in such a place!

"Ye promised ye would nae look!"

His tone was reproachful, but she knew that he was amused. "You are a vile, vain creature, Mr. Gibson," she said breathlessly.

"Are we back to that, and here ye were calling me Tom not three hours ago. A woman's a fey creature, for all a man may love her," he said in a wistful tone.

Aisleen took a deep breath and then another. Dignity. She would retain her dignity if it killed her.

Thomas watched her reach for the door handle. What could he say to send her spinning about again?

"I do nae suppose ye would consider staying to scrub me back?"

Sure enough, she stopped short but did not immediately turn back from the door. "Mr. Gibson," she enunciated with extreme care. "I will remain only if you promise not to tease me for the remainder of the evening."

"Fair dinkum." He sat down in the tub and found his knees at eye level. Water sloshed over the sides and ran across the dry planks to disappear into the cracks in between. Sudden misgiving sent his hand diving between his knees and under his left buttock, where he located a slimy semisolid. He dredged up the half-melted cake and sniffed it suspiciously. "Roses," he declared in amazement.

"My attar of roses soap," Aisleen said in dismay as she spun about. "I forgot to fish it out of the tub."

" 'Tis melted," he observed as he squeezed the soggy cake until the oily gel ran between his fingers.

She edged toward him, her hand outstretched but her gaze averted. "Give it to me."

He grinned. "Would ye be denying yer husband the soap with which to scrub the dirt from his weary body?"

She jerked her hand back at the mention of his body.

"I know, lass, I'm uncouth," he said with a gentle chuckle. "Poor wife, ye do have yer trials with the likes of Thomas Gibson. Ye must teach me different."

"I doubt that's possible," she answered shortly, but a smile tugged her mouth.

"*Musha*, if ye did nae think 'twas possible to mend me manners, then why did ye wed me?"

"Oh, do not ask impossible questions!" she answered impatiently and crossed her arms under her bosom, which Thomas could not help observing was a very flattering pose.

"If ye were to teach a man manners, truly, where would ye begin?"

After some thought she answered, "With your speech."

"Well, that's a fine thing," he answered, freely splashing water over the side of the tub as he lathered up. "What's wrong with the lilting voice of the old sod?"

Aisleen side-stepped to the chair by the window and sat down with her back to him. How would she have him sound? Certainly not like Major Scott or like Nicholas Maclean, with his Oxford vowels and London drawl. "I would not change so much how you sound as what you say," she admitted finally.

"Like me calling ye 'lass' and saying how grand I think

ye are, all pleasing and proper in yer starched ruffles? Ye remind me, sitting there, of a wee lass who's waiting to be tucked in for the night.''

The speech made her stomach flutter strangely. ''You've never said anything of the kind to me.''

''Then 'tis an oversight,'' he answered promptly. ''I like the way yer hair shines in the moonlight. And I think it's the greatest kind of sin for ye to hide the glory of it.''

''Now that is an example of what you should not say.''

''Whyever not?''

''It is too familiar.''

''Too familiar?'' His brow furrowed in mystification. ''Cannae a man say what he likes to his wife?''

''Not in polite society,'' she answered, though she could not swear to that statement as truth.

Thomas sniffed the attar of roses lather smeared on his palm, speculating that it must smell even better on Aisleen's warm skin. ''What, then, does a man say to his wife when they're alone?''

''Oh, I do not know,'' she answered irritably. ''Perhaps the weather or the evening meal, what he's heard in the marketplace, or the wife might comment on a book that she read.''

''The weather's been the same four days running,'' he remarked affably as he rested his chin upon his soapy knees. ''We have nae eaten yet. Bullock driver says there's rain in the mountains. What book would that be that ye've been reading, lass?''

Exasperation sighed out of Aisleen. ''You know very well that I have not been reading.''

''Then we've finished our talk.'' His black brows peaked. ''I do nae like polite speech, I'm thinking.''

''Polite conversation takes practice,'' she admitted. ''For instance, if you and I both read the same book then we could discuss it.''

"Nae. I'll not be reading a book."

"Why not? I have several volumes that I think you would find interesting."

"Are there pictures in them?"

"I do have primers, but I think you would prefer Defoe or Swift."

"I might, if I could read them, which I cannae."

"Cannae? Cannot?" Aisleen slued about in her chair. "You cannot read?"

Thomas ducked his head. "No."

The admission surprised her so much Aisleen did not even think of the fact that she was staring at a naked man in a tub. "Why not? Were there no hedge schools near your town?"

"Aye, there was. But me da was a fisherman, and when the catch was good he needed all his hands. A good catch would feed more bellies than all the words in all the books in all the world piled up together, so he often said."

"Perhaps." Aisleen considered her words carefully. "But there are other hungers in a man just as great."

He raised his head, and with a single glance he changed her innocent words into a weapon against her. "That is not what I meant!"

"I know," he replied mournfully. "And more's the pity." He waited the space of three heartbeats before saying, "About us, lass. We're man and wife. 'Tis time we acted the like."

Aisleen's fists clenched in her lap. "We are sharing our first real conversation. I think we were proceeding quite nicely."

"Then ye'd best be thinking again," he muttered. "I'm a man wed, and that gives me certain rights."

"Which you agreed not to lay claim to."

"Never did I!" he answered hotly.

Aisleen closed her eyes. So there it was, plainly said. She

could no longer evade the moment. "I would rather you leave me in peace," she said low. "Yet I have sworn before God to submit to you." She swallowed with difficulty before adding, "I beg you, do not use me as you would your whores!"

The pleading statement should have touched him differently, Thomas suspected, as laughter struggled in his chest for release. His whores! Did she believe him to have been the ram in the paddock before they wed? Poor wee thing. "I will be gentle," he said when he could speak.

"You will be as you must," she said bitterly.

Was he hearing her correctly? Was she agreeing to allow him the right to share her bed?

Aisleen rose to her feet. "Where is your nightshirt? I will fetch it for you."

"Do nae have one," he replied smugly.

She walked over to where her bag stood open and withdrew a garment. "This must do," she said under her breath. She averted her gaze as she approached the tub and held the garment out toward him. "You may wear this."

Thomas looked askance at the flimsy gown edged in lace and pink ribbons. "Lass, ye cannae be serious!"

She dangled the gown before him. "A gentleman would own a nightshirt."

"Never said I was a gentleman," he muttered, his arms folded stubbornly before him.

"A decent man," she countered.

"Ah, well. 'Tis me own experience saying the lasses would nae have their men be decent altogether."

"Do not speak to me of your other conquests. I am your wife!"

His eyes crinkled at the corners. "Then be a wife to me."

"You know what I mean," she said, taking a step back.

"I do and I'm nae liking it," he answered truthfully. "But for all that, I'm not against reason. So I'll put forth a bargain to ye, being that ye're so fond of bargains. I'll cover meself if ye'll come willing to bed as me wife.''

Aisleen blinked. "I—I don't understand.''

"Sure'n ye do, else ye'd not be fluttering them golden lashes at me. Whenever ye're hearing what ye do nae like 'tis always the same. Ye put a butterfly to shame with all that flashing and fluttering.''

Somehow this statement seemed more personal than all the others because he had gained knowledge about her of which she was not aware. She stared at him with enormous eyes, confused and more afraid than any time before. What she feared most was that he would learn all her weaknesses and someday turn them against her. The jumbled feelings stirred by the thought of submitting to him as his wife cavorted in her middle. How had matters come this far from what she hoped for?

"Trust me.''

She blinked. Trust him? Trust the man who had a mistress in Sydney, the man who had taken the cook's part against her, the man who had ravished her? Trust him? She shook her head in bewilderment and turned away.

Thomas watched her crawl into bed and pull the covers up under her chin as a child might. He stood and glared at the feminine nightgown lying by the tub. She could not expect him to wear it. And yet he had promised.

"Promised nae to bare meself,'' he murmured and stepped out of the tub, trailing water. In his bedroll he found a clean shirt and put it on, not at all concerned that it dampened immediately and clung to his wet body.

But when he had fastened the final button he did not move immediately to the bed where Aisleen lay with eyes gleaming darkly in the dim light. He walked over to stand before the window. It was a pleasant night, cool and clear, the kind best spent out of doors.

"Do ye like the stars?'' he asked softly.

"Yes," came her answer, even more softly.

"Took me years of gazing at the night sky to really feel at home here. The first time it happened I knew then I would never go back."

"To Ireland?"

"Aye. A part of me is there and always will be, but a man cannae bring back the past, and that's all it is to me now."

Aisleen turned toward him. In profile he did not seem so daunting a figure. "I cannot return home either. I suppose I knew it when I came, but I did not want to think of it."

"Did ye leave no one behind?"

"Yes."

"A man, perhaps?"

Aisleen's gentle laughter brought a smile to his face. It was nice laughter, like the sound of rain after a long dry season. "Were there so many, lass, that ye find me question impertinent?"

"Oh, don't you see? There were none at all," she replied.

"I find that hard to believe, ye being so fine a lady and all."

"Ladies without dowries or fancy titles are not regarded as eligible marriage goods," she answered drily. "I have neither fortune nor face. As for title, the Fitzgeralds of Liscarrol were well thought of only among their own, and that some while since."

"What did ye say!"

Thomas's startled tone made Aisleen jump. "About my family? It should be no surprise to you to hear my name."

"Ye mentioned a place," Thomas said cautiously.

"Liscarrol?" Aisleen bit her lip. "You've heard of it?"

"Aye." The syllable gave nothing away.

Aisleen cringed inside. He was only a little older than she. If he was from Cork he might know about her father, might even have met him. "Are you a Corkman?"

"Aye."

Again the avowal that said less than it might. She began to tremble. "You know of Liscarrol. Did you know the owner?"

"No, not the owner," Thomas said and suddenly turned toward her. "I no longer want to talk of the past. We're here, and that's all that matters." He moved toward the bed. "Ye're a Gibson now and 'tis past time ye remembered it."

The light floral scent of roses hung in the air as he approached the bed. Thomas grinned, wondering if he or Aisleen was the cause of the fragrant night. Like the bed in Sydney, this one was narrow with scarcely enough room for one. With Aisleen there . . .

The desire he had kept deeply buried during their journey swelled in release. It was not his wedding night, yet it may as well have been, for his foggy recollections of the other grew dimmer with each recall. Soon he would learn in passionate detail all that he could not remember. The size of the bed did not matter. Their mating needed only the width of one body.

Aisleen held her breath as he bent a knee upon the mattress. She had agreed. This was God's plan. Why did it terrify her so?

Thomas pulled the sheet free of her nerveless fingers. "Do nae fear nae," he said softly, reaching down to touch the pale oval of her face. "I'll not hurt ye this time. Ye'll see for yerself, lass. 'Tis meant to be a pleasuring for man and wife."

As he bent to her Aisleen caught sight of the strain of passion in his expression, tightening the skin until the bones of his handsome face were starkly outlined beneath. Strange wingbeats fluttered in her middle as his face neared, and she shut her eyes to the emotion too strong to be borne.

His mouth did not engulf hers as it had the first night. They met, touched, and then parted. The flicker of his tongue against her lower lip made her gasp, and he stretched his smile over the contours of her mouth as he kissed her again.

"I do love kissing, lass, and ye do it so well."

"I do not," she murmured truthfully.

"Then ye must learn."

He caught her by the shoulders and lifted her up until she lay slanted across his lap, her head resting in the crook of his arm. Laying a forefinger against her lower lip, he tugged. "Ye've a sweet, soft mouth, lass, but ye prim it like ye expect a dose of cod-liver oil when I kiss ye. Will ye nae smile for me?"

She stared solemnly up at him, too wary of the potency of the smile he favored her with to return one of her own.

"So proud and proper," he chided gently and bent his head once more.

His lips brushed lightly across hers, the gentle abrasion tickling until Aisleen smiled in spite of herself. Again and again, he moved his head back and forth, the firm arch of his lower lip gliding along the softer curve of her own. When he paused, it was to press the full impression of his mouth upon her own. She did not resist for, she realized in amazement, she wanted his kiss. In fact, she quite liked the kissing. The giddy, light-as-a-feather swimming in her head was perfect company for the swift-as-a-hare pounding of her heart.

When Thomas lifted his head there was happy puzzlement on his face. She was not cold after all. Encouraged, he kissed her more urgently, plying his tongue in the trough between her lips in hopes of tasting more of her.

Without quite meaning to, she conceded to his voiceless command, softening and then tentatively parting her lips for the subtle but powerful quest of his tongue. He touched her with the tip, stroking the roof of her mouth. In and out his tongue stroked, skimming the secret moistness behind her lips, licking up her taste.

A chiming tension in her chest so at odds with the spreading languor of the lower half of her body pulled taut the rope of indecision stretched across her thoughts. If it were this and only this, she could give up to the pleasure of his touch.

But it is more than pleasure, her secret self crooned against the regular chiming that was her heartbeat. *You wish it to be more. You must take care!*

"No!" Aisleen grabbed the wrist of the hand that sought the shape of her breast through the bed linen.

"No?" he questioned in a passion-muddled voice.

"You mustn't," she whispered, dry-voiced. "I will not be handled like a whore."

Thomas tensed. Her kisses had drugged him into believing that she, too, was welcoming the tide of passion surging up inside him. "A gentling touch only."

"I am no dumb animal! Do what you must, but do not expect me to be grateful to you for the taking of what I would not willingly give!" Aisleen scarcely recognized the speech as her own. Dear Lord! That waspish shrew could not be she.

But it was. Thomas had withdrawn from her and from the bed. When she dared to open her eyes he was standing above her, his face lost in shadow, but his voice was clear enough.

"Ye promised," he said accusingly, but in that accusation was the lament of a joy snatched away. "Ye are me wife!" It was the only answer left him, and he used it as a shield against his wounded pride.

Aisleen did not utter a sound, only turned her head away and closed her eyes. She did not move away as the sheet was lifted back, nor when she felt the hot, hard length of him slide down beside her. She only whimpered once, when he reached for the hem of her gown, skimming it upward over her knees toward her thighs.

"What?" he barked, thwarted desire turning to anger.

"The candle. Please," she whispered so softly that she thought he would not hear her. But he did. Reaching up, he snuffed it between thumb and forefinger before he moved to lie over her.

She wanted to lie still, to submit without opposition, but she could not bear his touch upon her naked skin. When his palm slid up over her thigh she again caught his wrist in both hands. "Don't touch me!"

"But I must—" Thomas began, only to realize that he was near bursting with need of her. No, he did not need to touch her or even kiss her for his own body's arousal. A few kisses had been enough, more than enough, stimulation for a man who had been waiting a week to reclaim his bride. But it would be hard for her if she did not want him. "For yer need—"

"For my need you would cease altogether!" she cried. "Please!"

The pitiful cry was too much even for his passion. Thomas jerked his hand from her hip and flopped across the bed onto his back. "Bloody hell! I'm no monster!"

Aisleen stared wide-eyed but utterly exhausted as she lay beside him. She had won. Yet she was inconsolably miserable. What she had wanted was for him to be kind to her, to make her smile. Now they were both miserable.

A dry sob racked her, and then another and another until she could scarcely catch her breath. Finally tears brimmed and coursed, running downward into her ears and onto his chest.

Thomas touched the droplet of water that fell upon his chest. "Do nae cry!" he roared.

Aisleen sat up, but Thomas caught her by the elbows and

roughly pulled her back down beside him. "Ye're me wife and ye'll sleep by me! That's little enough to ask!"

Too drained to protest, she lay meekly still, her tears suddenly gone. But the place where her heart should be ached as though the organ had been torn out by its roots.

Aisleen sat on the hard wooden chair staring vacantly out into the impenetrable darkness long past the last shout, and last bang of the door, and last tinkle of glass below in the tavern.

Behind her Thomas sprawled in sleep, completely filling the narrow bed with his heavy frame. Once in a while she heard a low, sonorous breath of deep sleep that bordered on a snore but failed.

What will I do? The question hung unanswered in her mind. The revelation that had come to her as she lay wide-eyed beside her husband was that this was how her life would be from now on, for the rest of their lives, until one of them died. How was she to endure it?

You've been defeated, my girl, she thought sadly. She would lie beside him but spurn his advances until he grew tired of her or she gave up the struggle. Either way, she was lost . . . because he did not and never would love her.

The answer was so simple she did not know why she had not discovered the source of her fear much sooner. From the first she had been attracted to him. The first sight of him had been like gazing on a glorious sunset or a magnificent oak, or the face of a man she could love.

But what was she to him? She was chattel, no better than his horse or sheep or shirt: there when he had a need for her, but uncherished and unmourned in his absence.

The sharp pain of loneliness knifed down between her

ribs and she bent forward, covering her eyes with her hands, and wept.

Colleen?

The whispering of the wind across the treetops was louder than the voice, but Aisleen stilled, tears still seeping between her fingers.

Colleen?

She held her breath, waiting for the moment to pass. It was not possible. After all these years, it was not possible.

Colleen?

The third sigh of her name contained within it a heartbeat, and Aisleen jerked her hands away from her eyes.

In the yard below the faint glimmer of a white shirtfront was visible under the ebon shadow of a tree. A breeze brushed past her cheek, carrying in it the scent of roses. And then he was close beside her, so close she could feel the life breath of him warming the night air.

She did not realize when she gained her feet or even when she left the room, tripping down the stairs in only her nightgown. But suddenly dew pearled her bare feet as she hurried toward the spectral shadow.

At first she thought he had disappeared, the glowing white lost in the violet shadings of night. But then the blackest shadow moved, the shape of a man separating from the ethereal opacity of darkness.

"*Bouchal?*" Aisleen questioned softly.

He paused, an alert silhouette.

Neither moved, each frozen in uncertainty. She thought he quickened first, but perhaps it was she. Suddenly she was in his arms, the arms of safekeeping.

Thomas awakened to the strange sensation of soft, cool lips plying his. One moment he held the soft, warm, womanly body of his wife in his arms. The next his eyes were open, and he knew he slept alone.

She stood by the window, a tensely erect figure staring out into the night.

"Aisleen?"

She did not move.

"Aisleen!" he called more sharply.

She jerked at the sound and then swayed as though she would swoon.

The clear, pure scent of roses, sharper than even the soap fragrance, enveloped him as he leapt from the bed to catch her. She did not quite collapse but rather leaned her weight fully against him as he embraced her, so that the swollen buds of her nipples thrust against his bare chest and the soft curve of her belly hugged his bare loins.

"It's all right, lass," he crooned into her ear. "Whatever it is, 'tis all right." He did not know why he said that, for he did not know what she thought or felt, only that she trembled as though emotion too big for her body sought release. He adjusted her in his arms, one hand going to the small of her back to press her lightly against him, the other bracing the width of her shoulders.

Aisleen squeezed her eyes tightly shut, not wanting to allow Thomas in but unable to deny the harder, rougher embrace that had replaced . . .

She raised her head and craned it around toward the window. Nothing, no one stood in the shadow of the tree below. It was gone. A dream. With a sigh of defeat, she sagged bonelessly against him.

Thomas scooped her up and carried her back to bed. She was cold to the touch, her skin chilled. He briskly rubbed her hands between his rough palms and then tucked her beneath the bedding, adding the warmth of his kiss to her unresponsive lips.

The sweet aching that had begun with another's kiss

lurked just under her skin, the careless brush of a finger enough to ignite it. It was the source of her body's betrayal during the dark hours of their wedding night. She could feel again the strummed vibrations of her wanton nature as her husband's hand moved up under her gown to the sensitive skin of her inner thigh. A deep moan of pleasure shuddered past her lips.

Thomas's self-discipline broke. He had to have her. She was his wife. He would take her gently, gently . . . if he could.

He climbed into the bed, lifting her gown up to bare her hips. Lush skin trembled under his touch, the subtle curve of her belly a tender swelling that he could not resist kissing. The sweet steam of her body filled his senses with attar of roses, fragrant musk, and woodland mosses. The taste of tears and sweat and salt became the sea, the sea that he knew from childhood. Desire twisted down tighter in his loins.

He moved quickly over her, prying her reluctant limbs apart with a firm but cautious hand. When he knelt between her thighs, a fleeting feeling of anxiety spun through him. The first time the amorous intoxication of rum had made him too eager. This time he would go slowly, gently, and pray that she would in some measure understand the gesture.

Aisleen clawed the bed as he entered her, the slow penetration more a torment than a torture. She knew the exact moment when her body relaxed enough to accommodate him. This was not invasion but a filling of the sweetly swollen center of her, a hidden void she had never before suspected.

Nails digging deeper into the tick, she bit her lip to keep from answering with loud cries of pleasure his deep, hard, slow thrusts. The instinctive need of her body to rise and meet him answered them instead.

Perspiration broke from their bodies, bathing them in the

slick wash of the emotional tsunami which he rode gratefully and she struggled to comprehend.

The cresting came too soon for both, but they rode together the bursting, foaming wave of desire.

Later, when he found the strength to move, he pulled her close and tucked her tenderly to him.

Thomas lay for a long time watching the indistinct silhouette of her face until he was certain she slept. When satisfied, he rose and went to the window to look out.

The night was still, the faint whispering of leaves in the eddy of mountain breezes the only sound and movement beyond the window.

Give to these children, new from the world,
. . . .
Rest far from men.

—A Faery Song
W. B. Yeats

Chapter Thirteen

Aisleen wiped the perspiration from her face, lifting aside the veil she had adopted to keep her face from becoming more sunburned. Ahead the drovers had brought the sheep to a halt when on the road beyond an argument had erupted. Beside her the cook sawed on the traces as the pair of bullocks who now drew their wagon bawled in protest and lumbered to a stop. Stock whip still in hand, the cook jumped down from the wagon and ran toward the fray.

She did not watch. During the morning there had been innumerable arguments among the travelers over the right of way on the mountain road. After the first few she realized that the frays ended as quickly as they began.

The general profanity of the argument subsided quickly as Aisleen gazed about. Over the last few days she had become inured to the crudities and blasphemies of the men among whom she lived, but she had not grown accustomed to the

startling beauty and breath-arresting sights of the Blue
Mountains.

In the beginning she had been amazed by the number of
people and vehicles traveling west. They had been alone
during the first leg of their journey from Sydney. Now that
they had reached the mountains they were frequently over-
taken by wagonettes full of waving children and grim-faced
parents, horsemen in expensively cut coats and finely tooled
boots, and itinerant workers on foot. Once an overland
coach had rumbled past, its passengers hanging on for fear
of their lives. One and all, the cook had informed her in one
of his rare moments of speech, they were headed for the
goldfields, with names like Blackman's Creek, Ophir, Hill
End, and Mookerawa, which lay west of the mountains.

The road was far from the fine highway she had expected.
The narrow passage through the towering peaks was often
harrowingly steep. Once they lost half a dozen sheep when a
sudden noise sent them stampeding over the edge of a sharp
turn in the road.

In reality the mountains were not blue at all. The vertical
cliffs that seemed at times to run straight to the sky were
sand-colored sandwiches of stone streaked rust-red or impurpled
brown. A blue haze rose from the thickly wooded bush of
the lower elevations. The oily green fragrance had been
pleasant at first, but after a few hours she began to feel as
though she were trapped inside a closet pomander. Today
the strong aromatic odor hung heavily in the air above the
canyons. Nearby the strange laughter from what the drovers
called "bleedin' kookaburra birds" could be heard in the
underbrush.

"G'day, lass."

Aisleen nodded shyly and stared ahead as Thomas stopped
beside the wagon. Since they had left the community at the
base of the mountains, they had not exchanged more than a
dozen words. She slept alone in the back of the cook

wagon, while he spent his nights with the drovers. Nothing seemed changed.

Yet everything had changed inside her. She could not look at him now without the desire to be truly loved by him rising uppermost in her mind. The knowledge left her profoundly shaken and more wary than ever before. He could not know of her feelings, yet she knew that he sensed a difference in her. There was an enigmatic question in his gaze. It was not lust or impatience or cockiness, but a quixotic question which she could not decipher.

"We're coming out of the worst of it," he offered with a ghost of his old smile. He looked distinctly uncomfortable as he said, "Would ye care to ride a bit?"

Aisleen nodded again, and the brilliant smile that she received in reward set her heart knocking against her ribs. The strength of her reaction embarrassed her. She was truly and thoroughly distracted to react so to his pleasure.

He moved his horse alongside the seat and reached for her hand to guide her. She slipped easily onto the horse's broad flanks and, without any encouragement from him, adjusted her skirts.

"Ye're nae afraid this time," he commented over his shoulder. " 'Tis good to know ye trust me."

It was a simple statement, but she realized the truth of it as he turned his horse and sent them cantering down the road. She *did* trust him about many things. It was herself that she had begun to doubt.

They did not travel far before Thomas slowed and turned his horse off the highway and down into a shallow gully. At once they were plunged into the shadows of the surrounding forest. Sunlight filtered through the leaves of spindly, pale-limbed trees and became a pale green opaline haze illuminating the underbrush.

"I've something to show ye that I discovered the last time

through,'' he said. "For meself, I cannae think of a more pleasant way to spend any part of a day.''

He reached back to pat his saddlebag and instead found the shapely thigh of his wife under his hand. He felt her stiffen but thought better of apologizing. "Ye're tempting, lass, and more tender than the gentlest lamb, I'd be swearing, but 'twas a joint of mutton I was reaching for.'' Reluctantly he moved his hand past her thigh to the leather pouch.

Aisleen said nothing. She could not think of a thing to say with the impression of his hand still tingling warmly on her skin. Why did she feel so giddy, so near laughter?

I am growing quite dizzy with the heat, she told herself, but that was not the truth. The shaded canyon was much cooler than the sunlit road. It was Thomas and his carefree manner that made her want to smile.

"Do ye like adventures?'' he questioned as they picked a path through the strange forest.

"I do,'' she admitted. "Are we to have an adventure?''

The disarming question made Thomas reach down and place a hand over her laced fingers splayed across his stomach. "As much as ye'd like.''

A burst of clear, sweet music from the forest redirected Aisleen's attention from his hand. "What was that?''

"A magpie most likely,'' he answered, idly brushing his thumb back and forth across the back of her hand. "Keep watch in the lower branches, and ye may be surprised.''

"What sort of surprise?'' she asked, remembering the dark eyes along the Parramatta River.

"Are ye afraid of the forest? Or is it only creatures with bright eyes in the dark that ye're afeared of?'' he suggested with laughter.

"I made a fool of myself, falling in the river.''

"Did ye think so, lass? I'd never have thought that, what with ye so angry with me method of saving ye.''

"I was ungrateful. I apologize."

He turned in the saddle to look at her. "Did I hear ye right?"

Caught unprepared for the brilliance of his smile, she heard an unusual huskiness in her voice. "I apologize for shouting at you. Thank you for saving my life."

"*Musha!* I never expected anything so surprising as that!"

In the face of his teasing she grew more ashamed than ever. She had been thoroughly churlish about the incident. "I am sorry," she murmured.

"No more, lass! Ye'll have me believing that I've tamed yer temper with no more than a ride through the woods." He winked at her and turned around.

Contented to allow him the last word, she turned her attention to the forest once again. The day was far from silent. The chirping of unseen insects, the strange dialects of unknown birds, and the soft squelch of the horse's hooves all reverberated under the high roofing of the forest. After a few minutes a bright shaft of sunlight appeared between the rows of tree trunks, and Thomas urged their horse in that direction. All at once they were thrust back into the sunlight and into a scene of wild, exotic beauty that was set between the steep walls of a red stone canyon.

Ropy vines high in the pale branches of the eucalyptus bound together the boughs which overhung the clearing. Huge ferns grew like trees on thick trunks while their lazy cousins matted the canyon floor and framed the branches of brilliant orchids wedged in the half-shadows of sprawling tree roots. Other trees thrust spikes of pink blossoms above the crowns of their branches. Tumbled canyon outcroppings formed a colorful backdrop for the great sprays of yellow blossoms rising from the slender, pendant leaves of trees the drovers called wattles. Even the deepest underbrush was faint green and flower-tinted.

Thomas dismounted by lifting his leg over the horse's head. Smiling, he reached for her.

For an instant he held her suspended, and the grin on his face told her that he was well pleased with his display of strength and her acceptance of his help. And then her feet touched the ground and his hands left her waist. He had done nothing more than was courteous and acceptable, yet she understood his purpose. He enjoyed touching her and wanted to continue to do so. She turned away, her breath hemmed in by disquiet that was not displeasure.

"Mind yer step," he cautioned. "Ground's uneven."

Aisleen slipped her hand into the one he extended and followed his lead as he lifted back a branch to allow them to pass. It was more quiet in the sun than in the forest, and gradually a merry tinkling made itself heard.

"There's water here!" Aisleen said as she looked up from concentrating on the path.

"Aye." He pointed ahead.

For a moment it was hidden by sunlight, so bright all else receded into optical shadows. Then she realized the source of the silver-bright flash. Forty feet above, a single silver-tinseled stream of water broke from a crevice in the canyon lip. Turning, twisting, tripping like precious molten metal, it fell into a pool between the rocks, which swallowed it in a gurgling hiss.

"A waterfall!" She approached the shallow, crystalline pool showing mossy pebbles at its heart. Seeking ever lower ground, the pool spilled over at one end and dashed over tumbled rocks and disappeared.

Kneeling on a rock, she dipped a hand in and brought a palmful of water to her lips. The bracingly cold drink tingled her teeth. When she was done she pressed her cool hand to her brow and then to each cheek.

"Too bad ye cannae enjoy yerself properly," Thomas said as he stood beside her.

She looked up at him. "Why not?"

"Well, first ye would be needing to set aside yer bonnet."

She reached up, untied the bow under her chin, and removed her bonnet.

"And slippers—though being a proper lady, ye may nae wish to pad about in the mountains without yer brogans."

She thought only a moment before sitting back on the flat surface of the rock and lifting her skirts to reach the lacing of her boots.

"Allow me," he offered and bent on one knee. His fingers skillfully plucked the laces, and then he lifted one foot to slip the boot free. "*Musha!* Ye've a wee foot and, what's more, ye've deceived me!" He held up the narrow, high-heeled boot and measured the two-inch heel with his fingers. There was a fierce scowl on his face as he looked up at her. "Ye're nae so tall as I believed!"

Aisleen pinkened. "It is the style at home."

"Aye, well," he grumbled as if resisting her attempt to mollify him. He slipped the second boot off and laid it beside the first. "A pity ye're so proper. There's nothing to compare on a warm day with paddling about in a stream."

Aisleen studied the tips of her black cotton stockings for, as she expected, there was a glittering in his eyes when she met his blue gaze again. As she bent to reach under her skirts his hand was there first, resting lightly on her knee. "I can do it myself," she said quickly.

"Aye, but ye'd nae get half the pleasure from it that I will," he answered in a voice that made her wish she had remained on the wagon seat beside the cook.

His touch was feather light as it rose above her cotton-clad knee, making all the more startling the moment when his fingers found the defenseless line of her garter and the warm, sensitive skin of her thigh. Her eyes widened before the blue stare that she could not look away from.

Slowly he slid a finger along the rolled cotton until he

found the knot. It came free with surprising ease. The lightly abrasive palm of his hand followed the natural descent of the stocking, molding the smooth curve of her knee as she held her breath against the sensation. She jumped as his hand slipped around behind to the warm moistness at the back of her knee but sat mesmerized by his touch as his hand rode the elegant swell of her calf to the trim curve of her ankle.

"One," he said, grinning wickedly as he held up his trophy.

"One is quite enough," she answered, but his hand was already gliding back under her skirts, reaching for the top of the second stocking; and then it, too, was peeled away at his leisure.

She heard in acute embarrassment a soft sound escape her as he paused to stroke the inside of her knee.

"Soft, so soft and tender," Thomas murmured. It was meant to be a test of her trust, not his command of himself. Yet his loins had tightened in anticipation as he explored her satin-smooth thigh. If only she would allow him to *see* a little of what he had touched a few nights before.

He rose quickly to his feet and turned away. "Now ye can enjoy the best that this place has to offer," he said over his shoulder and bent to begin pulling off his boots. He had not expected to react so quickly to the simple touch.

Aisleen sat a moment in agitated silence. She should not have permitted him to touch her. Somehow the moment had gotten past her and regretting it now seemed the height of futility. Her knees trembled beneath her gown, resonating from the strum of his fingers, and she wondered how long the sensation would persist.

Thomas drew his socks off and then reached up to unbutton his shirt. *Don't think about her soft-as-butter skin*, he told himself. *Just be glad that she did nae smother ye in a great pile of disapproving words.*

He did not approach her when he had drawn his shirt off. He knew how that would end. He hung his shirt on a branch and then found a large rock on which to sit a few yards away from the pool. Stretching his legs out before him, he folded his arms behind his head and reclined in the bright sun.

Surprised by his continued silence, Aisleen looked back over her shoulder. He lay among the ferns, his chest all sleek muscle and contoured bone. Black hair skimmed the bridge of his sternum and fanned out in delicate whorls to encircle his nipples.

She yanked her gaze away, a rush of blood stinging her neck and ears. She should be furious with him for flaunting himself. And yet annoyance and anxiety were not enough to keep her treacherous gaze from shifting sideways once more.

Yes, indeed, the flat, pinky-brown circles were masculine nipples. Her lids shuttered down. She had never before thought about a man's body. In fact, she was deplorably ignorant of human bodies, both male and female.

Her lashes fluttered as if under uncertain command and then parted. The faint gleam of sweat polished the narrow shallows between his ribs. Salty droplets snaked over the edge of his rib cage and into the hollow of his belly, gathering in a shallow, tremulous puddle that rode the ebb and flow of his breath.

The day was suddenly unaccountably warm. She curled a finger into the collar of her gown, seeking a cool breeze to brush her skin. Unconsciously she licked the perspiration from her upper lip. And then, when she had turned away from him, she loosened the first two buttons of her bodice.

Behind a forest of black lashes Thomas surveyed his red-haired wife. She was every bit as fascinating to him as he was to her. The bun she wore had slipped sideways. Poorly anchored strands buffeted up by the breeze danced and flashed and flickered against the rich cream of her neck. Watching the tip of her tongue peek through again to trace the arch of her upper lip, he imagined the feel of that luscious pink tip upon his hot skin. Doing so changed the profile of his moleskin britches.

When she turned away, the clean curve of her cheek, the smooth line of her jaw, and the intricate whorl of an earlobe were exposed for his view. He remembered the feel of her in his arms. He had been able to think of little else. Dozens of intriguing questions buzzed in his thoughts. Was she pink and cream all over? Did thin blue veins lace the globes of her breasts? Were her nipples coral or pink or berry red like strawberries?

He watched the gentle arch of her spine as she bent to trail a finger in the water, and desire dragged at the back of his throat. What he needed to slake his thirst she would not offer him. Not yet. "Will ye wade about?"

Aisleen smiled. The thought had been strongly in her mind. "Do you think I should?"

"Aye," he answered warmly. "Mind yer skirts, now."

Aisleen stood and, as she had done so often as a child, bent over and caught the back hem of her skirt and pulled it forward between her legs. When she brought it up and tucked it into her waistband the action pulled her skirts up above her knees.

"Oh!" The water was incredibly cold, stinging her ankles. Smooth stones shifted beneath her weight. She flung out her arms to keep her balance and teetered dangerously as another yip of alarm squeaked out of her.

Thomas opened his lids a slit.

The stones settled as she took a few careful steps. It had been so long since she had experienced the simple pleasure that she was determined not to lose the moment. Gradually she learned to keep her balance in the clear rush of the stream. Once she became accustomed to the bracing chill, she waded toward the foaming hiss of the waterfall.

Enjoy yerself, wife, Thomas thought, and closed his eyes.

The gurgling water seemed inordinately cheerful, as if nature herself were pleased by the day, and Aisleen found herself smiling for no reason at all. Cold tingled her feet and legs while the heat of the sun warmed her head. The contrary sensations met in her senses as a glorious collision of pure enjoyment.

She lost all sense of time; but when she finally waded back to shore, she saw that Thomas had laid out the meal from his saddlebag on a rock. He said nothing, but because he was watching her, she pulled free the tucked edge and her skirts fell, petticoats clinging to her wet legs.

"Ye've never been more pleasant to look upon, and for the life of me I cannae think why ye should deny the world the simple joy of it," he remarked with a grin.

"The joy of what?"

"Yer smile, lass. Ye're stingier with them than O'Flaherty was with his hens."

Aisleen came toward him on bare feet. "Who was Mr. O'Flaherty?"

"Ah, lass, now that's a tale worth telling." He pushed a wedge of cheese toward her and then reclined on an elbow, his legs stretched out. "O'Flaherty was the proudest man in five counties, that's who he was. Proudest of all he was of his hens. Why, he built them a coop on the side of his cottage when everyone else said it was best to let them roost in the eaves. But being a careful and prudent man, and times being what they were, and that before the famine . . ."

He paused, his eyes growing darker for an instant. "Ah, well, that's a different tale entirely. Eat."

Aisleen bit into the wedge of white cheese and was pleased to find the taste sharp but not unpleasant. She looked across at him. "Will you not finish the tale?"

He did not answer immediately, and after a moment she decided that he would not answer at all. But she was curious about him, and the camaraderie between them made it impossible to keep her curiosity contained. "What brought you out to New South Wales?"

Thomas reached for a bit of cheese and popped it into his mouth. "The answer may not please ye."

She looked away. "I did not mean to pry."

"Nae, lass, ye've every right to ask the question," he answered, but she noted the reluctance in his voice.

"Did the potato blight send you abroad?"

"Nae, I was gone a year and more before the beginning of the great famine, though, strike me, if I could have seen me leaving as a blessing at the time."

"How did your family fare?"

"I'm the last of me line," Thomas answered, the implication clear in his bitter tone. "I was the eldest, there being Katie and Maggie, Mary and Sinead all younger than me. Was some years before I heard that they'd perished, whether from starvation or pestilence I'll never know."

"And your parents?" Aisleen asked quietly.

"Broken hearts and a weariness of life have put many under," he answered.

Aisleen waited, but he seemed content to say nothing more; and she was too uncertain of him to ask further questions. When he offered it, she accepted the piece of damper covered with a slice of lamb. The taste of curry was new to her, but she was learning to appreciate the power of the spices the cook doused upon every morsel of meat a few days after the slaughtering of a lamb. It nearly masked the faintly rancid taste of the meat. They ate in companionable silence.

"So tell me about yer illustrious self," Thomas ventured when he had finished his meal. "I did nae think to wed the bloodline of gentry."

Aisleen looked up. It was there in his eyes again, the strange quizzing look that was too subtle to give a name. She had told him much. Did she dare share more? "We were once more than gentry. We were royal. Our blood's mixed with kings and tanists. Legend says there's the blood of the *Ard Righ* in our veins."

"*Wirra!* A man stands himself in great company to be counting himself among yer acquaintances."

She knew that he teased her and she did not mind. "Come, sir, you must have inherited so glib a tongue. Is there not a druid or perhaps a bard among your ancestors?"

His smile was full of secret humor. "I'd be lying were I to say different. But I'll not shame me forefathers by calling them as witnesses to me worth. Yet we were speaking of ye. Were ye a wee solemn thing as a child, all starched petticoats and lace and ruffles?"

Aisleen smiled. "I was the rarest sort of hooligan, if the truth were known."

"*Musha!* I cannae believed it. With a smudge of dirt on yer nose?" Aisleen nodded. "And a tear in yer best Sunday gown? Faith! Ye've destroyed entirely me image of ye." He leaned forward on his elbow to add in a whisper, "And glad I am to hear it, for I want me daughters to feel the heart that's beating in them."

Aisleen's smile wavered. His daughters. *Her* daughters.

Thomas saw the guarded look come into her face but continued. "Since the good Lord in His most mysterious of ways saw fit to spare me, I cannae keep from thinking that perhaps there was a purpose in that."

Aisleen watched him. "Do you not feel guilty that you lived while your family died?"

"Aye, there was a time when I hated meself thoroughly. But man is a curious creature. He can only hate himself so long. 'Twas me own fault I was not in Ireland to die with the rest of them. To me own way of thinking, the least selfish thing I can do for Da and Ma and the lasses is to live to bring honor to the family name."

Aisleen caught her lower lip between her teeth. "I failed even that."

"What is that?"

She shook her head. "You wouldn't understand."

"Perhaps I understand more than ye think," he answered with a knowing gaze. "Yer da was a miserable excuse of a man who tried to shift the blame for his own failure onto the frail shoulders of his wee daughter. 'Tis no reason for ye to blame yerself."

"What if the responsibility were greater; what if through no fault of mine my family looked to me to save and protect them?"

Thomas was quiet a long time. "What way could ye, a bairn, save them?"

Aisleen shook her head. As before, he had drawn out of her more than she meant to admit. "A foolish legend, that's all it was. In any case, it does not matter now. I've lost everything."

"All life is a struggle, lass. Did they not teach ye that in yer great schools of learning?"

"Aye," she answered. "They taught me to live on my own, to rely on no one, that recklessness brings punishment, and that being Irish is a curse that no amount of blessing will ever completely cure."

"Ah, well, 'tis glad I am to hear it that the English set so great a store by yer heritage," he answered sourly. "And when they were drumming into yer head these right and morally uplifting thoughts, did they tell ye also that when a thing is lost 'tis often only in the knowing how to look that a man can recover the loss?"

Aisleen gave him a quick glance, expecting his smile of amusement to be in place. But it was not. His face was solemn. "Some things cannot be recaptured," she said.

"What is it ye would have that ye've lost?"

Aisleen gazed at his handsome face, wondering why he could not read in her own face the desperate answer. "Perhaps," she said very softly, "it is a matter of never having had it at all."

He looked at her, and the world grew still, hushed. The breathless moment continued as if all life, even the breeze, had ceased outside his glance. "It's in the knowing how to look. Let me show ye."

The firm clasp of his fingers over hers brought Aisleen the first pang of misgiving, but she did not want to pull away from his touch. She wanted to trust him, wanted more than anything to believe that what she dared hope for was possible. But if it weren't—oh, if it weren't—then she would be utterly destroyed.

Thomas watched the shift of emotions across her face: the wariness, anticipation, reluctance, expectation, and then the tremulous hope that flickered unstably.

"Ye can make real whatever ye desire," he said. "If only ye believe."

Aisleen could not answer him. Too many unspoken desires stood on the precipice of her hopes and dreams. She prayed, *Let it be enough, now, this moment. Let me ask for no more than this.*

Wordlessly she watched him push aside the remains of their meal with a hand and then spread his shirt on the rock. Then he turned to her, his eyes a deeper blue than the sky, and he pulled her down beside him as he reclined on the shirt. He curved an arm about her, pressing her to his chest, and stilled.

For a moment Aisleen could not think, could only feel the thunderous pounding of her heartbeat. Gradually other more subtle things made themselves felt. Heat rose from the stone beneath her hip and shoulder while the sun blazed upon her cheek, her throat, and her feet. The musical gurgle of the pool serenaded the day. The piping notes of birdsong were repeatedly interrupted by raucous laughter from the kookaburra.

Then, overwhelming all else, Thomas himself invaded her senses. His heartbeat was a slow, steady throb under her ear. His warm skin cushioned her cheek. The scent of his skin distracted her more than the exotic fragrances of the bush. And the pressure of his arm at her waist encircled her with a protectiveness she had never, never before known. For the first time in her life she felt as if she belonged somewhere—here, in her husband's arms.

Serenity, so rapt and complete all else faded before it, enveloped her. She thought she would never let the moment go. Yet sleep came stealing.

She awakened in shadow. The stinging heat of the sun suddenly eclipsed. He stood above her, his features blotted out by the halo of sunlight behind his head. She sat up and grasped the hand he extended.

She did not speak and neither did he. He turned his face from her as he led her away from the rock. She saw then, away from the blaze of his eyes, that he was naked. She knew who he was, and yet he was a stranger. He paused at the edge of the pool and turned to face her.

He reached out to frame her face and lay his lips on hers. He tasted of sunshine. His hands, strong and gentle, moved from her face to her shoulders. Wherever they touched, her skin warmed and tingled. They moved to the neckline of her gown, and as they trailed downward her gown opened before them. With a wanton whisper the gown slipped past her hips to the ground.

Aisleen did not move to stop him. She could not. There was nowhere to go, nothing to say, nowhere to look but into his serious face. All will, all fear, all desire to be separate from him disappeared. He found the ribbons of her chemise. She had taken his advice not to wear a corset in the bush. A whisper of batiste pantaloons was all that lay between her and him. And then even that was gone.

He pulled her against him, and she sighed as the heat of his skin met the cooler plush of her own. He held her a long time, as though to impress upon her his own ease with his nudity. The soft breeze blew gently along her back, but where he touched her warmth spread through her, a rush of blood brought to the surface by the stroke of his fingers. She turned her face upward voluntarily, thirsty for his kiss.

He was as needy as she, and they kissed in urgent anguish. She thought the stroke of his tongue too much pleasure to be borne until he found the tender weight of her breasts. He filled his palms with the generous curves and closed his thumbs against the budded nipples to rub them gently.

She whimpered in pleasure, unable to believe, only to feel, the utterly devastating joy of desire. And there was more. His mouth left hers, skimming over her cheek, the side of her neck, downward to the breasts he held in capture. The corded velvet of his tongue sailed under one rosy bud before the hot, wet hollow of his mouth drew it in.

She wrapped her arms about his back, holding onto him against the buckling of her knees as he suckled her. She closed her eyes, adrift in the timeless luxury of sensations too intense to be disturbed by sight.

When, at last, he raised his head, the smile of pure pleasure on his face was more flattering than words. He placed her arms about his neck and then lifted her off the ground by the waist. She tightened her arms as his hands moved under her buttocks. He pulled her legs up astride his waist and locked her feet behind his back. The repeated contact of her loins against his naked waist made her tremble as he stepped into the pool.

He was surprisingly agile as he traversed the slippery

bottom, wading in deeper and deeper until the water eddied about their hips and mist from the waterfall sprayed them.

She shivered in laughter as the cold spray dewed them in rainbow droplets. He laughed with her, and then his lips found hers again and the heat of the kiss evaporated the chill.

His tongue met hers, taught it a lively jig that needed only the *bodhran* of their hearts for accompaniment. His embrace relaxed and she slipped lower until the hard length of him was pressed between her spread legs. Somewhere a distant fear chimed. This was wrong, wicked, sinful. And then he kissed her again and the chiming ceased.

His embrace tightened again, and she lifted herself against him in an unconscious need to assuage the throbbing of her lips, her breasts, her loins.

He entered her in one thrust, directing her movements as he murmured indecipherable assurances into the deep cleft of her breasts. Each push/pull of pleasure forced a small cry from her until her cries formed a hoarse chorus of joy.

She knew then that she had been lied to. They were wrong, those who said there was no magic. The magic was now, here, in this place, with this man.

He was a man born with the art of persuasion. She had thought that gift of charm lay in his words. But that was before she had known this pleasure in his arms.

His fingers dug urgently into her buttocks, his rhythm quickening as he joined her cries with short grunts of desire.

Aisleen held him tighter, and tighter, kissing his sweaty cheek, his brow, crying, laughing, holding him so tightly that she hoped to solder them forever as one. The final rotating thrusts of his pelvis plunged deeply into her. She knew it was the first time that they were really and completely one.

*   *   *

She awakened in the curve of Thomas's arm, her hair spread out under his head, the copper flood a dramatic backdrop for his ebony locks. She raised up on an elbow. There was peace in his sleeping face, and joy, and wonder. Her eyes followed the length of his arm until she saw the place where his hand lay. Beneath his spread fingers on the curve of her hip was the rose-red birthmark of her heritage. Had he seen it?

Even before she lifted her gaze she knew that they were not alone. *He* was there, as he had been outside her hotel window, this time a purple shadow behind the bright ribbon of the waterfall. He raised a hand in salute.

"Go away!" Aisleen whispered. "Please let us be!"

Croosheening in the voice of a *gean-canach*, the apparition replied, *"Nae, avourneen machree!"*

Thomas's eyes opened and the figure vanished. "What's wrong, darling of my heart?"

Aisleen glanced down at him in bewilderment. Those were the words the phantom had spoken. "Nothing," she lied and pressed her cheek into the curve of his neck.

"There's naught to fear, *macushla*." Thomas sighed. "If only ye would believe."

Aisleen could scarcely credit her eyes as she and Thomas rode double through the gently rolling countryside west of the Blue Mountains. Everywhere small plots of land were under cultivation. Wheat, corn, and vegetable plants thrust upward from rich red earth in neat squares of plowed fields. Sheep grazed in cropped meadows. Cattle ruminated in the shade of pale-green trees. The scene was not English in character. The sun was much too vivid, the sky too blue. Native trees of myrtle, eucalyptus, and wattle, with their sparse limbs and willowy trunks, drew a stark contrast to the dense, rounded silhouettes of the elm and oak forests of Britain. Yet there was the sense of prosperity and settlement carved out of the wilderness.

After more than a week in the bush Bathurst appeared to be a city in Aisleen's eyes. This was no mere collection of daub-and-wattle huts with stringy bark roofs. A genuine village emerged as they neared the settlement on the banks of the Macquarie River. The main streets were broad avenues whose traffic included smart enameled rigs and elegant carriages as well as the more serviceable buggies and travel coaches. Women dressed in the latest European fashion strolled on the arms of smartly dressed gentlemen. There were banks and hotels of stone as well as townhouses with neat patches of lawn.

Aisleen bit her lip in disappointment when Thomas rode past the more prosperous section of town. The beckoning temptation of the lace-curtained windows of one hotel had been particularly appealing. Soon, however, she realized that he did not mean to stop in the charming town at all.

"Where are we going?" she asked when the main street gave way to the surrounding farmland once more.

"To Hill End," he answered. "I thought, being that ye are gentry and a gently reared lass, ye should see what a common man of wit can hope to make of the bush."

"What of the sheep?" Aisleen protested, realizing that everything she owned was in the cook wagon.

"They'll not be catching up with us for a week yet," Thomas answered. "Jack's grazing them on some squatter's land, just out of sight of the man, of course. Fattened jumbucks will bring more at market than a road-weary mob."

It was nearly dark when she saw the glow of a community on the rise. The noise of a town under the influence of great revelry reached them long before they entered.

Soon they were surrounded by the camp city on the bluff of the Turon River, where gunfire and riotous laughter on the busy streets competed with the tinny notes of a piano and fiddles. Sea shanties and music-hall ditties spilled from the numerous pubs and saloons which lined the lanes.

Aisleen held tight to Thomas, growing more and more afraid of the din. He seemed to take it all in stride, shoving away with a boot kick the one drunk digger who dared to catch a handful of Aisleen's muddy skirts. When they at last turned off the storefront street into a dark and quiet lane, Aisleen slumped in relief and weariness.

All at once Thomas reined his horse in. "Here we are, lass."

Aisleen peered through the dark at the small white-washed frame house where an argand lamp glowed warmly in the curtained window. Her spirits rose at once, only to plummet again as he dismounted and reached up for her. They had forded many tributaries of the Macquarie River in their journey. The hem of her gown was stiff with dried mud, and underneath her petticoat was still damp. Her bonnet had wilted long ago, and she had no gloves.

"Aye, ye're a wee bit mussed, but Matt and Sarah will nae think the less of ye," he remarked as he helped her down.

"Who are they?" she questioned uncertainly as he tried to smooth the road dust from her skirts.

"They're nae gentry, if that's what's worrying ye," he answered as he tried unsuccessfully to perk up the soggy brim of her bonnet. " 'Tis a saying among bush folk that the Scotch own the land while the Irish own the pubs. Matt Mahoney owns the finest drinking establishment in Hill End."

With that dubious comment to bolster her spirits, Aisleen followed the push of his hand at her back as he opened the gate to allow her to enter the yard. A moment later his heavy knock brought footsteps to the door, and a man with blond curls and a full, bushy beard opened it. "Aye? Who's there?"

"Now is that any way to greet a man, I'm asking ye! Damn yer eyes, Matt, that ye'll nae be knowing the ugly mug of Thomas Gibson!"

"Tom!" The man swung the door wide in greeting. "Sarah! Come quick! It's Tom, and he's brought company with him!"

"Not company," Thomas replied as he led Aisleen forward into the light. " 'Tis me wife I've brought for ye to meet. Aisleen, this is Matt Mahoney. Matt, meet Mrs. Gibson."

"Did I hear you say you've married?" came the feminine query an instant before a woman appeared in the doorway of the room beyond.

She moved slowly, and the reason for it was readily apparent. Advanced pregnancy stretched the limits of the periwinkle blue gown worn by the dark-haired young woman.

"Sarah, me darlin'!" Thomas greeted with a hug that half-lifted her off her feet. He winked at her husband. "I can see how Matt's spent his time since I was here last."

Color suffused her cheeks as Sarah playfully pushed him away. "Why, Tom, you devil!" She looked at Aisleen with a warm smile. "Just look at what you've done to her! Hurry, Matt, put the kettle on to boil and you, Tom, fetch a blanket from the chest. Poor girl, she looks all in."

Before she could protest, Aisleen was enveloped in a maternal hug faintly scented with lavender.

"Welcome, Mrs. Gibson. You've been a long time presenting yourself. Tom had begun to think you would not appear at all."

With those enigmatic words ringing in her ears, Aisleen was welcomed to Hill End.

And he saw young men and young girls
Who danced on a level place,
And Bridget his bride among them,
With a sad and a gay face

—The Host of the Air
W. B. Yeats

Chapter Fourteen

Hill End: November 1857

Aisleen sidestepped the splash of mud thrown up by
the wheels of a passing dray and clutched her bundle
tighter to her bosom. Behind the dray came another,
forcing her to jump up onto the wooden banquette of a
storefront.

" 'Ere! Mind your step, lovey!"

Aisleen blocked the path of a pair of women dressed in
vivid shades of red and gold and holding silk parasols.
"Pardon me," she said and moved aside.

" 'Ere that, Cora? A lady!" the woman in the gold gown
exclaimed. "Wait a tick, luv." She grabbed Aisleen's arm
in a glittering beringed hand. "What brings you to Hill
End?" She paused, her mouth forming a crooked "O"
before she said, "Ye wouldn't be one of them actresses
from London?"

Aisleen shrugged off the woman's greedy touch. "Certainly not! If you will kindly allow me to pass."

"La de da!" the second woman sang. "Ain't we the lady with airs? Just so ye know, ducks, this lane here belongs to Polly and me. Shift yer wares somewhere else. Take my meaning?"

Harlots! "I'm sure I don't!" Aisleen answered indignantly and walked purposefully around them.

As she passed the storefront, a man with top hat and cane emerged. He tipped his hat in respect, and she nearly responded to his politeness with a smile until she saw that while he wore a frock coat and cravat, he also wore a golden loop in each ear and a drooping black mustache. When he smiled she was dazzled by the flash of a dozen gold teeth. This was no colonial gentleman but a Spanish digger who had made a strike. Averting her amazed gaze, she marched away.

His laughter did not disconcert her as much as it might a short time ago. She was becoming accustomed to meeting with the unexpected in this gold-diggers community. Each day in the bush brought instances of wonder or surprise or rude awakening. After little more than a week in Hill End she was even beginning to understand the lure that had brought the bold, the desperate, and the dreamers into the bush to prospect for gold.

It was in the air: the gambler's fever. For some it was the chance to begin a new and better life. For others the hope of canceling out a lifetime of misery and failure with a single lucky strike lured them west. Expectancy pervaded every instance of life in the community. It had brought to this bush frontier a human flood as diverse in ethnic and economic backgrounds as any port city in the world. Cornishmen who employed the tin mining methods to crack the stone walls of the sandy cliffs along the river, buckskin-clad Americans who handled a pickax and their fists with equal ease,

Spanish sailors and Chinese coolies, even European aristo-crats: one and all they had come to New South Wales seeking the elusive prize. All spoke a common language. From casual conversation to business deals, nothing long prevented people from the one and only satisfactory topic of conversation: gold.

A sudden cheer went up from the passersby on the street, and Aisleen turned to discover the cause. It was the armed gold coach, arriving to collect from the gold merchants and banks the latest cache of gold nuggets and dust. Four men in military blue uniforms rode atop the coach. She noticed several more in the dim recesses of the interior. Too late, she realized her mistake in pausing in the street as mud and water flew up from the coach wheels and splashed her skirts. Several young boys who did not mind braving the splattering ran behind the vehicle, waving and whistling in excitement.

She turned away, brushing ineffectually at her skirts. It had not rained since early morning, but the street ran with mud and water and the collected refuse of the sewers. Once more she regretted not heeding her husband's advice that she remain in their room until his return.

Her husband. Aisleen smiled. It seemed impossible that she should be made so happy by the thought.

Just like the men and women around her, she had gambled everything in coming thousands of miles to this wild, unfamiliar place in hopes of beginning a new and better life. Like most of them, she felt that her prize was just below the surface, around the corner, in the next turn of a stone. Yet the prize she sought was not gold. She had not even known what she was hunting for, could not even put into words the innermost secret longings of her soul until now.

She wanted to be loved wholly and unconditionally. And that love would be mined in her husband's heart.

"Holy Mother, make it possible!" she whispered as she turned a corner and stepped through the gate of the fence that ringed the Mahoneys' house.

"Mrs. Gibson, thank heaven!" Sarah Mahoney said when Aisleen walked through the door. "I nearly sent for the magistrate!"

"Whyever would you do such a thing?" Aisleen questioned as she set her bundle down on an occasional table and began drawing off her gloves.

"Matthew won't hear of me traversing the streets unescorted. You might have been abducted." Sarah fanned herself against the warmth of the December day. "What would I have said to Tom, had he returned and found you gone?"

Aisleen smiled indulgently at her. "Poor dear, I've worried you needlessly. I can assure you, I would not allow myself to be abducted."

"You cannot be too careful," Sarah maintained. "There's no end of swagmen, bushrangers, and diggers who would snatch a young lady right off the street. Just a month ago the magistrate sentenced a digger to six months' imprisonment for abducting the ten-year-old daughter of a fellow miner. The madman had offered to marry her, but the father refused. Can you imagine?"

Aisleen could not help wondering by her speech which Sarah considered to be the greater crime, the father's refusal or the madman's offer, but she tactfully refrained from asking. "What can I do to make you more comfortable?"

"Nothing, my dear. When you're in your ninth month you shall remember your question and my answer and you will understand. I do, however, find the thought of a thimbleful of gin to my liking."

Aisleen schooled her features to show no amazement at this request. "Of course. I'll fetch it." The Mahoneys were another in the seemingly endless collection of friends Thomas had made in his shearing days. Because of Thomas, Sarah had graciously offered them shelter until the flock arrived. It was not her place to criticize her hostess's predilection for gin.

When she had poured a small measure of the clear liquid into one of the crystal tumblers she brought it to Sarah. "Shouldn't you be resting? You know your husband does not like you to be too fatigued to sit with him after supper."

"Matthew worries far too much," Sarah replied. "You would think it was my first child."

This time Aisleen could not mask her surprise quickly enough.

Sarah smiled. "You are wondering about the others, since there is no child toddling about the parlor."

"No, I do not wonder at all," Aisleen lied. "And if I did, it is none of my affair."

"That is true," the woman agreed, "and because you have made such a pretty speech of it, I shall tell you. I have two lovely children in England, a boy and a girl, ages two and four. In fact, were I to return to my village in Somerset, I imagine I would be arrested as an adulteress."

Sarah peered up at Aisleen through her lashes. "Don't you wish to know how a mother could leave behind two darling lambs and a husband of some consequence, for he was, you see. My husband is a bishop with a stipend of no small sum."

"It's not my place to wonder anything at all," Aisleen answered, growing more uncomfortable with every moment.

"You must have been a good and discreet governess," Sarah replied. "Once I might have hired you myself if I could have trusted Sedgewick not to corrupt you. But then again, perhaps Sedgewick would not have had you because I believe I see in you an incorruptible soul. You are shocked down to your shoes by my frankness.''

''No, not at all,'' Aisleen murmured, wishing now only to escape to her room, but she was not to be so easily released from the woman's confidence.

''Sedgewick was a heartless seducer of women,'' Sarah continued serenely. ''His preference was for young, excessively silly maids who thought it a great privilege to pray in the presence of a bishop. The trouble came when they found themselves off their knees and on their backs.''

She paused to sip her gin. ''When the third maid left us in disgrace, sworn to secrecy against the incursion of God's wrath, I left Sedgewick. I wanted nothing belonging to him, not his children, his stipend, nor the contents of his house. I wanted freedom, and that is what I've found here in Hill End.

''You will think me the lowliest of degenerates because I was a parson's daughter and bishop's wife. But I tell you I have quite a high opinion of morality and think it should be observed in no small measure. I confess freely that Matthew and I are not wed, but I shall stare into the face of Saint Peter himself and dare him to bar me entrance unless Sedgewick is sent to accompany me to hell. In which case, I shall joyfully participate in Sedgewick's unceasing torment.''

Sarah raised twinkling eyes to Aisleen. ''Have you nothing to say, no thought on the subject?''

Goaded to reply, Aisleen said, ''I wonder that you would bring a child into the world without the protection of his father's name.''

''Oh, but he shall have Matthew's name, as I have taken it!'' A smile softened Sarah's expression. ''Matthew was transported in 'thirty-nine for stealing. An emancipist has little chance of making his way once he's received his papers unless he's willing to work twice as hard as the next. Because of me, Matt has worked thrice as hard. Now he's an innkeeper with money in his pocket and a proper roof over his head. He likes to believe that I'm the cause of his success and that the child is God's grace on us. Only a fool would deny it, and I'm not a fool." She patted her prominent belly fondly. "This child will be loved better and more completely than the others who have their heritage free and clear."

"But if you are not married—"

Sarah smiled serenely. "I had every legal and moral entanglement with Sedgewick, and it did not keep him from breaking his vows to me, the church, and the state. Laws do not hold a heart that does not wish to be held. Love only can make the abidance pleasant."

"Love can change."

"Love does not change. Trust, Mrs. Gibson, is that not what you vowed in your love of Tom?" Sarah's cream complexion pinkened. "Oh, I do so enjoy plain speaking! I don't mind telling you that I've gazed fondly on your Tom in more ways than is proper, being that I'm pledged to Matt. Not that he would have had me. He always said he'd know the one for him the instant he laid eyes on her."

Aisleen frowned. "Why should he say that?"

Sarah leaned forward over her considerable middle and beckoned Aisleen with a crooked finger. "I don't believe such things myself, being a proper Anglican, but Tom once said he was in league with pixies or some such Irish fancy."

"Did he?" Aisleen murmured softly, remembering Tom's reference to that very thing himself. "An Irishman with half Thomas's gift for blarney might claim as much. It's a common boast."

Sarah eyed Aisleen with a knowing look. "All the same, I'd say Thomas has had his share of luck, considering his beginning in the colony."

"What beginning would that be?"

Sarah's expression went blank. "Has he not spoken to you of it?"

"No."

"Oh, dear." Sarah lowered her eyes and began fanning herself. "I did not think, did not think at all. What a silly goose I am!"

She looked up, blushing as a naughty child might, and Aisleen wondered how this seemingly naive woman could be the adulteress, child deserter, and mistress she proclaimed herself to be. "Tom will tell you about himself when he is ready. You won't tell him that I mentioned it? Promise?"

"Of course not," Aisleen answered because it was the only thing to do. She turned and quickly picked up her bundle. "I bought cloth with which to make a new gown. If I hurry, I can have it cut out before the men return."

Sarah nodded, wishing that she had held her tongue. When Aisleen had gone into the next room, she glanced at her empty cup and then rose awkwardly to her feet. So Tom did not want his bride to know about his past. If he found out that she had nearly given away his secret, she would need more than a finger of gin to brave the storm.

"I like them very much," Aisleen answered. "It is not a matter of liking them. Sarah is diverting company, and Matt seems a man of good character. It is only that I think we are imposing upon their hospitality."

Thomas rolled from his back to his side to see his wife's face better in the moonlight. "Where would you have us go, lass? Jack's due in tomorrow or the next day. After that mob's sold to slaughter, we'll be heading home."

"What if Jack is late or the sale takes longer than you expect?" she answered.

"What is a few days?" Thomas reached out to roll her

onto her side to face him. "Can ye think more kindly of the cook wagon than ye do the bed underneath us?" His hand curved down over her buttocks to pull her tight against his aroused loins. "Would ye be allowing me this with Jack and the others about to hear our every move?"

Aisleen blushed under the cover of darkness as he bent to kiss the side of her neck. "You know I would not. But still, could we not find a hotel? Our presence gives Sarah extra mouths to feed as well as extra work."

"Mmm," he murmured against her ear. "Matt tells me that ye'll not be allowing Sarah to lift a finger when ye're about, that even the maid is complaining that ye're there behind her half the time. The house has never looked better. Why should Sarah be wishing ye to leave when ye work so diligently, and for nothing besides?"

Aisleen caught her breath as his tongue snaked into the hollow of her ear. "Thomas! You're being inconsiderate because you're too well pleased to have a bed to share with me to think of the consequences."

"Oh, but I know the consequences, lass," he whispered huskily as he thrust his hips provocatively against hers. "'Tis why I'm nae anxious to be gone from here. A few more days, ye salve your conscience for a few more days, cannae ye?"

Before she could answer, his mouth found hers, and it was a long time before Aisleen was free to think of anything more than the joy of his lovemaking and her own eager response.

"Can we leave in the morning?" Aisleen prompted when Thomas's dark head once again lay quietly upon her left breast.

"If Jack comes in," he muttered sleepily.

"Even if he doesn't I would prefer to find another residence."

Thomas lifted his head, peering into her night-shadowed face. "What's the matter, lass?"

Aisleen wet her lips. "Do you know that Sarah and Matt are not legally wed?"

He tried in vain to see her expression. "Who told ye that?"

"Sarah."

"And ye were that shocked with the hearing of it," he answered flatly. "Lord love us! Yer prudish ways are certain to be sorely abused while ye remain in the bush. Lass, ye'll not be living among the gentry and the genteel any longer. I've told ye before, there are different ways of thinking out in the bush. Ye'll come to see the right of it after a time."

"I don't know that I'll ever see the right of it—as you put it—if that includes sharing my home with criminals."

Thomas stilled. "Sarah told ye about that, too, did she?"

Aisleen sighed. "I know it makes me seem intolerant and self-righteous, but I cannot avoid the truth. As nice a man as Matthew Mahoney seems, I am not comfortable sharing my life with those of the criminal class."

"What if I were to tell you I, too, was once a criminal?"

Aisleen smiled. "Do not be silly! Of course you were not, and so there's no need to speak of it."

"How can ye be so very certain?" he questioned quietly.

"Well, you would have told me, wouldn't you? You have been nothing if not frank and honest in your dealings with me. I find I cannot fault you on any account. So you see, I trust you would not have kept so obvious an objection from me."

"How quickly ye've changed," he remarked absently. "Not a week past, I would not have been able to say with any clear dependability that ye found anything about me worthy of yer praise."

"So you will agree that we must leave?" she pressed.

Thomas lowered his head back to her breast. "I can't rightly think where we might go, so, for the present, we will remain. There's a shivoo tomorrow evening. We've been invited."

"A party," Aisleen murmured, thinking of the gown she had begun. With passing regret she thought of the lace and lavender silk taffeta gown her mother had made for her. It was still in the cook wagon along with most of the rest of her belongings. She would need to make her needle fly to finish a new gown from the material she had purchased earlier in the day.

Thomas turned his head away. His greatest fear had come to pass. Aisleen abhorred the thought of sharing the company of convicts, even one who demonstrated by his industry that he was a useful member of society. She had not asked what Matt's crime had been, had not voiced one word of sympathy for Sarah and her situation. Could she not see how much in love they were? No, she found their love shameful and tawdry because it was not sanctified by ceremony. What would happen when she learned the truth about his past? There was nothing she could do. They were wedded and bedded and . . .

He reached out a hand to span Aisleen's flat stomach. Perhaps a child would soften her feelings. She liked bairns. She had expressed great interest in Sarah's pregnancy. Aye, a bairn would soften the blow, if and when it came. Until he was certain that she was breeding, he would say nothing to her about himself.

His hand moved farther until the slight pebble-textured mark on her hip was under his fingers. He traced the shape of a perfect rosebud with his forefinger and smiled. His thorny rose-haired wife. Until she accepted herself, he could not tell her about himself. He wanted her love, completely and freely given.

*   *   *

The clearing was filled with dozens of men, women, and children. Laughter rippled across the night, rising and falling in counterpoint to the ebb and surge of voices. Punctuating the din were the barks of dogs. The aromas of roasting mutton, burning wood, and tobacco smoke misted the night air. Across the yard stood a huge open-ended barn, its interior lit by whale-oil lamps and candles. From the shed came the shrill whine of a bagpipe, the whistle of tin flutes, and the tattoo of a *bodhran* accompanying the lively sawing of an expert fiddler.

Aisleen smiled. The lilting, toe-tapping melody of the Irish jig was familiar. It had been many years since she had heard it, and the tune brought her a rush of pleasure.

Thomas jumped down from the Mahoneys' trap and reached for her. "Come along, lass. Ye once promised me a dance. Tonight I will collect."

"Oh, how I envy you," Sarah said as Aisleen stepped down. "I'm afraid I must content myself with sitting on the sidelines."

Aisleen smiled stiffly and said nothing.

Thomas stared at her in annoyance. She could not bring herself to be more than civil to the people who had housed her. With a prod of his hand, he forced her to start across the yard. "'Tis me hope that ye'll nae find everything tonight to be beneath yer interest," he said when they were out of earshot of their companions.

"I can't think what you mean," Aisleen replied, but she did know. She was behaving churlishly, but she could not help herself. Everything she had been taught rebelled against the scandalous behavior of their hosts. Why could Thomas not understand her reluctance to align herself with people who openly flouted the conventions of decency and propriety?

As they stepped up onto the hardwood floor of the shearing shed he caught her elbow in a hard grip. "There may be a fair number here tonight of whom ye will nae be approving. If so, I'll thank ye to keep the knowledge of it to yerself. These are me friends and I'll nae have them insulted, even by me wife!"

The harsh words were spoken barely above a whisper, but Aisleen trembled. He was very angry, angrier than she had realized.

"G'evening, Mrs. Fahey," Thomas greeted as he paused before a middle-aged woman who wore a violet silk gown over her ample figure. "May I introduce to ye me bride?"

"That you may," the woman answered in a cultured voice. The effect was spoiled as she suddenly barked in amazement, "Bride, did you say, Tom?"

Aisleen met the woman's inquisitive gaze with a smile. "Good evening, Mrs. Fahey."

"Gracious! A lady!" Mrs. Fahey's frank surprise widened her eyes. "Do relinquish her to me, Tom. You've the look of a man with a thirst yet to be quenched. Come along, Mrs. Gibson. We will speak of things that would not interest a man."

"Me very thoughts, exactly," Thomas answered. "Of a surety I'm thanking ye to be looking after me wife while I pay me respects in certain quarters." Without a word to Aisleen he sauntered off toward the group of men standing before a makeshift bar.

"Don't worry," Mrs. Fahey said as she snagged Aisleen by the elbow. "He'll come back when he's had his fill."

The thought of a drunken husband was not a comforting one, but Mrs. Fahey would not be gainsaid, and so Aisleen found herself steered toward a row of chairs which she had not before noticed.

Mrs. Fahey settled herself and patted the chair beside her. "Do let's become better acquainted, Mrs. Gibson. There's so little of society readily available outside of Sydney. Who are your people, dear?"

"I am a Fitzgerald," Aisleen answered calmly, though she was repelled by the woman's avid gaze.

"The name is not unknown to me. I once met a Captain Fitzgerald of Cork who resided in Melbourne with his lady wife. Are you, perchance, related?"

"No," Aisleen answered, casting an anxious glance toward the crowd. Sarah and Matt had entered the shed and stood chatting with Thomas. Reluctantly she brought her attention back to the woman beside her. Thomas had introduced them—the least she could do was make a good impression. "I am newly arrived in Sydney."

"Then you knew Tom before? In Ireland?"

"No. Mr. Gibson and I met since my arrival in Sydney. We met through the offices of Mrs. Freeman, matron of Hyde Park Barracks. Mr. Gibson was kind enough to take an interest in me."

"I see," Mrs. Fahey replied in a tone which Aisleen could not mistake. "Hyde Park Barracks is, as a rule, a sanctuary for domestic servant girls, is it not? Yet you are educated," she mused aloud, "and your manners are those of a genuine lady. But, my dear, there are so many parvenus in the colony one simply cannot be too careful, you understand."

Aisleen glanced toward Tom once again, wondering if the woman meant her husband or the Mahoneys.

"For instance, the couple conversing with your husband is a case in point. The woman is well spoken, but her husband is the crudest sort—a Vandiemonian, that one. I'm amazed the magistrate issued a liquor license to him. Of course, though we've eliminated convict transportation, it's nearly impossible to stem the flow of emancipists into the colony. I tell Mr. Fahey constantly that he should do more to hold the lines between the classes, but he will not hear of it."

Liking the woman less and less, Aisleen noted with

distaste the damp circles on the violet silk beneath Mrs. Fahey's arms and the faint vinegary odor rising from the woman's damp skin. "It must be very difficult for you," she murmured absently, thinking that Tom had gotten his revenge by setting the woman upon her.

"Mr. Fahey is quite a man of some distinction here in the west," Mrs. Fahey said proudly. "The Hill End branch of the New South Wales Bank is but one of the feathers in his cap. I don't mind telling you that its success is no little credit to him. The diggers are a mad lot, wildly extravagant with the gold they scratch from the earth. Why, if it were not for Mr. Fahey's persuasion, I do believe they would prefer to be swindled by the gold merchants and sly grog shopkeepers who roam the fields like vultures. A strike, large or small, means only a further opportunity for women, wine, and song. I will admit my surprise that your husband traded his modest strike for property."

She seized Aisleen's arm. "Have you seen his station? I'm told it is quite the most extraordinary piece of property in all the New England region of the colony!"

Aisleen held herself in check against the inclination to back away from the woman, whose features had grown alarmingly red. "Would you care for a drink, Mrs. Fahey? Perhaps a cup of tea?"

"Tea?" Mrs. Fahey flushed a deeper shade of red. "My dear child, a glass of Bengal rum would do quite nicely."

Aisleen's eyes widened, but she remembered her manners. "Rum. Of course. I shall fetch a glass directly." She stood and started across the floor.

Rum. Imagine, a banker's wife who openly consumed liquor in public! She was not surprised by Sarah's conduct, once she learned the woman's history, but Mrs. Fahey's intoxicated state quite shocked her. The morals of the entire colony were reprehensible.

"Mrs. Fahey gave ye up?" Thomas said when she

reached him. "I'd not have thought she'd allow ye to leave her side for some good while."

Glad that the Mahoneys had slipped away as she approached him, Aisleen confided in a shocked whisper, "That lady is quite . . . quite flushed."

"Is she now, and me thinking her a wee bit flummoxed," Thomas answered amicably.

"You knew she was drunk, and still you allowed me to be—?" Aisleen stiffened at his chuckle. He thought it a jest. "Where may I find a cup of rum?"

He glanced at his tin cup and then offered it.

She eyed him coldly. "It is for Mrs. Fahey."

"I was afraid 'twas so," he replied in a regretful tone. "Ye might learn a thing or two from a sip now and again. Ah, well. Ye do nae drink but ye do dance, Mrs. Gibson?"

She could not resist the challenge in his eyes. "Yes, I do, sir."

"Sir, is it? And how's that sound to a husband who's asked his bride to dance? 'Thomas' will do for dancing," he said carelessly before draining his cup and tossing it aside. "When we're home again, there's another name or two I've a mind for ye to call me."

He was smiling that charming smile that made Aisleen wish she had spurned his offer, for the music had turned toward the slower tempo of a waltz.

"Have I told ye what a charming piece of work ye made of that muslin?" he asked as his arm slid about her waist. Her right hand was caught up in his left, and then he stepped off into a turn. "Ye're so clever with words and with yer fingers. 'Tis a wonder ye're nae so clever when it comes to people."

"Perhaps I've had less experience with people," she rejoined. He was unexpectedly close, much closer than Monsieur Pardieu, the dancing master, had ever dared.

"Why are ye showing the folks yer quite nice face

screwed up as though ye'd been asked to swallow a dose of cod-liver oil?''

She blushed as she met his gaze. "I am concentrating. I have never before waltzed with a gentleman.''

"Good! I like knowing that there's many a thing ye've shared only with me, and yer body's the most important!''

Aisleen took a backward step to separate them, but with a neat turn, he brought her back to him, holding her closer than ever. "Please!'' she whispered in embarrassment. "People are watching.''

"And so they should, being that I'm dancing with the prettiest lass here,'' he answered unabashedly.

His body seemed to flow into every inch of space hers provided, as though he had no sense of separateness from her. The hand on her waist rose to the small of her back, arching her closer until she had to rely on its support or lean against his chest. There was nothing to do but give herself up to the moment.

His coat was unbuttoned, and the heat of his body flowed through his shirt, through her bodice, and into her skin as they danced. She felt breathless, less solid than before, skimming along in her husband's arms.

"Aye, it's nice, dancing. Me mother called it soaring with angels,'' Thomas agreed, reading her thoughts in her eyes.

He could not look away from those dark gold eyes wide upon his. Aye, he'd been right the first time. Her eyes were as rich and warming as any spirits he had ever drunk. Their power stirred his blood as rum had never done. She was as much a woman as any who danced beneath this roof.

Neither of them noticed his approach, but suddenly they were brought to a halt by a huge hand on Thomas's shoulder.

"Jack!'' Thomas greeted the human mountain. "Ye're in!''

"Good evening, Mr. Egan,'' Aisleen greeted warmly

because his arrival meant they would be moving on, away from Hill End and the Mahoneys.

Jack stared at her a moment, his craggy features as immutable as stone, and then turned without a word to either of them and walked away.

"I'll be back," Thomas said, leaving her before he finished the sentence to hurry after the man.

"Mrs. Gibson! Over here!"

Aisleen turned to see Mrs. Fahey hailing her from across the room. The woman beckoned a second time, and she could not find any alternative to rejoining her now that Thomas had deserted her.

For the next half hour, she was led from one knot of people to the next, introduced, inspected, prodded, probed, and commented upon until her nerves were frayed and her own armpits damp. Her smile had become a frozen monument to civility. She did not care for any of the people she met. Their avid gazes were all alike, speculatively resting on her face, her hands, her hair, as if they could glean some secret knowledge from their inspection of her. What did they want?

"Well, Mrs. Gibson, have ye enjoyed yer visiting?"

Aisleen spun about at the sound of Thomas's voice. "Tom!" she greeted and thrust a hand toward him. "Oh, yes, I'm quite weary—with the gaiety," she added quickly.

"Then ye will nae mind leaving early?" he questioned, grasping her hand tightly.

"No, not at all." She turned to Mrs. Fahey and the other ladies, and all at once she knew the reason for their interest in her. One and all, they were staring at her husband. It was written in each of their simpering smiles and coy glances. How many of them had he flattered and perhaps seduced over the years?

Not one. She knew it was the truth. They had sniped and

dissected her out of envy for what they had not experienced, and would never, experience in the arms of Thomas Gibson.

"If you ladies will excuse me," she said as she slid an arm through his. "It has been a charming evening." She looked up at her husband and was surprised to see that he was gazing at her, completely unaware of the thwarted passions he had aroused.

When they had left the shed and walked across the clearing toward the trap that had brought them, Aisleen wondered why he was cutting short the evening. "Was Jack's trip a success?"

"We'll be leaving in the morning," he answered shortly. "Jack says he'll see to the sale himself."

"If that is true, why could we not have left before this, as I asked?"

Thomas turned to her, his face stiff, but a sound attracted their attention before he spoke. Out of sight, beyond the Mahoneys' trap, a woman was softly sobbing.

"Ah, Sarah, don't be weeping so," came the voice of Matt Mahoney out of the darkness. "Do ye think I'd care what her sort has to say? Neither should ye."

"You didn't—didn't hear her," came the softer, hiccuped syllables of Sarah's reply. "No better than a *whore*, she called me!"

"What does a great cow the likes of her know?" Matt countered. "Talk, that's all it is, lass. Talk."

"It isn't working," Sarah answered. "I should have known better. I'll bring you to ruin if I stay. Even Tom's wife can't bear the sight of me now that she knows. Oh, Matt, I'm so sorry!" The weeping began again, clearer and harder.

Aisleen realized that Thomas stood staring down at her, and guilt pricked her. She had not spoken her thoughts aloud, but they had been the same as those expressed by the woman who had insulted Sarah. "I can be such a fool!" she whispered and pushed past Thomas.

Thomas moved aside in amazement as Aisleen headed toward the wagon where Sarah and Matt stood.

Aisleen rounded the trap without preamble and startled the pair.

"Mrs. Gibson!" Sarah said with alarm and pushed quickly out of her husband's arms to rub away the telltale signs of her tears.

Aisleen pulled a handkerchief from her sleeve and offered it. "Wipe your eyes, Sarah. It can't be good for a bairn to have his mother weeping so. You'll have him afraid of the sea, with all that saltwater sloshing about inside."

She turned to Matt. "I will not pretend that I did not overhear a part of your conversation, and I'm glad I did. The woman who insulted Sarah should be shunned. Whatever one's personal opinions, there is no reason for rudeness." She turned back to Sarah. "I apologize for my behavior earlier today. I feel very small and uncharitable and meanspirited at this moment."

"And so ye should!" Matt answered harshly, "being that ye're nae so grand a lady that ye did not wed yerself to an emancipist! Aye, yer Tom's the same as me. Ask him!"

Aisleen looked up as Thomas neared her. "Is it true?"

"Aye."

It was too dark to see her face, but Thomas felt his heart contract as she continued to stare at him. "I see," she said after a long interval.

Aisleen turned to Matt. "Is it not time to leave? Sarah must be worn clean through, and I myself feel an attack of the megrims coming on."

She scarcely noticed that Thomas took her arm to help her up into the vehicle, and she did not retain any details of the ride home. Only when she lay in bed, with the shutters closed against the usual carousal of the night, did she draw a deep breath. Matt and Thomas's voices could be heard droning on in the parlor.

She was wed to an ex-convict. What was his crime? Was he a thief, a smuggler? She shivered. Was he a murderer? Perhaps he was a political prisoner, an Irish loyalist, branded as a rebel by the English Crown. Yet if that were so, why had he not simply told her the truth?

Would ye have believed him?

Aisleen sat up with a start.

In the deepest shadow beyond the window something stirred. "Who goes there?" she whispered in Gaelic.

Ye know, came the answer deep in the silence.

The scent of heather and the sea wafted through the room, stirring the curtains drawn over the shutters.

"I don't believe in you!" Aisleen whispered as she held the covers tightly to her chest.

I know, came the regretful reply.

She knew the exact moment he disappeared. It was a fleeting instant before Thomas opened the bedroom door.

I broke my heart in two
So hard I struck.
What matter? for I know
That out of rock,
Out of a desolate source,
Love leaps upon its course.

—His Confidence
W. B. Yeats

Chapter Fifteen

Thomas rose from Aisleen's side at dawn, dressed, and left without a word. She waited until she heard the front door close before hurrying to dress. After a quick look right and left, she gathered her skirts in one hand and lifted a stockinged leg over the windowsill and climbed out of the bedroom window of the Mahoneys' home.

Alert to every movement, she rounded the house to gain the street from the alley behind. Hill End was curiously quiet in the mornings. The diggers always deserted the pubs and hotels for the goldfields before first light. She had debated all night what she should do, and by dawn she knew the answer. She must return to Sydney. She could not continue to travel with a man she did not know or any longer trust.

From the very first Thomas had lied to her. Because he was capable of one lie, he was capable of any and all duplicity. Sarah was wed to one man while she lived with

286

another. Thomas not only knew but approved. Had he, too, been wed before? Perhaps he had lied about his wealth. Of course, there was the corroboration of Mrs. Fahey that he had bought property, but he might have lied to others as well. Then there was the story of his having made a lucky strike in the goldfield. Why had he never told her that he was once a digger? Why had he not told her how he earned his wealth? What was he hiding?

These and many other thoughts had whispered and seethed in her mind during the sleepless night until, finally, she did not want to know the truth.

Or perhaps I am afraid of the truth. Aisleen steeled herself to enter the main street. The truth was that she was very near not caring what Thomas had done if only he would continue to be kind to her. She had known the depths of torment during the night while lying beside him, their bodies touching at shoulder, hip, and thigh, unable to turn to him or move away. She had trembled with the need to throw over all her scruples, morals, and pride for love. If she did, she would be lost to herself forever.

Aisleen blinked repeatedly as she walked up the street toward the Hill End Hotel, where she had seen a coach from Bathurst drop off passengers earlier in the week. It was better to flee before the temptation. She loved Thomas. It was the best and worst thing that had ever happened to her. She was no longer a spinster, forced to live her life without ever experiencing the passion between a man and a woman. That was small comfort to a shattered heart.

She approached the hotel entrance, where two men in expensive suits stood chatting. One tipped his hat, but the other merely surveyed her in an insolent manner. They parted so that they flanked the doorway, thus forcing her to pass between them to enter.

"G'day," the first man said as she passed him.

Aisleen ignored him.

The second man was not so easily dissuaded, she discovered when a large hand reached out and grabbed the back of her skirts and brought her to an abrupt halt. Furious to have been so ignobly detained, Aisleen turned to face him.

He was not much taller than she, but broad. The shoulder seams and sleeves of his jacket were stretched tautly over bulging muscles. He wore a flowing mustache. Above it his nose was wide and flat, as if a hand had shoved it against his face. His cheeks and brows were sickled with old scars.

"Me name's James Dennys, but you can call me Jim," he said with a grin.

"I will call for help if you do not release me immediately," Aisleen answered, undaunted. "This is a public street, sir, and I cannot be molested without it coming to someone's attention."

The man's face puckered up. "She don't know me, George," he said in offense.

The second man, small, more dapper in appearance, lifted his hat from his head. "This here is Gentleman Jim, the boxer. World heavyweight champion, he is, come to fight one and all in this backward colony. You're to be flattered that you've taken his fancy. He's dined with crowned princes, Jim has."

Aisleen favored the man with a polite but distant smile. "I'm sure that is all very nice for him; but if he does not remove his hand from my gown this instant I shall be forced to resist, and you may tell him that I've gotten the better of many a ruffian schoolboy!"

The speech was so absurd that Gentleman Jim was surprised into releasing her when she smacked him in the face with her purse. "There!" she cried and darted inside the doorway before he could react.

The hotel was small but surprisingly well decorated with paintings, velvet draperies, and horsehair couches which she noted as she crossed to the desk. "I wish to make arrangements to leave Hill End this morning," she said to the clerk. "When does the next coach leave?"

"Not long after he gets here," the young man answered.

"What time would that be?" Aisleen rephrased the question.

The young man shrugged. "Like as not, he'll be coming before dark, that is, if the river's not swollen. There's been rain east of here. Could be the river's flooded."

"How will you know if he's coming?"

"When he's here, he's here. If he ain't, he ain't."

With those words of wisdom ringing in her ears, Aisleen turned away and crossed the lobby to sit on one of the chairs which flanked the fireplace. She clutched her purse and heard the clink of coins inside. She retained most of the first month's wages Thomas had paid her, but it was not enough to buy passage on a ship bound for England. She would return to Sydney and seek out Mrs. Freeman's help. Once the lady learned of the curious circumstances of her marriage, she was certain Mrs. Freeman would agree that she had done the right thing in leaving her husband.

Her husband. Aisleen crossed her arms tightly over her stomach to keep at bay the flutterings of misgiving. She had been married under pretense. She had made a horrible mistake. But, unlike her mother, she would not remain trapped and miserable. She would not!

Her eyes constantly on the door, apprehensive that at any moment Thomas would stride through it, she did not miss a single person who passed by as the morning sky caught fire with the rising sun. The street filled slowly, businesses opening on their own schedules. Finally the curtains of the milliner directly across the street from the hotel were drawn back on a glass display window.

Aisleen frowned as she glanced at the gown in the window. It was strangely familiar. Suddenly she was on her feet. The gown was familiar because it was hers!

She crossed the busy street nearly at a trot, her eyes fastened on the lavender silk and white lace gown. There could be only one explanation for its appearance in a shop window. Someone had sold it!

She entered the store in a breathless rush, the words already falling from her lips. "That gown in the window! The lavender silk taffeta one!"

"Oh, yes!" interrupted the young man behind the counter. "It is lovely, isn't it? Knew right away we'd have no end of ladies vying for its purchase."

"You cannot sell it!" Aisleen replied. "It is mine!"

"Yours?" the man voiced faintly and then smiled. "Of course. You saw it first and you shall have it."

Aisleen took a deep breath. "Allow me to begin again." She pointed at the display window. "The gown you have there cannot be for sale because it does not belong to you. It is mine."

The young man's brow wrinkled. "I don't understand."

"Neither do I," she answered. "But that does not alter facts. The gown, together with the bonnet you display there, belongs to me. I do not know how they came into your possession, nor do I care. Please remove my belongings from the window and give them to me!"

"What's the trouble?"

Aisleen turned toward the voice and saw an older man in a top hat and frock coat who had entered.

"Mr. Russell!" the younger man greeted in a voice filled with relief. "This woman claims that the gown in the window belongs to her."

The older man removed his hat from a head of thinning white hair. "Yes, miss? I am the owner. If you have a complaint you may register it with me."

"Well, I have a complaint," Aisleen answered, pleased that he was a man of some breeding. "I do not know how these things came into your possession, but they belong to me.''

The man smiled sadly. ''My dear young woman. As so often happens, second thoughts often follow the first. I am not a hard-hearted man. I am willing to resell to you your gown. Edward?'' He indicated the gown, which the young man moved to take down.

''Resell?'' Aisleen questioned. ''There's no reason why I should purchase what I already own.''

The man's smile saddened. ''There is no need for a scene, my dear. I assure you, I have dealt with all kinds, all kinds. I am willing to return your garments to you for, shall we say, fifty pounds?''

''Fifty pounds!'' She drew herself to her full height, which was several inches more than his. ''Even if I possessed that much, I would not pay you a shilling for what is rightfully mine. If you do not hand my belongings over immediately, I shall seek a constable to aid me.''

''Very well spoken,'' Mr. Russell answered as he received the gown from his clerk. ''I am almost persuaded that a young lady of such culture might prevail upon the constable's sympathies and enlist his aid. However, the answer to him shall be the same. I paid for these items, and at a fair price, too.'' He absently rubbed the lavender taffeta of the skirt between two fingers. ''We don't often get this quality of goods.'' He looked up at Aisleen. ''Would you not prefer to reconsider? You must have been in extreme circumstance to barter your clothing away. If you've come into money, it is only right that you should repay me.''

Aisleen shook her head. Was she speaking to a madman? ''I never sold a single item to anyone. Those clothes were stolen, do you hear me? If you bought them, then you were duped.'' She caught the hem of the gown and turned it over. ''Do you see the name embroidered here? That is my name, Miss Aisleen M. D. Fitzgerald. This is my gown.''

"I never doubted it," he answered implacably. "But I've lived in the goldfields too long to accept that a seemingly proper young woman would never bargain away her clothing. For all I know, you spent your earnings on rum!"

Anger turned Aisleen's eyes into golden flames. "Sir, I do not know you; therefore I will assume that the sort of women with whom you do business may be as nefarious as you say." She wagged a finger under his nose. "But, sir, I am not that sort of person! It is my gown, and I shall take it back!"

"If you do, I will have no alternative but to have you arrested," Mr. Russell answered heartily, though he looked to the young clerk, quite taken aback by the slender young woman's forceful speech.

"Maybe she's telling the truth," the clerk offered. When his employer turned a flushed face to him he said, "Wasn't this among the lot that swagman brought in yesterday? Said he found the belongings floating in the river. Figured they'd been swept off a dray or a coach and washed downstream."

"A likely tale!" Aisleen scoffed. "Do you see water marks on the taffeta? You do not! Stolen, that's what they were! And you, sir, are guilty of purchasing stolen merchandise. Kindly hand over my belongings."

"Not so quickly," Mr. Russell answered. "I'm not a fool. You may be a party to a ploy to swindle me out of my money. Before I give them to you, I'll need proof that what you say is so."

"What sort of proof?" Aisleen demanded.

"The man who sold me these items promised to have several other articles to show me today."

"More stolen merchandise?" Aisleen suggested.

Mr. Russell frowned. "At the time I was too delighted to give the matter much consideration, but I suppose that is a possibility. No matter. I am expecting him momentarily."

He looked at her skeptically. "If matters are as you say, you will not mind waiting for him."

Aisleen went to the window and crossed her arms as she stared out. "Not at all!"

She did not have long to wait before she recognized two of the men on the street. Thomas and Jack came up the lane on the opposite side. She backed away from the window when they paused before the hotel. From the corner of her eye she saw Mr. Russell's interest in her action and knew what he must be thinking. Why would she behave in a furtive manner unless she had something to hide? Anxiety raced along her nerves as she held her ground. A quick movement might draw Thomas's attention.

To her consternation she saw two women approach the men and engage them in conversation. Further to her dislike, one of the women threaded her arm through Thomas's. The sound of his laughter filled the street as she bent and whispered in his ear. Aisleen's fingers flexed on her elbows and her mouth tightened. Thomas was flirting on a public street. How dare he!

The shop bell jangled as the door opened, but Aisleen was too agitated to give the customer notice. Suddenly Thomas looked up sharply and directly into her face. She knew she was hidden in the shadow of the shop, but she felt as if he had reached across the busy street and touched her.

For the space of several seconds she was pierced and pinned like a butterfly by that too-blue gaze. Her heart contracted as a hard tremor shook her. She loved him. She loved him so much the emotion shattered her heart, her pride, her will to resist. It wasn't right! He would ruin her, bring her to pathetic misery, and never even once feel the battering gale winds of love and tenderness and desire that buffeted her each and every time he looked at her.

Why was love not possible!

"Ye bitch!"

Aisleen spun about.

"Is this the man?" Mr. Russell prompted.

At first she did not recognize the grizzled old man in a plaid suit. But as his lips drew back from his teeth in a grimace of rage, she knew who it was. He held her green-and-red wool tartan gown in one hand, the hand with the missing thumb. "Cook! You thief!"

"Bloody pommie bitch!"

Aisleen never saw the fist that came flying toward her. She felt only the sickening connection of fist to jaw, the levering pain that jerked her head away from her body, and then the stunning wild darkness that engulfed her.

"Aisleen! Aisleen, me darling!"

Thomas knew that she was not seriously injured. The ugly blue-red bruise darkening her chin would heal. Yet he could not stop the churning in his middle as he held her limp body in his arms. Her stubborn little chin was not meant to withstand the brutal strength of a man's fist. "Aisleen, lass, please open yer eyes!"

Aisleen moaned. Her head felt too big, her lids too heavy to open. "Go away!" she murmured. "I don't believe in you. I won't!"

"What's that gibberish she's mumbling?" Mr. Russell asked as he bent over Thomas's shoulder.

" 'Tis the mother tongue of Ireland," Thomas answered shortly. "Give her some air!" He bent low to whisper in her ear in Gaelic, "I don't care if ye believe in me, lass, only come back and fight me if ye must!"

The words in the taunting lilt made Aisleen's eyes fly wide open. "Who said that?" she questioned in English.

"Ah, well, so ye've decided to come round, have ye?"

Thomas questioned with a smile. "Have ye nothing better to do than to lie about on a shop floor?"

"Cook! He stole my gowns!" She tried to sit up; but pain struck her a stunning blow between the eyes, and with a gasp she sagged weakly between the cradle of Thomas's thighs.

"Easy, darling." He brushed back a lock of bright hair from her face. "I'll be taking care of the cook before the day's done, of that ye can be certain."

"She looks all crooked," offered the clerk, which brought a glare from Thomas.

"I'll be thanking ye to keep away from his wife," Jack said with a weighty hand on the young man's shoulder.

The clerk backed away as if he had once been a victim of Jack's temper and hurried to put the width of the counter between him and the huge man. Jack bent down and stared at Aisleen's pale face.

Aisleen caught her lower lip to keep it from trembling. Jack had made her feel completely useless and foolish.

"Shouldn't give ye bother," he said at last to Thomas and stood. "I'll see to the cook."

"No." Thomas spoke the word quietly, but it stopped the gigantic man in midtread. "I be thanking ye to leave that pleasure to me. If ye'd take me wife back to the Mahoneys, I'd be that obliged."

He scooped Aisleen up in his arms and rose to his feet. "She's nae a sack of meal," he cautioned Jack as he handed her over. "She'll have a sore head some little time without ye frightening her to death. Keep her still until I get back."

Jack nodded once.

To her astonishment, Thomas left her without a word. Contrarily tears rose in her eyes, because she wasn't sad, she was furious!

"No tears!" Jack's basso voice boomed over her head, snapping Aisleen's head up. Pain skyrocketed up the column of her neck to explode in a shower of stars behind her eyes as she heard him say, "Can't swim!"

She shouldn't have been able to laugh—it hurt too much even to blink her eyes—but laughter bubbled out of her. So there was something that the great and mighty Jack feared, and that was a woman's tears. Had she known, she'd have cried a bucket of them on the journey over the mountains.

Mr. Russell offered Jack the carpetbag of clothing that the thief had left behind. "I am to suppose that I have lost the money I paid in good faith for these articles?"

Jack's silver gaze narrowed.

"Yes, of course. Foolish of me to inquire." Mr. Russell signaled for the lavender gown and matching bonnet, which his clerk reluctantly brought. "That is everything, I believe." He moved to open his shop door. "Good day to you both."

She knew they turned every head—Jack alone would have been enough to do that. Aisleen did not care. She had had a miserable night and a miserable morning. The sight of the coach from Bathurst rattling past was the last straw. The tears she had promised herself she would not shed broke free of the thicket of her golden lashes and streamed unchecked down her face. And so the main street of Hill End was subjected to the astonishing sight of a red-haired giant with a small, weeping, red-haired lady in his arms trailing a costly lavender silk and white lace gown.

"You're so very brave to have accosted the thief yourself."

"She's a damned fool!"

"Now, Matt, what sort of talk is that?" Sarah scolded. "I think she is quite brave." She smiled. "If a bit foolish."

Aisleen sat up in bed, her head supported in her hands. "I think I am a damned fool! Ouch! My head!"

"Jack went to fetch something," Sarah said with a lift of her brows at her husband.

"Oh, aye, I'll see what's become of him," Matt offered belatedly and left the room.

Sarah studied the young woman before her. With her hair falling about her shoulders and her chin darkly bruised and her eyes shining with the lees of tears, she was prettier than ever before. It was easy to see why Thomas loved her to distraction. "Where were you going this morning, before you nabbed the thief?"

Aisleen looked up guiltily. "Nowhere—that is, not precisely anywhere."

"How odd," Sarah remarked calmly. "I thought it must be something very important for you to climb out of the window."

Aisleen felt her cheeks warm with blood. "Did you tell Thomas?"

"Of course not!" Sarah leaned forward. "If you are so foolish as to throw over a man as fine as Tom, then you don't deserve him!"

Her gaze fell before Sarah's accusing one. "I wasn't throwing him over, exactly. I needed time to think. He wasn't honest with me."

"Did you ask him to be?" Sarah asked quickly.

Aisleen shrugged, a deplorable habit that would never have been tolerated at Miss Burke's Academy. "There has been no time."

"I see." Sarah pursed her lips. "I've kept my opinions to myself because they have not been asked for. I am not so presumptuous as to assume that you would find advice of mine worthwhile. As you know, I live a shameful existence in which I find inestimable joy."

Aisleen raised her head. "I do apologize, Sarah. I can't think why I behaved the way I did."

"I can." Sarah's expression thawed. "You behaved as I

would have had our situations been reserved. It was ill-timed of me to think that you could share with me things that you have not yet shared with Tom.''

''What things?'' Aisleen asked in genuine puzzlement.

''My dear, everything! What you hide behind that golden gaze could fill volumes. Don't think because I am a woman I am the only one who can see the shadows. They are driving Tom half-mad with curiosity and fear. Yes, fear. Do you think he brought you here by coincidence? He hoped you would confide in me, another woman who left her old life behind only to face the uncertainty and perplexities of a new one, what you could not confide in him.''

''Did he tell you this?'' Aisleen asked in amazement.

Sarah smiled sadly. ''You are so ignorant of men! Tom himself does not know why he is here. It was plainly written on your faces that you've yet to master the most basic conventions of marriage.''

Aisleen shook her head. ''You are wrong. I quite understand what I need to know of men. Thomas married me because I fit quite nicely his idea of a wife. I married him because I was desperate. Yet neither of us has gotten what we bargained for.''

Sarah nodded. ''I know. You've both gotten more, and you're frightened of it. Foolish child, don't you see that you've fallen in love?''

Aisleen shook her head and winced as pain radiated through her skull. ''I don't love him. I couldn't. I don't know what love is.''

Sarah opened her mouth, but Jack burst through the door at that moment with a tin cup in his hand and thrust it at Aisleen. ''Drink!''

The command impelled her to take a large swallow. For an instant there was only the cool feeling of liquid. The next instant the cool caught fire and flames traveled quickly down her throat into her stomach and back. She gasped but could not seem to draw breath. Tears started in her eyes. She choked and then expelled a fiery breath in racking coughs as the inferno raged.

"Rum," Matt offered from the doorway with a quick, apologetic look at his wife.

"Tom said to keep her quiet," Jack mumbled. "Rum'll do the trick."

"I don't—drink spirits!" Aisleen gasped. She tried to hand the cup to Sarah, but Jack's huge hand blocked the path. "Drink," he ordered.

Aisleen gulped, blinking back the tears of pain and anger that she doubted would move him to sympathy even if he did abhor them. "I won't," she said softly but quickly brought the cup to her lips as he made a move toward her. She took another swallow, igniting new flames in her throat, and she sputtered.

Sarah grabbed her wrist to temper her sipping. "Slowly. You'll make yourself sick." She looked up at Jack. "I'll see personally that she finishes every drop. If you hurry, you might find Tom before he finds the thief."

A look passed between Matt and Jack, and they left without a word.

When they were gone Sarah turned back to Aisleen. "Where were we? Oh, yes, you're a fool and a prude and a snob, Aisleen Gibson. And if you don't cease being all three immediately, you will soon learn what it is to live with regret for the rest of your life!"

Aisleen awakened to the sounds of a carousal. No, she had not been asleep, simply watching a spider spin its web in a ceiling corner. Her head felt woolly, yet lighter than air. If not tethered by the stem of her neck, she knew it would simply float away to bob gently in the corner near the spider. She giggled. Such a silly notion.

The contours of the room faded, stealing softly away until she was under the canopy of high-ceilinged bush. Below in the distance, the tents of hundreds of diggers lay in the skimpy shade of a few trees. But the noise did not come from the camp. It did not signal the joy of a strike. She turned her head slowly, aware of what was happening before she saw it.

He stood with his feet apart, his shirt hanging in shreds from his shoulders. One eye was swollen nearly shut, but the grin on his face was confident. At his feet lay the battered cook, bleeding from a dozen lacerations inflicted by a pair of fists. The cheers of the crowd urged the cook to try again, but he was sprawled unconscious. His vanquisher accepted the victory with a simple bow and then came toward her. The rest dissolved like images muddled by a stick thrown in a calm pond.

Aisleen found she could not move. The bed was at her back, but how was that possible? He came toward her slowly, limping badly, and she knew that his was not an easy victory. All the same, she felt no pity for him, only elation. Her first words to him surprised even her. "You're quite proud of yourself, aren't you?"

Aye, came his grinning reply.

"And so you should be," she answered cockily, "knocking the five senses out of a man half your size and twice your years!"

He paused a few feet from her and wiped his face on his arm. When he looked at her again his face was solemn. *So ye know now, do ye?*

"Aye," she answered softly.

Will it be making a difference?

"I don't know," Aisleen answered truthfully. "I don't understand it."

His smile was as warm and beckoning as sunshine. *When will ye learn that ye've no need to understand it, only to accept it?*

"You lied to me!"

Sure, and I should have said, macushla, ye're wedded to a man ye've known all yer life! he answered with a sad, sweet smile.

"It can't be!"

Ah, well, if it cannae be then it cannae be, he answered in gentle mockery. *I'll nae be pleading with ye for the believing of it. Some things cannae be had for the wishing of them. Others cannae be undone for the same.*

Aisleen stared at him, his blue eyes the bridge between the moments. "Why?"

He shrugged. *What the pooka writes, he himself can read.*

"That is no answer," she protested. "It is a childish riddle."

He smiled. *Ye once liked me riddles.*

"I was once a child. I'm no longer a child."

And don't I know it!

Aisleen turned her head away. It was not possible. She was dreaming, dreaming of a magic that did not exist.

'Tis yer saying it makes it so, colleen!

She turned back, but it was too late. He was gone. The walls of the bedroom had returned, the bed, table, and chair. Only the humming in her blood continued. Was she intoxicated? Yes, that was it. She had drunk a cup of rum. She was unquestionably, completely drunk!

Thomas had stopped to wash the worst of the blood from his face, neck, and chest before entering the house. Even so, Sarah gasped at the sight of him. "And me the winner!" he said before she spoke.

"Shame on you, Tom Gibson!" Sarah cried. "You've thoroughly enjoyed yourself while your wife has been beside herself with worry for you."

"She knows there's naught to fear," he answered easily, but his gaze moved to the bedroom door. "Is she sleeping?"

"I wouldn't call it sleeping," Sarah answered, "not when Jack's poured the better part of a rum keg down her poor throat. She's never taken a drink before, poor lamb, and when she's weathered the sore head that's sure to come, she may never drink again." She paused to wink at him. "You'll never have a better chance to make her listen to you. And if you'll take some advice, you'll tell her now what you should have long ago."

Tom dabbed the cut above his eye. "Not now, Sarah. She'll be too weary."

"Maybe," she answered. "But if she were my wife, I'd talk to her before she ran away a second time."

Thomas's gaze went back to the door. "I didn't know."

"Luck saved you a ride to Bathurst," Sarah added, hoping to goad him to action. "There's many a gentleman who wouldn't mind telling her how pretty she is and how much she stirs his heart."

Thomas glanced at her. "Ye're meddling in me business."

"So I am. Enough said, from me. It's your turn, Mr. Gibson, and high time!"

Thomas did not know what to expect when he opened the door, certainly not the sight of his wife sitting in bed with a warm smile of welcome on her face.

"Oh, you poor man!" she said. She raised a hand to touch the gash over his left brow. "Does it hurt?"

"Never a bit," he answered, more interested in the sights revealed by the slipping sheet. She was lying in bed naked! As he gazed at one ruby peak, he unconsciously wet his lips. "Do ye feel like a bit of conversation, lass? Ye're particularly fond of conversation."

Aisleen giggled. She knew it was quite improper to giggle even if one giggled in the privacy of her room with only her husband to hear. Highly improper, but she could not stop. Her fingers trailed down his temple to his cheek. "You're growing whiskers," she said in wonder as she rubbed against the grain of his new beard.

Thomas sat down carefully on the side of the bed, wary of this new Aisleen. "Aye, a man in the bush most often wears a beard. Ye'll nae be liking it?"

Aisleen curved her nails to catch the bristles. "I don't know. It will scratch, won't it?"

"Some women don't mind."

The change in her eyes was startling. From bemused gold to amber rage in a blink. "I won't have you walking down the street with another woman hanging on your arm!"

"Saw that, did ye?" Thomas smiled. "Then ye know it wasn't me fault."

"It was certainly your fault!" Aisleen snapped, but she couldn't hold her anger. Giggles bubbled in her chest, fermenting and then foaming over at the most inconvenient times. "Oh, Tom!" she gasped between giggles. "You mustn't make me angry. I don't like being angry."

Thomas smiled and reached out a hand to steady her by the shoulder. "Aye, and I've given ye grief enough this day. Poor lass, look at yer chin." He touched the bruise with infinite tenderness. "It must pain ye something fierce."

"It doesn't," she answered truthfully. "Jack gave me something for the pain."

His laughter was quite the best laughter she had ever heard, she decided. "Jack has the same cure for every ailment. I hope ye will not be thinking too badly of him come the morning."

Aisleen looked at him, at his black hair and blue eyes, at

the masculine contours of his jaw and brow, at his handsome mouth that she wanted very badly to kiss. "Love me," she whispered. "Please love me!"

"But I—"

He was unprepared for the strength of the arms she swung suddenly about his neck to bring his head down for her kiss. Her kiss was warm and wet and inviting, and he forgot everything but it and the warm silky body that thrust itself against him. Wrapping his arms about her, he followed her down into the bed.

Her hands were suddenly everywhere: at his belt, pulling it free from the buckle, at his shirt, unfastening buttons and tugging the tail from his trousers. Her breasts were impossibly soft against his chest, except for the hard nubs of her nipples.

He tried to be careful, not to jar her head, but she would not let him be gentle. She pulled him eagerly onto her, her kisses dragging at his mouth, devouring him in their hunger, seeking his breath before he could catch it. The heady intoxication of her passion brought to flame his own desire for her. Yet she was not satisfied with a return of her kisses. She wriggled under him until he lifted his head in puzzlement. She scooted up in the bed until she was half out from under him and then threw back her head and arched her back, offering him two swollen nipples.

He caught one peak in his lips and felt her shudder with pleasure. Bracing his elbows on the bed, he supported her back with his hands and began, one stroke at a time, to lick up from the shallows of her ribs to the summit, where he caught the nipple with a flick of his tongue. Each time she gasped until the lower half of each breast was slick and she quivered uncontrollably.

When she lifted her head, her face was deeply flushed, her hair tangled in her lashes, and her eyes two honeyed pools of passion.

"Ye're so beautiful!" he whispered. And she was, with a wild unstudied beauty that had nothing to do with light, or dressing, or composition of muscle and bone.

He lowered his head to rub his bristling chin into the soft curve of her belly, his hands sliding lower to buttress her hips. He had never touched a woman in this way before, had never known one long enough to hold and touch and possess as his fertile imagination might direct. His head moved lower, into the wild, fiery tangle that smelled of heather and sea mosses, and there he plied her with his tongue until she wept and shuddered and wept again, all for him.

He had not words for the emotion sweeping over him, just a deep primitive satisfaction that she allowed him these moments, this mastery that he had not even known was possible. His Aisleen, his "vision"—she was worth waiting for, worth fighting a hundred men for, worth anything for this!

When his own need for fulfillment levered him up across her once more, he had not words to express the need or the pleasure. He buried his face in her shoulder, lifted her hips while she, for the first time, parted her thighs without persuasion. He came into her easily and completely, a perfect match of soft, wet warmth and firm, hot flesh. She embraced him from within, welcoming him as no woman had, holding him as no woman had, pleasuring him as nothing ever had.

When it came, the fierce explosion of passion shook them both, left them gasping and shuddering and holding on to each other as the only reality in the world.

Afterward, as his head lay heavily upon her shoulder, Aisleen thought she felt the cold trail of tears upon her skin. But that was not possible. What did he have to weep about? It was she who was lost. She lightly stroked his head, smoothing the silky hair that lay behind his ear. "Do not weep, *avourneen machree.*"

"You make a fine pair! A black eye and a bruised chin! The folk of the New England district will know there's real gentry among them at last," Matt pronounced as he and Sarah stood outside the hotel the next morning to see their guests off on the coach for Bathurst.

"We'll heal right enough," Thomas answered and touched his tender eye. "Haven't had more fun in years."

Aisleen merely looked at Sarah, too miserable from her hangover to give much thought to her chin. "Thank you for everything," she said through stiff lips and gave the woman a quick hug. "You must come and visit us once we're settled."

"Don't know that we'll have the time," Sarah answered and patted her stomach. "Soon we'll be busier than ever. Matt's thinking of opening another public house far west of here at a place called Broken Hill. Some of the older diggers think it'll be the place of the next big strike."

Matt hushed Sarah with a hand over her mouth. "Can't tell the little woman a thing," he groused. "Before ye know it, there'll be a dozen sly grog shops going in under me nose."

"Don't suppose ye'd consider moving up north?" Thomas asked. "Not many of our kind in the district. We could do with some honest Irish neighbors, if ye know what I mean."

Matt smiled. "Maybe, when I've made me fortune and we're more settled." He glanced at Sarah, and she nodded at him.

"That's the ticket!" Thomas moved to help Aisleen climb onto the dray with extra seats that served as transportation to Bathurst. He climbed up after her and waved a hand. "G'day, Matt, Sarah! See ye next time through!"

Aisleen did not look back as they rounded the corner; she could not without shaming herself with tears. Once more she was being uprooted just as she was beginning to feel a bond between people and herself. Was it always to be like this?

"We'll be seeing them again," Thomas said beside her. "I've known Matt some years. He'll come round to me way of thinking, see if he doesn't."

"Were you transported together?"

For a moment Thomas said nothing, and Aisleen wondered if she had embarrassed him. They were not alone. They shared a seat with a huge woman with whiskers on her chin and a rummy breath.

Thomas reached out and took her hand, his eyes on the road ahead. "There's many a thing I should be telling ye, lass, but now is not the time. When we're alone together, I'll be answering yer questions, *all* yer questions. I swear it."

Aisleen leaned her aching head on his shoulder, and his arm came about her to hold her close. "That's me lass," he murmured in her ear.

Danger no refuge holds, and war no peace
For him who hears love sing and never cease...

—The Rose of Battle
W. B. Yeats

Chapter Sixteen

A lurch of the coach jolted Aisleen awake on the seat, but Thomas's arm was there at her waist to hold her steady. She looked into his face and smiled.

"Not much further now," he said. "We'll soon be stopping for the night."

She nodded and lowered her head back onto his shoulder, where she looked past him out of the coach window. The afternoon sky shone in vivid shades above the Blue Mountains. They had taken the regular coach from Bathurst across the mountains, a trip that Thomas informed her would take the remarkably short time of a day and a half when she considered that the journey with the sheep had taken more than three weeks.

After a moment she glanced at her fellow passengers. There was a thin woman in a deep-brimmed bonnet that hid her features. Beside her, a child of eight dressed in his Sunday best clung to her hand. To their right two rough, pipe-smoking diggers sat silently exhaling clouds of bilious cheap tobacco that circled the brilliant feathers they had stuck in the bands of their bush hats. They had not spoken, but Aisleen was aware that their gazes seldom left her. If Thomas noticed, he said nothing. She suspected that he *did* notice, for he occasionally patted the hard lump under his jacket which was the butt of his pistol.

Aisleen suppressed a yawn, delighted that she was not on the trail with Jack, who was following them on horseback and leading Thomas's mount. They were to meet on the eastern side of the Divide and then travel north to the New England district together. The coach was faster, more comfortable, and the meals served up hot and hearty at coaching inns. If she never saw the back of another cook wagon, she would not regret it.

As she snuggled down against him once more, Thomas smiled. The misgivings and uncertainty of the last weeks had left him. They had a great deal yet to learn about each other, some of it a filling in of the past, but he no longer doubted that they would survive the truth.

She loved him—at least she was beginning to do so. His welcome into her bed the night before would remain in his memory if he lived to be a hundred.

As for the other, he did not know what to think of it. In fact, he shied from an examination of it. If he thought about it too hard and too long, he might grow wary of her or of himself. It was not a natural gift, of that he was certain. As to its purpose, there seemed to be none. Accept and forget: that would be his advice to her. He would take it himself.

He bent and touched his cheek to Aisleen's brow, his gaze settling blandly upon the taller of the two pipe smokers, who seemed to find the curves of Aisleen's bodice of irresistible interest. With an easy movement he reached inside his coat and lifted his pistol so that the butt of it peaked through the opening. He saw the thin woman across from him stiffen in fright, but he merely smiled and nodded at her. His point had been made with the diggers.

The coach swayed on its leather supports, and the driver cursed the horses around a tight bend in the canyon road. All at once the driver's cry split the air, and the coach veered sharply toward the edge of the precipice as he fought to bring the animals to a halt. Aisleen slid forward on the seat with a cry of fright, but Thomas caught her, bracing them with a boot against the opposite seat.

"Ambush!" the driver cried over the protest of his passengers. "All out, lads!"

The diggers were the first to jump from the coach, and as they left, Aisleen saw the burning tree that had been dragged across the road.

Thomas reached for his pistol, but it was too late to prevent an attack. Half a dozen men rushed from the bushes that flanked the mountain side of the road.

"Bail up!"

The cry was followed by the crack of pistol shots and then the thud of a body as one of the diggers dropped onto the roadside.

The thin woman screamed, and the child with her wailed in fright as he threw himself into her arms. The remaining digger leaped back in beside the hysterical woman and winked at Thomas. "Bushrangers! Half a dozen!"

Aisleen clutched Thomas's arm. Thomas gave her a quick, reassuring smile and tucked his hand with the pistol in it into her skirts. "Say nothing."

A moment later the coach door was thrown open and the driver was shoved into the breach, a pistol at his temple.

"All out or he's dead!"

"If it's gold ye're after, lads, ye'll be finding it with the luggage on top." Thomas's voice was amused and slightly bored.

The digger fired a shot past the driver in the open doorway, and the bushranger was thrown back by the bullet that bored his forehead. The driver was thrust aside as a second robber turned his pistol into the coach's interior and fired. With a cry of pain the digger collapsed onto the terrified woman's lap.

Aisleen's screams were muffled by the weight of Thomas's body as he covered her. From the opposite side new shots entered the coach, and the digger jerked and moaned as several bullets found their mark.

"Bail up!" came the shout a second time.

"We surrender!" Thomas reached over and threw the dead digger's pistol from the window. "We've women and a child!"

A man moved into the breach of the open coach door, and a face out of a nightmare stared in on them. Aisleen gasped and recoiled. It was a travesty of a human being: the mouth wide and lipless, above a thin beard the cheeks seamed and furrowed, ravaged by the harshest elements of the sun and pitted by disease. The eyes were almost lost in a permanent squint. It was a face to be remembered with a shudder and a prayer, and when she turned to Thomas she saw her own revulsion reflected in his contracted pupils.

But he did not withdraw. A bemused smile flickered on his lips. "Sean O'Leary."

The man stared at Thomas; then a slow, gap-toothed grin spread over his face. "By hell and the devil! If'n it isn't me old friend Tommy!" The small man's wild eyes seemed to drink in Thomas, his grin widening to imbecilic proportions. "God rot me if I don't have ye at last!"

"I've heard ye were looking for me," Thomas said politely, but he did not release the pistol he held hidden in Aisleen's skirts. "Well, here I am."

"So ye are," the man answered and thrust his pistol in

the weeping woman's face. "Step out, Thomas, me boy. We've things to discuss."

"I think I'll be keeping me seat," Thomas answered and slid his arm free of Aisleen's grasp, leaving the pistol in her lap.

The man's squinty gaze shifted to Aisleen. "Be that yer lass?" Thomas shrugged. "Heard ye was wed a few weeks back." The man's tongue rimmed his gash of a mouth as he stared at Aisleen's red hair. "Haven't seen a lass the likes of her in fourteen years."

His gaze moved back to Thomas. "Ye were always the one with the most luck. Seamus and Michael died on the hillside above Schull Harbor. They were the lucky sort, too, to me way of thinking. Thought I'd been hanged, did ye, Tommy? Well, I wasn't! Now there's just ye and me, and the score will be settled between us."

Thomas stared at the man a moment. "Very well," he said in Gaelic. "For ye, Sean, I'll be stepping out." He pressed Aisleen's thigh hard to keep her from moving. "But I'll be asking ye, as one Corkman to another, to let the ladies be. Ye've no quarrel with them."

"Sean! For God's sake! Hurry up!" one of the bushrangers cried.

"Hold yer tongue!" Sean roared back, his pistol moving to point at Thomas. "Nae, I'll nae kill ye. 'Twould be too easy. I'll nae have ye die easy. Stand down, Tommy, lad. Stand down with me, just like the old days when we were rebels together against the English. Only this time, ye'll nae be seeing us grabbed!"

"No!" Aisleen clutched Thomas's arm as he rose to leave the coach. Sean turned his pistol on her, but she was too frightened for Thomas to judge the danger in which she also stood. She lunged for the pistol that was sliding free of her skirts and lifted it.

Thomas saw what she was about to do and deflected the

barrel with the back of his hand before jumping free of the coach.

"Thomas!" Aisleen cried, but he shut the door before she gained the exit.

For an instant his face was framed in the coach window. "I'll be meeting ye in Sydney, *macushla*. Tell Jack about Sean!" The next moment he was felled by a blow from Sean's pistol butt.

"Tom!" Aisleen threw her weight against the door, but the latch held. A moment later Sean's ugly face reappeared. "Ye'll nae see him again, lass! I'll be taking him to hell with me!"

"Drive on!" came a cry from beyond the coach, and all at once they began to move.

Realizing that she lay half-sprawled over a dead man's body, Aisleen rose to push herself back in one corner of the coach seat, numbed by misery and fear. She sat a short while in silence, scarcely aware of her surroundings as the wails of the woman and child filled the interior. But gradually the hysteria that raged across the small space drew her attention, and she stared at the woman. What was she wailing about? She had lost nothing to the bushrangers.

"Shut up!" she cried as the woman continued to keen wildly. "Shut up or I'll strike you!"

The woman halted abruptly to stare at her, but Aisleen turned her head away and began to weep softly. The weeping did not last long. Something must be done, but what?

Aisleen reached up and began pummeling the coach ceiling with her fists. "Stop! Stop at once!"

At first she did not think the driver would heed her pleas, but finally he brought the coach to a halt. The moment it stopped, she grabbed Thomas's pistol and climbed down.

"What'd ye be doing, miss?" the driver called as she stepped down. "We've another four miles before we reach the coaching station."

"I'm not going there. I'm expecting a friend along shortly."

"Are ye mad, miss? Those bushrangers could come this way, and where would you be?"

Aisleen pointed at her bags. "Leave our things at the next station. We'll be coming back for them."

The driver gaped at her. "I can't leave a woman passenger on the roadside."

Aisleen lifted her pistol. "Drive on!"

With an amazing string of profanity the driver whipped up his team, and the coach rolled on.

When it was out of sight, Aisleen wiped the perspiration from her face with a hand and then found a large rock on which to sit to wait for Jack. Her perch was out of the sunlight and away from casual view from the road, but it allowed her sight of anyone traveling the highway.

She did not know how far behind them Jack might be, but she suspected that he kept the pace fairly well. She refused to think about what she would do if he did not come before dark, or worse, took a different route that would not bring him along this road. Thomas had said there was only one pass over the Blue Mountains. He must come this way.

"He must!" she whispered fiercely.

The sight of a man on horseback did not kindle her hopes. Several had passed in the intervening two hours. It was the oversized length of the late-afternoon shadow he cast before him that drew Aisleen to the edge of the road.

When she stepped up onto the roadway he paused but did not seem surprised to find her standing alone on an empty road.

"G'day," was all he said.

Aisleen blinked back new tears. "We were held up by bushrangers. The one named Sean took Tom."

Jack looked up, his eyes narrowing against the sun. "How long ago?"

"Two hours, maybe nearly three," she answered, her hand held to shade her eyes. "Help me find him, Jack. Please."

When he looked down at her, Aisleen was surprised to see that he was smiling. It was not a pleasant smile, but it gave her heart. "Maybe Tom's dead."

Aisleen shook her head. "No, I'd know it."

Jack stared at her a long time, and she felt the weight of his stare like a heavy hand upon her head. Finally he nodded once and tossed her the lead reins to Thomas's horse.

She did not bother to tell him that she had never ridden alone. He knew that. She gathered the reins and then set her foot in the stirrup and hoisted herself inexpertly into Thomas's saddle. When she had pulled herself upright she looked across at the man who towered above her in his saddle.

"Which way?" he asked quietly.

Aisleen shut her eyes. How was she to find Thomas? Until this moment she had believed that Jack would help her find him. Now she understood that the burden was hers.

She touched the pistol she had tucked into her waistband. She was in a strange land, in unfamiliar territory. Where in all the wilds of the Blue Mountain bush did one search for a man?

There was no answer and so she simply turned her mount, handling the reins as she had watched Thomas do so often, and dug the heels of her boots into the horse's flanks to urge her mount back down the road. Jack followed her, walking his horse behind her and then riding abreast.

When they reached the site of the ambush, Aisleen did not stop. She did not glance at the dead body that had been left on the roadside. She did not think of what might be happening to Thomas. She turned her horse down the steep embankment off the road and into the twilight of the underbrush with Jack riding like an otherworldly sentry at her side.

*   *   *

"I'm not finished with ye, ye miserable, traitorous cur!
Just ye wait till daylight. Ye'll wish ye'd swung all them
years ago! I'll be giving ye ten stripes for every one of
mine, before I'm done with ye! See if I don't! Only enough
life'll be left in ye to hang!"

The maddened voice roared through her mind, but she
could not find the source. Bonds held her securely, and there
was no light when she tried to open her eyes. She was
blind!

Pain radiated through every fiber of her body, excruciating white-hot flashes of agony that she could not move from
or cry out to prevent. Face, chest, stomach, and back: the
blows came repeatedly until she knew she would die!

Aisleen sat up with a gasping cry. For a moment her
dream-blocked eyes saw nothing. And then she saw Jack
standing over her, his craggy face immutable as always.

"Tom dead?"

Aisleen shook her head. "No."

Jack watched her with a predatory gleam, but she did not
fear him. "Knew a woman once, same as ye. She saw
things, heard things. Never liked her."

Aisleen blushed furiously as he turned away. Is that how
she seemed to him—a mad woman who claimed to hear and
see things that no one else did? It was not true. She had
suffered a nightmare, nothing more. But she knew Thomas
was still alive; she could feel it inside her. Alive, but for
how long?

She scrambled to her feet. They had spent the darkest
hours of the night in the shelter of great, gloomy trees. The

thin light of early dawn lent an eerie, brooding quality to the air. The silence seemed pregnant with treachery and danger. She shivered with cold and dread.

"Cha," Jack muttered and motioned to her. She saw that he had made a very small fire over which he had swung his billy can. She gratefully took the cup he offered her.

"Bushrangers'll be moving soon," Jack offered as he hunkered down to douse his fire. He looked up at her, his eyes almost on a level with her own as she stood beside him. "They'll kill him before that."

Aisleen met his cold gray eyes. "Then we must find them first."

Jack nodded and pointed at the pistol in her waistband. "You're a shot?"

"I'll learn," she answered defensively.

She was not certain that she liked his gallows smile any better than his funereal stare. He reached out to touch her sore chin, and though she winced she did not back away. "Maybe Tom had the right of ye. Can't always count a man's flock by the sheep ye can see."

It was the longest speech she had ever heard him make, and she was flattered. "What do we do?"

Jack said nothing as he took the pistol from her waistband and examined it. He opened the revolver, took several bullets from his shirt pocket, and placed them in the empty chambers. Then, without speaking a word, he spun her about so that her back was braced against his chest. He took her right hand and wrapped her fingers about the butt, curving her forefinger over the trigger. He brought her left hand up to brace the pistol and, hunkering down over her shoulder, raised the weapon to her eye level and took aim on a tree limb.

"Two hands and squeeze!" he said, the ghastly whisper grating into her ear. "You aim to kill, every time. *Every* time. Heart or head. Nothing else!"

Aisleen felt the iron pressure of his huge hands over hers and smelled his stale tobacco breath and knew that had she searched a year she could not have found a more deadly companion. When he released her she looked at him askance. "You've killed men before?"

He grinned. "Not enough."

Aisleen's skin shrank against her bones. She was not afraid for herself. She understood that he was totally indifferent to her as a woman. She suspected that he did not possess the usual human lusts. He was curiously devoid of all passion. Nothing burned deep inside his pale eyes. She did not even know why he was helping her. But she was very grateful that he was.

"Will you use it?" He pointed to the gun she held.

Aisleen nodded. "What do we do now?"

He lifted a long arm and pointed south. Aisleen saw nothing. "Smoke," he said as though it were a complete explanation. "Saddle up."

They wound a slow path through the silent forest of the somber mountain, this time Aisleen trailing Jack. They did not travel far before he put up a hand and lifted one long leg over his horse to dismount.

Less easily, Aisleen slipped from her saddle. A dozen unanswered questions buzzed in her head, but it was too late. Jack was moving away on that silent tread she had never become accustomed to. She hurried after him, glad that his huge body provided a shield between her and what lay ahead.

When he halted suddenly, she nearly collided with him. He caught her by the shoulder and pointed again.

At first she saw nothing in the gloom, but gradually she saw the faint glow of a fire in the center of a ring of trees and then the dark humps of men sleeping on the ground. At the base of a large tree another body was slumped over. Her skin tingled as she looked up into Jack's face, and he nodded.

She clutched her pistol tighter. She knew she could not shoot a man. Everything in her rose up in protest at the thought. But she would fire in their direction and hope that it would frighten them.

Jack stood still so long a time she would have thought him made of stone had she not felt the tense alertness emanating from his huge frame. Finally he moved, veering off to the left. After quickly tucking up her skirts to keep them from dragging over twigs and rocks, she followed. They made a wide circle about the sleeping bushrangers as her heart hammered in her chest. Where was Tom?

Jack's long arm shot up suddenly, stopping her, and he pointed at the ground. Aisleen squatted down, too daunted to question his order. Where was Tom? Why was there no sign of him? Even as her thoughts raced round and round she saw Jack move forward into the shadow of a huge gum tree and seemingly disappear.

Aisleen swallowed repeatedly as she crouched in the near-dark. Insects clicked and buzzed and rustled close by. In the distance the *gawk* of a parrot was heard. The morning air hung cold and still and damp. Her face was sticky with the sweat of fear. And still nothing happened.

A man's moan, so low and muffled she doubted its reality, wafted over the clearing. Aisleen clutched the pistol tighter, willing her forefinger to grasp the trigger, but it would not.

A flash of memory that seemed another lifetime ago came and went. Had it been less than two months since she had pointed this pistol at Thomas in anger because he had demanded his rights as her husband? How foolish and empty the gesture had been. Now the danger was very real and very deadly. At any moment the bush would come alive with men who would not hesitate to kill. To save Thomas's

life she would do whatever was necessary. Her finger closed
gently on the trigger.

The second moan was louder but instantly cut off. Aisleen
shuddered as sweat trickled down between her breasts. Who
was hurt so badly? Was it Thomas? She could see nothing
though her eyes ached with the strain of effort. Where had
Jack gone? Did he intend to rush the camp alone?

A branch snapped nearby. The crisp *crack* of the wood
sent fear screaming along her nerve endings as her hands
flexed on the pistol she lifted. Other, softer sounds of
footsteps thudded the earth. Aisleen's arms trembled under
the weight of the weapon she held at eye level. Whatever it
was, whoever it was, could be halted by her shot.

A hulking grotesque shadow reared suddenly before her,
and Aisleen fell back with a muffled gasp, the hair bristling
on her arms. The grotesquerie resolved into Jack and the
inanimate man he bore on his back. "Tom!" she whispered
in shivering amazement. "Is he—?"

Before she could finish the question, Jack bent and
dragged her to her feet and roughly shoved her before him
back toward the way they had come.

Joy flowing through her, Aisleen beat a path for them
with her hands through the thickly laced bush. Resilient
twigs whipped back to lash her face, but she did not mind
the stinging pain. Thomas was alive! Of course he was
alive. Jack would not have brought out a dead man. Less
cautious than before, she hurried through the canopied
twilight of early dawn. Their horses had been tethered
nearby. She had not seens horses in the bushrangers' camp.
They would escape.

The pistol's report that rent the silence of the morning
brought Aisleen to a stumbling halt, but Jack was there
behind her to shove her along with a mumbled, "Get shot
with ye!"

The camp behind them exploded with sounds of curses

and running feet. Aisleen ran faster than she had ever run in her life, faster than up the hillside of Slieve Host as a child. The horses were so close. It did not matter if they were heard. Their pursuers would not be able to catch them once they were mounted.

"Bail up!"

The cry was familiar, but Aisleen did not slow her pace even as a wild shot flew past her and struck the trunk of a nearby tree. Jack was at her back, prodding her with his gun barrel; she feared failing him more than anything else.

The nervous whinny of a horse was the sweetest sound she had ever heard, she thought in the moment she burst into the glade where the animals stood. She ran for Thomas's horse, but Jack's cry made her pause as she lifted a foot into the stirrup.

"Mine!" and he gestured at the larger horse, where he had thrown Thomas crosswise over the saddle.

She had no time to argue. He grabbed her about the waist and slung her up on the back of his mount. The next instant reins were shoved in her hands. With a sharp turn, Jack reached for the reins of the second horse.

The report of a rifle startled the horses. Thomas's horse tore the reins from Jack's grip and bolted. Aisleen's mount reared, pawing the air in fright. She threw herself forward across Thomas's back to grip the horse's neck. She heard Jack curse, then the explosion of his pistol and a man's cry of pain as she clung breathlessly to the horse, frightened that at any moment she would be flung to the ground. Then, amazingly, the horse's head was jerked down and Jack's face appeared level with hers.

"Tell Tom we're even at last!" he shouted and smiled at her. "You're a good'n yourself!"

A pistol went off. Jack's smile froze. He whipped about, his own weapon aimed for the delivery of shot. Aisleen saw two men race out of the underbrush with pistols, the orange/red flares of explosion from Jack's weapon and theirs, and then the blinding white smoke of gunfire misting the air.

"Jack! Hurry," Aisleen cried, reaching out to shake the big man's shoulder.

He turned to her slowly, his smile still in place. So fierce was his grimace she did not at first notice the red roses blooming on his shirtfront. "Get shot of here!" he shouted and brought the flat of his massive hand down on the horse's rear.

The slap startled the horse, and it danced away from the man at a gallop as new gunfire split the morning. Aisleen cried out in protest, but it was useless. She could not control her mount. A single backward glance was all she had of Jack. He was still standing as a man rushed him. There were new shots and then a deathly stillness punctuated by the galloping hooves of her horse.

She had no time to think of what had happened behind her. Underneath her Thomas stirred and moaned, and she knew that he was wounded but not how badly. She had not had a single glimpse of him. She tugged on the reins but to no avail. The animal was too frightened to heed her tentative struggle and so she gave the beast free rein, holding Thomas across the saddle with one hand and clinging to a handful of mane with the other. She did not know where they were headed or how they would find the Great Western Road. She only knew that every stretch of the horse's stride took them farther away from the bushrangers and closer to safety.

The horse ran for miles, dropping into a trot when the bush gave way to the rough, broken country of a valley between the somber naked peaks of the mountains.

Finally the sound of rushing water attracted the animal's attention, and it gentled its stride to a walk that brought it to the banks of a stream.

Aisleen slid immediately from its back and caught the reins, gulping in breath after breath. Her throat was so dry that every gasp pained her lungs, and she was drawn with the horse to the edge of the riverbank in hopes of taking a drink. Instead she found herself on one side of a deep chasm through which a roaring river ran, its surface churned to white foam as it rushed down the narrow slope between rocky walls.

With regret she turned the horse back from the precipice and led it to the shade of a tree not far away. The horse followed her uncomplainingly, too weary and lathered with sweat to object. When she had wound the reins securely about a branch, she reached for Thomas to help him down. He had not moved or spoken but lay as Jack had tossed him, meal-sack fashion, across the saddle.

He was heavier than she expected as she tugged him feet first off the horse. When he slipped free, she was unable to balance his weight, and she sprawled with him onto the grass. He groaned terribly, and a shudder shook him.

"Oh, Thomas, I'm sorry!" Aisleen said as she scooted out from under him. "Let me help you." On her knees, she reached for his shoulder and turned him onto his back.

"Oh, dear God!"

He was unrecognizable. His face was a mass of blood, caked dry in places and with fresh, oozing wounds. His lips were puffed and broken, his nose a swollen lump of flesh. His eyes were sealed shut by the swelling that made his face seem twice its normal size.

Bile rose in her throat as she tore her gaze away to find other, less repulsive, sights. But everywhere she looked there was more evidence of torture. There were lacerations on his chest and arms. The ends of leather thongs still hung from his wrists where he had been tied. Where his ribs showed through the rents in his shirt there were long, blue-red bruises. He had been beaten mercilessly. How could he breathe?

She backed away. She did not want to touch him. She did not know this battered hulk of a man. He was not her lovely, handsome Thomas. He did not even seem human. She could not help him.

She turned away and choked. She was sick, over and over again, until there was nothing left but the dry heaving that turned to tears. She stretched full on the ground, unmindful of the beauty of the sunshine, of the green and brown tapestry of the valley, or of the silver laughter of the river racing by at her feet, and wept until she was dry.

So here ye are, with a real, thoroughgoing adventure before ye at last, and what do ye do? Lasses! Trust them to weep a sea over a little blood and spit every time!

Aisleen's head shot up at the sound of the mocking laughter and she glanced at Thomas, but he lay still.

The day cooled suddenly, the drifting of a cloud across the sun. The smell of the sea rode the softer air textured with mist. The tang of bog and the floral scent of heather invaded the day.

Is it that game ye're still playing? came the cocky retort. *Wirra! I should have known.*

Aisleen turned around very slowly. In the shade of a flowering wattle the familiar shadow stood. She glanced again at Thomas's prone body and then at the apparition. "Is Thomas dead?"

Musha! What good would that be to ye? Nae, the lad's sleeping deep, 'tis all.

"Then why . . . ?" Aisleen shook her head and looked down at her hands. "You've never shown yourself when Thomas was present."

Ah, well, being that he's a hard man to best, and that I've nae cause to come between a man and his wife, it seemed best.

Aisleen looked up again. He was only a wavering image in the distance. Behind him—no, through him—she saw the outline of a mountain. "Who are you? *What* are you?"

His voice was shaken by laughter. *Trust a woman to be asking foolish questions. I'm meself, of course!*

"You look like my husband."

Do I now? Well, that's nae so much a shame, would ye say?

Aisleen did not respond.

So it's to be like that, is it? Very well. Top of the morning to ye, colleen!

"No! Wait!" Aisleen scrambled to her feet and took a step toward him. The vision wavered as though rippled by a breeze and then steadied. "Why have you come?"

What answer would ye like, lass?

She hesitated. "Am I mad?"

Laughter shimmered the air, littering the day with bright petals of amusement. *No madder than the next, and saner than some!*

"Blarney!" Aisleen scoffed. "You never offer anything but clever words and useless riddles."

Can ye do better?

"In what way?"

There's the matter of yer man lying there neglected, for instance.

Aisleen paled, her eyes sliding guiltily toward Thomas's bloodied face and away. "I can't. I can't bear to touch him!"

Och, well! If ye cannae, ye cannae.

The glib answer made her squirm inside. She put a hand to her throbbing brow. "I don't know what to do!"

Of course not. That's why ye were lying there weeping and wailing for a Good Samaritan to make his appearance. A fine plan that is, lass. I'd as lief I'd thought of it meself.

Anger stung her. "Don't mock me! It's all very well for

you to speak, when you've not offered a single helpful suggestion. Go away!''

She turned and marched over to the horse, which stood patiently cropping the short grass in the shade of the tree that flanked the river. A quick survey of Jack's saddlebags reassured her. He had been well provisioned for his journey.

Jack. Aisleen leaned her head against the saddle. Was he dead? If not, he would come after them. But how would he know where to find them?

She thought then of what Jack would say if he *did* find them and discovered that she had not even attempted to tend Thomas's wounds. The idea so appalled her that she grabbed the billy can from his saddlebag and went to the riverbank. But the water was more than six feet below her, a sheer drop that allowed no method for her to climb down and fill the pail. She scanned the gorge, seeking a place where the bank was less steep, but she did not see one.

She stood there a moment, thinking. She needed a rope with which she could lower the pail into the water. A check of the saddlebags did not provide that. She found a knife in the provisions and began to hack at her skirts, tearing off long, thin strips which she then plaited together to make a stout rope.

She was quite proud of herself when she had fished up the first pailful without losing more than half the contents. She cut the legs of her pantaloons off just below the top of each thigh and, using a portion of the material, began to clean Thomas's face. The work was painstakingly slow.

Pail after pail of water turned red with blood as she gently sponged his wounds. When she had cleaned his face and body as best she could without moving him, she sat back on her heels and studied the results. His eyes were swollen shut and his lips were cracked, but she had no salve for them. Cuts gaped open above his brows and on the ridges of his cheeks. She had no sticking plaster with which to close them. She was certain at least two of his ribs were broken, but as she pressed her ear to his chest, she did not hear the betraying hiss of a punctured lung. He could not be moved until his chest was bound tightly.

Tears stung her eyes, but she blinked them back. What good were they? Because there was nothing else to do, she went once more to look through Jack's saddlebags. This time she picked up and recorded in her mind each item. There were small packs of rice, flour, sugar, dried peas, beans, dried beef, salt, and tea and—wonder of wonders—a small tin of lard. She took the tea and lard, remembering that once she had seen Miss Burke apply crushed tea leaves to a small finger wound one of her pupils had received while cutting her quill.

She knelt down beside Thomas and opened the packet of tea. Rolling the dried leaves between her fingers, she sprinkled it into the first wound over his left eye. When it was thoroughly dusted she pressed the wound firmly closed with her fingers and held it so for five minutes. When she removed her hand, the wound remained closed and unbleeding. She repeated the procedure until every wound on his face had been so treated, and then she opened the lard tin and smeared his lips lightly with grease.

Binding his chest was the most difficult task of all. Though he never gained consciousness, pitiable moans occasionally broke from him as she rolled him from one side to lay the remaining strips of her skirts under him. When she had pulled tight and tied the last piece of cloth, her face was damp with tears of sympathy.

It was midafternoon when she finished binding his wounds. Her back ached from tossing and hauling up innumerable pails of water, some of which she had given to the horse. Her head ached from working in the sun without a bonnet, which she had left behind in the coach. She was half-naked. A jagged ruff of skirt, petticoat, and pantaloons covered her from waist to knee, and a part of this she fully expected to lose to bandages by morning. Two things kept her from resting. She was hungry, and night was coming on.

Between the river and the mountains stretched a wide strip of woodland. She went there and gathered wood for a fire. When she had coaxed a blaze from the timber with Jack's flint, she sat back and hugged her knees a moment, grateful, this once, that she had been in the cook's company long enough to learn how to set a campfire. She made a tripod for the billy and hung it over the flame to make tea.

As she cradled Thomas's head in her lap the late-afternoon sky turned golden and then flame. From the forest a flock of parrots came to perch in the tree above her. Their bickering drew her attention away from the sunset, and she saw in amazement the equally brilliant plumage of the parrots, their feathers emerald and saffron with a blood-red patch of color on their rumps. They stayed only a moment, sounding to her city ears like a classroom of schoolgirls all talking at once, and then flew off, green wings flashing like emerald lightning in the sky.

When the billy boiled she sprinkled in the tea and set it aside a moment to brew. A cooling breeze blew in from the forest at her back, and she remembered with misgiving how cold the nights became in the mountains. She touched Thomas's cheek and found it warm but not yet feverish. He needed protection against the chill of the night, but there was only one thin blanket rolled behind the saddle. When she had tucked it about him she added another faggot to the fire to brighten the flame. Jack would come soon, she told herself, and when he did he would lead them to safety.

The tea tasted unbelievably good. When she had drunk her fill and chewed a bit of jerky, she soaked a piece of cloth in the tea and brought it to Thomas. Forcing his mouth open, she squeezed a little of it between his lips. He coughed and choked, the spasm jerking him forward, and a long, low groan sighed out of him as he fell back.

Guilt pricked her as she stroked his brow. She had only wanted to give him a drink. Perhaps later he would awaken enough for her to pour a sip down his throat.

Not long after, she spied in the distance several figures slowly making their way out of the forest. She jumped to her feet in hope. Were they men? It was too great a distance to tell. She raised her arms and waved frantically as she ran toward them. "Here! Here! Help! Help!"

They saw her at the same moment she realized that these were not men but animals, and each stopped short. The beasts had tall ears rather like a rabbit's. Clothed in almost black or gray fur, they sat upright. One creature scratched its chest with a small forepaw, and Aisleen smiled. They looked harmless enough and, eager for a better look at them, she moved closer. But they were not so curious about her. All of a sudden they sprang in every direction, jumping in long, bounding hops that took them back into the cloaking darkness of the forest.

Kangaroos! Thomas had told her an outlandish tale about such beasts, but she had not believed him. She half-expected to hear the mocking laughter of her ghostly tormentor; but she did not feel his presence, and as she made her way back to her camp, she felt very alone.

She gathered the wood for the fire close and then lay down beside Thomas. He was silent and still except for his breathing. She watched him a long time, ashamed of her cowardice in the face of his distress. She had wanted to run away. Now she felt only a fierce protectiveness toward him. She put a hand over his eyes, praying that they would be fine when the swelling subsided.

After a moment's reflection, she got up and poured out as much tea as the tin cup could hold and then went to fetch more water. The river water was very cool, and she soaked a piece of cloth in it and placed it over his eyes to help the swelling. As it became warm from his skin she wet the cloth, again and again, and placed it over his eyes.

When she was too weary to continue, she bent and kissed his mouth very gently and then lay down so that he was closer to the fire. She cuddled close to him to add the heat of her body and fell instantly asleep.

Surely thine hour has come, thy great wind blows,
Far-off, most secret, and inviolate Rose?

—The Secret Rose
W. B. Yeats

Chapter Seventeen

He floated in a thick dark sea of agony. The pain crested in endless seething waves that battered his face and chest and groin. In the beginning there had been fists and boots. Later the blows did not separate themselves but became a pelting of indefinable origin that left him sobbing and cursing to keep from shaming himself with pleas for mercy. There was none. Sean was mad, mad with the years of bestial service in the hellhole penal colony of Norfolk Island.

"Not my fault!"

He had not betrayed his friends all those years ago. Why had Sean believed the lying English? He and Sean had been saved from the hangman's knot not on his confession but by a quirk of fate that perhaps would never be explained. Was he to die now, after all the years of suffering and loss were behind him?

Aisleen. No! He shut his mind to thoughts of her. He must not do that to her. It would be too cruel. Too cruel!

Nausea swept him and he was sick. Then there was oblivion.

Silence. The blessed sound of silence. Nothing moved. He could not even draw breath. Was he dead?

He choked, the spasm his body's effort to keep him alive. He groaned as intolerable pains radiated out from his chest and groin. Broken ribs. Was his manhood shattered? Where was the sky? He whimpered. Blind!

The rich, fecund odor of soil mixed with the stench of vomit was his first impression upon regaining consciousness. He had been unbound and lain out on the ground. The aroma of crushed grass tickled his nose. Alive. But for how long? Cautiously he flexed his fingers. They were stiff, aching from the rheumatoid tension of the beating. But they were whole.

Nothing else seemed whole. He could not move arms or legs. His face ached. His teeth—he felt about in his mouth with the bruised edge of his tongue. Several were uncommonly loose, but there were no gaps. He would have smiled at his own vanity had it not hurt too much. His arms would not move. His eyes were glued shut. Was he blind?

Fear gripped him, turning his bowels watery. Blinded and left in the bush. It was a vicious revenge. There were a thousand ways to die. He might tumble down a chasm and break a leg or drown in a rushing stream. He was prey for wild boar, a dingo pack, any and every danger in the bush.

Panic released reserves of strength he had despaired of a

moment earlier and, pushing with his hands, he levered his torso up and away from the ground.

Fiery pain careened through his body. Knifeblades of pain dug into his chest. His breath burst from his body in a cry of agony. The ground seemed to rise up and slam his face with a stunning force.

There was a voice droning in his ear. It was a weeping voice, a soft, pretty, girlish voice. Aisleen's voice? No! He mustn't think of her. She must not know what was happening to him. She was too fragile, too gently reared to withstand the shock of it. She must never know how he died, when he died. The bond between them, the one he had discovered long before she had, must not bring her pain.

His mind floated between the worlds of consciousness and unconsciousness. Sometimes he felt the heat of the sun slanting down upon his face. Other times cool water—was it rain?—bathed him. His face was swollen, the skin stretched so tautly over the bones that he wanted to scratch it to gain relief, but he was too weak even to lift his hand. His mouth was dry, his tongue thickening.

Fear roiled in him again. He had heard that to die of thirst was the worst agony a man could know. It took a long time. His tongue would thicken until he could not swallow. He would choke to death.

Water! his mind screamed, tensing muscles that tortured his already aching body.

The cold touch of a tin cup's rim surprised him almost as much as the hand at the back of his neck that lifted his head. The water ran out around his stiff lips and trickled down his cheeks into his collar. He cursed the cup holder, tears of anger starting in his eyes. And then, blessedly, the cool, life-giving fluid spread across his tongue.

He swallowed, sucking noisily at the cup until the cooling relief bathed his gullet and pooled in his stomach. He felt it slosh gently just behind his lowest ribs as his head was lowered back on the ground. He wanted to thank his savior, but he had no strength left to form the words. No time before weakness reclaimed him in the half-world of stupor.

Aisleen sat with her chin propped on her knees as the sun set on the second day. Thomas lay beside her, asleep. She absently brushed away an insect that crawled across his brow and then threaded her fingers through his hair. She had washed away the blood, and his hair felt silky cool to her fingertips. His face was better, if purple bruises and angry red wounds could be considered preferable to blood and puffiness. If only she knew more!

She looked away, her hand still touching him. She had never in all her life felt less competent and more ignorant than in the past two days. She knew nothing about the plants that grew about her. Which ones were beneficial or harmful? Which were eatable, which should be avoided at all costs? She did not know in which direction to travel to find help or even if it were safe to leave Thomas to do so.

She turned to check the horse that she had tethered under a new tree, where the grass was fresh. She was not sure she could correctly resaddle a horse, so she had left the saddle in place, only to find that it was beginning to rub sores on the animal's skin. She had used a little of the lard to soothe the ones she saw, but that had drawn flies to the animal and she had had to wash it off.

Her ignorance appalled and angered her. It was not until the morning of the second day that she noticed the canteen on Jack's saddle contained rum rather than water. At least she had the sense to know that whiskey was good for healing wounds, and she had bathed Thomas's lacerations with it repeatedly. If only he would awaken.

As she stroked his brow Aisleen sucked her lower lip. She had gnawed it raw with worry. Why did he lie so still? Was he healing or dying? He had eaten nothing. It was all she could do to pour a little water down him without choking him. She was boiling rice and peas together to make a thick gruel in hopes that when he stirred again, she would be able to feed him a little of it. She had fashioned with Jack's knife a crude spoon from the peeling bark of a tree she had discovered in the forest while fetching firewood.

They were well supplied for at least a week, but even if they had had more, one thing was becoming increasingly clear. They could not remain here. She had not found a single bit of evidence of human life in her forays along the strip of ground between the river and the mountains. They might be stumbled upon tomorrow . . . or they might never be found.

But how could she move Thomas? She certainly could not lift him onto the horse. And if he did not soon regain consciousness enough to eat, he would be too weak to move when he did awaken.

She had slept too little and eaten almost nothing for fear that their supplies would dwindle too quickly. Every night sound startled her awake, and now there was another night before her.

Where was Jack? Was he dead or wandering about, just out of sight, searching for them? She had awakened the night before with the certainty so strong in her that she had run headlong into the forest shouting his name.

Aisleen cringed with the remembrance. She was a useless, frightened woman who did not know how to save the one person in the world who meant more to her than her own life. Even the voice that taunted her had deserted her.

No. To think like that was to give up to madness. Perhaps she was going mad.

A hard tremor of fear shook her. Her father had been correct. She was useless. Worry and weariness worked in her like yeast, expanding her fears, and she began once more to saw her lip between her teeth. Why had Jack given Thomas into her unskilled care? Had he not realized that she was incapable of caring even for herself? He should not have let them go alone. When Jack found them, if he did, he would probably blame her for Thomas's death. Because of her, Thomas would die. Because of him, she was stuck in an unfriendly wilderness which offered no clues to salvation. Because of this hostile country she was doomed to die, unmourned and alone.

She bent over her knees, suddenly sobbing and shouting, "I hate this country! I hate its people! And most of all, I hate you, Thomas Gibson! I hate you for lying there dying! I hate you!"

With her own cries ringing in her ears, she stretched out on the ground beside him, threw her arms about him, and fell asleep.

She knew she was not alone even before she opened her eyes and sat up.

They stood on the far side of the campfire, as still as statues. At first she thought they were some new form of wildlife. A second look told her they were human. The scant firelight picked up the gleam of their dark faces, chests, arms, and legs. Aborigines. She had seen a few of them on the streets of Sydney and Bathurst but never in their native habitat of the bush.

Her heart thumped high in her throat. She was outnumbered six to one. She reached for the pistol she kept tucked in her waistband. The movement drew the attention of one of the men, and he jumped across the fire and jabbed a sharpened stick at her middle.

Aisleen fell back before the onslaught, the pistol untouched. As she watched, a second man, short and so thin his arms and legs looked like shrunken leather strips, walked around the fire and bent over Thomas.

"Don't touch him!" she cried in anger as he nudged Thomas with a bare foot. Her guard raised his stick threateningly, but she did not care. "Don't touch him! He's hurt!"

The man looked at her sharply, his black eyes wide with interest. "Him wurry bad hurt?"

The question posed in English surprised her so much she smiled. "Do you speak English? Oh, thank heaven! This is my husband." She gestured to Thomas. "He was hurt by some very bad men. We need help. Can you lead us to the nearest settlement?"

The man's face split in a broad grin. "Him wurry bad hurt," he repeated and nodded.

Aisleen stared at the man with only a scrap of cloth covering his privates. "Do you speak English?"

He looked at her in puzzlement, and then he spied the billy over the fire. "You drink 'em tea?"

"No, that's rice and peas," Aisleen answered and went to lift the billy with its charred contents. The man looked in the pot and then sniffed it and shook his head. "You drink 'em tea?" he repeated.

"Tea. You want tea?" she asked. "I have a little left." She reached into the saddlebag and withdrew the packet of tea and handed it to the man. "Will you help us now?"

The man sniffed the tea and then nodded, smiling. He made a movement with his hand and a small young woman came forward bearing a fur rug, which she dropped at Aisleen's feet.

The man, apparently the leader, now looked across the grass, and though *she* could not see it, she knew that *he* had seen the horse. "Brumby?"

She did not know the word, but she understood the suggestion in his tone, and she would not give, sell, or trade him the horse. "No!" she said emphatically. "No horse!"

The man lifted his spear, but she was not frightened this time. The loss of the horse would mean certain death. Backing quickly away, she pulled the pistol from her belt and fired it above her head.

The sharp point of a spear poked her in the small of her back. She reacted out of instinct, swinging about and pointing her gun at her attacker. The loud report sent her backward a step as the man cried out in pain. She saw him grab his neck in surprise and then look at the blood that smeared his hand. Baring his teeth, he raised his weapon a second time, but a guttural grunt from the leader made him pause.

Aisleen backed farther away from the man brandishing the spear. "Go!" she shouted. "Go! Now!"

She did not expect to be obeyed. There were more grunts and clicking of tongues behind her, and at any moment she expected a lance to be driven into her back; but she did not turn away from the man she had wounded or lower her weapon.

A strange bird called deep in the forest. Suddenly there was absolute silence behind her. The man before her swiveled his head sharply in the direction of the sound as the call was repeated. Instantly he set off, racing across the grass and out of sight.

Aisleen turned toward the campfire slowly, not knowing what to expect. What she saw utterly amazed her. She was alone with Thomas. The others had disappeared as swiftly and silently as they had appeared. Had the birdcall been a signal that someone else, a white man, was approaching? Perhaps her fire had drawn the attention of a settler or swagman.

For a moment she allowed that irrational hope to bolster

her spirits. She stood waiting as still as a statue for several minutes. Should she fire the revolver again, just to make certain they could not mistake her direction? She lifted her arm to do so but then changed her mind. What if the natives were only temporarily frightened? If they came back she would need every bullet.

One minute became five. Five minutes stretched out to ten. Still no one came. New thoughts nagged her. If the aborigines had not been frightened away by other men, what would have made them leave? Were there beasts in the forest that even *they* feared? If so, how would she, an ignorant Irish lass, know how to cope?

Ye've nae done so badly, for an ignorant Irish lass!

Aisleen did not even look for him. She was too tired to cheerfully indulge the apparitions of her half-mad mind.

So it's to be that way, is it? Then ye'll not be wanting to know me news.

Aisleen closed her eyes. Dreams and mad schemes—she had inherited her father's madness.

Ye cannae stay here any longer, lass, and well ye know it. Ye may be certain of nothing else, but this ye know—there's bushrangers nearby. Now isn't that so?

Aisleen straightened up. She had forgotten. Of course! Bushrangers. She did not know how many had been killed by Jack before they . . . killed him.

"Oh, Jack!" She gave up a shuddery sigh. He was dead. She had known it all along but had been too afraid to admit it. She was afraid of so much. It had been too great a burden to think that she was absolutely alone. But it was true.

She looked back over her shoulder. There was nothing she could do before morning. If she put out the fire, they would not find her before dawn. By then, she would have devised a plan.

"Aisleen?"

The thick, coarse whisper brought her head snapping back. Thomas was lying with his eyes open.

"Tom!"

"Better? Is that better, darling?" she whispered, afraid even the sound of her voice might cause him further pain.

Thomas gazed at her in mute joy. His head rested in the curve of her left arm, her left breast the softest of pillows for his sore cheek. She had been spooning a nasty concoction of scorched rice and pea porridge into him, and though he had been able to swallow it, his teeth were still too sore for him to chew. Her hair hung down in straggly tangles on either side of her dirty face. The bruise on her chin had turned a greenish yellow. Her usually bright eyes were sunk deep in worry-bruised sockets.

He wanted to comfort her, to hold her close and tell her that she need not worry about him any longer, but his assurances would scarcely have been worth the effort. She had talked to him while she fed him, told him everything that had happened from the moment of his capture until he awakened a short while ago. The tale amazed him. He would not have believed it had he heard it after the fact.

No, there was nothing to be gained by empty words. He was completely useless to her as a source of protection. He was a burden to her. Careful examination of his body with her help had confirmed his suspicion that several of his ribs were broken. He suspected that his nose was also. His crippled leg had been kicked. As for his groin, well, he would never aim a kick at a man's privates again, unless they were Sean's.

He did not need the look in her eyes to tell him how badly his face was damaged. She did not seem to realize that a tear slipped unimpeded down her cheek once in a while. "It will heal," he had said as another tear appeared.

"Of course it will!" she answered in the crisp, no-nonsense tone he had not heard in weeks. "You attracted quite too many women before. Although in your case a few decorative scars might only season the appeal."

He smiled at her—at least he hoped it was a smile and not the grimace of pain that it felt like. "I love you," he murmured between stiff lips.

Aisleen blinked at him. What had he said?

"Aye, love," he said, seeing the disbelief in her face. "Didn't ye know it, lass?"

Her reaction wasn't what he hoped for. She burst into tears that scalded his tender skin as they dripped into his face. *Women*, he thought, closing his eyes. He would never understand them.

His eyes opened as he heard the jingle of a bridle. "A horse?"

"We've Jack's horse," Aisleen answered.

Thomas sighed and closed his eyes again. Jack was dead, had died saving his life. Perhaps Jack believed, as he had told Aisleen, that they were even at last. He would not have had the debt repaid in this way.

"Tom, we must leave here," Aisleen said when she thought he was falling asleep again. "Firing the gun as I did, I think it might have alerted someone to our presence."

Thomas regarded her in wonder. He, too, had thought of that but did not know how to broach the subject without frightening her more than she already was. He need not have worried. His wife had the makings of a bushwoman equal to any colonial-born miss.

"At dawn," he muttered.

"Yes, my thought," she replied in relief. "Can you ride?"

Thomas merely nodded. The thought of straddling a horse was best not contemplated just yet.

When he opened his eyes again it was to suggest that she put out the fire. He turned his head slowly to the left and smiled when he saw that the fire was out. She was a smart lass. He turned his head back to the right and leaned his head against hers. She was curled tightly against him under the cover of the cloak of opossum skins she had traded for their tea.

He had been alone in the world for so long he had forgotten the wonderful, heady feeling that came with loving and being loved. He would begin again. When they were out of danger they would build an empire to equal any. They would have children, lots of them, and grandchildren, and maybe, just maybe, he'd live to see great-grands. They would populate New South Wales.

He squeezed the hand she had slipped into his. First they had to reach safety.

Aisleen tried to quell her impatience as their horse picked a listless path under the high canopy of the bush. It had taken almost all Thomas's strength to hoist himself into the saddle. The horse had been skittish and well aware that it had been mistreated by these strangers. Feckless and contemptuous of their clumsiness, the animal had made a difficult task even harder by its uncooperative antics.

In the distance the craggy red peaks of the Three Sisters tantalized them. The Great Western Road passed directly by the formation, yet she and Thomas had not been able to find a method to cross to them. Thomas's remark that it had taken the colonialists nearly thirty years to find the first path through the mountains was not comforting.

As they came out of the trees along a narrow mountain

ridge they were confronted once more by a physical barrier. A steep precipice fell sharply away before them, dropping hundreds of feet to the bottom of a deep gorge. Immense rocks had tumbled down from the cliffs behind them and lay strewn at random all about.

Thomas sighed and Aisleen was quick to answer it with, "Are you in much pain?"

Thomas shook his head. He ached in so many places there was no sense in cataloging them. "We'll try up there," he said when he could speak without groaning.

For hours they followed the mountain ridge northward. Despite the discomfort and her constant concern for Thomas, Aisleen could not help admiring the wild beauty of the country through which they rode. Orchids and wild flowers unlike any she had ever seen dotted every shady hollow.

And birds. She did not believe that any other place on earth produced birds of such variety and splendid plumage. She discovered parrots more gorgeous than the red-rumped ones who had visited her the first night alone in the bush. Like a flower garden taken flight, they would swoop down across their path and then arch away. Jewel tones of ruby, sapphire, and emerald, gemstones of topaz and jade, sky pinks, mauves, and blues—all the colors of the spectrum had wings in the Australian bush.

When the sun had crossed its zenith and begun its slide westward, she could no longer support Thomas in the saddle. He had dozed off or fainted; it was impossible to tell. Her arms felt as though they would tear from their sockets. Searing pain raced up their length each time the horse misstepped.

The sound of running water was slow to penetrate her beleaguered mind; yet when she recognized it, she knew the horse had been drawn to it long before she heard it. Somewhere deep in the forest a small mountain stream ran. They would camp nearby for the night.

The sound of hoofbeats coming up quickly behind them brought her up sharply. "Tom!" she hissed close to his ear.

Thomas opened his eyes and at once knew why she had awakened him. He turned his head, but the overhanging bushes obscured his view.

"It could be help," Aisleen ventured softly.

"Maybe," he answered and took the reins from her hands. There was no need to elaborate further.

He turned the horse off the path into a dense portion of the forest. Less than a minute later hoofbeats came even with the place on the path where they had been. Suddenly the horse was reined in. The hair lifted on his neck as he quickly reined in his own mount. They were being followed. Only two people would have reason to track them: Jack or Sean.

He caught Aisleen by the arm and whispered quickly, "Slide off!"

Aisleen did as he directed. "Hide!" he ordered, motioning her toward a wall of ferns. Only then did she realize what he intended to do. "You can't! You're not fit to ride! Let me!"

But Thomas urged the horse up the path.

Aisleen pulled the pistol from her waistband and waved it after him, hissing, "The gun!"

He turned, winced, and waved her a cocky salute before kicking his horse into a gallop that took them quickly out of sight.

The muffled thudding of a horse's hooves sounded from the thick bush behind her, and Aisleen swung round. Above the top of a fern tree she saw a cabbage hat. Jack did not wear one. This was a stranger. Walking backward, her eyes on the hat moving in time to the horse's walk, she slipped behind the wall of waist-high ferns and crouched down.

She saw his face as he rode clear of the trees and paused. It was the bushranger named Sean. Anger and fear collided in her stomach as she stood and lifted the pistol. This was the man who had beaten Thomas nearly to death. He and his friends had murdered Jack. A single shot was all it would take to kill him. He was armed, dangerous. Thomas was hurt too much to withstand a struggle. A squeeze of the trigger, that was all it would take.

"G'day, miss." He turned toward her, his hideous face stretched in a smile. "Well now, is that any way to greet an Irishman, I'm asking ye?"

"Get out of here!" Aisleen shouted, her knees buckling in fear even though it was she who held the gun.

"Faith! And me about to offer ye me protection to see ye safely back to civilization." He looked about, smiling. "Or maybe ye already have a protector?"

"I'm alone," she said quickly.

His smile deepened. "Where's yer horse, then, lass?"

"I—I hid it." It was a poor lie. She swallowed. "I heard someone trailing me. I sent it ahead so that I could see who it was." She managed a weak smile. "You weren't as clever as you thought."

"Nor are ye, to be letting go yer horse in the bush." He rubbed the whiskers on his chin. "So, will ye be coming along quietly, or will ye make me chase ye?"

Aisleen steadied the gun, sighting along the barrel as Jack had showed her.

"Oh, now, ye will nae be doing that! Ye're too clever and good a lass to kill a man outright. Think of yer soul. What would ye be telling Saint Peter about the murdering of an innocent unarmed man?"

It was not his taunting that stopped her. She could not have shot him in any case. Thomas was away. It was the thought uppermost in her mind. The longer she detained Sean, the farther away Thomas got. "Stand down!"

Sean looked taken aback. "Ye've a thing or two to learn about a bushman if ye believe he'll be giving up his horse, even to as fair a *colleen* as ye, darling."

"If you do not stand down, I will shoot the horse," Aisleen replied and wondered if she'd have any more courage to do that. She thought fleetingly of the dog Thomas had shot and why. Yes, perhaps she would, for Thomas's sake. She took aim at the horse's head.

Sean threw a leg over his saddle and dismounted, still smiling. "I heard him running away. That'd be just like our Tommy, leaving a lass to face the crime he's committed. I'm in nae hurry. I'll be finding him again, never ye fear. He knows now how I'll be wanting him to die, and so he'll have that to think on between now and then."

As he talked he advanced on her. "Still, he should nae have left so pretty a thing behind him. Did he give ye that bruise? *Och!* Our Tommy's that careless a lad."

"Stop! Stop right there!" Aisleen demanded. She felt liquid with terror. Her arms ached from holding Thomas. The weight of the gun dragged them downward.

"I can see that ye're afraid of me," Sean said confidently. "There's nae need for it. Me quarrel's not with ye. Ye've only to show Sean O'Leary yer prettiest smile and he'll be as gentle as a lamb. I'd never bruise yer face, nae like I done to Tommy Fitzgerald."

"Fitzgerald?"

Sean's brows lifted. "Did he lie to ye about that, too? He's no Gibson, lass, though well I don't wonder he changed his name. He'd have known one of us would be coming after him. Hell could nae have held me back!"

"Thomas's name is Fitzgerald?" Aisleen persisted.

"Aye, Tom Fitzgerald of County Cork. Wrong side of the blanket, I'm told, but a bastard's bastard though he be gentry."

Aisleen saw his hand move to his waistband. "Don't! I don't want to shoot you, but I will! I swear it!"

"And ruin his fine handsome face!" came a reply in Gaelic.

The voice so startled her, Aisleen looked away from Sean.

He stood in the shadow of a distant tree.

"Tommy, lad, will that be ye?" Sean cried triumphantly and whipped his pistol from his trousers.

"Top of the morning to you, Sean!" he said.

"Bheirim don diabhal sibh!" Sean cursed and fired.

"No!" Aisleen's finger tightened on the trigger, and the gun in her hands recoiled from the explosion. She heard a man's cry and then she was running, running toward the spot where Thomas had stood.

She heard Sean cursing and his running footsteps, and knew that she had missed. "Tom, look out!"

Sean caught her from behind, by the ragged edge of her shredded skirts and whipped her about. "Ye bloodthirsty bitch!" he cried and struck her full across the face.

She staggered and tripped, the gun flying from her hand as she sprawled. She was up on her knees in a moment, groping for the lost weapon, but his boot caught her in the stomach and flipped her over.

"No, ye don't!" Sean cried. "And I'll not even waste a bullet on ye!"

Gasping for breath, Aisleen watched helplessly as he beat the bush until he found what he wanted. "A good head bashing will do for the likes of ye!" he muttered as he bent and picked up a fallen branch and lifted it over his head.

Aisleen stared up at him as he neared, waiting for the blow to descend, when suddenly Sean's expression altered. Surprise replaced murdering rage. He turned and looked at his arm. It was crawling with large, blue-green ants. He tossed the branch away and began to howl like a demented creature.

Aisleen rolled away, more frightened by his actions than by her own death. He was dancing in place, screaming and tearing at his arms with his fingernails. And then he was tearing at the rest of his clothing. When he tore open his shirt she saw that he was half-covered with ants. She looked down and saw them swarming across the ground toward him . . . and her.

She turned and ran, Sean's screams resounding in her ears.

"Aisleen!"

She stumbled blindly toward the cry until, suddenly, Thomas was before her on horseback.

"Ants! Terrible stings! They're killing him!" she cried as he bent an arm toward her. But she did not need his help. She hurled herself upward with a boost from the stirrup. "Hurry, please! Take me away!"

Thomas took one backward look. Sean was on the ground, his body twitching as he was covered by a black sea of insects. There was nothing to be done.

"I'll never sleep in the bush again!" Aisleen protested for the hundredth time as she stirred the peas boiling in the billy. It was late evening and they had made camp in the open, away from treacherous underbrush that concealed more than beasts.

Thomas lay quietly. "I'm sorry, lass, that ye had to witness it. 'Twas almost like a plague sent straight from heaven, now wasn't it?"

Aisleen gagged but swallowed back her bile. She had been sick enough for one afternoon. "You never saw him?" she questioned softly.

"How could I, when I was hiding a hundred yards away? 'Twas his shot that brought me back, with me heart in me throat, I can tell ye!" He turned to look at her. "As God is me witness, I never thought Sean would see ye, not when he had me on horseback to follow!"

Aisleen moved back from the campfire and bent to kiss

him. "I know that, Tom. It was me who stopped him. You didn't have a weapon. He'd have shot you in the back, given the chance. I couldn't allow him to do that."

"Ye couldn't allow—" Emotion blocked his throat. He looked up at her, his smile a little crooked. "Whyever not, lass?"

She smiled at him. "Didn't I tell you? It's because I love you."

She had not said it before, not out loud. It sounded good, it sounded fine, it sounded safe.

"I'm that honored that ye'll be trusting me with yer love," Thomas said after a moment.

She was not surprised he used the word. "I do trust you, with all my heart, forever."

A long while after, when dinner was finished and she had cleaned his wounds and Thomas lay sleeping easily in her lap, Aisleen raised her eyes and found the shadow standing under a nearby tree, where she knew he would be.

"It was you in the forest," she said simply.

So it was, he admitted. *This'll make an end to us, lass.*

"Why?"

Because, ye great stupid girl, ye've found what ye've sought yer life long!

"A riddle!"

Musha! If ye cannae be satisfied with that after all these years then ye do nae deserve a reply!

Aisleen regarded him thoughtfully. "Who are you?"

Two halves of a whole, lass, two halves of a whole. When ye've solved that, ye'll have the answer!

He winked out like a snuffed wick, and she knew that he was gone forever.

"Good-by, *bouchal.*"

*   *   *

"She ain't dead. She's sleeping!"

Aisleen popped her eyes open to find two young boys staring solemnly down into her face.

"Gor! What'd I say?" said the older of the two.

She sat up. "Who are you?"

"Name's Robert. This is Hugh. Who are you?"

"I'm Mrs. Gibson and this is my husband." She shook Thomas's shoulder. "We've company, Tom. Where do you boys live?"

Robert pointed and Aisleen smiled when she saw the answer. They had camped within hailing distance of a good-sized settlement.

"You lost?" the younger boy questioned.

"We were," she replied.

She saw the boys exchange glances and then the older one bend to whisper to the younger boy contemptuously, "Pommies!"

Give to these children, new from the world,
Silence and love...

—A Faery Song
W. B. Yeats

Chapter Eighteen

Hill End: January 1858

"Tell us again about fighting off the abos!" Matt Mahoney encouraged and was enthusiastically seconded by those who sat near the table of honor on the dais.

Aisleen shook her head. "I'm afraid it was much less glorious than it sounds."

"I should say it would pale beside the accomplishment of dispatching a notorious bushranger," Magistrate Owens interjected. "My dear Mrs. Gibson, you shall be known far and wide as the young woman who broke up a gang of Vandiemonians single-handedly!"

Aisleen blushed and glanced at Thomas, who sat by her side at the front table. "I was not alone, Mr. Owens."

"I was the extra burden weighing her down," Thomas offered with an indulgent smile. "She deserves every bit of

351

praise for what she's done, and I'll not have her shirking the hearing of it for modesty's sake.''

"Fair go, luv!" came a cry from farther down the banquet hall.

"And never be forgetting she were a lady to the end!" offered the coach driver, who had been invited because of his presence at the beginning of the adventure. "Her husband captured at gunpoint by a murdering band of bushrangers and what does the lady do, I ask ye? She bails me up with her husband's pistol and asks, as polite as ye please, to be set down so that she may go after the thieving rogues!"

Thomas squeezed her hand. "She faced dangers many a man would quail at the thought of meeting."

Aisleen's admirers sat in rapt silence as Thomas continued to regale the company with stories of her exploits in the Blue Mountains. The stories had taken on a life of their own and with each telling became more outrageous and audacious. Entrusted to Thomas's eloquent care, she was certain they would reach mythic proportions in no time.

She gazed about the room. This was a party in her honor, thrown by the grateful inhabitants of Bathurst and surrounding communities. To her great embarrassment she had received a letter of commendation from the governor of New South Wales. She spied Mrs. Fahey sitting near the rear of the room talking at a fever pitch with two other ladies. Pleased to have been noticed, Mrs. Fahey waved a lace handkerchief at her. Aisleen smiled and nodded and looked away.

She was tired. The day of festivities had palled hours earlier. She felt like a carnival freak paraded down the center of town for people to gape at and poke for clues as to the reasons behind her extraordinary adventure. If not for Thomas and the obvious pleasure he took in her celebrity, she would not have allowed the banquet to take place. The room was thronged with strangers who might wish her well, but that was because they did not understand how guilty she felt. She did not deserve their praise. She had not been brave or clever or fearless at all.

She felt tears prick the back of her eyes as they had done often in the month since their arrival back in Hill End. Sarah had fussed over her until she was afraid the woman would make herself sick. It was Thomas who concerned her.

She glanced repeatedly at him while he spoke. His face was nearly healed, the swelling all but gone. To her satisfaction and his own not inconsiderable Irish pride, he would soon be as handsome as ever. The broken nose? It was a badge of courage of which many a schoolboy would boast.

He seemed healthy enough, but he had had to resort to a cane since his recovery. With all the attention lavished on them as they recovered, they had not had a single evening of peace. Her mind seethed with unanswered questions.

At first she had been too worn and weary to give them much thought but, after a day of constantly being referred to as Mrs. Gibson, she wanted very badly to question Thomas about Sean's statement that his name was really Fitzgerald. Was that possible?

As Thomas finished, spontaneous applause broke out, rippled across the tables, and washed back in thunderous waves.

"Will you not say something in your own words, Mrs. Gibson?" asked a man down front with pencil and pad.

Aisleen shook her head with a mute plea to Thomas.

Thomas rose to his feet. "Ladies and gentlemen, me wife and I thank ye for yer considerable good wishes. We'll be remembering this hour fondly for the rest of our days. But as we've a far journey to make, and being that we begin at dawn, we'll be asking yer indulgence in allowing us to depart. Of course, the champagne, being that it's free, will continue to flow till the last bottle's drunk!"

With a hand under her elbow, Thomas deftly steered her past all but the most persistent admirers. The reporter from Sydney he clipped with his cane.

"Heavens! I thought we'd all stew in our own juices," Sarah declared when she and Matt had joined Thomas and Aisleen in the cart for the drive home.

"Aye, 'tis a fine warm night!" Thomas commented as he drove the cart through the main street of Hill End. "Aisleen, lass, are ye too weary for a starlit ride?"

Aisleen shook her head. "Not at all."

"Sounds fine to me!" Matt agreed heartily. "Ouch! What was that for!"

"Matt Mahoney! Have you lost entirely your romantic streak?" Sarah scolded. "They wish to be alone, you great clod!"

"Oh. Oh!" Matt answered as reason dawned. "Well now, I'll not be standing in the way of a man and his wife. Set us down by the gate, Tom, and a good night to you both."

Once they left the Mahoneys at their home, Thomas drove out of town at a leisurely pace. They did not speak. It did not seem necessary. Aisleen had tucked her arm through his and leaned her head against his shoulder. Only her fingers clenched on his sleeve betrayed her discomfort. He drove them out toward the river down below the noise and lights of the mining camp.

The sky was dusty with stars, hot points of diamond light in a gauze of cosmic shimmer. The cart rolled up a rise to a cliff overlooking the Turon River, and here he reined in and set the brake.

"Tired?" he questioned quietly as she sat up away from him and released his arm.

Aisleen shook her head as she stared straight ahead.

"Weary of celebrations?"

This time she nodded.

He smiled because he understood her reluctance to speak. It was as though they were strangers, or friends who had just been reunited after a long separation. He felt it, too, the strain of not knowing what to say or in what order things should come. She had confronted and bested a man who had wanted her husband dead, and she did not even know the reasons why. So many questions must be asked and answered. The wrong one first might spoil everything.

"I've never really told ye about me life before I came to New South Wales. Would ye care to hear a bit of it?"

Aisleen nodded wordlessly.

"We were fishermen, as I've told ye. And ye may suspect that it was a sometimes tedious business for a lad with spirit and a high opinion of himself. Why should he be pulling fishes from the sea when there were worlds abroad to conquer? Oh, aye, a fine opinion Tommy had of himself. He dreamed away many an hour of his youth, a-plotting and a-planning. Still, there came a time, about his fifteenth summer, when he saw that his homeland might be the place for adventure as well."

Thomas paused, letting his thoughts range back over the years. "What a fine warm summer night that was. The sky so clear and black a man could nae see his hand before his eyes before moonrise. Some of the local lads thought it a night for mischief. The English were sitting and quaking with fear lest the very soil they trod split open and swallow them whole. 'Twas so easy to set a bit of powder by the munitions hut. A long time after, I wondered where we'd have stopped had we not been caught. We might have taken to murdering redcoats. 'Twas a natural enough inclination after an easy victory. Perhaps the English judge was right to sentence us to be hanged."

He shrugged. "In any case, hanging was preferable to

being torn apart by the jaws of the great bloodthirsty hounds they set on us that night.''

"Your leg?"

"Aye. And may the dog who took me flesh have choked on it and died!''

Aisleen shivered. At last she knew why he had shot out of hand the kelpie that had attacked her. "Sean O'Leary was with you that night?"

"Aye, Sean was with us. He wasn't a village lad but a rapparee who roamed the countryside stirring up the hot-blooded among the local lads. He was experienced in bedeviling the English. I didn't see any of them after the sentencing. Me leg festered and they thought I'd die on me own. 'Twas me da who bribed the courts to commute me sentence to transportation. Until a few months ago I thought the rest had been hanged. When I heard there was a man looking for me by the name of O'Leary, I knew it could be no other but Sean.''

"He thought you'd betrayed them," Aisleen said softly.

"Well now, I guess I'll never be knowing for certain what the English told Sean and the others. I'd not like to think they all died believing me to be a turncoat.''

She felt the tremor that passed through him where their shoulders touched. "They couldn't think that, Tom, not if they knew you.''

He was silent a moment. "Well, that's how our Tom came to the colony, aboard a convict ship in chains.''

Aisleen turned to look at him. His face was a sharp profile before the night. The familiar sight brought a sudden pulsing somewhere deep inside her. She had nearly lost him. Beside that anguish, his convict background was ashes. "Did Tom have his adventure, after all?''

He turned to her, the corners of his mouth bowed in his cocky smile. "Aye, I did." He paused. Perhaps later he would tell her about those first years. But not just yet. "I was a man with a willing hand, and as me grandma often said, a bit of luck out of being born. Turned me efforts to shearing when I'd earned me emancipation papers. Became a ringer in a short while, me own boss. I needed that.''

Aisleen smiled, understanding the need to be independent after her years at Burke's Academy. ''Where did you meet Jack?''

''I knew him five years, but I'd be less than honest to say I knew Jack Egan a whit better than yerself, lass. He was drowning when we met. That great frame of his was nae meant to float, and so I told him when I'd hauled him out of the Hawksbury during a flood.''

''Was he a farmer?''

Thomas's laughter startled the horse. ''Lord love us! Jack was a bushranger! He'd held up the coach from Sydney not an hour before the bridge washed out, and him on it.''

Aisleen's lips twitched. ''He always did rather remind me of a highwayman. Mercy! What company you keep, Thomas Gib—''

''Ah, so it's that we'll be discussing next.'' Thomas reached out and touched her face. ''Ye know me history, lass. So ye'll be understanding me reasons for changing me name.''

''Because you did not want it known that you were a convict?''

''So me family back in Cork would not have to suffer because of me foolishness. The record of me conviction was for Tom Gibson. 'Twas why it took Sean so long to find me.''

''And your real name?''

Thomas rubbed her chin with his thumb. ''Ye know it.''

''Fitzgerald.''

''And so it is.''

''Why didn't you tell me before?''

''Well now, lass, we weren't well acquainted, ye and me.

It was hard enough to coax ye into marriage without asking ye to believe that ye were marrying a cousin."

Aisleen sat up straighter. "Our marriage. If you are not Thomas Gibson then we are not legally wed!"

"Ye're vexed," Thomas said calmly. "I suppose what ye say is true, in a manner of speaking."

"In a manner—! You lied to me, not once but repeatedly," Aisleen cried. "I'm not your wife, I'm your—your mistress!"

"I confess up to the reality of it," Thomas agreed pleasantly. "And I don't mind saying that the situation holds a certain fascination for a man. But being a honest soul, I'll save ye from a life of sin by offering to wed ye a second time."

Aisleen twitched her skirts away as if in anger and said primly, "I would not marry you if you were the last man on earth!"

"Aye, and I would not be asking ye, for there'd be none to join us," he retorted in high humor. He could not see her face, but he thought he felt the warmth of her smile. "But we're among civilized folk, lass, and it won't do. Maybe we'd nae give a lamb's tail about what others say, but there's the bairns to be considered. I don't much fancy the name bastard being attached to a child of mine."

"I'm not bearing a child of yours," she replied.

"Aye, but ye will, lass. We're well matched and ye love it so!"

"Go away, you horrid man!" she said, slapping away the hands that reached for her. "You're not well enough to bedevil me in that manner. Besides, until we're properly wed, you'll take no more liberties with me!"

"Lass, there's no liberties I could be taking in any case this night."

Aisleen remembered the dark bruises that ringed his groin. "Will you, that is, are you getting better?"

"Oh, lass, if ye could see yer face!" Thomas hooted in glee.

Aisleen put her hands up to cover her cheeks and then snatched them away. "You can't see my face."

"Maybe, but I know what ye're thinking, and just the knowing of it tells me I'm healing well enough."

To his surprise, she did not laugh or further berate him but burst into uncontrollable sobs. He watched her in amazement, certain that the hysteria would end as quickly as it began. When it did not he reached out and drew her against him, but she did not want the harbor of his shoulder. She twisted away and when he tried to pull her back, she elbowed him, and with a soft gasp he released her.

Aisleen spun about on the seat. "Oh, Tom, I'm sorry! I didn't think—"

Thomas had raised a hand to his still-tender middle. "Never mind. If ye will be denying me even the comforting of ye, then I'll nae touch ye again."

Aisleen gasped in a hiccupy breath. "You do—don't understand."

"That's the glorious truth!"

"It's too much. The marriage. Your name. The fears. The death of Jack. And Sean. And now the colony gone mad with celebrating, which I don't deserve!" She took a deep, steadying breath and faced the truth. "I am a coward."

Thomas grinned at her. "Ye had a bad fright, lass, and sorry I am for all of it. But to say ye were not grand and brave is a lie."

Aisleen shook her head. "I was frightened witless. I couldn't bear to touch you at first. You were bloody and sick, and I was repelled. And later, when the natives came, I nearly killed one of them out of quaking fear, not because I was strong enough to protect you. I started at every rustle of bush. Cried every time I burned myself. Quaked in my boots through every night. I couldn't saddle the horse, couldn't carry you any distance, didn't know which direction to go for help. No, I was too much of a coward to leave your side. And Sean—if the ants hadn't attacked him, he'd have killed me. That's the truth about your heroine!''

"Did ye miss anything?" Thomas asked kindly.

She lifted her head from her hands. ''Jack died because I was too frightened to use your pistol. I should have stayed and fought.''

"Anything else?"

"I'm not brave! I don't want to be a legend!"

Thomas took out of her hand the handkerchief she drew from her purse and patiently wiped the tears from her cheeks and chin. ''Blow,'' he ordered and then wiped her nose. When he was done he gathered her close once more, ignoring the twinge in his ribs, and tucked her head under his chin. ''Ah, lass, you're the most contrary creature as ever God put on this earth. Ye'll send me to me grave puzzling over ye, which is no more than I deserve.''

"You mock me," she whispered.

"Ye're a Fitzgerald, so ye should be knowing what yer fate was to be. The rose mark is the answer.''

Aisleen stilled. "You know about that?"

"The legend of the Fitzgerald rose? Now what kind of an Irishman would I be not to be knowing the history of me own clan?''

Aisleen lifted her head. "You know the stories of Meghan and Deirdre?"

"Shall I tell them to ye?"

"No, no, that won't be necessary. But if you know them, then you know that I failed to keep the bond of the legacy.''

"How's that?"

"Oh, it's all so silly. The rose birthmark, the sign that I would save the Fitzgerald line. The castle Liscarrol was the Fitzgerald legacy handed down from Deirdre. My father went to his grave hating me because I could not prevent its loss.''

"Now how were ye to do that?''

Aisleen felt the cold wind of failure at her back but resisted it. "It's only a legend. There's no magic.''

"Forgive me if I don't agree, lass.''

Aisleen turned to look at him.

"Ye saved me life. That may seem an inconsiderable achievement beside the deeds of our ancestresses, but, faith, if it doesn't seem a grand thing to this Fitzgerald!''

His words, spoken with a careless charm with which only he could imbue them, struck her a hammer blow. She had saved him, perhaps haltingly, even against her will at times, but she had done it. For that she was famous. An accident. No magic; no mythical creature had reared up to save . . .

"Tom, do you believe in fairies?''

Thomas smiled. "Aye. One's whispered in me ear for years.''

"A boy?''

"Nae, a lass with a sharp edge to her tongue and a perverse streak that will nae bend to reason.''

Aisleen lowered her eyes. *Did she ever say she loved you?* she questioned silently.

There was no answer. There was nothing but the faint jingle of the horse's bridle and the slurred hiss of the river and her own breath.

Suddenly she realized that there should be no easy reassurance, no charmed reply to lend a helping hand across the chasm of distrust and fear of her own self. She was done with childish fancy. She was a woman in love. Love was not a game for pixies and fairies. It was a very real and singularly human emotion. Love made a man and woman two halves of a greater whole.

She raised her eyes to his face and her hand to his cheek. "I love you, Thomas Fitzgerald. Take me home.''

Thomas turned his head to lay a kiss in her palm. "Was I ever after telling ye the name of me station? No?"

Liscarrol Station: June 1861

The wind whipped through the New England highlands of New South Wales tucked in between the Gara River and Black Mountain. Aisleen stood on the veranda of her home, looking out across the stark beauty of the wintered valley, where gray-white clouds scudded across the shoulders of the nearby hills. As she watched, the first flakes of snow drifted down. In another hour it would be daylight. Tom was due home any day now.

A gust of wind dragged at her nightgown, and she folded her woolen shawl more tightly about her shoulders. She was quite proud of the shawl, for she had spun the thread and knitted it out of Liscarrol wool. Tom had laughed at her efforts, saying his wife could afford to buy whatever she needed, but she was not a fool. They were land poor, their investments in sheep and dairy cattle. Tom knew almost nothing about milk cows, but she had lived among herdsmen as a child and was willing to lend a hand. Their milk and butter was already being sold in Armidale, Uralla, and as far away as Tamworth.

Overhead, shutters slammed back against the upstairs window.

"Close those this instant!" she cried. She marched down the front steps and out into the early morning. She spied two black heads peeping out between the balusters of the second-story veranda and cupped her hands about her mouth. "Revelin! Killian! Back in bed this instant!"

"Ma! Ma! Look! Snow! It's snowing, Ma!" came the barrage of replies.

"Aye, so it is," she answered. "And which of you wants to be ailing and poorly so he cannot play in it come morning?"

"Ah, Ma!" came the chorused reply.

"Back inside, the pair of you, before your da comes riding in and sees you lurking about in your nightshirts. I'm sure I don't want to think what he'll have to say about it!"

The twin black heads, so like their father's, disappeared from the railing.

"Now that's a fine thing, frightening bairns with talk of the great ogre their sire is."

Aisleen spun about, new-fallen snow loosened from her shawl by the action. "Tom!"

He jumped from his saddle and picked her up by the hips to swing her around.

"Put me down, you great lummox!" she cried, playfully beating him with her fists. "I'll not be handled so freely in my own yard!"

Tom paused, staggering as though he might pitch over with her, and then slowly allowed her to slide down. By the time her feet touched the ground, she had forgotten the snow, forgotten her phony anger, forgotten everything but that she had not seen him in more than a month. Her arms had looped themselves about his neck, and she pulled his head down to meet her kiss.

His lips were cold, but his tongue was hot.

"Oh, Tom! A whole month!" she said breathlessly into his ear when finally they had warmed themselves with the passion of kisses.

"And here I am thinking it was worth every minute of it if this is how I'm to be greeted," he answered, straining against her until she could not mistake the source or magnitude of his pleasure.

"You're incorrigible!" she exclaimed and playfully bit his ear. "Oh! No! Tom!" she squealed as he caught her by the waist and hoisted her up over his shoulder. "Put me down!"

"Aye, I will. Inside," he answered, calmly walking to their front door with an arm about her hips to steady her and the reins of his horse in his other hand. He paused long enough to hand the horse over to the boy who raced out from the barn.

"Glad to have you back, Mr. Fitzgerald," the boy said, his eyes growing as big as soup plates as he stared at the missus collapsed over the mister's back in a fit of laughter.

"A lass will be taken this way from time to time when she's missed her man too long," Thomas explained with a smile. "Ask yer da. He'll tell ye what's to be done."

"Conceited wretch!" Aisleen reared up and tried to wiggle free, but Thomas held her fast, adding a second arm about her hips.

Once on the veranda he marched around the house to the back bedroom and opened the shutters and stepped in.

The room was dark, the fire nearly out. He picked up a log from the rack and stirred the embers before dropping it in.

"Do you suppose I could be released now?" Aisleen inquired above him.

Thomas marched over to the big brass bed that had been his wedding gift to her and, bending forward, rolled her off his back and onto the mattress.

She lay where she fell, arms outstretched and skirts twisted. Thomas smiled down at her as he peeled off his sheepskin coat. "A man could travel many a mile and not see a more welcome sight," he murmured as he reached to tug his shirttail from his trousers.

"In three years you've learned nothing of manners or civilized behavior," Aisleen scolded, but her eyes strayed in warm interest over the muscled chest he revealed as he peeled off his shirt.

"Aye, I've a thing or two to learn about manners," he answered and unbuckled his belt. "I'm none too gentle with porcelain tea cups and lace-edged napkins."

"We don't have lace-edged napkins," she answered as she watched his trousers slide free of his thighs. With mingled disapproval and exhilaration she saw that he did not wear the woolen underwear she had bought him for winter.

"We do now. In me saddlebags."

"What?" she asked distractedly as he reached under her skirts and gently spread her knees apart and then stepped between them.

"Is something on yer mind, lass, that ye're nae listening!" he questioned as he reached higher. "Why, lass, ye're naked!"

Aisleen blushed as his hand roamed her belly. "It's not usual to wear pantaloons under one's nightgown."

His grin was devilish as he bent over her and carried the edge of her gown up with his hands. The new log had caught flame, and the firelight danced over her skin. "Ye've filled out a bit. I like that. Bairns have given ye the deep bosom and broad hips a man can hold on to." His large hand, showing dark against the lush skin of her belly, moved up to lightly squeeze a taut-nippled breast. "Lass," he breathed hoarsely, "I've missed ye."

"Me, too, Tom." They had done this so often, made love so many times that she had lost count. But this moment of desire was no less sweetly fraught with anxious anticipation than the first. She reached down and stroked his thigh lightly, reveling in the feel of the silky hair that furred him.

His hand moved from her breast, trailing slowly, slowly charting with a single finger an invisible line from her ribs to the valley of her belly and then the mossy mound below, which he tenderly probed.

Her breath caught and her hand moved, found him, and closed. She heard his sigh of pleasure at her knowledgeable handling. She had learned so much from him, of loving, and trusting, and being loved. Yes, he had taught her even that, how to accept being loved. And he loved her so well. Not just with his body but, in this moment, she needed him as much as he needed her.

A month was too long to be away, Thomas decided as he bent a knee on the bed between her parted thighs. The twins were nearly three. By spring, when he had to go to Sydney, they would be old enough to travel with them. He would take them all. But first and now, he would take his wife.

He came into her swiftly, entered her with an unexpected urgency that drew a gasp from her. He could not stop, not now. His hands dove under her buttocks to lift her up to make his access easier, deeper. Again and again he plunged into her inviting heat, glad for the welcome of her. It was a quick, grappling pleasure that he had learned to his amazement that she enjoyed as much as he. When need be, she looked every inch a lady, all lavender and lace and prim bonnets. But there was sand in her, and strength, and a wantonness he needed.

He heard her gasps of joy in gratitude as he felt the summing of his own pleasure. Hard and quick, like a gallop across the meadow, and his sweet, dear Aisleen keeping pace.

He was distracted to hear her laughter even before he got back his own breath. "What's wrong?" he groused.

"Your boots! You *sthronsuch*! You left on your boots!"

The room brightened slowly while Aisleen lay beside her sleeping husband. She wouldn't tell him just yet that she was pregnant again. He would feel guilt over his rough play, and she had no regrets. She had needed him high and hard inside her. It was a confirmation of life, of all that they were and were to be. He had not lied to her, after all. She had a home, a husband, a new life. How foolish she had been to fear this.

In the last three years she had learned to forgive every trespass in her life. She had even forgiven herself. How sad it was to know that her father had never known the peace and security of this kind of loving. How grateful she was that she had not been able to persuade her mother away from finding it with Patrick Kirwan.

The magic of life lay in finding and keeping love. And if her world was strangely haunted by the most amazing of coincidences, she was too wise to ponder them.

She rose up on an elbow and looked down at Thomas, her hand straying over his chest and down into the black tangle that began below his belly. She lightly kissed his chest and he moved, his legs sprawling wide.

It was there as always, tucked inside his upper right thigh, the exact duplicate of her own: a single rose-shaped birthmark.

She bent and kissed it. *My bouchal. Two halves of a whole*.

"Da! Ma?"

Two glossy black heads peered in through the doorway as Aisleen jerked the sheet up. Perhaps she'd name her daughters Meghan and Deirdre.

GLOSSARY

1. *Aisleen*—Gaelic name: vision.
2. *Ard Righ*—High King.
3. *Avourneen machree*—Darling of my heart.
4. *Bail up*—"Hold up!" Used during robbery (Australian).
5. *Beltane*—First day of May.
6. *Bheirim don diabhal sibh*—"The devil take you!"
7. *Billy/Billy Can*—Metal can used for brewing tea over open fire (Australian).
8. *Bouchal*—Boy.
9. *Brumby*—Wild horse in Australia.
10. *Bushranger*—Bandit who preyed on travelers and isolated homesteads, often an escaped convict.
11. *Cha*—Tea (Australian).
12. *Colleen dhas*—Pretty girl.
13. *Coolyeens*—Curls.
14. *Crosheening*—Whispering.
15. *Dag*—feces (Australian).
16. *Damper*—Unleavened bread.

369

17. *Daoine sidhe*—Fairy people.
18. *Deeshy*—Small.
19. *Dilse*—Love.
20. *Dingo*—Australian wild dog.
21. *Dinkum*—"Fair and square." (Australian).
22. *Dodhran*—Irish drum.
23. *Drover*—Person who drives sheep or cattle from property to property.
24. *Emancipist*—Ex-convict, one who served his time.
25. *Gean-canach*—"Love talker," an Irish fairy.
26. *Grazier*—Sheep or cattle rancher.
27. *Jackeroo*—Stationhand on a sheep or cattle station.
28. *Jumbuck*—A sheep.
29. *Kelpie*—Australian sheep dog with dingo blood.
30. *Larrikin*—Tough young man.
31. *Macushla*—"My darling."
32. *Musha*—"In truth!"
33. *Ooh*—"Oh!"
34. *Ochone*—"Oh my!" (Irish).
35. *Pommie, Pom*—English woman or man.
36. *Pooka*—Irish fairy.
37. *Poteen*—Illicitly distilled whiskey (Irish).
38. *Rapparee*—Irregular soldier; guerrilla fighter (Irish).
39. *Ringer*—Champion sheep shearer.
40. *Sheila*—A female.
41. *Shivoo*—Spree or party.
42. *Skean*—Irish dagger.
43. *Sly grog*—Liquor sold illegally in Australian gold fields.
44. *Squatter*—Large-scale grazier who owns a station.
45. *Sthronsuch*—"Lazy thing!"
46. *Sundowner*—Tramp who avoided work by arriving at a station at sundown.
47. *Swagman*—Hobo, itinerant worker; carried personal belongings in rolled blanket, a swag.

48. *Tanists*—Second in command to Irish clan chieftain (Irish).
49. *Tucker*—Food (Australian).
50. *Vandiemonians*—Escaped convicts from Van Diemen's Land in the 1850s who robbed the gold diggers of New South Wales and Victoria.
51. *Walkabout*—Travel; nomadic wanderings (aboriginal).
52. *Wirra*—"Oh!"